Praise for
The Wishing Tide

"Everything I love in a novel: a coastal setting so rich you can practically taste the salt in the air and feel the sand underfoot, an old inn, and a deeply felt and explored love story with a smart, relatable heroine and a handsome hero with a mysterious past. Atmospheric, suspenseful, and very romantic." —Erika Marks, author of *It Comes in Waves*

"Beautiful and haunting. The mystery sucked me in from the first page and I was swept up in Lane and Michael's story. . . . I could not read it fast enough!" —Anita Hughes, author of *Lake Como*

"Set on a desolate, storm-tossed North Carolina barrier island lush with family secrets, madness, and ghost stories, this lyrical novel will haunt you from the first page to the last."

—Barbara Claypole White, award-winning author of *The In-Between Hour*

Praise for
The Secrets She Carried

"Barbara Davis wowed me with her flawless blending of past and present in *The Secrets She Carried*. Her compassion for her characters made me care and her haunting tale kept the pages flying. A poignant, mysterious, and heartfelt story."

—Diane Chamberlain, author of *Necessary Lies*
and *The Secret Life of CeeCee Wilkes*

continued . . .

"I was swept into Adele's heartbreaking life and her devotion to those she loved."
—Susan Crandall, author of *Whistling Past the Graveyard*

"I read Barbara Davis's debut novel, *The Secrets She Carried*, deep into the night—one minute rushing to discover how the mysteries resolved, the next slowing. . . . Adele Laveau's haunting voice and Leslie Nichols's journey toward understanding lingered long after I read the final page of this engrossing tale."
—Julie Kibler, author of *Calling Me Home*

"*The Secrets She Carried* is a beautifully crafted page-turner with many twists but a simple theme: No matter how far you run, you can't escape your past. Part contemporary women's fiction, part historical novel, the plot moves seamlessly back and forth in time to unlock family secrets that bind four generations of women. Add a mysterious death, love that defies the grave, and the legacy of redemption, and this novel has it all."
—Barbara Claypole White, author of *The Unfinished Garden*

"This beautifully written novel tells a tale of epic romance, one that lasts through the decades and centuries. All centered on a plantation home in small-town North Carolina, love stories unfold as the novel progresses through both past and present, and hidden secrets, once thought long buried, slowly reveal themselves. It's a beautiful story, and Davis does an amazing job telling it." —*Romantic Times* (4½ stars)

"Davis's writing is heartfelt and effective." —*Kirkus Reviews*

"Davis has a gift for developing flawed characters and their emotionally wrenching dilemmas. The small-town setting, full of gossip and prejudice in the Depression years, feels realistic . . . a very satisfying tale." —*Historical Novel Society*

Nancy read then
Loved It
Sue 🙂

Also by Barbara Davis

The Secrets She Carried

The *Wishing* Tide

BARBARA DAVIS

NAL
ACCENT

NAL Accent
Published by the Penguin Group
Penguin Group (USA) LLC, 375 Hudson Street,
New York, New York 10014

USA | Canada | UK | Ireland | Australia | New Zealand | India | South Africa | China
penguin.com
A Penguin Random House Company

First published by NAL Accent, an imprint of New American Library,
a division of Penguin Group (USA) LLC

First Printing, September 2014

LIBRARY OF CONGRESS CATALOGING-IN-PUBLICATION DATA:

Davis, Barbara, 1961–
  The wishing tide / Barbara Davis.
    p. cm
  ISBN 978-0-451-41878-4 (paperback)
  I. Title.
  PS3604.A95554W57 2014
  813'.6—dc23   2014016209

Printed in the United States of America
10 9 8 7 6 5 4 3 2 1

Set in Carré Noir Std
Designed by Alissa Theodor

For Tommy, my absolute everything . . .
for helping me find my wings

Acknowledgments

To my lovely agent, Nalini Akolekar—thanks for making it all so easy. Every writer should be so lucky! To my editor, Sandra Harding, who is never too busy to be a cheerleader. Words can't express what a privilege it is to work with such a pro.

To Lisa Rosen, Matt King, and Doug Simpson, wonderful authors all, who week after week provide fresh eyes and invaluable feedback. I couldn't have done any of this without you.

To Barbara Claypole White, Diane Chamberlain, Susan Crandall, Julie Kibler, Anita Hughes, Laura Drake, Barbara Longley, Normandie Fischer, and all the amazing writers of woman's fiction who have been so very gracious in their support of a struggling new voice. I'm blessed to know you, and grateful beyond words.

And finally, to Debbie Threlkeld Wittstein, and my friends from Tradewinds and Changing Tides, Pompano Beach High School classes 1976–79, who've been faithful supporters from the very first page of my very first novel. I love you guys. We may be scattered to the four corners of the earth, but we're never out of reach.

They say the people you need appear in your life just when you need them, and I must say this has been especially true for me. I've been blessed with such an amazing team of supporters, family, friends, and professionals, whom I can never repay for their kindness and generosity. The writer's journey is said to be a lonely one, but I have never felt alone.

Chapter 1

Mary

Through my fault.

Through my fault.

Through my most grievous fault.

The sea, it seems, has become my priest, the punishing, faceless thing to which I confess my sins, silent witness to my self-inflicted wounds. We're alike in many ways, a restless beating of water and salt, a shifting and seething of secrets, of treacheries. Reckless. Dangerous.

The tide, you see, is a fickle thing: stealing in, sliding away, always, always turning. She comes while you're not looking, a silent, liquid thief, only to rush away again, retreating from the shore like a coward. She gives sometimes, too, though, in fleeting, unexpected moments, yielding up her treasures and her dead—but never, ever her secrets.

And so here I sit on the dunes in my carefully mismatched clothes, hour after hour, day after day, frozen in my looking back. *Do not look behind you . . . lest you be swept away.* That is what scripture says. Only there is nowhere for me to look *but* back. No future. No redemption. Like Lot's wife, I am turned to salt, my tired eyes trained on the blue-gray horizon, where sea meets sky, where my yesterdays meet my tomorrows, a ragtag eccentric, watching and waiting for something that never comes.

Oh, I'm quite aware of how ridiculous I am. I'm called Dirty Mary by the locals, though Crazy Mary would be more appropriate. I'm not dirty, but I am crazy. I have the pills and the scars to prove it. I don't mind the name. It keeps people at a distance, which is exactly how I like them—the more distant, the better. I have no wish to share myself with anyone, you see, to unwrap either the then or the now, the before or the after. I move alone through the world. It's better that way—safer.

There are more like me—many, in fact—who hide behind masks and write their own fairy tales. Bright or dark, it makes no difference. We would not have our true selves stripped bare, would not have cold eyes peering between our emotional blinds. Our sins and follies are ours alone, to mourn or rewrite as we choose.

I have chosen the latter.

I pay no attention to the buffeting wind, or to the sand gusting up from the dunes. Mother Nature, it seems, is bent on pitching a bit of a blow. Penny. They're calling her Penny. High time, too, I'd say, for that good lady to show what she's made of. We should all do that now and again, unleash a bit of ourselves—a flash of lightning, a growl of thunder—just to prove to the world and the White Coats that we haven't been beaten, that beneath our cool, glassy surfaces we are still forces to be reckoned with.

I know about reckoning. I have lived through the reckoning.

I think of that time now, that other time, that other storm, and the day my life took its final, irrevocable turn toward disaster. I let my eyes wander briefly down the narrow strip of beach, down to Starry Point Light, hazy and chalk white in the windy distance, startled, as

I always am, by how little things have changed since that awful day. And I wonder how this can be—after all that has happened, after all I have lost. It matters little now, I suppose. And so I say let the storm come, with its wind and whipping sea. Let it take what it will. For me, the sea has already done her worst.

Chapter 2

Lane

Of all the rooms at the Cloister House, Lane's favorite was her writing room in the northeast turret. She loved the smoothly curved walls and high, curtainless windows, how the light played over the smoothly worn floorboards and turned the jars of sea glass along the sills into chalices of pastel jewels. But most of all, she loved the view, nothing short of spectacular when the day was clear and bright but even more breathtaking at night, when stars filled the sky and the moon turned the sea to quicksilver.

But tonight, as she peered over the rim of her cold cup of tea and listened to the wind gusting in off the Atlantic, there was nothing to see: no moon, no stars, nothing but the rhythmic sweep of Starry Point Light and her own reflection in the wavy panes.

They didn't have tropical storms in Chicago. Penny would be her first. There had been scares, of course, close calls that caught the attention of the locals and even sent a few scurrying to prepare, but they'd been incredibly lucky, something to do with El Niño. Now it seemed their luck had run out. Not that she was worried. She'd been through plenty of firsts in her life, plenty of lasts, too, and had managed to survive them all. More than five years had passed since she landed in Starry Point, the last in a sandy string of islands along

North Carolina's Outer Banks. At the time it seemed an unlikely place for a Chicago girl to end up, a small spit of land tethered to the world by a series of narrow, sand-swept bridges. But something had whispered as she crossed that last bridge, something that said this spit of land, with its charming old lighthouse, pastel-washed bungalows, and sleepy Victorian village, this place at the end of the world, might be the perfect place to begin again. And begin again she had.

Running a bed-and-breakfast had never been her dream. In fact, until she laid eyes on the Cloister, the idea had never crossed her mind. She'd had no idea where to start, but with a failed marriage, a failed pregnancy, and a failed novel to her credit, one more failure wasn't likely to make much difference one way or another.

She liked to pretend it was the view that captured her heart—powder white dunes and teal blue seas, Starry Point Light standing tall and formidable in the distance—but that wasn't the absolute truth. Those things kept her guest register full during the season, but for Lane the Cloister's appeal had to do with its twin Romanesque towers and rough-faced gray stone, wholly unexpected and starkly at odds with Starry Point's wooden shingles and white picket fences.

I'm all wrong, it seemed to say. *I don't belong here.*

Yet here it stood, proud, indomitable—a survivor. And now it belonged to her. For the first time in years, perhaps in her life, she was in charge of her own life, with no one peering over her shoulder, ready to pounce on her slightest mistake. And if running it took most of her waking hours, so what? For now, that was enough. And when the season ended—three weeks early this year, thanks to tropical storm Penny—there was time to pursue her freelance work: scribbling articles about things she'd never done and places she'd never been.

Lane's teacup came down with a clatter as a fresh gust of wind slapped at the windows, rattling the old panes in their frames. Everyone said that waiting was the worst. Everyone was right. Snapping off the lamp, she rose from her desk and headed downstairs.

In the kitchen she rinsed her cup and saucer, then decided to make one last round to check the locks. She had already checked once, right after the Burtons went up for the night, but these days it didn't pay to take chances. As if a late-season storm weren't excitement enough for one small town, a recent rash of break-ins on the normally sleepy island had the good people of Starry Point bolting their doors and demanding answers.

Nine break-ins reported so far: all petty, and all unsolved. But in a town where sand-sculpture contests and chowder cook-offs qualified as excitement, they might as well have been armed home invasions. And now, with her last guests fleeing inland tomorrow morning, she would soon find herself alone for the entire winter.

The thought was vaguely unsettling as she took one final peer through the curtains. Across the street, the Rourke place stood grave and forlorn. The once-fine house was empty now, and had been for years, its rear windows boarded after a fire ravaged the upper floors and took the life of five-year-old Peter Rourke. In the dark the place looked grand enough, when you couldn't see the overgrown shrubs and shabby lawn, or the faintly scorched brick above the third-story windows. She stifled a shiver, as she always did when her eyes lingered on the Victorian-style greenhouse hunkered against the north side of the house.

She had ventured inside once, not long after moving to Starry Point, had stood in the center of the ruined conservatory, choked with weeds and saplings, more than half its small square panes in shards on the packed earth floor. It had given her the creeps then, and it still did. But it made her a little sad, too.

It was a shame that a home that once belonged to one of Starry Point's most beloved mayors had been allowed to go to ruin. For years, the Preservation Society had been vowing to restore the place and open it to the public, but as far as she could tell, little progress had been made in that direction. In the meantime, years of neglect had taken their toll, until all that remained was the hollow echo of the home's former grandeur. And yet it remained a favorite on Starry Point's seasonal walking tours—mostly because locals insisted the place was haunted. Lane didn't believe it, of course, but it had become clear that owning a bed-and-breakfast across from the local haunted house wasn't exactly bad for business.

She was surprised when the banjo clock in the hall sounded a single, throaty peal. How was it already one a.m.? The Burtons would be up in five hours, ready for breakfast and anxious to stay ahead of the weather. She didn't blame them. According to the news, Highway 12 was bumper-to-bumper all the way to the mainland. She only had one more window to check.

Lane went still when she saw the light, a wide, milky beam floating past the first-floor windows of the Rourke House. She'd heard people use the expression *frozen to the spot* but had never experienced it firsthand—until now. Her heart thumped heavily in her ears as she squinted through the curtains, following the beam's steady progress and trying to make sense of what she was seeing. Then, as suddenly as it had appeared, the light was gone.

The police cruiser pulled up along the curb and cut its lights. Lane watched from the window as the officers emerged from the car, relieved that Donny Breester hadn't decided to answer the call. But then, Starry Point's chief of police wasn't one to put himself out when there was nothing to be gained, and after five years of trying—and failing—maybe he'd finally grasped that when it came to Lane Kramer, there was *absolutely* nothing to be gained.

She watched as the pair split up, then melted into the shadows at the back of the abandoned house. When they reappeared an impossibly short time later, she hurried out to meet them. The night air was thick and hazy with salt and chillier than she'd expected. She shivered as she made her way to the street, wishing she'd put more on her feet than a pair of flip-flops. Rick Warren and Gary Mickles were waiting for her at the base of the drive. Rick holstered his flashlight and tipped his hat. Gary spat, hooked his thumb between his paunch and his duty belt, and said nothing. Neither looked especially happy that they'd been called.

"Did you find anything?" Lane aimed the question at Rick, the less annoyed-looking of the two. "The light disappeared, but I never saw anyone moving away from the house. I've been watching since I hung up with dispatch."

Rick was scribbling in a small notebook. "No sign of anyone around back," he muttered without looking up. "No signs of forced entry. All the windows are still boarded. So unless somebody had a key—"

"There was a light," Lane said again, shivering now, and painfully aware that she was standing outside in a bathrobe. "It moved past the front windows, right to left, then back again."

Gary craned his neck in the direction of Starry Point Light and waited for the beam to sweep back around. "There's your intruder right there," he snorted.

Lane stared at him, incredulous. "You think I saw the beam from the lighthouse?"

Mickles spat again and hitched up his drooping belt. "Moves past those windows just like you said. Mystery solved."

Lane bit back the remark on the tip of her tongue and turned to Rick. "The light I saw moved slowly. And it moved from right to left, not left to right. It wasn't the lighthouse. It was . . . something else."

Rick jotted a final note in his book, then flipped the cover closed before stuffing it back into his pocket. "Light can do tricky things, Mrs. Kramer, especially late at night."

Especially late at night? What was that supposed to mean? Were there special laws of physics that kicked in after dark?

"Rick, I've lived here for five years now, and I can promise you that if the beam from Starry Point Light came anywhere near those windows I would have seen it before tonight. If you don't believe me, stand here and watch it for yourself. The beam's too high, and it moves in the wrong direction."

Mickles snorted again, clearly impatient. "Maybe the light looks different from over at your place. I read somewhere that light can bend."

Even Rick thought it was a stupid answer. He shot Mickles a look that told him to be quiet. "I don't know what you saw, Mrs. Kramer, but I can tell you there's nothing there now. We've checked the place out top to bottom and there's no way anyone was in that house tonight."

"So you're saying I imagined it?"

Mickles let his breath out through his teeth, heavily scented with the onions he'd obviously had for dinner. "Don't feel bad. Every time the wind blows these days, some woman's picking up the phone and dialing 911. You haven't got anything to worry about over here, though. So far all the incidents have been on the sound side. Hey, maybe you saw one of them ghosts that's supposed to live there—the boy, or the old man."

Lane stifled a groan. It was clear that nothing she said was going to make these two take her seriously.

Warren must have sensed her frustration. "How about I arrange for a car to drive by from time to time and keep an eye out? I'd be happy to do that if it'll make you feel better, but in all honesty, I can't imagine anyone wanting to get inside that old house. Everyone knows it's been empty for years. I'll send that cruiser around, though." He tipped his hat. "You have yourself a good rest of the night."

Lane fumed as she watched the cruiser's taillights disappear down

Old Point Road. They thought she was a hysterical female, a woman living alone, given to bouts of paranoia. But they had agreed to send a patrol around. That was something, at least. She turned to look again at the Rourke House—not a sign of life or light now—and wondered if Mickles might not be right. Maybe her imagination *had* been working overtime, conjuring things that weren't there. But no, in her mind she could still see the light. Someone had been in that house.

Chapter 3

Morning came too soon for Lane. It had been well after two by the time she'd crawled into bed, and she'd spent another hour tossing, trying to explain away what she'd seen, and failing completely. The fact that the Burtons would be pulling out in less than an hour did little to brighten her mood. In the five years they'd been staying at the Cloister, Dan and Dottie Burton had become like family, sending newsy e-mails along with the latest travel pics, and lately, drawings had begun to arrive in the mail from their granddaughter, Shelly. The most recent, a somewhat abstract rendition of her new puppy, Tango, stared back at her with bright green crayon eyes as she closed the refrigerator door.

Lane couldn't help smiling. They had been her very first guests, a sweet, comfortable old couple, married so long they'd actually started to resemble each other, and often finished each other's sentences. She could hear them upstairs now as she pulled out a handful of silverware and prepared to set the table—opening and closing bureau drawers, making a final check for items left behind, followed by the steady bump of suitcases being lugged downstairs. It would certainly be quiet when they were gone.

After filling the cream and sugar, Lane stacked a tray with mugs and carried it to the small sunroom just off the kitchen, where high arched windows usually offered a stunning view of the beach. Today, the view was anything but stunning. The sea was a heaving mass of gray-green swells, and the sun was nowhere to be seen, lost in a sky of scudding pewter clouds. She frowned at the windows, washed the day before yesterday and already hazy with salt spray. After the Burtons were gone she wouldn't have to wash them until March if she didn't feel like it.

"Yoo-hoo!"

Dottie Burton's cheerful greeting brought Lane around with what she hoped was a warm smile. "Morning, Dottie. All packed and ready to hit the road?"

Dottie was a young sixty, plump and pretty in a lived-in sort of way, with a quick smile and the slow, sweet drip of Nashville, Tennessee, in her voice.

"Dan's putting the bags in the trunk as we speak. I hate that we're having to desert early. Really, we'd be happy to pay you for the other three days."

Lane filled a mug with coffee and passed it over. "Don't be silly. It's not like I lost a booking. The season's over."

"And tomorrow you'll have this big old place to yourself." Dottie heaped a third spoonful of sugar into her mug and began to stir. She took it sweet, like her tea. "It must be a relief not to have to cook for anyone but yourself, to just eat a sandwich over the sink if you feel like it. By the way, what smells so amazing?"

Lane lifted her nose and sniffed, then remembered the breakfast casserole she'd stuck in the oven. "Good Lord! It's the breakfast if I haven't burned it."

Dan appeared as Lane pulled the casserole from the oven. He spotted the coffeepot on the table and made a beeline for it. "Pretty nasty out there," he said into his mug. "Windy as the very devil, and I don't like the look of that sky. No, sir."

Lane took another quick peek out the window. "Let's get you fed and on the road, then." The casserole was crispy at the edges, but salvageable. She served up two plates and carried them to the table, then topped off their coffee. "I made muffins, too, so you can take some with you. If the weather turns and you have to pull off, at least I know you won't starve."

Dottie looked up from her plate. "Do you think it's going to get that bad?"

Lane bit her lip as she eyed the sky through the kitchen window, but she gave the woman's plump shoulder a squeeze. "It's only a tropical storm. Just some wind and rain, maybe a few trees down, but then, I'm no expert. I've never been through one of these. They haven't made us leave, so that's a good sign, right?"

Dan shot his wife a look that said *eat faster*.

When the breakfast plates were in the sink, Lane bagged a half dozen still-warm muffins and filled two to-go cups with coffee. They said their good-byes on the front porch—a handshake from Dan, a hug and a kiss on both cheeks from Dottie, along with promises to send pictures of the new grandbaby when he arrived in spring.

"You write lots of pretty articles this winter, honey. I'll be looking for them. And maybe if you get time you could go see your mama for the holidays. I don't like to think of you here by yourself on Thanksgiving and Christmas."

"I'll be fine," Lane assured her. "And up to my ears in deadlines by the time the holidays roll around. Please promise you'll be careful. Pull off if it gets bad, or turn around and come back. Your room will be waiting."

Lane waved from the porch as the Burtons' silver Buick backed down the drive. As the car disappeared from sight, her eyes slid across the street to the Rourke House. Suddenly, she felt silly. In the light of day there wasn't anything remotely sinister about the place. And yet as she stared at its windows, rimed with years of salt and dust, she couldn't shake the memory of last night. She shivered again as she turned to go inside, reminding herself that the police had promised to keep an eye on the place.

In the kitchen, she poured herself a cup of coffee and dished up a serving of the now-cold breakfast casserole, thinking of Dottie as she ate it over the sink. With the Burtons gone the inn felt empty. But then, it always did when the last guest checked out: a peculiar blend of loss and relief as time slowed and she traded her innkeeper persona for pen and paper.

And who knew? Maybe one day she'd actually get around to visiting some of the places she wrote about. For now it was enough to hibernate, to burrow in, away from the world, and put words to paper, even if it was only an article here and there. Her name would appear in print from time to time, and now and then a check would appear in her mailbox, money in exchange for words. For a person of limited talent, it was really all she had a right to expect.

After tidying the kitchen, then stripping and straightening the Burtons' room, Lane laced up her muck boots, donned a heavy fleece jacket, and slipped a bag of stale bread into her pocket. The wind hit her hard as she stepped out the back door, damp and full of blowing sand. Standing with her feet braced wide apart, she shielded her eyes and scanned the beach, wondering whether she should skip her usual morning walk to the light.

Aside from last year's weeklong bout with flu, she'd made the mile-and-a-half trek to the light every morning for five years. She found clarity in the daily walks, like a kind of moving meditation that lifted away the fog and set the stage for the rest of the day. She saw no reason to let a little wind—or even a lot of wind—cheat her of that. She was contemplating going back for gloves when an unexpected flash of color caught her eye, a bright bit of purple against the dreary seascape.

But it couldn't be. Not today, in weather like this.

Standing on tiptoe, Lane peered past the back gate, stunned to see that the ragtag old woman was, in fact, seated in her customary spot on the dunes. She had appeared for the first time only a few weeks ago, a rarity since most beach walkers disappeared the minute the warm weather did. Even die-hard Starry Point natives—Old Pointers, they called themselves—rarely ventured onto the dunes past October, and this was the middle of November. Yet, each morning like clockwork, she continued to appear, clutching her purple bag and staring out to sea, as if watching for something no one else could see.

Today, she sat huddled against the wind in an oversize Windbreaker and a lumpy gray sweater, clutching the ever-present bag as if the wind might take it. They had never spoken, or even made eye contact, though Lane had always been curious about the woman's story. For the slimmest of moments Lane considered approaching, but something in the rigid set of the old woman's shoulders seemed to forbid it. Instead, she braced against a fresh blast of wind and zipped her jacket to her throat.

The gate wailed as she dragged it open, then clanged shut noisily when the wind snatched it from her hand. The woman flinched, whipping her head in Lane's direction. For an instant, eyes of indistinct color met hers, wary or confused, Lane couldn't say which. Then, as quickly as the gaze had settled on her, it withdrew, lost again out to sea.

Determined to give the old woman a wide berth, Lane lowered her head and set off across the dunes. She wanted to pretend the encounter hadn't unnerved her, but it had. It seemed everything unnerved her these days: old women, the wind, phantom lights in vacant houses. Maybe it was the weather. She'd heard somewhere that low pressure did strange things to cats and pregnant women. Why not innkeepers with active imaginations?

Whatever it was, she was determined to shake it. She doubled her pace, but it was far from an easy go. The dunes were already taking a beating, and the blowing sand made it hard to see. Overhead, a pack of gulls circled and dipped, screeching for the bread in her pocket.

"You know the drill, boys," she said to them. "Not till we reach the light, and then you have to share."

A single gull broke from the pack, wings flashing white as it swooped low, then lifted away with a shrill cry—the equivalent, Lane supposed, of a child stomping from the room. By the time she reached the lighthouse, dozens more would have taken its place.

Ahead, Starry Point Light braced for the coming storm, sturdy and steadfast after a century's worth of rain and wind and surf. The gulls were gathering in earnest now, circling in noisy anticipation as she turned onto the jetty and covered the last few yards. The rocks were too wet to sit on, but the wind was easier on the leeward side of the light. Dragging the bag from her pocket, she crumpled a slice of bread and tossed it into the air, watching the feeding frenzy as the wind took the crumbs.

The air was a blur of salt and sand as she glanced back down the beach, so hazy she could barely make out the roofline of the inn, tucked back from the dunes. Originally built in 1896 as a convent, the Cloister had weathered its share of storms; it had weathered its share of incarnations, too, serving, after the nuns left, as everything from a boys' home to a record storage facility and most recently a women's health clinic, until the pious new mayor had it shut down for permit violations.

The Cloister.

Even the name had struck a chord the first time she heard it, conjuring thoughts of peace and quiet, of seclusion—of escape. She had closed in just two weeks, plunking down nearly every cent of the divorce settlement before she had time to change her mind. It felt rash at the time—rash and good—to finally have something that was hers, and hers alone. Her mother had been horrified when she finally broke the news. But then, when had Cynthia Kramer *not* been horrified by something her oldest daughter had done?

And then there was Bruce, the real reason she'd left Chicago.

Their marriage had been doomed from the beginning, despite her husband's meteoric rise to become head of Chicago General's cardiac surgical unit and all the trappings that came with such a title—the egos, the parties, the pretty young nurses. It had ended, not with a bang but with a whimper, after she'd miscarried their first child.

Her fault, of course—somehow everything was always her fault—the warm gush of scarlet soaking through her lemon yellow slacks in the middle of lunch, the sudden horror, the moment of knowing. She had come to in the hospital, the child—the little girl who was to have been named Emma—gone. Bruce was there when she opened her eyes, his first words not expressions of care or concern, but of accusation. *What did you do?*

Her marriage had died that day, along with her child, and yet, for nearly a year after, she had worn her good-wife face as it all came unraveled: through his desertion of their bed, the transparent late nights and spur-of-the-moment conference weekends, the hamper of dirty shirts reeking of someone else's perfume.

Lane shivered involuntarily, though whether the reaction had to do with the memory of those dark days, or with the blast of sea spray that suddenly gusted in off the waves, she couldn't say. In the time it had taken to reach the jetty, the wind had risen considerably, its constant rush melding now with the hiss and roar of the waves, until one had become indistinguishable from the other. The sea, too, was on the move, the tide pushing in, boiling up onto the rocks in a ceaseless swirl of green and white. If she stayed much longer, she was going to end up soaked.

With the bread gone and the gulls disbanded, Lane shoved the empty sandwich bag into her pocket, tugged her hood up onto her head, and made her way in from the jetty. At least the wind would be with her on the way back.

The rain started around two, just as Lane was returning from a last-minute run for supplies. She darted inside with an armload of bags, trying not to dwell on the sullen clouds shredding overhead. Every radio station up and down the dial seemed to be blasting information: storm coordinates, wind speeds, projected surges on Manteo, Nags Head, Duck, and Starry Point. She had turned it off. No point worrying about the numbers now. She was as ready as she was going to get.

Sam Redman had come by yesterday and taped all the windows with big ugly X's. Better than nothing, he had grumbled when she told him she'd never gotten around to pricing the storm shutters he recommended four years ago. She had also misjudged when to start thinking about things like water, canned goods, and batteries. Unfortunately, Old Pointers were well acquainted with the ins and outs of storm preparation and hadn't made the same mistake. By the time she got to town, the Village Mart looked as if it had been set upon by a pack of zombies, plundered of everything but meat and produce.

She'd had no luck with batteries but had at least managed to scare up a few gallons of water and a lone jar of peanut butter. Crunchy wasn't her favorite, but it would have to do. She had fuel for the Coleman stove, two loaves of fresh-baked bread, and a huge pot of soup cooling on the stove. She might end up sitting in the dark, but she wasn't likely to starve.

After recording a "closed for the season" message referring callers to the inn's Web site, she brewed a mug of Earl Grey and carried it upstairs, resigned to nailing herself to the chair in her writing room until she completed a first draft of the vintage soap-making piece that was due next week.

The first day of the off-season was generally one of her most productive, when she was finally free to mold the ideas that had been percolating all summer, to lose all sense of time without a care for anyone else's needs. No bread to bake, no beds to change, no constantly being available for guests.

But today was different somehow. Even her writing room failed to inspire, despite last night's careful preparations. Folders filled with research and interview notes were stacked to her right, scraps of ideas captured on pastel-colored sticky notes were arranged to her left, and in the center, her laptop awaited only the touch of a button to bring it to life. All that was missing was inspiration.

As always, when her creativity was playing hide-and-seek, Lane reached into the desk for the old sketchbook, tucked carefully in the center drawer. From the moment one of the contractors had discovered it in a dusty nook beneath the stairs, the book had held a strange fascination for her. She had scoured it for a signature or date, anything that might offer some clue about its origin, but there was nothing. Now, after five years, she knew every scuff and scar on the leather cover, every smooth place worn along its spine, every gorgeous, lushly colored sketch: fairy-tale images of castles and princes and fair-haired damsels, each framed with an intricate vine of white flowers, like something from a child's storybook, but all done by hand.

Even now, Lane's fingers moved with a kind of awe as she turned to her favorite illustration at the back of the book, faded with who knew how many years, but still enchanting. It was a two-masted schooner in the throes of a storm, its sails in shreds, its keel shattered on a jagged rise of rock, and on the shoals, a bare-breasted woman with a shimmering tail and creamy white shells woven into her flame-kissed hair.

The drawing had disturbed her the first time she ran across it, its doomed ship and storm-tossed sea too real, too much like life with its storms and its choices. Be brave or yield. Lane knew about yielding, about slowly letting yourself go hollow, until one day you looked in the mirror and no longer recognized the woman staring back, and wondering where you'd gone—or if you'd ever really been there at all.

Maybe that was the real reason the image fascinated her, why little by little a kind of fable had rooted itself in her thoughts: a cautionary tale about a woman too weak to fight the tide, who chose to end her days in a great stone tower overlooking the sea. Purely fictional, of course, but sometimes—like now—her fingers itched to write that story. But she wouldn't. Not this year. Not ever. Because doing so would mean having to confront her own long list of shipwrecks, and when all was said and done, she simply hadn't the courage. Safer to stick to her articles and play with words she knew wouldn't burn.

Sighing, she closed the book of illustrations and slid it back into the drawer, feeling the old familiar ache. It came less often now, but today it had come with a vengeance. Not sadness exactly, but the numbing awareness that this was all there would ever be. Once upon a time, she'd dreamed of so much more, of love and marriage and children, of somehow leaving her mark on the world. Now, as she stared out past the dunes, she saw that even the footprints she'd left in the sand a few hours ago were already gone, blown over—as if she'd never been there at all.

She sipped her tea, too sweet since it had gone cold. She hated herself when she was like this, pouty and discontent, wallowing in the past. If she wasn't careful she'd soon find herself in the clutches of a full-blown sulk. Hardly the way she'd envisioned her first day of creative freedom.

Shake it off, Kramer. This is ridiculous. Not to mention exactly what Bruce would want.

The thought of Bruce reveling in her self-pity was enough to light a fire. Powering up the laptop, she reached for a folder with WILD AND SWEET VINTAGE SOAPS printed neatly on the tab. Before she could open it, a bit of movement caught her eye, a quick blur of purple. Surely it wasn't. Pushing up out of her chair, she peered down at the beach. The old woman had been gone when she returned from the lighthouse, removed, Lane assumed, to safer and drier ground. Now here she was again, hunched on the dunes in a blowing gray rain. Clearly, the poor thing wasn't well.

By the time Lane dragged on a pair of shoes and scrambled down two flights of stairs and out the back door, the woman was already on the move, crabbing her way up the dune and past the back gate. If she noticed Lane at the open door, she gave no sign, her drenched white head hunched into her collar as she skirted the boardwalk and cut across the vacant lot that bordered the inn.

With no thought for a jacket, Lane slipped out into the rain and through the gate to follow. She had no idea why, or what she might say if she were discovered creeping up behind her. She only knew the woman had no business being out in this weather. Moving furtively, she held back a few steps in hopes of avoiding discovery, but it was no good. As she turned the corner of the yard, the woman suddenly rounded on her.

For the second time that day, Lane found herself caught in that strange gaze, a mingling of panic and challenge. But this time it lingered, questioning. *Friend or foe?* it seemed to ask. The moment stretched, an uncomfortable eternity as they stood eying each other, soaked through and buffeted by the wind. Lane felt a prickle along the back of her neck, as if words had somehow passed between them, though the old woman stood as still and mute as stone. She should speak, she knew, say something, but her lips felt suddenly numb, useless.

It might have been a minute or an hour, but finally the old woman turned away, scuttling with startling speed across the grassy lot, vanishing behind a tall thicket of red cedars out along the road. Moments later, she reemerged on a bike, an ancient, rusty contraption with an enormous basket in front and a jaunty pink DayGlo flag in back.

Lane stood shivering at the edge of Old Point Road, arms wrapped close to her body, blinking fat drops from her lashes as she watched the bright plastic flag gradually fade from sight, praying the poor woman had a safe place to ride out the storm.

Chapter 4

Mary

A close call. Too close.

I see her every day, scuttling down the beach to feed the gulls—the Inn Lady. She's a bright, pretty thing, but sad, too, I think, and just a little broken. But then, everyone is fighting some private war, grappling with some missing piece, carrying some unseen burden. She hides it well enough with her quick step, always in a hurry, always one step ahead of something only she can see or feel. And yet I see it plain. To one well acquainted, there is no hiding grief. It stains, you see, seeping deep into your flesh, like a brand. A shame in one so young and lovely, but then, I was young and lovely once, too. Life plays no favorites when she sets out to break a heart.

Until today the Inn Lady has stayed away like the others, seeming to pay me no mind, though more than once I have felt her eyes between my shoulder blades. I always feel their eyes. But hers are different somehow, even when standing nearly face-to-face. It has been a long time since anyone had the boldness to look me in the eye, to risk a true seeing. Oh, they glance in my direction, but they're afraid of what they might see, a mirror, perhaps, of the future, should life go suddenly and terribly wrong. But it couldn't ever happen to them. They're good, clean, decent people. And so their curiosity, and their sympathy, too, if they ever had any, turns into something hard and mean. They turn away, disgusted, while a little part of them thanks their maker it isn't them.

But this woman is different. There was no disgust in her gaze, only curiosity and something like compassion as our eyes held for that long, rainy moment. And now, as I pedal away like the mad-woman I am, I feel I have received a great kindness, perhaps the greatest of my life.

How strange that such a gift should come at the hands of a stranger, rather than the hands of someone who claimed to love me. But then, they're all gone now, those loved ones. Swept away, burned away, blown away.

Through my fault.

Through my fault.

Through my most grievous fault.

Chapter 5

Lane

By nightfall Penny had begun to push her way onshore. Rain lashed steadily at the windows, the wind a sharply rising keen that made the panes rattle like old bones. Lane ladled soup into a bowl and popped it into the microwave, struggling to keep her mind on what she was doing and off where the old woman might be at that moment. They had set up a shelter in the community center. Maybe she was there.

But what if she wasn't?

It was hard to imagine the woman she had encountered this morning voluntarily shoehorning herself in with a bunch of strangers. In fact, it was impossible. A thought struck her, or rather, an image, a beam of light moving past empty windows. It was possible. It even made sense. The police swore there were no signs of forced entry, but they couldn't have been very thorough in the few minutes they'd spent at the back of the house. They could easily have missed something.

While the microwave whirred she padded to the front parlor, peering through the curtains, past strips of soggy masking tape. Old Point Road, the empty stretch of oyster-shell macadam that brought tourists to the Cloister, was deserted now, the road swamped after hours of steady rain. Lane watched anxiously as odd bits of detritus cartwheeled down the street: fallen tree branches, an aluminum trash can lid, a sodden chair cushion she'd missed when securing the yard yesterday. Across the street at the Rourke House, nothing seemed amiss, no light of any kind, no bike with a bright plastic flag. Lane didn't know whether to be relieved or concerned as she let the curtains fall back into place. It was a hideous night for anyone to be out, particularly an old woman. Not that there was anything she could do about it now.

In the kitchen, she thought of the Burtons as she poured a glass of Pinot and pulled her soup from the microwave, hoping they'd made it back to the mainland before things got too bad. She was about to slice herself a thick slab of bread when the lights sputtered and the kitchen went dark. The bread knife was still in her fist as she whirled around at nothing, the pins-and-needles prickle of adrenaline hot along her arms and legs, breath held in the sudden absence of household whirring and ticking.

It took a moment for Lane's heart to resume something like its normal rhythm, and several more to accept that the lights weren't coming back on any time soon. Feeling her way to the parlor, she fumbled with a pack of matches and lit a few candles, then groped about in the half-light to lay a small fire in the hearth. She supposed there were worse things than dinner in front of the fire, even if she was alone.

In a few minutes the blaze was going nicely, washing the walls with wavering amber light. Lane sipped her wine and stared into the flames. Candles, firelight, a stormy night—like something right out of a book. Only in books heroines didn't schlep around in sweats and stretched-out socks, or wear their hair in grubby ponytails. Groaning, she took another sip from her glass. The only thing missing was the eleven cats.

Her head shot up when she heard a knock at the front door. Who on earth—? Before she could finish the question, the knock came again, more insistent this time. Perhaps the Burtons had turned back after all. Or the old woman—?

Carrying a candle to the window, she pressed her forehead to the glass, hoping to be able to see out to the drive, but could make out nothing but sheets of gusting rain. When the knock came a third time she turned the dead bolt and eased the door open as far as the chain would allow. The silhouette standing on her porch was too tall to belong to either of the Burtons.

"Can I help you?" she asked through the crack.

"I hope so. I'm looking for a place to stay."

It was a male voice, deep and tired, and unless she was mistaken, a little annoyed. Lifting her candle, she tried to put a face with the voice. It didn't do much good. All she could make out was a square jawline and a pair of very broad shoulders.

"I'm sorry, but the inn's closed for the winter. You can try the Windjammer. Take a right up at the stop sign and head back into town. You'll see the blue neon sign."

"No sign," the voice shot back over the wind. "Power's out everywhere. Are you sure you can't put me up? The roads are a nightmare."

Lane had heard that voice before. It belonged to every traveler who'd been behind the wheel too long, so road weary they'd happily pay suite money to sleep in the pantry if it was all she had available. Unhooking the chain, she eased the door open another few inches, just wide enough to let the candlelight spill out onto the porch.

If the man objected to her scrutiny, he gave no sign. He stood there, one arm braced against the doorframe to steady himself against the wind. She put him at well over six feet. Forty, maybe, with longish hair dripping onto the collar of his jacket, and some kind of satchel slung over one shoulder. Okay, maybe he wasn't an ax murderer. On the other hand, who knew what the well-dressed ax murderer was wearing these days?

"I'm really quite respectable," he assured her, as if reading her thoughts. "I'm a professor at Middlebury College. I'm looking for a place to ride this thing out, and maybe park for the winter. I promise, the scariest thing in my bag is a collection of stories by Edgar Allan Poe."

"I don't have any power," Lane said, knowing it wouldn't dissuade him.

He glanced past her, to the parlor with its candles and cozy fire. "Looks like you're managing. Besides, I don't need lights to sleep, which is all I want in the world right now. You can charge me double if you want."

Lane felt herself softening. He was drenched to the bone and obviously exhausted. She could put up with him for one night, she supposed, until the storm passed and the roads were clear. Pulling back the door, she waved him in with her candle.

He wasted no time stepping into the foyer. Shrugging the satchel from his shoulder, he let it slide to the floor, then unzipped his jacket, revealing khakis and a dark blue sweater.

"Is there somewhere I can hang this? I don't want to drip all over your floor."

Lane took the coat, giving it a good shake over the entrance mat before hanging it on the rack beside the door, then motioned for him to follow her to the reception desk in the den. "Let's get you checked in. The worst of the storm should blow over by tomorrow. Then you can find other lodgings." She had taken several steps before she realized her guest wasn't behind her.

"Professor?"

He gave no sign that he heard her, standing almost eerily still, his head tilted back as he surveyed the parlor's coffered ceiling. Lane cleared her throat, and he jerked his head in her direction. "Oh, sorry. Right behind you."

At the desk Lane gave him a registration card to fill out, situating her candle so he could see. She'd have to key him into the system in the morning. No way to run a credit card, either. When he finished with the card he slid it back. Lane looked it over. *Michael Forrester. Middlebury, Vermont.* Nice penmanship. That was good—no serial killer handwriting.

"I'll let you have the Tower Suite at the regular-room rate since it's just one night and you're the only guest," she informed him, then launched into her standard first-time-guest speech. "All the rooms are nonsmoking. Breakfast is at nine, though with no power I'm not exactly sure what that might be. If you need anything, press two on your room phone and you'll get me. Well, no, you won't, actually, with the power out. I guess you can just bang on the ceiling. My rooms are just above yours on the third floor."

"I won't need anything except a bed. Would you like me to pay you now?"

"We'll take care of it in the morning when the power's back up."

"How long's it been down?"

"About thirty minutes." Lane saw him glance at the tray in front of the fire, at her wineglass and half-eaten bowl of soup. "Have you eaten, Mr. Forrester?"

"Not since lunch. I was trying to beat the storm. By the time I hit town, everything was closed."

"I've got some soup on the stove, but it might not be hot. And there's fresh bread, if you're interested."

"I don't want to put you to any trouble. I've already interrupted your dinner."

"It's no trouble. Your rate includes dinner, such as it is. Sit and I'll bring it out. Can I bring you a glass of wine?"

Dropping down onto the couch with something between a sigh and a groan, he stretched his legs out in front of him. "Wine would be great."

Even by candlelight it didn't take long to fill another bowl and slice off a hunk of bread. She carried the tray in and set it on the ottoman beside her own. "It isn't much, but at least it's still warm."

Michael Forrester rubbed a hand over his face, stretched the kinks from his neck. "Thanks, Ms.—I'm sorry, I don't believe I got your name."

"It's Kramer," Lane supplied sheepishly. "Sorry. I usually do the introduction thing at the desk, but everything's a bit...out of sync. Call me Lane."

Settling cross-legged on the floor, Lane reached for her wine, covertly watching her guest over the rim of her glass as he eagerly spooned up his cold soup. She could see him more clearly in the firelight. His dark hair was pushed back from his forehead, longish and still damp, not a bad look on the whole. He had a good face, too, high cheekbones and a firm, square jaw, a chin that hinted slightly at a cleft, with just enough scruff to keep him from being pretty. He probably wasn't as old as she'd originally thought, either, just tired.

He surprised her by looking up from his bowl and lifting his glass. "My compliments to the chef, whoever he is. This may be the best meal of my life, and I'm not just saying that because you're giving me a place to sleep, or at least not entirely."

Lane returned the salute, certain that she detected a faint trace of Boston in his voice. She'd become a dialect expert since opening the inn. "*He* is me, Mr. Forrester. And you should have tasted it when it was hot."

"Yeah, well, hot soup is overrated, especially to a starving man. And please call me Michael." His mouth curved in an attractive way. "Dinner in front of the fire calls for first names, don't you think?"

Dinner in front of the fire. Yes, everything certainly was...out of sync. It wasn't as though she never dined with guests. She did, in fact quite often, but it was usually with people like the Burtons, couples who felt more like family than patrons. This didn't feel like that. Suddenly, she was keenly aware of her baggy sweats and slouchy socks, her lazily scraped together ponytail. Maybe it was too dark to notice that she looked like a slob, but she doubted it. There'd been more than enough light for her to give *him* the once-over.

He was mopping up the last of his soup now, folding the last bite of bread into his mouth. It was silly, but with his long legs stretched out before the fire and a wineglass at his elbow, he seemed to belong right where he was. And yet there had been moments when she'd caught him glancing almost uneasily about the parlor, as if he'd rather be anywhere else in the world. What was his story? she wondered. Where had he been heading, and what was so important that he'd take to the road on a night like this? A critical job interview? A dying relative? An illicit rendezvous with a lover?

It was on the tip of her tongue to ask, but she'd always maintained a strict policy against prying into the private lives of her guests. If they volunteered, well and fine, but she knew not everyone's story was a pretty one. And so she wouldn't ask. Instead, she offered to refill his glass.

Michael made a sound of assent, lids heavy as he stared at the flames licking up from the hearth. "Nice fire. You should probably throw another log on, though."

"I didn't want it to get too hot."

"Trust me, it's in the forties outside. With no power this place will be like a refrigerator by morning."

Lane looked at him, surprised. She'd just been thinking the same thing. "It's because of all the stone."

"And the leaky old windows."

"Architecture professor?" Lane prompted, knowing full well she was breaking her own rules.

Michael blinked heavily, clearly trying to process the question. Finally, he shook his head. "No, but I've had some experience with old places like this. There's a reason there are fireplaces in every room." The words trailed away in a stifled yawn.

Lane stood, fishing a room key from her pocket. "I think I'd better show you to your room while you can still make it up the stairs."

"Please," Michael half groaned. "No stairs."

Lane smothered a smile. He'd meant it as a quip, but the words were laced with genuine fatigue. "I told you, I put you in the Tower Suite, the best room in the house. The only catch is you have to climb a few stairs."

Michael squinted up at her with one eye shut. "How many stairs, exactly?"

"I don't know. I never counted. But I promise you, the view's worth every one."

Another groan as he got to his feet and stretched to his full height. Lane wasn't sure why she was startled. She'd noticed his height the moment she stole a peek at him through the still-chained door, then again when he was hunched over the desk filling out his registration card, but now, with him standing right in front of her, she realized he must be at least six-four. For a moment she envisioned him asleep in the Tower Suite's four-poster with his feet dangling over the edge.

"All right, innkeeper," Michael muttered thickly as he stooped to retrieve his satchel. "Lead the way."

"You'd best grab a couple of those candles to take up with you," she told him. "It'll be pitch-dark upstairs."

How anyone could think of sleep in the middle of a storm like this one, Lane would never know, though clearly it was all Michael Forrester was thinking about. Before she could grab her own candle, he started up ahead of her, preventing her from leading the way as he had just suggested. Never mind—she'd tell him where he was going when they reached the landing. Except he didn't seem to need directions. Like a man with a compass, he made an abrupt right at the top of the first flight, then continued on to the end of the corridor.

Lane eyed him closely as she stepped around to unlock the door.

"Are you sure you haven't stayed with me before? You seemed to know exactly where you were going."

"You said the Tower Suite on the second floor. This is the second floor, and even in the storm I could see the tower when I pulled up. Also, the sign on the door kind of gives it away."

She felt foolish as she looked at the plaque on the heavy oak door, clearly engraved with the words TOWER SUITE. Gary Mickles said every woman in town was a nervous wreck. She hated to say it, but maybe he was right. Maybe the recent crime wave had unsettled her more than she realized, and soon she'd be checking under beds and sleeping with the lights on.

"Nice," Michael pronounced as he followed her inside, though she had the distinct feeling he was just being polite. "Very . . . authentic."

Lane had to agree. Of the inn's twelve guest rooms, the Tower Suite was her favorite, richly appointed and period-perfect. She loved to show it off, probably because she'd spent more time and energy on it than any other room. Or maybe it was because aside from her own apartment on the third floor, the Tower Suite offered the most spectacular view of the coast and lighthouse.

Tonight, though, there was no view to brag about, only a merciless wind on the other side of the blackout curtains. The wind was louder here, too, on the second floor, howling in off the water. Maybe she should have put him on the first floor, in a room that fronted the street rather than up here, taking the brunt of the storm. In the end she doubted it would matter much. By the look of him, he'd be asleep before she made it downstairs. And by noon he'd be back on the road, on his way to wherever.

"The suite has a private bath," she said, always the start of her spiel, "and an amazing tub, if you're up for a soak. There's probably still some hot water. Your toiletries are in this basket, and there are extra towels in the cabinet, along with a dryer and iron, not that they'll do you much good."

Michael nodded, but she could see that he'd appreciate it if she skipped the full tour and just hit the high points. "There's a small sitting room in here," she said, moving to the doorway of the small tower room at the southeast corner of the suite. "Normally, it's a stunning view, though I'm afraid there's not much to recommend it tonight."

He surprised her by stepping past her into the center of the small turret room, the first real interest he'd shown. He stood with his back to her, his hands in his pockets, staring at the heavily curtained window. "I'll bet you can see all the way to the light from here, watch the sun float up out of the sea and turn it silver in the morning. And at night, when it's very clear, I bet those stars hang over the water like fairy lights."

Lane felt a prickle along the back of her neck. His voice had gone so strange. And yet the words were exactly right, as if he'd snuck up behind her one day at her writing desk and peered out over her shoulder.

"How on earth can you describe something you've never seen in such perfect detail?"

Michael turned, his face all angles in the candlelight. "Did I?"

"Perfectly."

He shrugged. "I'm a writer. Well, a literature professor who writes, at any rate. We tend to have rather vivid imaginations. Surely you can describe places you've never actually seen?"

Lane nodded. She did it all the time, in her articles. But this felt different, visceral, a product of memory rather than imagination. But then, she supposed one ocean view was much like another.

He said nothing more as he strode past her, just waited patiently while she turned down the bed and made a quick check of the mini-bar. She was halfway to the door when she turned back.

"I almost forgot. The curtains are blackout. I put them up because of the light, which some guests find charming, and others . . . well . . .

don't." She tugged the cord lightly. "As long as you keep these closed, you won't even know it's there." She took a last look around the room, then handed him the key. "Breakfast is at nine. Will you be needing a wake-up call?"

Michael shook his head. "I'm a light sleeper and an early riser. Thanks, by the way, for putting me up like this. I don't think I had another ten miles in me."

Lane ducked her head in response and stepped out into the hall. As she pulled the door closed, she wondered what it was about Michael Forrester that made her linger in the hall a moment longer than was necessary, listening for—what? She had no idea. Finally, she started down, knowing she'd be up all night, tending her candles with one ear on the wind, waiting for some sign that the storm was beginning to abate, and wondering how much damage Penny would leave in her wake.

Chapter 6

Michael

Michael didn't move for several minutes, waiting until he was sure Lane Kramer had moved away from his door. What was she waiting for? The metallic snick of a pistol magazine sliding into place? A cryptic call to his comrades in Prague? He'd seen the sidelong glance she threw at him when they reached his door, the wary look of surprise when he startled babbling about the view from the turret room. She was suspicious—but of what exactly? He scowled at his own shadow on the far wall, stretched and ghoulish in the wavering candlelight, a grotesque shadow puppet. He supposed it was a wonder she'd let him in at all.

She had certainly done the place up right; he'd give her that. Even in the meager light, the room was like something from a glossy travel rag. She'd kept the elaborate woodwork, softening it with unfussy fabrics and period furniture with clean, straight lines. The result was both understated and authentic, no mean feat for a place as pompous as the Cloister. Her doing, he wondered, or a decorator's?

Finally, reluctantly, he forced his feet to move, slow, tentative steps, as if he expected the gleaming floorboards to suddenly open up and swallow him. He felt a queer kind of vertigo as he ran light fingers over the chair rail and beadboard, wrapped them briefly around the clear, satiny coolness of the mercury-glass doorknob, as if he'd entered a kind of time warp. From the bathroom door he walked off four careful paces, then leaned all his weight on his front foot until he was rewarded with the familiar give and groan of old boards. Everything changed. Everything the same.

And wasn't that exactly what he'd been afraid of?

The pretty little redhead, though—that was new. Women like that—long-limbed and green-eyed—had no business at the Cloister. But then neither did he anymore. What the hell could he have been thinking? He'd turned the car around not once but twice, ready to abandon the entire idea. And yet here he was, in the middle of a tropical storm for crying out loud, with no idea what he hoped to accomplish.

Too tired to bother with laces, he pried off his shoes, heel to toe, a practice that still earned him the odd scolding from his finishing school–mannered mother whenever he ventured home to Boston, which wasn't often these days. Dumping his canvas tote on the bed, he moved to the window, pulling back the heavy blackout curtain—fast, like yanking off a bandage. Nothing but pelting rain and the thin whistle of the wind squeezing itself into the chinks between window and frame. And then came the beacon, blue-white through all the whirling wet noise, illuminating and terrible. Sister Mary Constantine's all-seeing *Eye of God.*

Letting the curtain fall back, he turned away. He wanted to believe it was normal to be here, simple nostalgic curiosity. But deep down he knew it for what it was—unfinished business. Somewhere along the way, he'd taken leave of his senses. But then, that had been fairly predictable, hadn't it?

His parents would be livid if they knew he was here. No—scratch that. His mother would be livid. His father would simply shrug it off, as he shrugged off most things Michael did. Still, this little quest of his was hardly worth a family squabble. Maybe he should call the whole thing off. It wasn't too late. He could pull out the minute the roads were clear, watch Starry Point recede in his rearview mirror once and for all, and no one would be the wiser. But he couldn't decide any of that now. He needed sleep, the deep, dreamless variety that dumped you into a black hole and let you crawl out when you were good and ready. He couldn't remember the last time he'd slept like that. No, that wasn't true. He *could* remember—he just chose not to.

With a jaw-cracking yawn he yanked off his sweater and tossed it on a nearby chair, then fished a few essentials from his tote: toothbrush, toothpaste, and a well-thumbed edition of Poe, which he placed on the bedside table out of sheer habit. For once, he had neither the stamina nor the need to read before bed.

He brushed his teeth by candlelight, briefly tempted to take advantage of the fancy shower and what remained of the hot water to wash off the road grime before he slipped between his hostess's neatly pressed sheets. In the end, though, the knobs and jets presented more of a challenge than he was willing to tackle in the dark. Cold water in the morning would have to do. He'd probably need it to wake up anyway.

Beside the bed, he emptied his pockets into a small driftwood bowl: keys, cell phone, loose change—and a small button of faded pink satin. He'd excavated the button from a leather case he kept in his dresser back home, where he stashed the bits of his life he no longer had any use for: the diamond cuff links he had received as a graduation present but never wore, the rosary of shiny black beads that had failed to aid his boyish prayers, the class ring from Exeter with its bloodred stone, still bright as the day he'd received it. All symbols of the person others expected him to be.

Except for the button.

The button was real—the only memento he had of who he really was. He lingered over it briefly, the fabric worn thin at the edges, barely pink at all now. Most people had actual memorabilia, albums filled with photos, chests stuffed with baby clothes and discarded toys. He had a button. The candlelight flickered red against the backs of his lids as he closed them, fighting the dizzying barrage of memory—bourbon fumes and the sour pong of vomit, terror mingled with revulsion.

For a moment he stood stock-still, shoulders bunched high and tight, as if the T-shirt he was wearing had suddenly grown several sizes too small. When he finally managed to shove the memory away, he opened his eyes and tossed the button into the bowl with his keys. As he blew out the candle and collapsed into the antique mahogany four-poster, he tried to remember why he'd ever thought it was a good idea to come back to Starry Point.

Chapter 7

Lane

Lane sat bolt upright on the couch and glanced blearily at her watch—seven forty. It took a minute to remember what she was doing in yesterday's clothes, and why she'd slept on the parlor sofa instead of upstairs in her bed. Finally, the fog cleared and she began to connect the acrid scent of fireplace ashes with the candles scattered about the room. She'd gone up to her room, had even tried lying down, but to no avail. The relentless wind and rain battering the third-story windows had simply been too much to take. Sometime around two she had given up, groping her way downstairs, where the noise seemed less ominous and the windows seemed less likely to blow in. It must've been around five thirty when she snuffed the candles and finally managed to close her eyes.

She felt stiff and gritty as she got to her feet, already dreading the cold shower she knew was in her future. Clearly, the power was still out—not a hum or whir to be heard. That was going to make coffee a challenge, and she couldn't remember ever needing coffee more than she did this morning. God only knew what awaited her outside.

Sighing, she bent to collect the wineglasses from the coffee table. Glasses. Plural.

Damn.

She'd forgotten about Michael Forrester, asleep upstairs in the Tower Suite. The last thing she felt like doing at that moment was playing hostess. Oh well, there was fruit and fresh bread. She'd heat some water on the Coleman stove for tea. That was going to have to do. Right now she needed to see what kind of mess she was dealing with and find out whether there was anything left of the dunes. Yanking on her jacket and duck boots, she unchained the front door and ventured out onto the front porch.

Penny might have moved on, but she'd left no sunshine in her wake. Low gray clouds dragged by overhead, somber and still spitting rain. And while the wind no longer posed a threat, the breeze off the Atlantic was stiff and chilly, tangy with salt and the scent of freshly severed tree limbs.

Battered was the first word that came to mind as she stepped off the porch—plenty of downed trees, branches scattered over the lawn, but it wasn't bad, considering. Certainly nothing like the devastation she'd been dreading. The mailbox was gone, blown who knew where, and a heavy tree limb lay across the driveway, blocking the path of a charcoal gray SUV with Vermont plates. She wondered how long it would take Sam to come by with his chain saw.

Moving around the side of the inn, she further surveyed the damage. The wind had peeled back a section of the shed's tin roof, curling it back on itself like an apple peel, and one of the windows at the back was smashed out, but other than that the inn itself looked as if it had escaped any serious toll. Not so much as a cracked pane of glass, and only a handful of slate shingles off the roof. Those wouldn't be easy to replace, but all in all her relief was profound. She made a mental note to price shutters the minute things were back to normal. She'd worked too hard and invested too much money—all of it, in fact—to see it blown away in a single night.

She was on her way back around front when she saw Michael standing at the edge of the road. "Good morning," she said, slipping into hostess mode as she reached him. "Did you manage to get any sleep with all the wind and racket?"

He turned, unsmiling. "I did, as a matter of fact."

He had showered and shaved, and smelled of the Belgian sea soap she used in the guest baths. His still-wet hair was combed straight back off his forehead, curling slightly against the damp collar of his light blue button-down. Once again, Lane found herself painfully aware of her own appearance: the remnants of last night's ponytail, the sweats she'd been in now for almost twenty-four hours, and— God help her—duck boots and sweat socks. From where Michael Forrester stood she must look like some kind of . . . bag lady.

Lane's gaze shifted briefly toward the beach behind the inn. It was the first time since opening her eyes that she'd given the old woman a thought. How had she weathered the storm, and where? It was a disturbing thought, but after yesterday's uneasy encounter Lane doubted she'd ever see the woman again. Shaking off a twinge of guilt, she dragged her eyes back to Michael.

"I'll work on some breakfast as soon as I give my handyman a call. He'll pop over and get that limb out of the way so we can get you back on the road."

"Give him a call . . . how?" Michael asked with annoyingly dry amusement. "The phones are out and I've got no signal on my cell. Towers must be down. They'll be down several days, too, if there's any real damage. You wouldn't happen to have a radio, would you?"

Lane grimaced. "I do, but no batteries."

Michael's brows shot up, a blend of surprise and censure. "Did no one ever tell you that when you live on the Banks, water and batteries are Hurricane Prep 101?"

"I got the water," she explained defensively. "But the batteries were gone by the time I got to the store. It's not like there's a Walmart on every corner, you know. This isn't Boston."

Michael's eyes narrowed on her. "What's Boston got to do with it?"

"It's where you're from, isn't it? At least it's where you *sound* like you're from."

"My parents are from Boston," he corrected evenly. "I live in Middlebury, which is in Vermont. And we have only one Walmart in the entire state, though we do know that when there's a storm coming, batteries are the first things to go."

Lane cast about for a reply but couldn't think of one. She was too busy wondering what she'd said to make this stranger's mood turn sullen. Perhaps he'd mistaken her question for prying, but it was perfectly normal, almost required, for an innkeeper to chitchat with guests about where they were from.

It didn't matter. Apparently he wasn't interested in a reply. Fishing a set of keys from his pocket, he crossed the lawn and slid in behind the wheel of the charcoal SUV. He turned the key without cranking the engine, then fiddled with the radio buttons until he found a station. Lane stepped to the edge of the drive so she could hear.

Modest structural damage. All of Starry Point without power and likely to remain so for several days. Sections of Highway 12 washed out or impassable in many locations. No way on or off the island. Stay tuned for a list of shelters and medical aid stations in your area.

"Sounds like your basic mess," Michael said as he switched off the radio and got out of the car. "Could've been worse, though, I guess."

Lane was barely listening. She was too busy wondering what she was supposed to do with Michael Forrester. She had no power, no hot water, and since she'd planned on spending the next four months alone, she hadn't much in the way of food. But she couldn't turn him out, not when everything on Starry Point was shuttered, and there was no way to get back to the mainland. There was always the community center, although she was pretty sure turning a guest out to go to a shelter would be considered bad form, not to mention the review he was certain to post on the inn's Web site.

He was standing at the end of the drive now, hands buried deep in his pockets, his shoulders hunching uncomfortably as he stared across the street at the Rourke House. Lane pushed her bangs out of her eyes as she gave the old house an uneasy once-over. It was hard to know exactly what to chalk up to years of neglect, and what had resulted from the storm, but none of the damage looked serious. A shutter lay splintered on the front walk while another dangled precariously from the second-floor window. Several branches were down in the yard amid a scattering of shingles.

"It's a little bit creepy, isn't it?" she said gravely as she came to stand beside him. "It's been empty for years. I guess it's not surprising, though. Not too many people looking to buy a house that's cursed."

Michael's head snapped in her direction. "Cursed?"

"Its residents have a nasty habit of dying. Back in 'twenty-nine a man hanged himself in the attic, a banker who'd lost all his money in the crash. Then a while back, in the seventies, I think, the mayor bought it. One day he went out sailing and never came back. Pieces of his boat washed up several days later. A year after that there was a fire on the upper floor and a little boy died. No one's lived there since. If you listen to the locals they'll tell you it's haunted."

"And if I listened to you?"

Lane was startled. Not by the question, but by the intensity in his voice when he turned to ask it. She opened her mouth, prepared to tell him about the light she'd seen in the window two nights ago, but something stopped her. If she wasn't careful she was going to start sounding like the locals, up to her ears in ghosts and things that went bump in the night. She stole another look at the place, its empty windows and gloomy air of dissipation stirring the old familiar sadness.

"If you listened to me I'd tell you it's an amazing old house with a very sad history. And that I don't believe in ghosts."

"No?"

"You say that as if you do."

Michael shrugged, a deep, uneasy bunching of the shoulders. "There are all kinds of ghosts, Miss Kramer."

"Lane."

"Right," he grunted as he turned away. "Lane. Now, I think you said something about breakfast?"

And just like that, the conversation was over. He was already halfway up the drive, offering no opportunity to delve into his mercurial mood. Not that his mood was any of her business. She had a few ghosts of her own, and she'd just as soon keep them to herself. She could only assume he felt the same.

Breakfast was a simple affair: bread and honey with a bowl of fresh berries, washed down with a surprisingly decent pot of tea. Michael didn't seem to mind. He ate quietly across from Lane, browsing an old copy of the *Islander Dispatch*, licking honey from his fingers as he turned the pages.

"Mr. Forrester," Lane began tentatively. "We seem to have a bit of a situation here."

Michael folded down the corner of the newspaper and peered at her. "Have we?"

"As I said last night when you showed up, the inn is closed for the season. And as you can plainly see, I'm not exactly prepared for guests."

"During a hurricane? No, I wouldn't think so. Yet here I am, I'm afraid—at your mercy."

Lane cleared her throat and tried again. "My point is, last night you mentioned that you were looking for a place to—park for the winter, I think was how you put it—and I just wanted to make sure you understood that as soon as the roads are clear you'll need to find other lodgings. I could make a few calls if you wanted to stay here on the island."

"I thought I'd just stay here."

"Mr. Forrester, I—"

"Michael."

"Michael," she corrected. "Maybe I wasn't clear. I don't take guests between November and March. I'm closed."

"Perfect. It'll be nice and quiet, exactly what I'm looking for. I'm on a sort of sabbatical, trying to finish up the research for a book I've been working on for about five years now. A closed inn is ideal."

"Except for the part where it's *closed*," Lane shot back, putting emphasis on the last word. Then she realized what he'd said. "Did you say you're writing a book?"

He nodded. "A biography on Dickens."

Lane saw a chink and went straight for it. "Good, then you'll understand. I'm a writer, too. Well, not a real writer. Just freelance stuff, magazines mostly. But the winter is when I do most of my work. I won't have time to look after a guest."

He tapped his chin thoughtfully a moment, then carefully folded the *Islander Dispatch* and set it aside. "What is a . . . *real* writer?"

The sudden change of subject gave Lane momentary whiplash. "What?"

"You said you weren't a real writer. I'm curious to know what that means."

"I just meant the stuff I write isn't—I don't know—important."

"Ah, as opposed to tedious biographies about dead Victorian authors?"

Lane blinked at him, not sure how to answer.

It was Michael who broke the silence, his words flavored with a smile she could hear but not see. "I won't be any trouble."

She rolled her eyes as she began hastily gathering plates and silverware. "Of course you will. There'll be meals to cook, beds to make, showers to scrub."

"I've been making my own bed since I was six. I know my way

around a frying pan. And I am perfectly capable of scrubbing my own shower. In other words, I'm extremely low maintenance. All I need is a bed and a quiet place to work. I promise to be invisible. You won't even know I'm here."

Lane pulled in a deep breath and let it out very slowly. If he was trying to be annoying, he was certainly succeeding. And yet there was something disarming in his tone, as if he was deliberately trying to charm his way in. She hadn't been charmed in a very long time. She wasn't sure she liked it. She stood abruptly with the stacked dishes and headed for the sink, trying to think of a way to end the conversation once and for all.

But Michael wasn't giving up. Gathering the teapot and empty cups, he followed her to the sink. "How about this—you're stuck with me anyway until the roads are clear and the power's back on. Until then, I do my writer thing, and you do yours. If I'm a bother you have my permission to toss me out on my ear. If not, I get to stay. As a bonus, I'll help with some of the cleanup until your handyman can come around."

Lane turned to face him, towering above her now, and disturbingly close. "Why here?"

Michael set the teapot on the counter, then slid the cups into the sink full of soapy water. "Well, for starters I'm already here. And I guess because I like it. It feels like . . . home."

Lane peered up at him skeptically. "It feels like Vermont?"

"No, not like Vermont. And sure as hell not like Boston."

Something in his face told Lane not to press the matter. She was probably crazy for even considering his proposal, but it would be a nice windfall, maybe enough to pay for the storm shutters she was going to have to order before next hurricane season. And in light of the recent break-ins and the strange goings-on across the street, it might not be such a bad idea to have a man around. If—and *only* if—he kept his promise to be invisible.

"There are rules," she informed him firmly.

"Let's hear them."

"I don't allow smoking anywhere on the premises. The third floor is my residence and is off-limits to guests. Breakfast is provided, but not lunch. Dinner is included for an additional fee and I'll need to know at the beginning of each week if you'll be dining here so I can shop accordingly. Should you opt to dine elsewhere on a particular night, you will still be charged for the meal."

She had barely finished delivering the last edict when he extended a hand to seal the agreement. "Done. And now, if you'll excuse me, I'm going to see if I can scare up something to board up that broken shed window."

Lane felt a lingering sense of misgiving as she watched Michael slip out the back door and disappear in the direction of the shed. When he was out of sight she tugged on her jacket and ventured out onto the beach, picking her way through a tangle of sea grass and battered pink and purple morning glories. The storm had hit at low tide and she was relieved to see that the surge had left the dunes relatively, though not completely, unscathed. Squinting down the beach, she could see what appeared to be a cooler and other bits of debris snagged against the jetty.

It wasn't pretty, but it could have been so much worse. As she turned to go back to the inn, she paused for one last look, hoping for some sign of the old woman. For the first time in weeks there was no telltale flash of the mysterious purple bag.

Chapter 8

Mary

I dreamed last night, of a fine-set table, of exquisite lace and bone white china, of bloodred wine in thin crystal glasses, of handsome princes smiling through candlelight. The dream is not new. I have dreamed it before, the table with all its fine things, all its lost things, but not for a very long time. I did not want it to come, but it was insistent, like the storm outside, keening at my window to be let in.

While Penny raged outside the thick walls of my small safe world, another storm raged in my head, howling out of dark corners where I hide my most precious things—and my most terrible. I did my best to fight it, thrashing and tangled in my narrow bed, defying it, begging it to leave me in peace. But I knew it would not. The tide came in, as it always does in my dreams, swirling at the panes, pushing its way in, smashing its way in. I was not ready. I am never ready. Too late to save anything. Everything, everything, swept away.

The tremors have stopped now, the storms, real and imagined, at last gone by, leaving their small ruins before moving on. Beyond my window the world is fresh and clean, made new by the washing of water. And yet I find I haven't the strength to face this new day. I fumble two pills from their little brown bottle and swallow them without water—I'm a practiced pill-taker, you see—then crawl back beneath the safety of my covers. I will not go to the dunes today. My wounds are suddenly too fresh, my heart too raw. Let the sea keep its secrets while I tend to my bruises.

Chapter 9

Lane

Two days later, Lane opened her eyes with the sun streaming across the sheets, and the immediate sense that something was different. Propping herself up on her elbows, she looked around, eventually spotting the slow, steady turn of the fan blades over her bed. It was all she could do not to hoot out loud. No more cold showers.

God bless Benjamin Franklin, Thomas Edison, and anyone else who had to do with the modern conveniences of electricity. She all but skipped to the bathroom, where she flipped on the shower, waiting until the water grew warm, and then hot. She was out of her T-shirt and boxers in under a minute, thinking as she stepped into the steamy glass enclosure that hot water was undoubtedly the most unappreciated commodity on the planet.

She lingered, letting the scalding water needle her skin until it was tingly pink and just starting to prune. Two days of ice-cold showers had left her with a new appreciation for small daily rituals like hair conditioning and leg shaving, not to mention the luxury of actually being able to see what you were doing.

"Coffee!" she bellowed cheerfully as she passed Michael's door on her way to the kitchen.

The last few days had been a challenge to say the least—cold soup, peanut butter sandwiches, iced tea without the ice. Now, for the first time in more than seventy-two hours, she was able to cook an honest-to-God meal on an honest-to-God stove, to enjoy hot food on plates not made from paper. To his credit, her guest had remained true to his word about being low maintenance. He had eaten the makeshift meals without complaint. In fact, he'd eaten them without much conversation at all. Afterward, he would disappear with a handful of candles, presumably up to his ears in the cartons of books he'd unloaded from the SUV and carried up to his room.

Lane caught herself humming as she moved about the kitchen. There was an almost Zen-like feel to the tasks of chopping and whisking as she started the breakfast, simple pleasures she hadn't bothered to notice for a very long time, and would probably forget again in twenty-four hours. For now, though, the routine things felt very good indeed. By the time Michael wandered in, the table was set and the potatoes were already in the pan.

"What smells so amazing?"

"Home fries with onions." She held up a mug. "Coffee?"

"Please."

He wore a navy sweater with a crest on the pocket and well-creased khakis—a pricey version of academic casual. Lane tried to imagine him hunched over the tiny ironing board she supplied in the closet of every room, studiously pressing that crease into his pants, but she couldn't, perhaps because she suddenly realized he was staring at her. Understandable, she supposed, since this was the first time he'd seen her look anything like respectable.

She was used to having guests in her kitchen, asking questions about the island and chatting about their plans for the day. In fact, she rather enjoyed it. But this silent audience of one made her self-conscious as she served up two plates and carried them to the table.

"Now, that's a breakfast," Michael said, offering a rare smile as he stirred a dash of sugar into his coffee.

"Certainly better than bread and jam," she said, returning the smile as she slid into the chair across from him. She'd had to toss out just about everything from the fridge, but the eggs and some of the veggies had survived, allowing her to create a pair of fairly impressive omelets. "Sorry, there wasn't any cheese. Tomorrow I'll go to the village and see what I can scare up. It'll probably be several days before trucks are allowed through, so I expect the pickings will be slim. Hot meals from now on, though. I promise."

"As far as I'm concerned you can just keep making these. Most bachelors are good with eggs in any form."

Single—or at least not married. It was more than he'd volunteered about himself in three days. But then, she'd guessed as much. No ring, and on his own for the entire winter. Not that he couldn't have a girlfriend or fiancée tucked away somewhere. She had a momentary flash of a twentysomething sorority brunette in a twinset and tasseled loafers. Or maybe she was thinking of Melinda Bingham, the Pilates-sculpted wife of Bruce's college roommate, with her Volvo and her perfect twins. Lane shook off the thought with a mental shudder. The last thing she wanted to think about was Bruce's friends—especially the lofty Professor Bingham.

Looking down at her hand, she realized she was still stirring her coffee and had been for a very long time, her spoon clinking absently against the side of her mug. Setting the spoon on the edge of her plate, she cast about for something to say. She ended up settling for the obvious.

"How's the research going?"

If Michael heard her he gave no sign, his eyes busy wandering the kitchen as if he were trying to remember where he'd left something. Eventually he must have felt her gaze on him.

"Sorry, did you say something?"

"I asked how the research was going."

He rolled his eyes and waved the question away. "It's going. Let's leave it at that. How about you? How are the...unimportant... articles coming along?"

Lane felt her cheeks go warm. There was a teasing flavor to his words, and something else, too, that bordered on censure. It made her uncomfortable.

"It's going fine, actually, in light of all the distractions. That's the thing about writing the unimportant stuff. You know a month after it hits the stands, no one's going to remember a word of it, so there's very little pressure. Today, I'm putting the final touches on an article about vintage soap makers. Tomorrow I'll be starting a piece on microbreweries." She forced a lighthearted grin. "No deep thought required."

"Is that how you want it, or just how it is?"

"How I want it?"

"Is it that you don't have any deep thoughts? Or that you just don't feel like doing the work?"

He was using his professor voice, and Lane didn't appreciate it one bit. She didn't need a lecture from a stranger, especially one for whom she'd grudgingly agreed to inconvenience herself.

"It fills the time during the off-season," she replied coolly before pivoting to a safer subject. "I was thinking, since it looks like you're going to be here awhile, we could fix up an office for you. There are some old desks in storage on the third floor. We could haul one down to your suite and set you up in the turret room. The view—"

"I'd rather use the library off the front parlor," he said, cutting her off. "The desk is huge, which means I'd have plenty of room to spread out. I figure as long as the inn is empty I won't be in anyone's way. And it's full of old books. I'm comfortable with books."

Lane couldn't help frowning. What kind of person passed up an ocean view for a dark, windowless room, even if it was lined with old books? The literary kind, she supposed, who chose to spend his sabbaticals researching dead Victorian writers.

"I don't have a problem with it," she answered with a shrug. "But are you sure? The view is spectacular. You can see all the way to the lighthouse. It really is quite breathtaking."

Michael paused, his coffee mug halfway to his lips. "One man's breathtaking is another man's distraction, Ms. Kramer."

Once again she stared at him, not sure if he was teasing or in earnest. He'd delivered the line as if it were from some dark Shakespearian play. *It wasn't, was it?* In the end, she chose to let it go. Writers were known for being a bit manic about their routines. Some couldn't write without music; others required absolute silence. Some could write in the midst of utter chaos, while others shut themselves away from the world, sometimes for weeks on end. She'd heard tales of lucky pens, hats, scarves, and rocks, all of which seemed ridiculous to everyone but the writers who staked their creativity on them.

"Good, then," Michael said, picking up his fork again. "I'll bring in the rest of my boxes and get set up."

They lapsed into silence as they finished breakfast. Lane continued to study him through lowered lashes. He was an enigma, undeniably gorgeous, and at times even charming, and yet there was a frostiness about him, too, a careful wall he erected whenever it suited him. Perhaps he saw her attempts to be sociable as an annoyance. He'd made no secret of the fact that his main reason for wanting to stay at the inn was that with it closed there would be no one to bother him. Well, if that was the case, she had no problem giving Mr. Forrester all the space he wanted.

With breakfast over and the kitchen clean, Lane threw a batch of applesauce muffins in the oven, then set to work on a shopping list—or, more accurately, a wish list. There really was no telling what she'd find on the shelves, or if the Village Mart was even open yet, but as long as she had rice, beans, and pasta in the pantry they weren't going to starve. Next, she zipped several bread heels into a sandwich bag and pulled on her jacket. She was eager to get back to something like her normal morning routine—breakfast, dishes, walk to the light, then up to her writing room. But first she needed to tell Michael she was going.

He had wasted no time making himself at home, she saw as she stepped into the den, his laptop and books already spread over the softly polished library table he had pressed into service as a desk, a teetering stack of thick texts within easy reach on the seat of a green leather wingback. She really could see why he'd chosen to work here. It was a man's room, gleaming with dark wood and softly worn leather, stately and proper right down to the globe and lectern she hadn't had the heart to leave in storage. And he looked good standing there, right somehow, in front of the dark shelves, a pair of volumes tucked beneath his arm.

"Don't tell me you actually found something that might help with your research."

Michael started, looking vaguely guilty as he stepped away from the shelves. "Not really, no. But I have to say you've got a pretty impressive collection here."

"Thanks, but I can't take credit. They were here when I bought the place. Well, not here. They were up in storage. I salvaged what I could, but a lot were moldy. Others fell apart the minute I touched them. God knows how long they were up there in the heat and damp."

Michael let his eyes drift back to the shelves. "What happened to them? The damaged ones, I mean."

"I had to toss them. It broke my heart to do it. All those classics, even some first editions, all ruined. It would have made the nuns sad, I think."

He made a sound like a snort. "Sad nuns—now, there's a cheerful thought."

"You should look through the binder in your room. There's some history in it about the inn. It's called the Cloister House because it was a convent at one time. Then, in the late sixties, I think it was, the church converted it to a boys' home. I've always assumed the books were part of the curriculum. One day I'll get through every one."

"That sounds fairly ambitious."

"Oh, but I've already started. Here, I'll show you."

She pointed to the top shelf. "I've read all those, and I'm up to *Anna Karenina* on the second shelf. *Madame Bovary* is next. Rather racy reading for schoolboys, though, I must say."

"Maybe the top shelves were off-limits for the boys, and the racy stuff was for the nuns."

Lane laughed but realized he was serious. "You know, I never thought of that, but it makes sense. I always imagined nuns as stern and stoic, their noses always stuck in their Bibles or their prayer books, but who knows what they really do in their free time? They're human, after all."

"So rumor has it."

There it was again, that weighty, Laurence Olivier stage voice he'd used at breakfast, gruff and thick with cynicism. Or was it bitterness? Rather than ponder the matter, Lane decided to change the subject. She wandered back to the table and examined several more books he had pulled from the shelves—*Bleak House* and *Little Dorrit*.

"I see you migrated right to Dickens. *Great Expectations* was always my favorite. I fell in love with it in eighth grade. I bet I've read it ten times."

A tic appeared along Michael's jaw. "That's when I read it, too. It's my least favorite of all his books, actually. A bit gothic for my taste, but then, my interest in Dickens, and the focus of my book, has more to do with the social commentary of his writings, on his view of the inequities suffered by the poor, especially the children, than with mere entertainment."

He had slipped into professor mode again, delivering what Lane felt certain was part of his first-day-of-class lecture. "See, right there," she said, wagging a finger. "That's what I mean by important stuff. He was making a point, focusing attention on a problem. And now you're doing the same thing."

Michael nodded somewhat grudgingly. "As a boy, Dickens experienced those things firsthand, and they formed the foundation for his life's work. The shame is the same problems still exist today. We pretend we're civilized, but we're not so very different in how we treat the poor and ignore the sick, or the way we herd up displaced children like stray cats bound for the shelter." He paused and looked briefly away. "Which is why there isn't room in my treatise for broken hearts and crumbling mansions. Or for crazy old women who set fire to the house."

Lane blinked up at him, not sure whether to be impressed or insulted. He'd sounded more like a politician than a literature professor just then, filled with righteous zeal and compassion for his fellow man. Was he this passionate with his students? she wondered, because he was certainly nothing like any of the lit professors she'd ever had.

The silence stretched while Lane groped for something to say. "All righty, then," she blurted finally. "I suppose now that we've established our differences in literary taste, I should do what I came to do, which is to inform you that I usually walk down to the lighthouse every morning. I should be gone about an hour. There are muffins cooling on the stove, and I made a fresh pot of coffee should you want a refill."

"Thank you," Lane heard him murmur as she slipped from the room to leave him to his research, and wondered why it was that every time they had a conversation that lasted more than five minutes, he ended up saying something that got under her skin.

Chapter 10

Michael

Michael knew, as he watched Lane disappear, that he'd gone too far. He'd treated her like one of his students. Worse, he'd come dangerously close to insulting her taste in literature. He hadn't meant it to come out the way it did, but sometimes he forgot that not everyone spent their days hiding in the pages of old books. When he was a child books had been his sanctuary, a refuge from the bullies and the memories he couldn't outrun. Later, his friends were others like him, academic types more comfortable with dead writers than live people, who preferred words on a page to real life.

It hardly made for satisfying relationships, as Becca, his on-again, off-again girlfriend, had icily pointed out while packing up her DVDs and exercise mats three months ago. Truth be told, he was relieved when it ended. Keeping up with a twenty-seven-year-old yoga instructor had been both exhausting and mind-numbing, a manic whirl of health lectures and vegan cooking classes, all ironically lubricated with far too much chardonnay. He should have known better. In fact, he had. But she'd been someone—something—to fill the void, to distract him from the growing realization that the life he was living belonged to someone else, someone who wasn't even real.

Drifting back to the shelves, he slid the weathered volume of *Great Expectations* free and ran his palm over the front cover, cool and vaguely waxy. It had been beautiful once, moss green leather, embossed lettering, richly marbled endpapers. Now the lettering was gone, the leather badly scarred after God only knew how many readings. Not surprising, though. Boys didn't take care of their own things, let alone books that belonged to someone else.

He opened the volume tentatively, savoring the musty scent of old book: dust and ink and slowly decaying paper. After coffee, it was his favorite scent in the world. Flipping to chapter twenty-seven, he scanned the pages until he found the passage he sought. It was one he knew by heart.

In the little world in which children have their existence, whosoever brings them up, there is nothing so finely perceived and so finely felt as injustice.

Yes, he'd been abrupt with his hostess, and less than truthful about the reason he disliked *Great Expectations*, but what was he supposed to do? Spill his guts to a virtual stranger? Explain that as a boy the story had torn him apart, giving him nightmares that left him drenched and weeping in his narrow bed? That even now thoughts of the tragic Miss Havisham filled him with revulsion? Lane would never understand. How could she? His hostess saw *Great Expectations* as a literary classic. He would always see it as something else.

Chapter 11

Lane

Lane stepped out onto the deck and sucked in a lungful of air. It was breezy and cold, even for November, but she didn't care. Today would be her first walk since Penny had blown through, and after her recent conversations with Michael she needed to walk off a little steam, though she wasn't as angry with him as she was with herself. It was becoming clear that letting him stay had been a mistake. She had allowed a silly light in an empty house to get under her skin, and now she was stuck with an unwanted guest who was growing more irritating by the minute.

Sure, he was brilliant and good-looking, and probably very well-heeled, but he was also moody and opinionated—and secretive. No, not secretive exactly, but definitely reclusive, and in a mysterious and brooding way she didn't have time for. She couldn't deny that he'd been a big help, boarding up the shed window and doing his best to flatten out the mangled roof, tacking it down to prevent further damage until Sam could get by to replace it. He'd even cut up the fallen tree in the driveway with a rusty handsaw he found in the shed and hauled it all out to the street.

She had to admit he'd surprised her. In his professor clothes he didn't look as if he'd know which end of a nail was pointy, let alone possess the talent to perform all the tasks he had. Lucky for her he was handy, since it didn't look as though Sam was going to be able to get by for several weeks. The Cloister might have sustained only minor damage, but houses farther up the beach, many of them little more than cottages, had taken a much harder hit. Several had been reported a total loss.

Zipping her jacket higher, she headed for the narrow boardwalk, prepared to set out, when she spotted the old woman moving purposefully past the back gate toward her customary spot on the dunes. The sight sent something like relief tingling through Lane's limbs. She was safe. Even more surprising, she was back.

Where had she come from? Did she have family on Starry Point? It seemed unlikely. Based on the white hair and stooped shoulders, she had to be closing in on eighty, and no family worth their salt would allow a woman that age to roam the dunes while a tropical storm moved onshore. No, everything about the poor woman screamed *alone*.

Lane made up her mind in an instant. She couldn't just keep pretending the woman's presence on the dunes was normal. Instead of heading for the lighthouse, she turned and marched back into the kitchen. It took several minutes to find the old green thermos in the cabinet over the fridge, a few more to rinse it out, then fill it from the fresh pot of coffee she'd just made for Michael. Three muffins still warm from the oven went into a white paper bag, and a pair of paper cups went into her jacket pocket.

She let the gate clang noisily as she stepped out onto the narrow boardwalk but received not the slightest reaction. There was no greeting, no recognition of any kind as she came to stand beside the woman, but neither did she make a move to flee. That was progress at least. After a few minutes Lane dropped down beside her on the chilly sand and fixed her eyes on the horizon, waiting. She couldn't say how many waves washed in and then out again before the woman's gaze finally shifted, settling on her.

Lane kept very still, pretending not to notice that she was being stud-ied, and hoping she didn't look like a big old do-gooder here to hand out charity muffins to a bag lady—which was exactly what she was.

"What is it you want with me?"

Her voice was a surprise, quiet and almost melodic, not at all what Lane had expected. "I brought muffins and coffee," she said, holding up the thermos.

"Why?"

"I thought it would be neighborly."

"I'm not your neighbor. I'm no one's neighbor."

"Okay, then, to be friendly. I thought you might be cold."

Eyes the color of a storm-tossed sea regarded her from a face that on closer inspection appeared more weary than weathered. She had been beautiful once, Lane realized with a start, but the years had been hard on her. The bone structure was still visible, though, high cheekbones and a straight, almost patrician nose. But a web of fine lines fanned out now from those strange, almost translucent eyes, and a deep V had embossed itself between her brows. Her hair, probably blond at one time, was now the color of old ivory, brutally cropped just below her ears. There was no way to guess her age, but it was obvious now that she was nowhere near as old as Lane had originally thought, just worn down by a life that had clearly not been easy.

"My name is Lane Kramer," she offered tentatively. "I own the inn."

The woman barely nodded, her eyes on the thermos.

Lane fished the paper cups from her pocket and carefully filled one. "There's cream and sugar in it," she said as she handed it over. "I wasn't sure how you took it."

A mute nod was the woman's only reply.

After sipping from her own cup, Lane handed her a muffin. "I made these this morning. They might still be warm."

With something resembling a nod of thanks, the woman took the muffin, peeling back the fluted paper cup before pinching off a bite and popping it into her mouth. Lane couldn't help staring at her hands, smooth and strangely beautiful for a woman her age, long tapered fingers that moved with a delicacy that seemed at odds with her huddled posture and lumpy clothes.

"Mary."

It had come out as little more than a grunt, delivered without so much as a turn of the head, but for now it was enough.

They ate their muffins slowly, and in silence. Lane pretended to watch a pair of gulls play tag along the shoreline while secretly stealing glimpses of the woman beside her. What was it she saw beyond the breaking waves? Lane followed the pale wide-eyed gaze out to sea, to the place where the water turned a flat shade of navy, then melted into a cold, cloudless sky, but there was nothing.

It caught her off guard when Mary popped the last of her muffin into her mouth and wordlessly held out her cup. Lane topped off both their cups, then tucked the empty thermos between her knees.

"I've seen you out here in the morning," Lane said, dipping a toe into the heavy silence. "You sit here every day, like you're watching for something." Mary gave no indication that she'd heard. After a few beats Lane prompted her. "Are you . . . watching for something?"

The stooped shoulders rose and fell, rose and fell. Finally, her blue-veined lids fluttered closed. "Nothing you can see, my girl. Nothing anyone can see."

Lane turned to stare at her. The answer seemed to come from far away, from another time and place in this woman's life, but it begged more questions than it answered. And there was something else, the faintest hint of an accent, though it wasn't one Lane could place, a singsong quality that fell just short of a lilt, not English or Irish, but something like it. Though she couldn't be sure since she'd never heard it for herself, Lane suspected she was hearing what locals called a Hoi Toide brogue, common among Outer Banks natives. More perplexing, though, was how to respond. She had no idea what Mary's words meant, only that the way they'd been said made the hair on the back of her neck prickle.

"What?" Mary blurted, obviously picking up on Lane's confusion. "Have I got lipstick on my teeth?"

Lane wasn't sure whether to apologize or laugh out loud. "I'm sorry. I didn't mean to stare. I just—"

"You think I'm not used to people staring?"

Once again Lane found herself at a loss for words. "I'm sorry, really."

Something flickered in Mary's eyes, a new emotion Lane couldn't read. She shook her head. "You're a pretty thing, aren't you? Lovely hair. I knew someone once with hair like yours. She wasn't as pretty as you, though. Or as kind. You needn't worry, my girl. I didn't take offense. You're curious, not unkind. I already know that about you."

"How?"

"The coffee," she said simply. "You wear your scars on your sleeve, and I've learned that people, women especially, who've been knocked about by life are generally either terribly mean or terribly kind. You're the latter."

Lane's cheeks warmed despite the biting wind. It was a wonderful compliment, but unsettling, too. How could this woman, a complete stranger, possibly know she'd been *knocked about by life*? Was she really that pathetic, or did this woman have some kind of second sight? She'd never really believed in things like that, but it was rapidly becoming clear that Mary wasn't your average bag lady.

"How did you know I'd been . . . knocked about by life?"

Mary smiled her sad smile again. "It's to do with the way you walk, my girl."

"The way I walk?"

"You go at it with a vengeance. Keep your head tucked and your shoulders hunched, as if you expect life to land another blow at any moment, and all you want is to run away."

Lane nodded. The words stung, though whether that was because they'd hit too close to home, or because she was ashamed of not concealing her weaknesses better, she honestly couldn't say. Either way, it was sobering to be seen so clearly by someone who knew nothing about her life.

And what of Mary's life, this vagrant who roamed the dunes clutching a bag of purple cloth? There were so many questions she wanted to ask the woman. Where did she live? Was there anyone to look after her? But something made her hold back. She'd only just broken the ice. To pry now might spook her, this time for good. And for reasons Lane couldn't begin to understand, she knew she didn't want that to happen.

"I'm glad you came through the storm okay," she said, pivoting to firmer ground. It was a bland but safe topic, though she secretly hoped Mary might volunteer details about where she'd actually been while Penny was blowing across the island.

The V deepened between Mary's brows, her blue-green eyes suddenly clouded. "Storm? What storm?"

Lane blinked at her. "Penny?" she prompted gently. "The tropical storm that hit a few days ago? I was worried that day I watched you pedal off in the rain."

"Oh, that." Mary waved off her concern, but something in her eyes warned Lane that she was lying, or at least not telling the whole truth. "A little wind, my girl, nothing more. There are all kinds of storms, the kind we weather with our eyes closed, and the kind we're not meant to weather at all. Sometimes, though, we cheat life. Sometimes we come through when we're not meant to." Her gaze slid away then, back toward the watery horizon. "Though I suppose in the end we pay for that, too."

Again, Lane had no idea what Mary was talking about but felt certain it had nothing to do with Penny, or anything else that could be tracked on a weather map. She longed to delve deeper, to know what had brought this inexplicable woman with her lilting voice and faded beauty to such humble circumstances, but the pain in her gaze was too raw, still fresh after what she suspected had been many years.

Mary was gone again, Lane realized, lost in her memories and her watching. She'd leave her to it, then. Standing, she tucked her thermos under her arm and dusted the sand off her backside. "I'd best get back. I've got some work to do."

Mary barely nodded, her eyes fixed out to sea.

Lane held out the bag with the last muffin. "Take it. I've got more in the kitchen."

Something that might have been gratitude glimmered in the old woman's eyes as she accepted the offering. Lane watched, fascinated, as she dragged the cherished purple bag from beneath her coat—a tattered Crown Royal bag, she realized with surprise as Mary tucked her offering away and cinched the drawstrings tight.

When it seemed she would say nothing more, Lane took a step toward the inn, then turned back. "I walk down to the lighthouse every morning. I could bring coffee again tomorrow if you like."

Mary's frown deepened to something like a scowl. "Don't trouble yourself. I hate coffee."

Lane nodded, cheeks hot with embarrassment. The woman had only been humoring her, politely tolerating her charitable intentions. She turned to go.

"I'm very fond of tea, though," Mary called over her shoulder before Lane had taken a step. "Milk, not lemon, but only a touch."

It was a peculiar exchange to be having with a bag lady on a beach, Lane knew, more like something you'd overhear in a richly appointed drawing room, but she wasn't about to try to sort that out now.

"Can I ask you something?" she said instead, shielding her eyes with one hand. "You said a moment ago that you hated coffee, and yet you drank it and then asked for a second cup. Why?"

A smile trembled on the old woman's lips, thin and a little sad. "Because, my girl, I'm terribly kind, too."

Chapter 12

Mary

What on earth am I doing? I shake my muddled head as I watch the Inn Lady climb back up the dunes, her green thermos snug beneath her arm, and wonder if I've lost what little is left of my mind. Letting people in is a bad idea. A dangerous idea.

They sidle up next to you, all syrup and smiles, ask all the right questions, say all the right words. And then while you aren't looking, they open you up and take you apart, poke at your wheels and your gears, until they realize they have no stomach for what they've found—and then they leave you.

And each time they do, you scrape up the pieces and find a way to put yourself back together. Only somewhere along the way, a few gears go missing, and then a few more, until one day the little that's left comes flying apart, and all your warped wheels and broken springs are laid bare to the world. And perhaps you deserve that kind of scrutiny. Perhaps it's even good for you. They tell you it is.

But I can't do that again. I won't.

And yet here I am, risking exposure—and worse. How would pretty little Lane Kramer react if she knew where I'd spent the better part of my years—if she knew what I'd done? Would she turn away like the rest? I don't believe she would. Because in a way I can't explain, way down in my marrow, I know this woman. She's safe, not broken like me, only a little bruised around the edges, and those bruises, wherever they've come from, make me sad for her, in a way I suspect people were once sad for me. No one is sad for me now. And that's as it should be.

Still, it's a frightening thing, this sympathy—unfamiliar territory. My heart has been frozen for so long I can scarcely remember the last time I felt sorry for anyone but myself. Still, I feel it now, thawing like a glacier that's drifted too far south, leaving me exposed and uncertain on this slippery new ground. I don't know Lane Kramer's story, or who left her black-and-blue. I only know I'm willing to risk the finding out.

Chapter 13

Michael

Michael sat at the dining room table, sipping a glass of Chianti and listening to the sounds of dinner being served up on the other side of the kitchen door. Lane hadn't volunteered what was on the menu when she suggested they dine together, but whatever it was smelled amazing. After this morning's somewhat strained conversation in the library, the offer had come as a bit of a surprise. She had seemed distracted when she returned from her walk, her face grim and set, but then who could blame her? He had sworn he'd be no trouble, and so far he'd been nothing but. He was lucky she hadn't booted him out on his ear. Instead, she'd invited him to dinner.

Lane was still wearing her apron when she pushed through the swinging door connecting the kitchen with the inn's formal dining room. He stood to help with the tray, but she shooed him back into his chair, then proceeded to set out garlic bread, salad, and an enormous bowl of pasta.

It all looked wonderful, but at the moment Michael was more interested in the woman who had prepared it. Her face was just inches from his as she leaned forward to set out the dishes, though most of it was concealed behind a curtain of deep red hair, the kind of hair you wanted to touch just to prove it was real. She really was quite lovely, long-limbed and slender with enormous gold-flecked green eyes and a dusting of pale freckles across the bridge of her nose. He hadn't noticed those before, but suddenly he had a flash of her as she must have been as a girl, the freckles more pronounced, the auburn hair wound into a pair of heavy braids, all knees and elbows and eyes. He found himself wondering if she'd been happy then—and if she was happy now.

She sighed softly as she untied her apron and tossed it aside, then slid into the chair across from him, her cheeks still flushed from cooking.

"Wine?" Michael inquired, poised to fill her glass.

Lane shook her head. "Best not. I still have some writing to do."

Michael waited for her to take the first bite before picking up his fork to dive in. "This is amazing," he said after a few bites. "There's a little place outside Boston, La Campania. Best Italian I've ever eaten. But they've got nothing on you."

She waved off the compliment. "There's still no meat to be had, but there were some vegetables in the bins that were still halfway decent, so I opted for the primavera. I'm never, ever out of pasta."

"Are you Italian?"

"Lord, no. I was a Campbell before I married Bruce."

"Bruce?"

"My ex."

"Oh," he said, feigning relief. "I thought maybe you were stashing him somewhere."

"Hardly," Lane said with a roll of the eyes. "Have you got one? An ex, I mean."

Michael thought of Becca sorting through the CD tower in his living room. Could you call someone your ex if she required only one cardboard box to pack her possessions when she moved out?

"No," he said finally. "No ex."

Michael wasn't sure she'd heard him. She was nibbling on a piece of bread, staring off into space. He hadn't meant to bring up a sour subject, but the look on her face suggested he'd done just that. His suspicions were confirmed when she grabbed the bottle of Chianti and splashed some into her glass.

"I didn't mean to pry. I'm sorry."

"You asked if I was Italian," she said between sips. "That's hardly prying."

"Would it be prying to ask how the articles are coming along? I haven't been in your way, have I?"

Lane shook her head as she chased a chunk of zucchini around her plate. "No, you haven't. And they're coming along nicely, thank you. What about you? How's the research going?"

"Tedious. So pretty much as expected."

"You don't enjoy research?"

Michael helped himself to more salad and began carefully herding olives to the edge of his plate. "I think I'm just tired of working on this book."

"Then why write it?"

"Ever heard the phrase *publish or perish*?"

Lane nodded.

"Well, that's why."

"I thought you were crazy about Dickens and his social commentary on the poor and downtrodden."

Michael caught the slightly snarky reference but let it pass. "I am, which is precisely the point. The more I work on the thing, the more I realize it isn't the book I meant to write."

"I don't understand. It's your book. Write it the way you want."

Michael eased back in his chair, sipping his wine while he considered Lane's remark. If only it were that easy. If only he believed he had that kind of say over his career and his work. But he'd learned early on, and was still learning, that the hallowed halls of academia

carried their share of drawbacks, particularly for the son of a promi-
nent Boston attorney whose shockingly generous gift to the school
had conveniently arrived one month before he was hired.

He'd been trying to prove himself ever since, trying to overcome
the niggling suspicion that he was sitting in someone else's chair, that
he'd usurped the job of someone who might have been more deserv-
ing, though not as well connected or well-heeled. The worst part was
that he honestly couldn't say whether he would have landed the position had his father not mailed the check. He did, however, know
what everyone else thought.

"Can I ask you a question?" he asked, setting his glass aside.

Lane nodded, but her gold-flecked eyes were suddenly wary.

"This place—the inn—do you enjoy running it?"

"Very much. Why?"

"And your articles—you like writing them?" Her brow furrowed
and he could tell she was trying to surmise where these questions
were leading. "I guess I'm trying to figure out how you know if you're
where you're supposed to be in life, or if you're just, you know, tread-
ing water."

The words seemed to catch Lane off guard. She set down her fork
and blinked across the table at him. "I'm not sure if you're asking the
wrong question, or just the wrong girl. I mean, how does anybody
know that?"

He planted his elbows on either side of his plate and folded his
hands beneath his chin. "Did you always want to do this?"

"The inn? No, never. But I knew the minute I saw it."

"And it's enough? Even though it's not what you always dreamed
of doing?"

Michael saw at once that the question made her uncomfortable.
She lifted her glass to buy time, sipping deeply. "For now," she said
quietly. "Yes, it's enough."

"Hmmm . . . why don't I believe you?"

Lane's brows shot up. "Now I'm a liar?"

"Don't get mad. Believe it or not, this is actually about me, not you. Lately, I've been feeling like I'm living in someone else's skin, showing one face to the world, but staring at someone completely different when I look in the mirror."

"I know a little something about that."

"I don't know. Maybe it's because I never really chose a path. Well, I chose, but for all the wrong reasons. I confused running away *from* something with running *toward* something, and I'm starting to wonder now if that ever really works. I've been thinking about making some changes in my life, following my dream or my North Star or whatever people call it."

"Do you know what your dream is?"

"I do, or at least I think I do. And I can tell you it's a million miles from what my family thinks it should be."

Lane lifted her glass in mock salute. "At last, something we have in common."

"Really? What did your parents think *you* should be?"

Her eyes lifted over the rim of her wineglass, meeting his. "Married."

"Oh," he said, swallowing his surprise. He'd expected her to say something else. "And what did you want to be?"

"A writer," she blurted without blinking. "The kind who tells stories that make people laugh and cry and think about life."

"Important stories?"

Lane drained her glass, then stared down into it. "Important stories, yes."

Something in her voice made him want to reach for her hand, an uncomfortable reaction he managed to check. "Then why didn't you?"

"Oh, I did once."

Once again her answer surprised him. "And what happened?"

"He caught me."

"Caught you? Who?"

"Bruce. He hated that I wrote. He thought it was a colossal waste of time. So I used to sneak around. I'd work when he was at the hospital, or away at a seminar. One day he found part of the manuscript in my nightstand. I didn't want the pages lying about, so I rarely printed what I was working on, but I was having trouble with a scene and I thought if I printed it out it might help." She shrugged as she reached for the Chianti and refilled her glass. "He found it."

"And then what?"

"He pretended he thought it was funny, but he was furious that I'd gone behind his back."

"And whose fault was it that you *had* to go behind his back?"

"Mine," she said, the lone word flat and strangely devoid of emotion. "With Bruce everything was my fault. Everything. Always. It got to where I was afraid to make a move for fear of getting it wrong."

"Did he . . . hit you?"

She looked at him then, or through him. There was something hard and faraway in her eyes. "There are more ways to be abusive than just using your fists."

"I'm sorry," he said quietly, because he truly was. A writer's ego was a fragile thing, especially early on. It required support and careful nurturing if it was to have any hope of surviving those early uncertain days. She had obviously gotten neither.

"Did you keep writing?"

"For a while, yes. Until I figured out Bruce was right and I was just wasting my time."

"But how do you *know* you were wasting your time?"

"Kenny Bingham, one of Bruce's buddies, who worked in the lit department at Northwestern, assured me that I was. Bruce snuck him a copy of my manuscript to critique."

Michael stifled the grimace he felt tugging at his lips. He could already guess what was coming. He'd seen it firsthand, elitist profes-

sors bent on doing their duty by the literary establishment, brandish-
ing their opinions like swords, and riding roughshod over the dreams
of budding writers in the process. He'd managed to resuscitate a few
of those dreams, the ones he'd gotten to in time, but some had been
past saving, too bitter and disillusioned to try again. He suspected
Lane Kramer was one of the latter.

"And...?" he prompted, when it became clear she wouldn't volunteer more.

"And...he politely advised me to find a new hobby. Apparently
I'm a talentless hack. Oh, and I'm unoriginal. I have no voice or style
of my own. I do, however, have a gift for mimicking other, more talented writers, though that should in no way be confused with having
actual talent."

"Lane, there's no such thing as original. Everyone borrows,
whether they know it or not. Hell, some steal outright. It sounds to
me like this Kenny whatever-his-name-is actually paid you a compliment, even if he didn't mean to. Writing like other talented writers is
a very good thing indeed."

Lane sniffed. "That isn't how Bruce saw it."

Michael pushed his plate back in disgust. "So that was it? You
took one stuffy-ass professor at face value and gave up?"

Lane tilted her glass and drank deeply, then gazed absently into
the bloodred dregs. "I thought you stuffy-ass professors knew everything."

Michael couldn't help laughing out loud, partly because the words
had come out slightly slurred, but mostly because the premise of the
statement was utterly ridiculous.

"First of all, literary critique is purely subjective. One man's trash
may truly be another man's treasure. *War of the Worlds* was called
horrid, and a nightmare. Stephen King was told that *Carrie* would
never sell. And one publisher actually told F. Scott Fitzgerald that *The
Great Gatsby might* work as a book, but only if he got rid of Gatsby."

"Yes, well, I'm not F. Scott Fitzgerald."

"How do you know?" He could tell the question annoyed her, but he didn't care. "My point is the so-called experts don't know a bloody thing. We have an opinion, that's all."

A thick curtain of hair fell across her face as she reached for the wine bottle and refilled her glass. It wasn't a new occurrence; her hair was always falling across her face. But now, suddenly, he saw that the gesture wasn't wholly accidental. She used it to shield herself from probing eyes. He wasn't sure how he'd missed it until now, but to-night there was no hiding the fragile, eggshell quality that hovered about her, as if a wrong move or word might break her.

"I'm sorry," he said quietly. "I'm doing it again, aren't I? Sticking my nose in where it doesn't belong."

"No, this is different." She tipped her head to one side. "But why are you being so nice all of a sudden, so . . . supportive?"

Michael pondered the question a moment. They hadn't had many conversations since he arrived at the inn, and the ones they did have hadn't gone very well. Now, without meaning to, he stood accused of being nice.

"Because your husband was an ass," he said finally, and without apology. "Or perhaps it's because I think you have a right to your dreams, and the right to pursue them in whatever way you choose."

Lane smiled, a brief curl of the lips that was gone as quickly as it had appeared. "I can't tell—are we still talking about me, or have we switched back to you?"

It was Michael's turn to smile. "Point taken," he conceded grimly. "Though I honestly don't know the answer."

Chapter 14

Lane

Lane closed her eyes briefly as she washed up Michael's breakfast dishes, her cheeks warming at the memory of last night's dinner conversation. Two glasses of Chianti and she'd poured out her life story to a veritable stranger. Jesus, maybe Mary was right. Maybe she did wear her scars on her sleeve.

She had risen early to get her morning walk out of the way, then manufactured an excuse to skip breakfast with Michael. He hadn't seemed to mind. In fact, she might even have detected relief in his coolly distracted nod when she told him she was having breakfast with a friend later on. And it was mostly true, if you counted blueberry scones as breakfast, and Mary as her friend. Besides, she hadn't been the only one making free with personal details last night. She suspected Michael might be feeling a little sheepish, too. The good news was that in a few months they'd never see each other again.

The front door buzzer interrupted her thoughts. It would be Dally. A moment later came the scrape of a key in the lock, followed by Dahlia Morgan's signature greeting.

"Hey-howdy!"

"Back here in the kitchen," Lane hollered.

Dahlia Morgan bounced into the room with her usual burst of twentysomething energy, fueled in part by the enormous cup of Stop-N-Go coffee she never seemed to be without. Lane couldn't blame her, though. For a single mom juggling three jobs, not to mention online classes to become a massage therapist and something called a Reiki practitioner, it was probably the only way she managed to keep all the balls in the air. Still, even with megadoses of caffeine and a mother who helped out with Skye, Dally's four-year-old daughter, Lane honestly didn't see how she kept going.

Skye was just one of the reasons Lane kept Dally on during the off-season, though with no guests she usually cut her back from four days to one. The other reason, and perhaps the real one, was that Dally had been there for her from the beginning. She had lived next door to the cottage Lane briefly rented during early renovations. Skye's father had been abusive, and while Bruce had never laid a hand on Lane, Dally had had no trouble recognizing a woman who'd lost her confidence and needed to get her feet back under her.

She'd introduced Lane to yoga, and had nearly drowned her with herbal tea, but more important, she had listened and understood. Not to mention, when it came to keeping up with local affairs, her weekly visits were better than a subscription to the *Islander Dispatch*. She had a talent for picking up every scrap of Starry Point gossip worth knowing, and even a few that weren't.

Dally doffed her lime green jacket and draped it over a chair. "I haven't been by since Penny, but it looks like you fared pretty well. I saw the big tree all cut up out by the road, though. It didn't do any damage, did it?"

"No. It fell across the driveway. How about your place?"

"Not bad. The landlord came by and boarded us up. Mom was terrified, but Skye slept through the whole thing. The worst of it was going three days without power."

"And the Village Mart's still pretty bare, which makes meals a bit of a challenge."

Dally grinned as she snuck a scone out of the basket on the counter and nibbled off one of the corners. "Long as I can boil water, we're fine over at my place. We're plenty used to ramen and Kraft mac and cheese."

Lane refilled her mug, then crossed the kitchen, scowling at Dally as she dropped into a chair. "You do know that child's going to end up with rickets one of these days, right? Just because you think broccoli's some sort of government plot doesn't mean Skye can't eat a green bean every once in a while. I swear, for an earth-mother type you're the most unhealthy eater I know."

"Lord, now you sound just like Mama."

"Your mother's a smart woman."

The floorboards creaked briefly as Michael appeared in the doorway. "Who in the world are you talking—" He broke off, his face suddenly sheepish. "Oh, sorry. I didn't realize . . ."

"Michael, this is Dally Morgan. Dally, Michael Forrester."

Michael nodded politely as he backed out of the doorway. "I forgot you said you had a friend coming by. Excuse me."

His footsteps had barely receded when Dally pounced. "Who. Was. That?"

"A guest."

Dally folded her arms, her dark brows arched skeptically. "In November? Since when?"

"Since he knocked on my door in the middle of tropical storm Penny."

"And you let him stay? Well, of course you did. I mean, look at him. He must be seven feet tall."

"I promise you his height had nothing to do with it. He's a college professor on sabbatical. He needed somewhere to finish researching a book he's working on."

"So he's a writer, too? And no ring. How perfect!"

"It's not—" Lane glanced at the doorway, then dropped her voice. "It's not perfect at all. In fact, it's a bit inconvenient."

"Having a smart, hunky guy stay with you? Yeah, I can see how that would be a real hardship."

Lane shot her a look of exasperation. "Maybe it's me, but twenty-eight seems a little old to still be boy-crazy."

"I'm twenty-seven," Dally shot back as she pushed another bite of scone into her mouth. "So, how long is Mr. Tall, Dark, and Hunky staying?"

Lane stifled a groan, knowing what would come next. "He'll be here through the off-season."

"Through February?" Dally counted off on her fingers. "That's four and a half months. Eighteen weeks."

"I'm glad to see those online courses are helping sharpen your math skills. And yes, I know how many weeks it is. I also know where you're going with this, and you can stop."

Dally blinked wide brown eyes at her. "What?"

A grin threatened but Lane swallowed it, replacing it with her best stern face. "Don't play dumb, Dally. You stink at it. He's a guest—a *paying* guest."

"Okay, fine. But what's the big deal? He's here. You're here. What's wrong with mixing business with pleasure?"

"Nothing's wrong with it. I'm just not interested."

Dally slouched sulkily in her chair. "Suit yourself, but I've worked for you for over four years now, and unless you've been holding out on me, you haven't had so much as a date. Don't you think it's time?"

"For what?"

"Oh, for crying out loud. Now who's playing dumb? To get back on the horse, silly. Think of it as one of those no-risk ninety-day trials."

Lane set her cup down with a firm shake of the head. "No, thanks. I'm still chafed from my last ride. I'm not looking for a new set of saddle sores. Michael is here because with all the break-ins around town I thought it might be a good idea to have a man around."

"Hmmm." The eyebrow notched up again. "You never struck me as the nervous type."

Lane ignored the sarcasm. "The other night I was looking out front. I think I saw a light in the house across the street."

Dally suddenly sat up straight. "The Rourke place?"

"It looked like a flashlight, but whatever it was I can tell you it made me nervous. The worst part is the police don't seem one bit interested. In fact, I'm pretty sure they don't even believe me."

"Wow . . . creepy."

"I know what I saw, Dally. Someone was in that house."

Dally fingered the crystal amulet around her neck. "Maybe there's some truth to all those rumors—the banker back in the twenties, and then that poor little boy. Sounds like some pretty negative energy to me."

Lane made a face. "I know you believe in that stuff, but I'm pretty sure this light was man-made."

Dally shrugged. "Well, the good news is there haven't been any new break-ins since right before the storm. Maybe the culprit left the island."

"I'd love to believe that. But even if it's true I'm afraid I'm stuck with Michael Forrester until March."

Dally rose, carrying her empty Stop-N-Go cup to the trash on her way to the stairs. "Honey, all I can say is I'd love to have your problems. Now, if you'll tell me which room the professor is staying in, I'll go up and change his sheets and towels."

"I put him in the Tower Suite."

"Wonderful. I'll rifle the nightstand to make sure there aren't any pictures of a girlfriend lying around—just in case you change your mind between now and March."

Lane rolled her eyes, calling after Dally as she disappeared up the stairs, "You know I only put up with you because I can't stand doing laundry."

Dally's voice drifted back down. "I do. And you know I'm only here for the baked goods."

Chapter 15

L ane grimaced as she filled a thermos with tea, then bagged up
several scones. She could hear Dally clomping around upstairs,
hauling fresh linens from the supply closet, dragging out her
mop and cleaning rags. Finally, the vacuum cleaner switched on, its
muffled whir mingling with the gutsy strains of "Before He Cheats,"
belted out in Dally's typical wide-open, off-key fashion. Lane shot a
glance toward the ceiling, hoping the racket wasn't bleeding into the
den. Somehow Michael didn't strike her as a country music fan, not
that Dally's rusty voice bore the slightest resemblance to Carrie
Underwood's—or to anything like music, for that matter. She should
probably check before she headed out to the dunes, and maybe ask
Dally to postpone the concert.

Padding through the parlor, she stepped to the doorway of the
den and delicately cleared her throat. Michael's head snapped up, a
vaguely uneasy expression on his face as his hand shot out to lower
the screen on his laptop. Lane frowned. Maybe he was one of those
very private writers, or maybe in the world of academia you had to
be careful about letting anyone see your work. She'd heard it could
be dog-eat-dog.

"I'm sorry. I didn't mean to sneak up on you. I was just wondering if Dally working upstairs was bothering you. She's not particularly quiet, and she . . . uh . . . likes to sing while she vacuums."

Michael cocked his head briefly to one side, then shook his head. "I didn't even notice until you said something, so I guess not." His eyes scanned the length of her, lingering on her jacket and duck boots. "You're going back out? I thought you'd already been for your walk."

"I have. I'm just heading out to the dunes for a bit."

"A bit chilly for a day at the beach, isn't it?"

"I won't be long. I'm just meeting a friend. There's fresh coffee in the kitchen if you want it, and blueberry scones on the counter."

"I'm fine, really," he said, with another of his cool nods. "Low maintenance, remember?"

Before she could step away he had retrieved the pencil from behind his ear and was already scribbling in the margins of a crowded yellow legal pad. Lane was glad. She didn't feel like explaining Mary to him, perhaps because she had no idea how or where to begin. Sooner or later, though, if the visits continued, he was going to wonder where she went every morning, and then she was going to have to find a way to explain her fascination with a perplexing and perhaps troubled old woman she knew less than nothing about.

At the back gate she paused to admire the way the day was shaping up. This morning's chilly mist had finally burned away, leaving behind a sky of sharp, cloudless blue. Beyond the dunes the sea lay as smooth and shiny as quicksilver, the air scrubbed clean of everything but salt. It was hard to believe only a week ago Penny had been bearing down on them.

Mary was perched in her usual place, wearing a lightweight jacket instead of the orange scarf and lumpy peacoat Lane had grown used to. Her shoulders were squared and slightly stiff, signaling that she was aware of Lane as she picked her way up the vine-covered dune.

"I brought tea this time," Lane announced cheerfully.

Mary nodded, cool but noncommittal. Lane knew better than to wait for an invitation to sit, so she dropped down onto the sand. Producing the pair of paper cups from her jacket pocket, she carefully filled one and passed it to Mary, then held out the bag of scones.

Mary peered inside with a delicate sniff. "Blueberries?"

"Blueberry scones, yes."

Mary pulled a scone from the bag and ventured a small bite. "I used to pick blueberries when I was a girl . . . a millennium ago."

The words felt thin and wistful, as though they had traveled across many years and many miles. Lane let them be, content with imagining the woman beside her, weathered now and life-weary, as a young and carefree girl. The vision came with surprising ease. She saw bright aqua eyes, cheeks that were lineless and dewy, a face as fresh as a summer peach. Her hair, cropped now and leached of color, restored to its original gold, tumbling past slender shoulders in thick wayward waves. It was only the mouth that gave her trouble. No matter how hard she pressed her imagination, the mouth simply refused to smile.

Had Mary ever been happy? It was just one of the things she longed to know. She wanted to know if the woman had a last name, if she had family, or at least someone to look after her. She wanted to know where she had come from so suddenly, and where she pedaled off to each afternoon when she left the dunes. Mary was unlike anyone she'd ever known, an erratic blend of wisdom and confusion, a woman who spoke in riddles and knew things she had no business knowing. In a word, she was fascinating. But it was much too soon to go charging headlong into the woman's life. Her questions would have to wait.

For a while they sipped their tea in silence, listening to the soft tumble of the sea, washing in and pulling back, trailing ruffles of lacy foam on the packed wet sand. Lane feigned fascination in the brown-and-white pattern of a turkey wing shell. Finally, she felt compelled to break the silence.

"So . . . ," she said, dragging the word out, hoping to make it sound nonchalant. "You're new to Starry Point."

It was a kind of compromise, a question that wasn't *really* a question, which meant it didn't necessarily count as prying. Mary took her time, sipping her tea while she followed the drunken progress of a ghost crab zigzagging along the sand. Finally, her head swiveled, her eyes leveled keenly on Lane.

"And what about you, my girl? You're not from here, I think."

Lane blinked twice, then pressed her lips together to suppress a smile. The sly old thing hadn't batted an eye as she neatly turned the question around. "No. Chicago. I bought the inn five years ago."

"Chased all the little gray doves away, did you, with their beads and their crosses?"

Lane's brow wrinkled briefly until she realized Mary must be talking about the order of nuns who had once lived at the Cloister, though she seemed a little mixed up about the timeline.

"The sisters were long gone by the time I came. In fact, the place had been vacant for years. Before that it was a record storage facility."

"And in between there were the boys."

"Yes, the boys' home, which was run by the nuns. But that's still going way back. I believe the nuns relocated to the mainland sometime in the late eighties so they could build a more modern facility."

Mary's eyes kindled suddenly. "How terribly charitable of them."

"You don't like nuns?" It seemed a ridiculous thing to ask, but there was really no other way to interpret Mary's statement, or the tone she'd used when she made it.

"I don't like do-gooders!" she snarled with startling heat. "Nuns or any other kind. People who pretend to care when what they really are is a pack of meddling bitches, peeking in your windows and then whispering behind their hands. Oh yes, they mean well with their prayers and their casseroles. Love thy neighbor, and all that swill. Must look out for the children."

Lane stiffened, astonished by this sudden outburst, and by the disturbing change that had come over Mary. Angry splotches of color mottled her cheeks. Blue-green eyes, placid as the morning sea only moments ago, were stormy now, narrowed and seething. She had started to tremble.

"Mary?"

Mary jerked her cropped white head around, her expression so fierce Lane couldn't help flinching. And then, for no reason Lane could fathom, the old woman seemed to wilt, as if the air had suddenly gone out of her.

"Oh dear, I'm sorry. I've frightened you, haven't I?"

Lane was at a loss. She had never handled anger well, not her mother's and certainly not Bruce's. But that had been a different kind of anger, the silent, frosty kind, not this thinly veiled brand of fury.

"You didn't frighten me," Lane lied. "But all of a sudden you seem..."

"Crazy?"

"I was going to say upset."

Mary shrugged, her eyes fixed once more on the rolling waves. "For me the two are often the same." She surprised Lane by reaching over and patting her hand. "No worries, though. I'm all right now. Mustn't regress. What's past is past." Her head swiveled back to Lane after a beat. "It is, isn't it?"

Lane fumbled with the thermos, refilling her cup as she tried to decide how to respond to this inexplicable jumble of words. "Yes," she said finally, because she could think of nothing else, and because it was true. The past was the past.

"Good," Mary said. "That's what I thought." Her smile turned wistful before fading entirely. "Life is lived in chapters, my girl. Fairy tales and horror stories all strung together like beads on a string. When one chapter ends—when fate conspires to tear us from our own book—we've no choice but to begin again, to invent a new version of ourselves. And we pretend that version is all that has ever been, all that will ever be. We pretend we're safe. Until the tide comes rushing in again, and we must swim for our lives once more."

Lane suppressed a shiver. Fairy tales and horror stories? It seemed there was no way of predicting Mary's mood from one moment to the next. She had no idea what the woman was talking about. She only knew it was unsettling.

"Yesterday, you said you were watching for something," Lane ventured cautiously. "Something no one else could see. Will you tell me what that something is?"

The silence that stretched between them was a heavy one, thoughtful and weighty. Finally, Mary sighed. "The truth, my girl, is what I wait for. Only the truth."

Lane released her breath slowly, exasperated but not wanting to show it. "And no one else can see the truth?"

"Not the truth I mean, no. At least they haven't yet. They're not likely to, either."

"And why is that?"

"Because most people can't see past their noses—or choose not to. They see what they want to, what's easy. And I suppose it's just as well for me that they do."

"Have you . . . you haven't always been . . . on your own, have you?" It wasn't what she wanted to ask, but they both knew what she meant.

"You mean have I always been a pratty old bag lady?" She smiled then, her teeth surprisingly white and even. "No, my girl. No one begins this way. It's a place you arrive at, a bottom you sink to when life pushes you under one too many times. You paddle toward the light for a while, because you want to believe you can save yourself. But then one day you see it all true, and you simply let go. You stop fighting."

Lane wasn't sure if Mary's eagerness to call herself crazy eased the tension or heightened it, but the door was open now and she was too curious not to delve deeper.

"But how did—? What happened?"

"Why, I fell in love, of course. How is it we women always un-ravel? Always a man, isn't it? He was a handsome rake who had a way with words, just like in the fairy tales—and in the horror stories. But that's a story for another time."

Again, fairy tales and horror stories.

"Tomorrow?" Lane prompted hopefully.

"Perhaps." Mary pulled back the sleeve of her jacket to glance at a chunky digital watch studded with buttons. "Tacky, isn't it?" she said, holding it out when she realized Lane was staring. "But what can I do? My Rolex is in the shop and one must stay on schedule when there are pills to be taken. Mustn't frighten the others."

Lane did a mental double take. Rolex? Pills? How was she sup-posed to reconcile those two words? And who were the *others*, and why should they be frightened? Unfortunately, there was no time to ask; Mary was handing back her empty cup, gathering herself to stand.

"Well, I'm off. My turn in the kitchen, and they don't like it when we're late."

Lane stood, too, and walked with her as far as the gate, left to ponder a whole new set of questions as she watched Mary pedal off on her bike. *Late for what?*

Chapter 16

Mary

I have always been ... different ... though I did not always know it. No, that isn't quite true. I've always known. Even as a child one knows these things instinctively. What I should have said was I didn't always understand it.

One of the fey, my Welsh grandmother used to say with a keen, dark eye. Fey. Such a charming little word, bright and otherworldly. For years I thought it meant fairy-born. Then one day I came across it in a story and realized it meant something quite different. It meant touched, crazy—cursed. Even then, my grandmother knew that there was something not quite right about me. And looking back, I believe I must have frightened my parents. They never left off watching me. Something to do, I suppose, with my mother's sister, who was always given to bouts of depression and threw herself from a window when she was sixteen.

I wasn't supposed to know about that, but I did. An *accident*, they called it, rather than what it was—a blot on the family name, an unredeemable sin against God. Perhaps it's why they sent me to the nuns. They had no faith in doctors. But they did have faith in the Almighty. And Lord help me, those little gray birds did their level best to mold me into a blank, colorless replica of their kind, to empty me of me, to make me over for God. They brought their prayers and their beads and their candles to bear, but in the end I would have none of it.

Would now that they had succeeded.

Taking the veil would have stood in the way of so many sorrows. Not for me. I would ask no reprieve, nor do I deserve one. My sorrows are of my own making, my yoke to bear for what remains of this life, and, I suppose, the one beyond. But for those whose lives were mine to cherish, lives that were lost instead, I heartily wish I had chosen differently. Instead, when happiness beckoned, shiny and false, I closed my eyes to the truth and ran toward disaster with arms wide open. So much lost in the name of love. So much in ruins.

Through my fault.

Through my fault.

Through my most grievous fault.

Chapter 17

Lane

L ane was surprised to find Michael in the kitchen when she returned. She'd forgotten him somehow while talking to Mary. He was refilling his coffee mug, a scone caught between his teeth so that his hands were free. When he finished pouring he removed the scone, then picked up a scrap of paper off the counter.

"Your friend Delilah asked me to give you this note as she was leaving."

Lane began unlacing her duck boots. "It's Dahlia, actually—Dally for short. What does it say?"

Michael squinted at the note. "Well, it appears to be scribbled on the back of this month's electric bill. Let's see . . . Ninety days risk free. If not completely satisfied, simply return the unused portion for a full refund." He frowned as he handed the note over. "It's signed with a little smiley face."

Heat prickled in Lane's cheeks as she glanced at Dally's scribble. Laundry or no laundry, it was definitely time to fire that girl.

Michael was making short work of his scone as he spooned sugar into his mug. "So, did you have a nice visit?"

Lane glanced up at him, feeling awkward and still vaguely annoyed. "What? Oh yes."

"Coffee?" he offered, jerking a thumb toward the pot. "I'll bet you're freezing."

"No, thanks." She held up the thermos. "I brought tea, and it's actually nice out. Almost balmy."

Michael grunted. "Call me crazy, but maybe next time you could invite your friend in, rather than sitting out on the dunes freezing your tail off. You wouldn't need the thermos."

"Oh, she'd never come inside."

Michael's brows drew together. "Never come inside? What kind of friend is that?"

Lane stepped around him and crossed to the sink, busying herself with emptying and rinsing the thermos. She really didn't want to get into explanations about Mary, at least not until she had a better handle on the woman.

"She isn't exactly a friend," Lane corrected, trying to keep her tone light. "She's more of an acquaintance really, but for some reason we hit it off. She's sort of... special."

Michael's spoon went still in his coffee. "Special... how?"

"Well, sort of like a bag lady, I guess. Her name is Mary."

"Mary what?"

Lane shrugged again. "I have no idea. She just started showing up on the dunes a few weeks ago. Rain or shine, she's there every morning. I don't know a thing about her except that she hates coffee, and sometimes she seems like she's not all there. She rides a rusty old bike with a DayGlo flag on the back and carries this purple cloth bag around with her everywhere she goes." Lane paused, a smile slowly forming. "And she calls me *my girl*."

"You mean she's crazy."

Lane's chin lifted a measure in response to the word. "I'm not going to say that. But she *is* different—and sad. Day after day, she just sits there staring out at the ocean, waiting."

"What's she waiting for?"

Another shrug. The gesture seemed to perfectly sum up her brief relationship with Mary. "Truth. At least that's what she said when I asked her. Every time I ask a question, I wind up with ten more."

"Lane, do you really think this is wise?"

"Wise?"

"Getting mixed up with someone you know nothing about."

"I run a bed-and-breakfast, Michael. I make a living getting mixed up with people I know nothing about."

"That isn't what I'm talking about."

"Then what are you talking about?" It came out snippier than she'd intended, but as usual, something in his tone was getting under her skin.

"I'm just saying maybe you should think twice before getting involved with someone like that."

Lane felt her anger bubbling close to the surface. "Someone like what?"

"Unstable, unhinged—hell, call it whatever you want. There are people who want help and there are people who are just looking for a crutch to prop them up between disasters. You seem like a nice person. I'd hate to see you get sucked into someone else's self-induced hell."

"How do you know I will?"

"Because that's what happens. People like this Mary of yours are like human quicksand. You give them a hand and they drag you in with them. The woman could be dangerous for all you know."

"Don't be ridiculous. Mary might be a little . . . confused, but she's not dangerous. In fact, there's a sort of gracefulness about her, even if her clothes don't match and her hair looks like it's been hacked off with a pair of hedge clippers. I think she was probably quite beautiful once. You can tell by just looking that life's been hard on her. She looks so tired, poor thing, and so alone."

Michael set his mug on the counter, his expression steely. "Lane, trust me. You need to steer clear of this woman. Maybe you haven't had experience with her type, but I have, and I can promise you, you'll be sorry if you let yourself get pulled in."

Lane studied him a moment, the bunched shoulders and grim mouth, the hands fisted tightly at his sides. Where was all this coming from? From the moment she laid eyes on him, she'd pegged him as well off, but prep-school, country-club well off, not heartless-bastard well off. Clearly she'd gotten it wrong.

"I'll take my chances," she answered finally, rolling her eyes for emphasis.

"Fine. Just remember I warned you. Before it's over you're going to wish you'd listened. These people lure you in with their sad stories, and then they take you right down with them."

"Take you where?"

"To whatever sick place they go to in their heads. They like company, so they grab on to you and they don't let go."

Lane couldn't help thinking about the look on Mary's face when she had spoken about trying to save herself, and of eventually letting go—of sinking to the bottom. It was a terrible image, and a sad one, but the woman wasn't a monster.

"For God's sake, Michael, you've never laid eyes on the woman and you're talking about her like she's the Creature from the Black Lagoon! She's a tired old woman who's had a hard life, and my guess is she could use a little compassion. Something tells me she hasn't found much lately, if ever."

"I see," Michael said, raking a hand through his hair. "This is some mission of mercy, then, an act of Christian duty?"

Do-gooder. The phrase popped into Lane's head, fresh from Mary's rant. Since when was trying to help someone a bad thing?

"How about a simple act of human kindness?" Lane snapped, not bothering to hide her annoyance. "Or is that out of fashion these days?"

Michael held up his hands, signaling a truce as he backed toward the door. "Just be careful, is all I'm saying."

He turned and left the kitchen then, his coffee forgotten on the counter, leaving Lane to wonder what the hell all that had been about.

Two hours later, Lane was in her writing room still trying to put the final polish on the microbrew article that was due in two days. She wasn't making much progress, distracted by the sparkling blue horizon, pondering what truth Mary hoped to find there.

She was also thinking about Michael, or maybe stewing was a better word. He had chutzpah, that was for sure. In little more than a week he'd found a way to question her taste in literature, her willingness to put herself on the line as a writer, and now her judgment in friends. But it wasn't only that he'd weighed in with an opinion on something that was none of his business; it was the intensity with which he had voiced that opinion, the look in his eyes approaching panic, as if she'd just told him she'd shared a thermos of tea with a terrorist. It reminded her of Bruce, who had never trusted her judgment in anything.

Glancing at her watch, she realized it was time to start thinking about dinner. Michael Forrester might be a royal pain in the ass, but he was still a paying guest. And it wasn't as if she was getting much writing done anyway. After tidying her notes she headed for the door. She was startled to find Michael on the other side, hand raised as if about to knock.

"Oh, sorry," he said, stuffing the hand into his pocket. "I didn't mean to scare you. I came to say I'm sorry."

Lane fixed him with wide, unblinking eyes. "Sorry for what?" She knew damn well what he should be sorry for, but she wanted to hear him say it.

"For sticking my nose in your business—again. I came to ask if I could buy you dinner."

His appearance at her door had definitely caught her off guard, but his offer of dinner was an even bigger surprise. "I was just on my way down to the kitchen."

"Look, I know what you think, but I promise I'm not the jackass I appear to be—or at least not all the time. In fact, some people actually like me."

"Parents don't count," she replied frostily, though she felt a grin tugging at her lips. He looked so serious, and slightly ridiculous, too, towering in her doorway all sheepish and sorry.

It was Michael's turn to grin. "Damn good thing. Mine would hardly make my case."

Folding her arms, she made a show of looking him over. "Oh yes, I can see how you'd be a terrible disappointment—handsome author, esteemed college professor. Yes indeed, a total failure."

She realized at once that she'd hit a nerve. She could see it in his eyes, a fleeting shadow that was there and then gone. Still, he covered well enough and even managed a smile.

"I'll take that as a yes, then."

Lane dropped her hands, ready to protest, but suddenly the idea of dinner out was a tempting one, even with a guy who drove her crazy. She couldn't remember the last time someone had prepared a meal for her, served her, and then done the dishes.

"I'm not sure what's reopened after the storm. I guess I could call around to a few places. It's all pretty casual on the island, so don't expect much."

"Low maintenance, remember? Come find me when you're ready. I'll be in the den shutting things down." He turned and took two steps, then turned back. "And thanks for the second chance."

Lane closed the door and leaned against it, wondering if this was a good idea and trying not to think of the smiley face at the bottom of Dally's note.

Chapter 18

The Blue Water Grille wasn't much to look at, a squat shack painted blue, with a red tin roof and a pair of bedraggled window boxes. That hadn't stopped it from earning local landmark status, or from drawing a crowd every night of the week. Even on a Wednesday the place was packed to the rafters, the small square of pocked asphalt choked with cars anywhere they could find or make a spot. The unseasonably warm weather wasn't hurting business, either, pulling in locals eager for one last meal beside the sea before a chilly winter drove them inside.

The front door beckoned, propped open with an enormous rusty anchor. The hum of people unwinding at the end of the day—conversation, clinking glasses, and sporadic bursts of laughter—drifted out to greet them as Lane trailed Michael up the weathered wooden steps. It was a strangely pleasant sound, lively and warm and far too foreign of late. Suddenly, she found herself eager to be a part of it, to let down her guard and have a little fun—if she still remembered how.

She eyed the chalkboard sign just inside the door: NO SHOES. NO SHIRT. NO PROBLEM. Cliché, perhaps, but in all likelihood true. It had taken some time to adjust to the concept of *island time*, a world away from the high-octane pace of Chicago's city dwellers, where fashionable up-and-comers were forever checking their watches, hurrying *from* somewhere or *to* somewhere, always running late for something. But on Starry Point the days were different. Most of the things that seemed important back in Chicago carried little weight here. Life had its own rhythm, its own ideas about what mattered. At first the pace felt wrong—too careless, too loose. But then, little by little, the sand and the salt had crept into her veins, and she had realized how very right it all was.

The hostess gave them the option of a cramped corner table near the kitchen, or waiting a few minutes until the repairmen got the last of their equipment off the deck. She warned that with the sun going down it might be a little chilly until they lit the kerosene heaters, but the upside was that the band would be setting up shortly and they'd have great seats. Michael and Lane nodded simultaneously toward the deck. They didn't have to wait long.

The deck was a maze of empty picnic tables. Michael took the menus the hostess offered and picked his way to a table along the railing, shooing a chubby gull who surveyed them with glassy, hopeful eyes. The sun was definitely on its way down, the cooling twilight thick with the scents of salt and seafood and beer, the light a pearly shade of lavender where it fell across the scarred tabletop.

Lane folded her arms along the edge of the table and let her eyes follow the smooth curve of empty beach. She'd come to Starry Point five years ago, and yet there were still times when the raw beauty of the Carolina coast caught her off guard: pristine stretches of sugar white sand, sea oats bending softly in the breeze, tireless waves that had been churning against the coast since time began. It didn't take long to see why the Blue Water was a favorite with locals and tourists alike. Sitting here while the light died and the sea went flat and gray was more soothing than any tonic or pill could ever be.

"This is nice," she said dreamily. "Like a postcard."

"I think it was you who said I shouldn't expect much," he reminded her as he grabbed one of the laminated menus. "So, what's good?"

"I have no idea. I was going to ask the waitress."

Michael cocked an eye at her. "I thought you said this place was a landmark. Are you telling me you've never eaten here?"

"Never."

"How is that possible?"

"Well, for one thing, running a bed-and-breakfast doesn't leave a lot of time for dining out. You're too busy taking care of everyone else's food."

"All right, I suppose I'll give you a pass," he said, but in a way that made her think he really wasn't. "How 'bout we keep it simple—beer and a bucket of steamed clams to start?"

Their waitress was a perky, twentysomething blonde with Merthiolate-colored streaks running through her hair. She introduced herself as Jessica—Jess for short—then promptly forgot Lane was at the table, pinning her appreciative blue gaze on Michael as she rattled off the specials.

"We'll take a couple Yuenglings and a bucket of clams," he said as he handed back the menus. "And could I get some extra lemon, if it's not too much trouble?"

"No trouble at all," Jessica drawled, showing off perfect white teeth as she stuffed her order pad back into her apron.

Lane could almost swear she saw the girl toss a wink in Michael's direction as she turned to leave. Apparently *Jess* didn't have a problem with men who were almost twenty years her senior. Or at least not the ones who looked like Michael. And why would she? He was amazing-looking, the perfect blend of scruff and polish, sexy and smart—like now, when his square jaw was all stubbled and the breeze ruffled through his dark hair.

She wondered briefly if he was aware of the effect he had on women, then decided he must be. The man owned a mirror, surely. And if that wasn't enough, she felt certain there were classrooms full of wide-eyed coeds back in Middlebury more than willing to confirm the power of his considerable charms.

"Warm enough?" Michael asked, startling Lane from her somewhat unwelcome thoughts.

She nodded, plucking at her turtleneck and jacket. "You learn to layer when you live at the beach. In Chicago, if it's cold when you wake up, it's going to be cold when you go to bed. Here, the weather changes hourly, especially at this time of year."

"Speaking of Chicago, I'm curious. How in the world did you find your way to Starry Point, and why? Or is that being nosy again?"

Lane smiled. "It is, but I'll tell you anyway. After the divorce I couldn't stand all the hand patting and pitiful looks, not to mention the endless attempts to fix me up. So one day I packed a bag and drove away. When I found a place I liked, I stopped. When I got bored, I moved on. Then I found Starry Point and I knew I wanted to stay. It felt like the edge of the world—one road in, one road out. That was appealing."

"And does it still feel like the edge of the world?"

"It does," she admitted, scraping at her beer label with her thumbnail. "And one road in and out is still appealing."

"Do you ever miss home?"

Lane's head came up sharply. "This is home." The words landed harder than she'd meant them to. "And the answer is no. I don't miss Chicago. My mother was furious when I left."

"Chicago or Bruce?"

She gave a halfhearted shrug. "Both, I guess. She thought I should stay and fight for my marriage. After all, it's not every day a girl catches a surgeon."

"She liked your husband?"

"My *ex*-husband, thank you very much. And yes, she did. At least she liked being able to brag about her son-in-law, the doctor. Social status is very important to my mother. She liked the parties we threw, and the men that came to them. After my father died she started collecting husbands—and last names. Cynthia Campbell Daniels White. She finally hit the jackpot with number four. He's an attorney."

Michael grinned. "So is my father, although I'm not sure my mother would say she hit the jackpot."

"Your parents aren't happy?"

"Now who's being nosy?"

Lane leveled her gaze on him. "It's my turn."

Michael inclined his head, conceding the point. He swirled the last of his beer and drained it, then held up the bottle along with two fingers as Jessica passed by. "I suppose *unhappy* isn't really the right word. They're just, I don't know ... dutiful. My whole family is, actually. Except me."

Lane took a swallow of beer, recalling the fleeting shadow in his eyes when she had teased him about being a disappointment. Still, it was a strange thing to say to someone you barely knew. "You don't consider yourself dutiful?"

"If I was I'd be an attorney now, like my brother. And a junior partner in my father's firm. But I wanted to teach, or thought I did."

"How'd your father take that?"

"Let's just say the announcement went over like the proverbial lead balloon. When he realized I was serious, he said he'd make a few calls. He had connections in Cambridge, and if I was hell-bent on teaching, the least I could do was do it at a prestigious university. I asked him not to make the calls. I wanted to get it for myself, and the truth was I really didn't want to stay in Boston. So I applied at Middlebury and got the position. Two weeks after I unpacked my boxes, I found out my father had sent a hefty donation to the school. I guess he didn't think I was impressive enough without his money."

There was no missing the bitterness in Michael's voice, or the steady tic that suddenly pulsed along the side of his jaw. "I'm sorry," she said quietly.

"Don't be. It's water under the bridge. My father pretends he's not disappointed. I pretend I'm not angry. And my mother pretends the whole thing never happened. Problem solved."

Lane was more than a little relieved when the clams and second round of beer arrived. She barely knew what to say about her own family relationships, let alone someone else's.

They ate with gusto, sopping up garlicky broth with hunks of warm bread, sipping ice-cold beer as the sun went down and the deck tables steadily filled. In the corner, beneath a skeletal aluminum frame that was meant to be covered with canvas, and probably had been until Penny blew through, a trio of musicians began running a series of sound checks while a busboy scurried between tables, lighting the stainless-steel patio heaters.

A few minutes later the crowd broke into raucous applause as the band opened their first set with "Brown Eyed Girl." Several couples got up to dance between the tables. By the second verse everyone in the place was singing along. Lane said yes to another round. Not because she wanted another beer, but because she wasn't ready to leave. It felt good to be out, good to know that she still knew how to enjoy herself.

She barely heard her cell when it went off in the middle of "Hotel California." She scowled as she pulled the phone from her pocket and checked the number. Perfect timing, as always. Apparently their conversation had conjured her mother out of thin air.

"My mom," she hollered to Michael over the thumping music. "I'm just going to step down onto the beach a minute so I can hear. I won't be long."

It was quieter down on the sand, but not by much. Lane bit her lip as she tapped the screen to answer the call, instantly wishing she had just let it go to voice mail. She grimaced at the sound of her mother's voice.

"Lane—honey? What in the world is that racket?"

"It's music, Mother. What's up?"

"Robert and I just got back from New York, and I called your sister to tell her I was home. She said something about a storm?"

Lane took a deep breath and let it out very slowly. Of course she'd called Val the minute she got home. "It was a week ago, Mother, and I'm fine, thanks."

"Lane, you know I don't like you living in that old castle all by yourself. Anything could happen and there wouldn't be a soul to take care of you."

God, not again.

"Mom, it's not a castle; it's an inn. And I can take care of myself. I have been for years now. And if it makes you feel any better, I'm not alone."

There was a long silence on the line, and then, in a whole new tone, "Do you have . . . company?"

Lane bit her lower lip, already hating herself for what she was about to do. "Yes, I have company, and we're in the middle of dinner, so I should get off."

"I didn't hear you. Is it a man? Where did you meet him?"

Frustrated, Lane plugged her ear with one knuckle and raised her voice a notch. "Yes, it's a man, and he'll be at the inn through the off-season, so you can stop worrying about me." It wasn't a complete lie, and if it got her mother off her back—and off the phone—she wasn't going to feel guilty. In a few months she'd invent a messy breakup and the whole thing would be forgotten.

"Who is he, Laney? Is he from a good family? What does he do?"

"He's a professor," she yelled into the phone. "Mother, I've got to go. I can barely hear you."

"I just want you to be happy, honey. You let Bruce get away. Men like that don't grow on trees, you know."

"Well, let's all thank God for that, shall we?"

"I heard he's seeing someone," her mother said, ignoring her sarcasm. "And that it might be serious."

"I'll pray for her."

"I just thought you should know, in case . . ."

"In case what? In case I want to go crawling back?" Okay, time to get off before she said something she regretted. "Look, I've really got to go. I told you, we're out to dinner."

"Why don't you bring him home, Laney? Your sister can come for the weekend, bring the kids. It would be nice."

Nice? Lane shuddered at the thought. Yes, bring him home by all means, parade him in front of her mother and Val so they could grill him about his prospects, then vote thumbs-up or thumbs-down. Maybe they could go through his wallet while he was sleeping, check the balance in his checking account. Sweet Lord, what was she thinking? This entire conversation was a farce, and Michael Forrester wasn't a prospective anything.

"I'll have to get back to you," she said, fighting to keep her voice even. "He's working on a book, so it's probably not a good time for a trip. I'll, um—I'll call you next week."

"Can't you at least tell me his name and a little about him?"

There it was, the old familiar wheedling that was supposed to pass for concern but was really nothing more than good old-fashioned nosiness. It was all Lane needed to go teetering over the precipice of good sense and good manners.

"His name is Michael, Mother," she shouted in exasperation over a series of earsplitting drum licks. "And we're having quite a lot of sex!"

The words hung sharply in the chilly salt air—too sharply. Lane glanced up, realizing for the first time that the band had stopped playing, and that every head on the patio had just jerked in her direction—including Michael's.

Lane leaned against the passenger door of Michael's SUV. Her head came up at the sound of his voice. She wasn't sure which was worse: the fact that she had blurted such an outrageous lie in front of dozens of strangers or that she had lacked the courage to return to the table, choosing instead to slink out to the parking lot and sulk.

"Is . . . everything okay?" The question was a tentative one, as if he were addressing a child who'd just pitched an enormous tantrum.

"Everything's just peachy," she muttered, folding her arms tight to her chest. "Why do you ask?"

"No reason, really."

He wasn't being snarky, just comically low-key. That made it worse somehow.

Reaching around her, he opened the car door and waited for her to slide in. They rode home in silence. For Lane, it was torture. She'd been prepared for the outburst, the angry looks, the *what the hell was that about?* grilling, not this unsettling, unreadable quiet. She supposed he'd pack up his papers and books now and hightail it out of town. And who could blame him? She'd acted like some stalker nut job, and just that afternoon he'd been crystal clear about how he felt about nut jobs.

She should try to explain, she knew, but every time she attempted to string the words together in her head she realized how absurd they would sound. What could she possibly say that would explain lying to her mother about a nonexistent romance with one of her guests, particularly one who'd barely glanced in her direction? Anything she said would only make her look more pathetic.

She was out of the SUV almost before it rolled to a stop in the driveway, wanting only to get inside and up to her apartment. Michael trailed a few paces behind, pausing at the door to kick off his shoes and hang up his jacket. Instead of following her to the stairs, he hovered in the doorway of the library.

"I've got a little reading to finish before I go up," he said evenly. "Thanks for . . . an interesting evening."

Lane couldn't stand it anymore. "Aren't you going to ask me about what happened back there?"

He shrugged, then shook his head. "I don't have to. Your mother was making you crazy and you wanted her to back off. No biggie. The band finishing up when they did, though—that was a bit unfortunate."

He was letting her off the hook, and she was more grateful than she could say, but she had to say something. "I'm not . . . I mean, I don't usually—"

"Forget about it. Seriously. I'll see you in the morning." She had just turned to mount the stairs when he spoke again. "There is one thing I need to know."

Lane turned back, steeling herself for whatever was coming.

"You told your mother we were having quite a lot of sex. You never said whether or not the sex was good."

The remark was so unexpected that Lane actually managed a grin. For the first time since her phone had gone off in the middle of "Hotel California," she felt the knot of embarrassment in her gut loosen. "What can I say?" she said, with a wink and a shrug. "There are some things a girl doesn't even share with her mother."

Chapter 19

Michael

Michael stood quietly in the kitchen doorway watching Lane fix breakfast. She wore gray sweats with a hole in the thigh and a faded Northwestern T-shirt, the same outfit she'd been wearing the night he arrived. Only then, he'd been too exhausted to notice how beautiful she was. He wasn't too tired now. And he hadn't been too tired last night. In fact, he couldn't help wondering where the evening might have ended up if Lane's cell hadn't gone off when it did. Just as well, really. He wasn't in the market for anything serious, and unless he missed his guess, Lane wasn't the hit-and-run type.

As if sensing his presence, she turned. There were smudges beneath her eyes, he saw now, as if she hadn't slept well, or at all. She poured him a mug of coffee and mutely handed it to him, hiding behind her bangs in a way he now recognized as avoidance.

"Good morning," he ventured, stepping into her line of sight so that she had no choice but to meet his eyes. Her cheeks went a lovely shade of pink.

"Good morning," she answered thickly, before sidling back to the stove. "Breakfast is almost ready. The paper's there if you want it."

Michael dropped into the kitchen chair he'd come to think of as his and opened the Thursday edition of the *Islander Dispatch* to scan the headlines. The last remaining section of Highway 12 damaged by Penny was scheduled to reopen. Manteo residents were making a stink about historical preservation in the wake of storm rebuilding. Two new break-ins had been reported last week on Starry Point's sound side, leaving residents up in arms and demanding action from local authorities.

"Two new break-ins last week," he said, to make conversation. "Sounds like the natives are getting restless."

Lane set a plate in front of him—a mushroom omelet, melon slices, and a muffin of some sort—then settled across from him with her own.

"I don't blame them. It's been going on for months now, and the police don't seem to be taking it very seriously. At least not the ones I dealt with."

Michael peered over the corner of the paper. "You were broken into?"

Lane's face was thoughtful as she nibbled a slice of melon. "Not broken into, no. But there was definitely some suspicious activity. When I called them to check it out they acted like I was imagining things."

He pointed to the article. "According to this the incidents have all been on the other side of the island."

"They were quick to point that out. But does that mean whoever it is hasn't been here, too?"

"I didn't realize you were worried about this."

"Not worried, exactly. But it's annoying. You could tell they didn't want to be bothered. It doesn't exactly inspire confidence."

"No, I don't guess it would. If you want I'll check all the windows, make sure they're secure. It says here that that's how they're going in—through the window."

Lane smiled gratefully. "That would be great. I was going to ask

Sam, my handyman, to come take a look, but Dally says he's up to his ears since the storm. I'd be happy to pay you."

"It's a favor, Lane. I don't let people pay me for favors."

"Well, thank you." She took another forkful of omelet, then checked her watch. "Wow, I need to get a move on. If I don't get some writing done today I'm going to miss my deadline. And I do not miss deadlines."

Michael glanced up from his plate. "Never?"

"Never." The word came with a firm shake of the head. She stood with her plate and drained her mug. When Michael stood, too, she motioned for him to sit back down. "You're a paying guest. I'll let you check my windows, but that's where I draw the line. I never let guests wash their own dishes."

"Never?"

She grinned at him. "Never."

"You seem to have a lot of rules. Do you always follow them?"

Her eyes clouded briefly, as if the question had thrown her. "It makes life simpler, don't you think?"

"I think too many rules make life boring. I also think sometimes you just have to toss the rules and go a little crazy."

"Last night wasn't crazy enough for you?"

It was Michael's turn to grin. "I'll have you know I enjoyed last night very much. Do you know the crowd actually clapped for me when I got up to come after you?"

Lane hid her face with both hands. "Oh God . . . I'm so sorry."

"I thought we got past all that last night. No apology necessary. Now, seriously, what can I do to help? I'm looking for an excuse not to get to work."

Her cheeks were a deep shade of pink when she dropped her hands. "I guess you could wash up the breakfast plates while I brew the tea for the thermos."

Michael brought his plate to the sink and turned on the tap. "You're off on another mission of mercy, then, I take it?"

The look she shot him was part warning, part exasperation. "I thought we got past that, too. It's just tea, Michael."

"It's just tea *now*. Soon it'll be more. It always turns into more."

He saw her hands go still in the tea tin, eyes closed as if mentally counting to ten.

"Michael," she said eventually. "Is there something—? Did something happen to make you feel the way you do? I mean, you've never laid eyes on the poor woman, yet you have her pegged as some sort of monster. I guess what I'm saying is, you don't seem like a guy who'd be so, well, judgmental."

Michael shrugged his shoulders, feeling the old familiar tightening, the unseen puppeteer tugging at the strings of his past. "I told you once to chalk it up to experience."

"Yes, but you didn't say what kind of experience."

Picking up the sponge, he went to work on a plate. He wasn't going there. There wasn't any point. She'd made up her mind about this Mary woman. His story wasn't going to change that, and it really wasn't any of his business.

"What do you say we just leave it there, okay?"

Lane's gaze lingered briefly, plumbing his expression for clues. After a few moments she seemed to give up. "I will if you will," she said, and turned back to her tea.

With the kitchen chores complete, Lane stepped into her duck boots and zipped on her jacket. Michael waited a few minutes after hearing the back door close. It wouldn't do to be caught prowling about in Lane's rooms. The last thing he wanted was to have to explain himself. For starters, who the hell would believe him?

When he was convinced she wasn't coming back, he made his way upstairs to the third floor. No need to creep, he reminded himself. She was out on the dunes and would be gone at least an hour. Still, he tiptoed like a thief, pausing before the door to her apartment to fight down a prickle of conscience. It was probably locked anyway. Then again, anyone naive enough to let a homeless woman into her life probably wasn't cautious by nature. When the mercury glass knob turned in his fist he honestly didn't know whether to be relieved or disappointed.

The third-floor apartment was clean and spare, like its owner, but soft, too, decorated in hues that echoed the sea and sky. Sunlight spilled in through the open curtains, puddling brightly on the softly washed floorboards. He'd need to stay clear of the windows, he reminded himself, though he briefly stepped close enough to steal a glimpse of Lane's penny-bright head on the dunes below. The bag lady was beside her, hunched and lumpy in an oversize coat, her chopped white hair standing on end like some kind of mad halo.

The sight of her, a complete stranger, and yet familiar in some bone-deep way, made him take a step back, assailed by a sudden wave of vertigo, a clammy sense of his past unspooling, reaching for him. He wanted desperately to look away, to erase the woman's image from his mind, too terrible, too similar, a flesh-and-bone symbol of what and where he'd come from, but somehow he couldn't drag his eyes free.

Lane thought him hard. She was right about that, but he had his reasons. Good ones. He'd done his best to warn her, but she refused to listen. She didn't know what he did, that women like this new friend of hers could be unstable, even dangerous. And when they finally came apart—and they always did—they latched onto whatever, or whoever, was closest. But then, maybe he was glad she didn't know. No one should have to know the things he did.

More shaken than he liked to admit, he forced himself away from the window, stepping to the doorway of what he knew to be Lane's writing room—round with plenty of windows and a knockout view of the Atlantic. He had one just like it in his own room, though he never used it.

Like everything else about her, Lane's workspace was impeccably ordered, her desktop cleared of everything but a pencil cup, a stack of color-coded folders, and a handful of sticky notes, carefully arranged. Even the wastebasket was empty, he noted, thinking of his own over-flowing receptacle in the den. A place for everything, and everything in its place, right down to the artfully arranged jars of sea glass she had lined up along the windowsill.

His eyes strayed beyond the thick, wavy panes. It was hard to ig-nore the view, the stark white column of Starry Point Light standing against a blinding blue sky, gull wings flashing over silver-tipped waves, like something from a calendar—if only he could see it that way. Instead, he envisioned himself with his face pressed against that same glass, watching boys scramble along the beach and out onto the jetty, boys who wanted no part of new inmates, especially one with tassels on his shoes and initials on his sleeve. And then when the sun disappeared and all was dark beyond the glass, the light would come, scouring blue-white over cold plaster walls at precise six-second inter-vals, glancing, here and gone, off the blue-veined lids of boys sleeping row upon row.

He shoved the memory down as he backed out of the doorway and crossed to the narrow set of bookshelves in the sitting room— the real reason he'd come. In his day they'd been crammed with children's adventure books, well-thumbed copies of *Treasure Island* and *The Swiss Family Robinson*. Now they were artfully arranged with slick-jacketed contemporary fiction. Pushing several aside, he groped blindly until he located the tiny latch. He had to admit he was surprised as his fingers closed around it. He had known before climb-ing the stairs that there was a good chance the bookshelves had been torn out during renovation, that the hidden passage had been discov-ered and sealed. But here it was, just as it was the day he left.

He felt the gratifying snick of metal against metal when the latch finally gave, then held his breath as he leaned on the heavy wood panel until it slowly creaked inward to reveal a narrow passage not much wider than his shoulders. A whiff of damp wafted up out of the dark, along with a barrage of memories. Dragging a flashlight from his back pocket, he ducked into the opening. The bare tread squealed beneath his weight, with just enough give to make him wonder if he should abandon the expedition altogether.

Thirty years ago these stairs had held his weight, no problem. But he wasn't a boy anymore, and while he was no expert, he suspected termites could do a lot of damage in thirty years. For a moment he imagined Lane returning from the dunes to find the passage door open and him lying at the bottom, neck twisted at an unnatural angle. He closed his eyes, chasing away the image, then forced his feet to move, following the flashlight beam down the century-old staircase.

The air in the passage was wet and cold, thick with mildew and God only knew what else. Michael felt his way with the flats of his hands, hugging the wall of cool, crumbling stone as he crabbed his way down one painstaking step at a time. To this day he had no idea why the passage existed, though there had been plenty of theories. The most salacious was that the stairs had been built so the good sisters could slip out now and then, to keep clandestine assignations with the priests from St. Mark's, and then, nine months later, to smuggle out the babies that resulted from those assignations.

Another theory, equally ridiculous, was that when the weather was warm the sisters used the passage to slip down to the beach to cavort and skinny-dip by the light of the moon. And of course there was his personal favorite—and one not completely out of the realm of possibility—the stairs were used to dispose of the bodies of boys who crossed Sister Mary Constantine one too many times.

His legs were good and wobbly by the time he reached the bottom and located the slender doorway that had once opened up onto the library, sealed now with a frame of rusty bolts and a padlock that clearly hadn't been opened in years. The door was the reason he'd asked to use the library in the first place. Unfortunately, he'd found the downstairs passage paneled over, which left sneaking into Lane's apartment his only option.

Kneeling on one knee at the bottom of the stairs, he groped about until he found what he was looking for, a small recess beneath the last step—the ideal place for a boy to hide cherished possessions from prying eyes. For just a moment he felt a twinge of the old dread, the fear that at any moment Sister Mary Constantine would throw open the door to the passage and catch him sneaking around where he didn't belong. But he wasn't that boy anymore, and in all likelihood, Sister Mary Constantine had met her maker years ago.

Ignoring the knot of anticipation in his gut, he cut through the maze of sticky cobwebs with his flashlight, then aimed the beam into the narrow space.

Nothing.

He wasn't sure why he was surprised, really. There was no telling over the course of thirty years how many of the Cloister occupants might have discovered the hidden passage, any one of whom could have stumbled onto his carefully concealed treasure and tossed it like so much old junk.

It wasn't junk, though. In fact, the book had been his lifeline, the last vestige of the life that had been torn away from him, and a refuge from the older boys who'd beaten him because they didn't like his clothes and his last name. They had taunted him brutally about the book, threatening to wait until he was asleep and then burn it. And they would have, too, if he hadn't come across the passage one day and secreted it beneath the stairs for safekeeping. After that, no one ever saw him with the book, but every day for nearly two years he would creep down those plunging stairs with his pocket flashlight and turn the pages, pretending that someday everything would be normal again. It wasn't, though. And now the book was gone.

There hadn't been time to go after it when they came for him, no time for good-byes or explanations, either. His things had been quietly packed while he was at breakfast, and before he knew what was happening he'd been belted into the back of his uncle R.B.'s big black car, heading for Boston. For years he'd wondered if the book was still there, collecting dust while mice gnawed at the pages and the colors slowly faded. And then, for a time, he'd forgotten about it—until the dreams started and refused to leave him alone.

For nearly a year now, virtually every night, he had come awake with a start, his nostrils filled with the dank, musty air of the passage, his fingers still registering the feel of the leather cover, the smooth, heavy pages, as if he'd actually retrieved the book and spread it open on his knees, instead of only dreaming it. The whole thing seemed ridiculous now, a silly, childish obsession, but the truth was he felt the loss more keenly than he liked.

At least he knew now, and it wasn't really such a monumental deal. It was a book—a silly book full of silly pictures, a pointless boyish memory. But deep down it *was* a monumental deal, and he knew it. Not only for the boy he'd been, but for the man he was now, a man who bore the scars of another life, and the guilt that came with failing those you loved. He wasn't sure how finding the book would have helped with that; he only knew he'd hoped it would. Instead, the memories seemed to sting more than ever. Training the flashlight on the stairs, he started back up, wishing to God he'd never come back to Starry Point.

Chapter 20

Lane

Lane kicked off her shoes, wriggling her heels into the soft, cool sand of the dune, savoring what would likely be her last chance of the season to go barefoot. The breeze off the water was warm and briny, more like April than November, as she sat beside Mary, sipping her tea and nibbling the pumpkin bread she'd baked earlier that morning.

Perhaps it was only wishful thinking, but she couldn't help feeling as if some sort of barrier had fallen, that when she had appeared with her thermos, Mary had been almost happy to see her. And yet she had seen the brief flash of wariness as the precious purple bag was snatched up and furtively stashed beneath Mary's jacket. Trust, it seemed, was still an issue, and might always be, no matter how many thermoses of tea they shared. The realization made Lane sad. It must be a terrible thing to move through the world believing everyone meant you harm.

"Mary," she said gently, breaking the silence. "I want you to know that I would never take your bag. You don't have to hide it."

Mary lifted her nose with a delicate sniff. "Of course you wouldn't, and I wasn't hiding it. I just like to know it's nearby. I don't dare lose it, you see."

Lane knew she should let it drop but couldn't help herself. "Why? What's in it?"

Mary opened her mouth, then seemed to change her mind. Instead, she dragged the bag back into view, plucking a moment at its frayed strings before reaching in and pulling out a fistful of something.

Lane peered at the frosty bits of blue and green held out for inspection. "Sea glass?"

Mary didn't answer at first, engrossed in picking through the smooth pastel shards with her index finger. "There's been quite a lot lately. But then, the pickings are always better after a storm." She glanced up then, her gaze suddenly clouded and distant. "All sorts of things have been known to wash up after a storm."

"I've heard that, yes," Lane responded awkwardly, not knowing what else to say. She hated that Mary always seemed to keep her off-balance, that she never knew quite how to take the things she said, or at times, if they were even talking about the same thing.

Unscrewing the thermos, she poured the last of the tea into their cups while Mary stashed her sea glass. "You know," she said finally, hoping to bring Mary back from wherever it was she had strayed. "I collect sea glass, too. I keep it in jars on the windowsills of my writing room." She turned, pointing to the tower windows. "Right up there. See? That's where I write."

Mary's gaze cleared a bit. "You write stories?"

"Well, sort of. I write articles for magazines. I just finished one about soap making. Now I'm working on one about beer."

Mary blew on her already tepid tea, then sipped. "I used to make up stories," she said in a voice laced with sadness. "Beautiful stories, for my princes. But they're gone now. I lost them."

Once again, Lane found herself completely in the dark. "Your . . . princes?"

"Yes, my girl," she said, her voice suddenly soft. "Two darling princes with smoky eyes and dark wavy hair. They loved me once, a long time ago. I was their queen, you see. But they're gone now. All gone."

Sons. She must have had sons once. "Gone where, Mary? I don't understand."

"No, you wouldn't understand. No one would. I was pretty once. Hard to imagine it now, but I was. Once upon a time I was fresh and young, and men fell at my feet. I danced at balls and wore gowns and jewels, and they all courted me."

Okay, maybe not sons. Lovers perhaps? "Are we still talking about the princes?"

"No, the men," she answered distantly. Her eyes had taken on that flat dark look again, like the sea when the clouds suddenly eclipse the sun. "I could have had any of them back then."

Lane's gaze slid to the woman seated beside her in tattered, mismatched layers. It was hard to imagine her wearing jewels, dancing at parties. And yet her delicate hands and lilting voice, her tinkling silvery laugh, all spoke of another woman, another life. Could any of it be true, or were these merely the ramblings of a wistful old woman wanting to remake the past? It took every ounce of fortitude Lane had not to ask that very question, to silently sip her cold tea and leave Mary to weave her story in her own way, and in her own time. After a moment she was rewarded.

"They told me they loved me—all of them," she said with a smile that was both coy and bitter. "I knew better than to believe them, though. Except for *him*, with his dark hair and his smooth words. *Him*, I wanted to believe. And so when he kissed me and whispered in my ear, I pretended he meant it. And I gave him what he wanted. Any fool could have guessed what would happen next." She paused to drag in a shuddering breath, then sighed out the rest. "Any fool but me."

Lane bit her lip and looked away. Was that it, then? A child conceived out of wedlock? A decision over the child's fate, lamented after all these years? It was hardly a new story, although in Mary's day it probably hadn't occurred as often or as openly as it did today. Still, it seemed a stretch to imagine such a thing pushing a woman over the edge—unless she'd been poised there to begin with.

"I can still see his face when I told him about the baby," Mary went on. "Like he'd just heard the door to a jail cell slamming shut. He didn't want it—or me. But my family made a stink. In those days a boy married a girl when that kind of thing happened. And deep down, I was just a little bit glad. Foolish girl—I thought I could make him love me."

"But you couldn't," Lane said softly, knowingly. She'd made the same mistake.

Mary shook her cropped head grimly. "He meant to be an important man, you see. And he needed me to be an important man's wife. Only I wasn't. I was a child, silly enough to believe in once upon a time—in fairy tales and happily ever after. I didn't know how to be what he wanted me to be, and I didn't want to learn. I thought he should love me for me."

Lane stared down at her hands, at the faint impression in her ring finger, still visible though the divorce had been final for almost five years. The story was all too familiar. "He should have," she said quietly. "He should have loved you for you."

"Ah, but he couldn't, and I should have known it. We were different creatures, he and I, always at odds. He wanted money, and to be important. I wanted only my castle and keep, my king and my princes. But now I've lost it all—my castle in ashes, my princes lost forever."

"Your husband—what happened to him?"

"Why, a woman happened, of course. He left like a coward, slipped through my fingers and disappeared. That's when I let go, when there was nothing left to hold on to. I let them do what they wanted after that. I became what the White Coats call ... tractable. That means you eat what they put in front of you, swallow whatever pill they put in your palm, lie still while they peer inside your head, and pretend you don't mind them raking through all the things that broke your heart."

Lane closed her eyes, repressing a shudder as a series of gruesome images flitted through her head—white coats and leather restraints, padded walls and straitjackets. Did they still use straitjackets? She started when she heard Mary's laugh, a high, thin peal that sent an ice-cold prickle needling down her spine.

"Oh, I've seen that look before," Mary said, with something like glee. "You're thinking I really am crazy. Well, my girl, I've never pretended I wasn't." She reached for Lane's hand then and patted it, her voice suddenly somber. "Come, now, don't look so startled. You've known it all along, haven't you? Besides, you have a right to know the truth."

"The truth?"

"I am what they say I am. Everything, and a little bit more besides. Dirty Mary, the Starry Point Hag—and those are the nice things. Now, now, don't look like that. I've been called worse, and probably deserved it, too." Fumbling beneath her jacket, she produced the purple bag again, this time spilling a cache of pill bottles into her lap. "There, now," she said, pointing. "There's what I can't afford to lose. My pills—blue ones, yellow ones, white ones, and every day I wonder if this is the day they'll stop working. I won't go back. I'd rather die first. That's why I take them, you see, so they'll let me walk around free."

"But why would you have to—"

"I killed a boy once."

Lane felt the blood drain from her face.

"The doctors said it wasn't my fault—the judge, too. But it was. Of course it was. A boy died, so it has to be someone's fault. Little boys don't just die."

"No," Lane answered numbly. "They don't."

"Still, they put me away for a long time—for safekeeping, they said—so I wouldn't try to hurt myself again. Dangerous, they said." She scrubbed absently at her wrists, then shrugged. "Maybe I was. Yes, of course I was."

Lane went still as Mary's words sank deep. She had killed a boy. When? How? The questions trembled on her lips, but the truth was, she didn't think she wanted to know any more. How could she speak so nonchalantly about the death of a child, as if she'd dinged someone's car in the parking lot at the Village Mart? Dangerous—the word rattled around like a loose pebble in her head. What if Michael was right?

Once again, Mary seemed to read her thoughts. "You needn't worry, my girl. You're quite safe. I made a mistake, lots of them, in fact, but I'm not a monster. At least not the kind you're thinking of. I didn't have to knot up my bedsheets and shinny out a window to get free. They let me walk right out the front door."

"How long ago?" Lane asked when she could finally trust her voice.

"Since they let me out?"

"No. Since the boy."

Lane was surprised when Mary stiffened, then crushed the empty paper cup she'd been holding in her fist. Apparently the woman had no problem bringing up her past, but she didn't like being questioned about it.

"A lifetime," was the answer she finally gave. "I'm not that woman anymore. She died that night, too. And there was no one to even miss her." The color was gone from her face and she was trembling, her eyes shimmering with unshed tears.

Lane laid a hand on her arm. "Mary, is there someplace— Can I take you home, wherever home is?"

Mary jerked her head emphatically. "I have my bike," she said stiffly, and began stuffing the pill bottles back into her bag. She avoided Lane's gaze as she stood and handed back the crumpled paper cup. "I'm going now. I'm going to be late. I told you, they don't like it when we're late."

And with that she was off, scrambling up the dune with her head down as she headed for the street, leaving Lane to wonder for the second time that morning if perhaps she should have heeded Michael's advice.

Chapter 21

Mary

They say I'm not mad, at least not in the worst way one can be mad, but surely they've gotten it wrong. Only a fit of madness could explain what I've just done. Without a moment's thought, I have dragged the worst of my sins out into the light, thrown back the curtain on the woman I have struggled long and hard to bury. And for what? For penance? Sweet bleeding Jesus, as if living through it all has not been penance enough.

Confession, they say, is good for the soul, but that's just a load of manure shoveled by those who want to know your secrets. I should know. I've been confessing for years. Not to the priests or the nuns, or even to God. I gave up blathering to them long ago, when I finally realized no one was listening. No, I don't believe in God. It's best not to for people like me. It wouldn't do, you see, to lay what I am at the feet of a benevolent God. Better, I think, to count myself, and those like me, as unfortunate accidents of nature, the splicing of cells gone terribly awry.

Instead, I've done my confessing to the White Coats, who all claim they will heal me, if I will only tell them again what happened that terrible night. And so I tell them. And then I tell them again, though all this confessing has done nothing whatever for my soul. It is only the sea that understands, the sea that shares my secret, the sea that truly knows what set all the horrors in motion.

And now someone else knows. Or at least knows part of it.

If only I had stopped with the pills. Plenty of people take pills. Plenty of perfectly sane, perfectly safe people take pills. But then I had to bring the boy into it. Poor, dear thing; there was no missing the revulsion on her pretty face in that instant when I blurted out the truth. Oh, she hid it well enough, because it's in her to be kind, but there's no sense in trying to fool myself. I've been on the receiving end of that look too many times not to recognize it when it's staring me in the face—like I'm something to be scraped off a shoe.

She was polite to the end, of course, offering to take me home, but that will be the end of it. The morning tea will stop, and she'll begin taking the long way round the dunes when she sets out on her morning walks. Who can blame her, really? No one wants to take tea with a crazy woman, and certainly not one with the blood of a young boy on her hands.

Chapter 22

Lane

Lane struggled to focus on the final edits for the article that was due tomorrow, but in her mind she was out on the dunes with Mary. She'd had hours to digest the startling declaration and she still couldn't put a finger on exactly what it was she thought or felt.

"I killed a boy once."

She'd said it just like that, without preamble or qualification—and very nearly without remorse. But Lane sensed there was much more to the story. There had to be. A car accident, perhaps, or an unwanted pregnancy quietly disposed of. But then why not say so? What kind of woman made such a confession without at least trying to explain it—unless it was true?

Michael's warnings echoed again in her head. Without ever laying eyes on the woman, he had pegged her as possibly unhinged, even dangerous, and she had flatly dismissed him. Now it was beginning to look as though he'd been right. Mary had been institutionalized, labeled dangerous by her own admission. But dangerous to whom? She claimed it was to keep her from hurting herself. Did that mean she had tried, or had they only been afraid she might? She also claimed she hadn't been held responsible for the boy's death. Was that because she was truly innocent, or because she'd been found not guilty by reason of insanity?

Insanity.

The word made Lane shudder. She could only imagine what it must have been like for Mary, kept for years in a small room with a heavy door, a tiny square of reinforced glass too high up to see out, rendered carefully docile with a regime of pills, enduring visits from a revolving door of anonymous doctors—*the White Coats*. It was a horrible image, like something out of the movies, and yet she couldn't seem to shake it.

But something about Mary's story didn't feel right, like a book with some of the pages missing. It was clear that life had left the poor woman with her share of scars, the kind that ran deep and never quite healed, but it hadn't broken her. Even now, after all the losses and horrors she'd clearly suffered, there was a depth to her, and a wisdom, a canny understanding of how the world really worked, that contrasted sharply with Lane's idea of insanity.

But what of the princes? The castles? The jewels and fancy balls? Was she supposed to believe all of that as well? It all seemed rather unlikely, the product of a colorful and clouded imagination. And yet something in those cool blue-green eyes, so distant and yearning, made Lane almost believe there was some small scrap of truth in the tale.

Lane stood, prowling the small space of her writing room. She'd be lying if she said she wasn't hungry to know the rest. But was that really wise? Was there room in her life for this troubled woman? She honestly wasn't sure. Sooner or later she was going to have to make a decision—and probably sooner. It wasn't going to be easy. As far as she knew, Mary was alone in the world, without friends or family, and while they hadn't known each other long enough to grow truly close, it was hard to deny that some sort of bond had formed, even if that bond seemed only to be based on mutual pity.

Perhaps she should talk to Michael, since he prided himself on being something of an expert. But no, only this morning they had agreed to avoid Mary as a topic of conversation. Besides, she already knew what he'd say, and she wasn't in the mood for an *I told you so*, even if it was starting to look as though she deserved one.

Dropping back into her chair, she opened the center drawer of her writing desk and eased out the old green sketchbook, laying it open on her lap. Slowly, carefully, she thumbed through the heavy pages, hoping to lose herself in the intricate details of the sketches, but it was no good.

Restless, she closed the book and slid it back into the desk. It was too early for dinner, but that didn't mean she couldn't suggest to Michael that they go back to the Blue Water. They could sit on the deck and drink a few beers, and she could pretend the conversation with Mary never happened. Unfortunately, after last night's rather embarrassing fiasco, it would be some time before she'd consider showing her face there again, if ever.

The dull buzz of her cell phone vibrating on the desk spared her having to relive that night. She frowned when she saw her sister's number come up. Val called on Christmas and her birthday, and it was neither of those. Something must be wrong.

"Val, what's the matter?" she answered without preamble.

"Why does something have to be the matter? Can't I just call my favorite sister every now and then to say hello?"

Lane felt the first prickle of suspicion. "You can, but you never do. And I'm your only sister, Valerie."

"That's pretty cold. And the phone lines run both ways, you know."

Suspicion quickly morphed into guilt. She had a point. "How are the kids?"

"They're fine. Carla is taking piano, and Cameron is driving us crazy asking for a dirt bike. Daniel thinks he's old enough, but it's me who'll have to patch him up when he falls off the thing. And he will fall off."

"Well, you know what they say. Boys will be boys."

"I guess." Val laughed, a tight, stilted chuckle followed by an awkward pause. "So..."

"So..." Lane held her breath, waiting for whatever was coming.

"Mom said she talked to you the other night."

Michael. She should have guessed.

"She said something about a guy staying with you for the winter. Michael, I think she said his name was."

"And she conned you into calling and putting on the sweet sister act."

There was the scrape of a lighter, the huff of smoke being exhaled. "All right, yes, she did. But what's wrong with that? Honestly, Lane, by now I think you'd know it's just easier to let her have her way."

"Her way?" Lane echoed, stunned. "With *my* life?"

"Okay, not her way, then, but you know what I mean. Sometimes you have to compromise and just make her happy."

"Like you did, Val?"

Lane regretted the words the instant they were out of her mouth, but there was no way to take them back. Silence stretched over the line, frustration mingled with apology. They'd had this argument too many times. And they would almost certainly have it again.

"We're different, Laney," Val said finally. "We always have been. I didn't have to compromise. I wanted the same things she wanted for me. But you fought her every step of the way, and you're still doing it. She only gets how she gets because she loves you."

Lane closed her eyes and counted to ten before answering. "Look, I'm glad you're happy and that your life has turned out so perfectly, and I don't mean that to sound nasty. But the last time I compromised to make Mother happy, I wound up miserable. I'm not doing that again, ever."

"Okay, okay, I get it. I'm sorry I pissed you off. It's not why I called. Can I at least tell her that you and this Michael person are happy? She might stop bugging both of us if she thinks you're serious about someone."

"Sure, Val. Tell her whatever you want. In fact, tell her we're on our way to pick out china. I've got to go."

Lane didn't feel a bit guilty as she ended the call. Let her mother think what she wanted. It served her right for meddling. And Val should know better than to get involved in their mother's schemes.

Chapter 23

Lane took the dripping skillet Michael handed her and wiped it dry. Despite her protests, he had insisted on helping with the dishes after dinner. He claimed he wasn't in the mood to go back to work, but she suspected it was more than that. He'd been quiet during dinner, chewing mechanically until his plate was empty, with barely a word between bites.

A good hostess would have tried to lighten the mood with pleasant conversation, but something told her he'd rather be left to his thoughts. And to be honest, she didn't feel like being entertaining. She couldn't get Mary out of her head, and she was still stewing over her conversation with her sister.

"I feel awful about you doing your own dishes," she told him, reaching for the sponge in his hand. "We're about through here. I can finish up."

Michael jerked the sponge out of her reach and proceeded to wipe down the counter. "You act like this is a first for me. I'll have you know I'm a world-class pot scrubber."

Lane eyed him dubiously. "I have a hard time imagining you up to your elbows in soapsuds."

"Well, you don't have to imagine it, do you? You've just seen it for yourself."

Lane dried her hands, then handed him the towel. "That's true. In fact, I've seen it twice now, but that isn't what I meant."

"Then may I inquire what you *did* mean?"

"Only that you strike me as coming from the kind of family that always had a maid."

Michael tossed the towel at her with something like a smirk. "I should take that as an insult, but I can't. We did have a maid, also a cook and a gardener. But that doesn't mean I haven't scrubbed my share of pots."

Lane tried to stifle a grin but failed. "And where was that? Yachting camp?"

Michael's eyes went flinty. "Something like that, yeah."

Lane bit her lip, feeling as if she should apologize, though she had no idea what for. She watched mutely as he returned to his wiping, his mouth drawn thin and tight. It reminded her of yesterday, when she'd teased him about being a disappointment to his parents. Despite the gardener and the maid, she was beginning to suspect that growing up a Forrester hadn't been all sunshine and lollipops. "I'm sorry. I didn't mean to—"

"Forget it. It's water under the bridge."

Turning the sponge on the stovetop, he set to work with a vengeance. Lane watched him from the corner of her eye as she spread her towel over the edge of the sink to dry. "I was thinking of taking a walk down to the lighthouse," she announced, when the silence finally grew awkward. "You're welcome to come along."

He wouldn't, of course. In the two and a half weeks he'd been here, he had yet to venture past the back gate, let alone out onto the beach. Just as well. She needed to clear her head, to walk off some of her tension, and in Michael's current mood he wasn't likely to be much help in that department.

"Can I have a minute to change shoes?"

Lane blinked at him a moment, then dropped her gaze to cover her surprise. "I thought you didn't like the beach."

Michael's mouth twitched at the corners. "Ah, you were just being polite, weren't you? And secretly hoping I'd say no."

"Don't be silly," she assured him, flustered that he'd seen through her so easily. "Just let me grab a jacket and I'll meet you on the deck."

She was still kicking herself for inviting him along when she stepped outside. He was leaning against the railing, wearing jeans now, instead of khakis, his loafers swapped out for a pair of worn Top-Siders. He appeared not to notice her at first, his eyes raised to the top of the weathered stone turret, to the windows of her writing room. She cleared her throat softly.

"You've done an amazing job with the place," he said, stuffing his hands deep into his pockets. "You've made it feel . . . welcoming."

Lane smiled graciously, wondering if she had imagined the almost proprietary tone of voice. "Thanks. You should have seen it when I bought it. It looked like—"

"A dungeon?"

Lane's gaze narrowed. There it was again, that vague tone of familiarity, mingled with something like bitterness. "I was going to say fortress, but I suppose dungeon works, too. Everything was so dark and depressing. And yet the minute I laid eyes on her, I knew what she could be. It took just about every cent I had, but I don't regret a single penny."

Michael looked away, out toward the horizon. "It takes a special person to change the soul of a place," he said, his eyes still on the sea.

Something about the words—or maybe it was the way he'd said them—made Lane go still. "The soul of a place?"

A smile briefly touched his lips, fleeting and almost wistful. "It sounds crazy, I know, but I believe buildings, old ones especially, possess a kind of soul, collected memories that live on in the plaster and the floorboards. All the good and bad that's ever happened, it stays—like people."

"You think buildings are like people?"

"I do. And so do you. Just now, when you were talking about the inn, you called it a her."

"I was just—"

"You were referring to its personality. A building's personality hinges on its experiences. Again, just like people."

Lane found the thought more than a little disturbing, particularly when she thought of the Rourke House. Suddenly, she understood what Michael meant the day after the storm when he told her there were all kinds of ghosts.

"Like the house across the street," she said quietly. "Where the little boy died."

Michael shoved his hands in his pockets and looked away, his shoulders suddenly bunched up tight. "Yes," he said. "Like the house across the street where the little boy died."

Without thinking, Lane laid a hand on his shoulder. "Michael?"

"I'm fine," he said, and ducked away from her touch.

"Are you? You look like you're in pain."

"It's nothing. An old injury that acts up sometimes." Turning away, he headed for the gate. "If we're going to walk we'd better do it."

Lane followed him through the gate and out onto the narrow boardwalk, regretting her invitation more than ever. There was more to this mercurial man than met the eye, and although he might be gorgeous, she wasn't at all sure she wanted to know what it was.

The breeze was chilly as they broke from the shelter of the dunes, the sun nearly gone, leaving in its wake a swatch of pink and silver sky. Dusk had always been her favorite time of day, but moving to Starry Point had given her an entirely new list of reasons to appreciate it. She loved the way the sea went quiet and glassy at the end of the day, the pearly gold quality of the light as it backlit the clouds and set them on fire. Tonight, though, she was wound too tight to enjoy any of those things. Out of habit, she ran her eyes over the dunes, looking for Mary, but there was no sign of her.

She set out for the lighthouse at a brisk pace. Michael matched her stride for stride, apparently not interested in further conversation. She was grateful for that at least. He'd been right about her not wanting him along. It wasn't personal. She just needed a little time to empty her head, to rid her thoughts of Mary and the dead boy, to focus on nothing more than the blood pulsing through her limbs. Instead, she had company, and sullen company at that. When they finally reached the jetty she checked her watch. They'd made good time.

She was halfway out onto the rocks when she realized Michael wasn't behind her. "Aren't you coming?" she called over the thrum of wind and waves. "Standing on the end of the jetty is the best part. Or are you afraid you'll get splashed?"

Michael eyed the narrow finger of rock but made no move to follow. "I'm not afraid of getting splashed."

"Then what? Don't you swim?"

"I'm a grown man. Of course I swim."

Despite his words, Lane couldn't help noticing his body language—legs braced, arms locked stiffly at his sides. Seconds ticked by, but he gave no sign of changing his mind. Shrugging, she turned away. If he didn't want to come, that was his choice. She wasn't going to hold his hand.

Seagulls wheeled overhead as she picked her way over the jutting boulders, their numbers swelling exponentially by the time she reached the jetty's end. "Sorry, boys," she muttered to the noisy gray and white horde. "You'll have to wait till morning."

"Wait for what?"

Lane swung around, startled. Between the wind and waves, and the greedy cries of the gulls, she hadn't heard Michael approach. "I was talking to the birds," she said. "I bring bread every morning. I guess they're spoiled."

Michael tipped his head back a moment, following the gulls as they circled and dove in the rapidly dying light. When he brought his attention back to Lane he was almost smiling. "Bread for the birds. Scones for the bag lady. You're quite the soft touch, Ms. Kramer."

She eyed him sharply, but his face was unreadable. "I thought we agreed we wouldn't talk about Mary."

"I'm not talking about Mary, at least not directly. And I honestly didn't mean for that to sound snide. What I was trying to say is that while I don't necessarily approve of your choice in friends, I do admire your motives. You're kind, and I like that about you. I wanted to tell you that. Mostly so you'd stop looking at me like I'm some kind of heartless monster."

Lane's mouth worked silently before she realized she had no idea what to say, or even which of his remarks to respond to. In the end she let both the compliment and apology pass, choosing instead to drop down onto the rocks and tip her face to the breeze. She didn't want to reopen their discussion of Mary. Not because she was convinced Michael was wrong about her, but because she was beginning to fear he might be right.

"It's getting dark," Michael said. "We should probably get back."

"We've got time yet." She patted the rock beside hers. "Sit with me awhile and wait."

Michael made no move to sit. "Exactly what is it we'd be waiting for?"

Lane shrugged, her eyes still locked on the horizon. "I don't know. The truth, maybe. A friend told me it was out there somewhere." But as she fastened her gaze on the fading crease between sea and sky, she wondered if she would ever really know the truth about Mary—or if she even wanted to. Some truths were just too terrible to be spoken aloud.

Suddenly, she was aware of the chill, of the damp seeping into her bones. Scrambling back up onto her feet, she stuffed her fists into her pockets and turned to go.

Even in the fading light, Michael looked confused. "Where are you going?"

"You're right. We should get back."

"What about the truth?"

"I changed my mind," she mumbled as she angled past him, keenly aware of his eyes as she made her way back down the jetty.

Chapter 24

Lane raised a hand to shield her eyes as she stepped out onto the deck and into the morning sun. She hadn't slept particularly well, churning through a series of dreams that left her more exhausted than when she'd fallen into bed. The only upside was that she'd opened her eyes knowing exactly what she needed to do about Mary. She might not like what she heard; in fact, she was almost sure she wouldn't, but she couldn't just walk away without giving the woman a chance to tell the rest of her story.

She was huddled in her usual spot, wrapped in her lumpy coat and orange scarf, her arms clasped tight about her knees. A small scrap of purple showed from beneath her coat, the ever-present purple bag kept close for safekeeping. Despite her second thoughts, Lane tucked the thermos of tea beneath her arm and climbed the dune.

"You came," Mary said without looking up. "I didn't think you would."

Lane folded herself down onto the chilly sand and drew her knees up to her chest. "I almost didn't," she answered bluntly. "But I need to know what happened to you, what made you . . . how you are."

"What made me crazy, you mean."

"No," Lane shot back more sharply than she'd intended. "That is *not* what I mean. You keep saying that, but I don't believe it's true."

Mary sat in stony silence, her eyes trained carefully out to sea, clearly wrestling with memories she wasn't ready to share. But it was for precisely those memories that Lane had come.

"You keep saying you're crazy. Is it true, Mary? Are you crazy?"

Mary lifted one shoulder in a halfhearted shrug. "There's all kinds of crazy."

Lane felt her patience beginning to thin. She'd come to hear the truth, not play word games. "Fine, have it your way. Just tell me. Should I be afraid of you? Are you dangerous?"

Mary turned her head slowly, her stare queerly vacant. She blinked a few times, then held out her hands, turning them palm up. The long, slender fingers could have belonged to a piano player or a sculptor, but a killer? It didn't seem possible.

Lane reached for them, folding them into her own. "You don't have to be afraid, Mary. Not of me. I just want to know what happened. After yesterday . . . after what you said . . . can you understand why I need to know?"

Mary nodded almost imperceptibly as she stared at their clasped hands. When she finally lifted her eyes to Lane's they shimmered with unshed tears. "You don't have to be afraid of me, my girl. Truly, you don't."

Lane managed a tremulous smile. "No, I didn't think so."

Mary pulled her hands free and wiped both her eyes on her sleeve. "Pour us some tea, then, if you like, while I think where to start."

Lane did as she was told, pouring out the tea and handing her a cup. But Mary seemed in no hurry to begin. She blew on her tea, ventured a cautious sip, then blew some more. Her hands trembled around her cup, though whether this had to do with the cold breeze blowing in off the water or with what she was about to say, Lane couldn't be sure.

"You've heard of Hope House," she said finally, a statement rather than a question.

"It's a halfway house on the south side of the island."

"That's right. I live there."

Lane fought to keep her tone even. "You had a drug problem?"

"No drugs," Mary said, shaking her cropped white head emphatically. "At least not the kind you mean. There are people like me there, too. People who have been . . . through things. Oh, there were pills, too, but they were the legal kind. Pills to wake me up. Pills to put me to sleep. Pills to make me happy. Pills to keep me calm. Back then, they didn't know what they do now, that mixing all those drugs can make rather a mess of a person. I knew, of course, but no one was listening to me by then. Especially not my husband."

"Oh, Mary . . ."

"He needed me to behave, you see, to stop . . . embarrassing him. He had a right to that, I suppose. But they were killing me, all those doctors and their pills. Little by little I felt myself unraveling, disappearing. Eventually I stopped caring about anything."

"If they weren't making you better, why keep taking them?"

Something close to a sneer tugged at the corners of Mary's mouth. "Better means different things to different people, my girl. To the White Coats and the families, it means quiet and well behaved. It's got nothing to do with the patient, and whether we care if we take another breath or not. It's about not being a nuisance. I took the pills because my husband threatened to take my children and put me away. I couldn't lose my children. They were all I had left, you see. And so I took the pills—until I couldn't bear it anymore."

Lane fought down a shiver. "You tried to hurt yourself."

"I wanted the pain to stop. Not for me, but for my boys. For my princes."

"The princes," Lane said. "They were your sons?"

Mary pressed a fist to the center of her chest, her throat bobbing with unshed tears. "They were my world. The oldest called me *my lady*, as if I were his queen. It was our little game. Poor lamb—he didn't deserve a mother like me, ranting one minute, in a stupor the next, embarrassing him in front of his friends. I wanted to spare him— spare them both—that shame."

Holding out an arm, she dragged back her coat sleeve. The scars were livid and blade-fine against her flesh, a heartbreaking map of despair. "I couldn't remember which way you're supposed to do it— up and down or straight across—so I did both. They found me before I could finish the job. Death cheated me, but it was my boys who suffered for it. They're gone and I'm here—a much more fitting penance than hell, I can promise you. I know about hell, you see, because I've been there. And I won't ever go back. Not ever."

Something steely had crept into Mary's voice, something that made Lane pull back a little. She stole another glance at the web of scars, and thought about the desolation it must have taken to drive a person—a mother—to do such a thing. Who had found her? *Please, God, not one of her sons.* She couldn't bring herself to ask. Instead, she reached for Mary's hand.

"I'm so sorry that you've been through so much. And that you had to go through it all alone. Your husband doesn't sound like a very kind man."

"He wasn't *unkind*," Mary answered with a queer sort of detachment. "Only weary of me. I think it might have been in him to be kind, somewhere deep down, but he never quite got the hang of it." She smiled sadly. "Things got bad when the babies came, especially the second. It all came apart after that."

Lane bit her lip, almost afraid to ask. "Came apart how?"

Mary looked up, her eyes pale pools of misery. "He left. They all did. Then the wagon came for me. That was thirty years ago."

"Thirty years?" Lane didn't bother to hide her shock. "You were institutionalized all that time?"

"No, my girl, not all of it, but for a good piece. I was a guest of the state for a long while, before I learned what they wanted from me and decided to go along. Eventually I was deemed, how did they put it ...?" She paused, tapping a slender finger on her chin. "Ah yes, no longer a threat to myself or others. After that, I was moved to a nicer place where I was allowed outdoors a little each day, supervised, of course. I was there six years, I think. It's hard to keep track. Then I went to a place near a lake where they let me teach crafts twice a week. And then one day they said I was ready."

"Ready for what?"

"For the real world. I moved around a bit, looking for somewhere to land, but I couldn't seem to get my bearings. No landmarks, you see, in this new world. And without landmarks, solid things to hang on to, one tends to wander. Eventually I ended up at Hope House. A social worker arranged it all. That was four or five months ago."

Lane ticked off the months on her fingers. That explained her sudden appearance on the dunes. "Do you have family anywhere?"

Mary sighed and looked away. "No, my girl, I've no family. Not anymore."

A heavy silence stretched between them that neither seemed in a hurry to break. While Mary stared at the horizon, Lane struggled to digest it all. A loveless marriage, a suicide attempt, the loss of her home and her children—it was heartrending and incomprehensible. And yet she had no doubt every word was true. The proof of it was etched into the very lines on the woman's face, an indelible sorrow no amount of time could erase. And yet there was one more thing Lane had to know.

"Mary, the boy ..."

Mary's head came up sharply. "I won't talk about him. I can't ... I don't remember."

"But just yesterday, you told me—"

"I was mixed up. I get mixed up sometimes. I remember things wrong." She had begun to tremble, her eyes flashing and darting as she continued to babble. "I can't remember. They took it away. I let them take it away."

Take what away? Nothing she was saying was making any sense. Mary was holding her head now, in both hands, rocking slowly back and forth, her mouth twisted in silent agony. Lane closed her fingers around Mary's wrists and dragged her hands down.

"Who, Mary? Who took *what* away?"

"Everything," she moaned. "All of it. They took it all with their wires and straps."

"Mary, I don't understand what you're saying."

"The lightning," she said finally, wearily. Hugging her arms tight to her body, she rocked harder. "I wanted them to do it. They told me it might take my memory, and I didn't want to remember anymore. I was so tired of remembering. And so I let them do it. They strapped me down and gave me some kind of shot—and then they sent lightning through my head."

"Lightning through your—" Lane's voice fell away as an image slowly formed, of a gurney with leather straps and carefully placed electrodes, muscles gone suddenly rigid. The thought sent a blade of cold down her spine. She had no idea they even did shock therapy anymore. But then, it had probably been years ago. She laid a gentle hand on Mary's arm only to have it shoved away.

Blue-green eyes locked with Lane's, narrowed like a cat's. "I know what you want," she ground through clenched teeth. "You want me to remember. You all want me to remember!" She struggled to her feet, upsetting the thermos as she turned to head up the dune. "Well, I won't. You can't make me go back. I'll never go back!"

Lane scrambled after Mary as she stumbled up the dune. "Mary, wait! No one's trying to make you go back. I promise. I just wanted to understand. I'm sorry!"

Without warning, Mary rounded on her, cheeks shiny with tears. "Keep away from me," she sobbed raggedly. "You're just like the rest of them, always wanting to talk when what I need is to be left alone and allowed to forget. Can't you understand that? Can't any of you understand?"

She whirled away then, scuttling past the gate and across the vacant lot. After a moment of indecision Lane followed her out to the street, but it was too late. She was already pedaling away, leaving her purple bag in a heap near the curb.

Chapter 25

Mary

God help me, I told her the truth. I did want to forget. And for a while I nearly managed it. Or the White Coats did, in their mercy, with the help of chemicals pushed into my veins almost around the clock. For a time, I had no memory of the tortured screams, the loathing and accusation in a young boy's eyes, the blare of lights and sirens as they came screaming up the drive.

Too late—dear God, too late.

But that wasn't until later, at the hospital. Before that I could only watch from a distance as my life came apart thread by thread. He was so still when they carried him out, so still and...unrecognizable. I did that. It was true. I knew it was, but I never meant—

Oh God, I wanted to go to him, poor dead boy, to peel back the dead-white sheet and shake him awake, to say I'm sorry, so terribly, terribly sorry. But they had already strapped me down, were already pushing me into the back of the ambulance. And then there was only the hollow shrill of sirens and the sickening flash of red light as they took me away.

A full week passed before they withdrew the sedatives and let me drift back to the surface, back among the living and a world where everything was black and empty, where I had become a monster, a killer, strapped to my bed like an animal. I ask to please see the boy and then to be allowed to die. I was denied both.

For seven years, long after the straps were gone, I was punished with that awful night, each morning when the sun slanted through the iron bars at my window, and I realized where I was and why, each afternoon as I sat in the day room, staring at the others and wondering how many of them had killed a child, and each evening, as I lay down and closed my eyes and heard the plaintive screams of that poor dying boy.

Tuesday afternoons were the worst. That was my day to report to the office of some White Coat or other, always precisely at two o'clock. Each week, I would be reminded by at least one fellow inmate to paste on a smile, to lie and say I was getting better. Only I never smiled, and I never lied. I wasn't like the others, you see. I didn't want to get out. I had nowhere to go, nothing left in the world to entice me toward freedom. I was afraid. Afraid of the dream. Afraid of myself. Afraid of what I might do if they let me out.

And then one Tuesday, after a rather unpleasant episode in the day room, and a new regime of experimental medications, one of the White Coats suggested the lightning to me. Electroconvulsive therapy, he called it, which was apparently enjoying something of a renaissance. It sounded terrifying, the vengeance of the Lord administered in a controlled and sterile environment. I didn't care. By then I was well acquainted with the Lord's vengeance. When the White Coat warned me that long-term memory loss was a potential side effect, I signed his sheaf of papers without reading a word.

It worked for a time, or at least partly. I woke feeling like a jigsaw puzzle with some of the pieces missing, fragments of memory fitted in where they didn't belong, others continually shifting, so that it was impossible to pick them up and examine them. Eventually, though, I realized it wasn't like a puzzle at all, because lives are not still. They change and flicker, like a moving picture, but now mine had some of the frames cut out. I wondered if they would come back, or if I even wanted them to. Would they knit together like broken bones, flare back to life like a fire not quite quenched?

I missed my princes. Gone, all gone.

Through my fault.

Through my fault.

Through my most grievous fault.

Chapter 26

Lane

Lane stared out the kitchen window at the rain-swept beach, her paring knife forgotten over the tomato on the cutting board. Two days and still there'd been no sign of Mary. Two mornings without seeing her figure huddled on the dunes, two days of waiting for her to return for her bag full of pills.

More than once, she'd been tempted to drive over to Hope House, to check on her, or at least drop off her medication, but something told her Mary would be less than thrilled to see her. Perhaps it was the look on her face when she'd shrieked at Lane to keep away. But she couldn't sit by and do nothing. The whole thing had been her fault. She had prodded and pried, pushing for the truth until Mary had finally come undone. The least she could do was make sure she'd gotten home safely. Tomorrow—if she didn't appear tomorrow, she would ride over to Hope House and at least drop off her meds.

Michael would try to talk her out of it, of course, ticking off all the reasons it was a bad idea, but then she already knew them all. Still, he'd been pretty decent about the whole thing. After stumbling into him in the kitchen with tears streaming down her face, she'd had no choice but to come clean about Mary's unraveling.

His reaction had surprised her. Before she knew what was happening, he had pulled her into his arms, holding her tight while she blubbered out the whole horrible ordeal. She'd left out the details—the dead boy and the attempted suicide—they weren't hers to share, even if she had managed to understand Mary's agitated gibberish, which she hadn't. By the time she'd stopped crying she had painted a pretty clear picture of just how thoroughly Mary had unraveled. Exactly as he'd predicted she would. And yet he hadn't said I told you so, at least not in so many words. Nor had he tried to talk her out of worrying or feeling guilty. Instead, he had held his tongue and listened with an empathy she hadn't expected.

Lane didn't turn when she heard the scrape of his shoes as he entered the kitchen. He moved to the stove, giving the pot of spaghetti sauce a quick but unnecessary stir.

"She's not likely to be out there in this, Lane," he said, eyeing her as she stood staring out the window at the blowing gray drizzle.

"I know. I know. I just keep hoping. I've decided to ride over to Hope House tomorrow if she doesn't show up in the morning."

"Do you really think that's a good idea?"

She forced a thin smile. "I knew you wouldn't think so, but I have to go. I at least need to get her medications back to her."

"Then just do that. Drop off the meds and then walk away from the rest of this. It's eating you up and it's not your problem. Or your fault."

Lane set down her knife and slowly wiped her hands. "I pushed her, Michael. I knew she was in trouble, and I just kept pushing. So yes, it is a little bit my fault."

Michael said nothing as he busied himself with a corkscrew and bottle of merlot. She was grateful to him for that, and for the glass of wine he eventually pressed into her hand. It was the third night they'd cooked together. She knew he was trying to keep her thoughts off Mary, to keep her from stewing in her own guilt, and she appreciated the effort.

"Look, I know you're just trying to look out for me, but I have to do this. I couldn't live with myself if something's happened to her."

He nodded somberly. "Well, if I can't change your mind, can we at least change the subject?"

"What should we talk about?"

Michael lifted the lid off the spaghetti pot and peered down into the rolling water. "Well, for starters, we could talk about why this pasta's taking so long. I'm starving."

Lane took a sip of merlot and went back to preparing her salad. "It's been kind of nice having someone to cook with these last couple days. You're actually not too bad in the kitchen."

Michael snatched a slice of cucumber from the cutting board. "This isn't going to be another crack about me growing up with a cook, is it?"

"No, it's a serious compliment. Bruce didn't know which end of a spatula was which."

Michael shrugged. "I'm a bachelor, and I need to eat. As far as Becca was concerned, the well-stocked kitchen required just two ingredients—wine and yogurt. Beyond that, it was up to me."

Lane raised her eyebrows questioningly over her wineglass. "Becca?"

"A woman I dated for a while. A yoga instructor. She's in L.A. now, I think, which is probably a good place for her."

"You don't like California?"

Before Michael could respond the front door buzzer sounded, three quick, impatient bursts. Michael set down his glass and headed for the parlor. "I'll get the door. You drain the pasta. I don't care if it's still crunchy. I'll eat it anyway."

Lane laughed as he disappeared. She paid no attention to the faint murmur of voices coming from the parlor as she spilled the pot of spaghetti into the colander. A few minutes later she heard Michael clear his throat as he returned to the kitchen.

"Laney...honey...look who's here."

Lane grunted a bare acknowledgment, negotiating the colander of pasta with a face full of steamy bangs as she threw a glance over her shoulder. For a moment she was too stunned to make sense of what she was seeing, but gradually she wrapped her head around the sight of a petite brunette with her arm looped through Michael's.

"Mother...what on earth are you doing here?"

It was a ridiculous question, or at least a rhetorical one. She knew full well what her mother was up to. She had come to meet Michael, the man who was spending the winter with her daughter—the man with whom she was purportedly having copious amounts of sex.

Cynthia stepped forward to brush an airy kiss on her daughter's cheek. "Well, what does it look like, Laney? I came to spend some time with my little girl, and to see how they stuff a turkey down South."

Turkey?

Mystified, Lane blinked at her mother. Then, finally, it dawned. It was the middle of November; Thanksgiving was next week. She'd grown so used to the inn being empty at this time of year that she barely marked the passing of the holidays anymore. There didn't seem much point when it was just her. Only, as far as her mother knew, it wasn't just her anymore. As far as her mother knew, she'd be spending Thanksgiving with her new boyfriend.

A prickle of panic tingled along the back of her neck at the thought of having to confess the truth, that the handsome Michael Forrester was a paying guest and nothing more, their supposed romance a mere fiction born of frustration and one too many beers. It had seemed harmless enough at the time, ill-considered, certainly, but necessary. How was she supposed to know her mother would hop a plane and show up unannounced?

Cynthia was looking her over with critical eyes, and a bit of a pout. "Aren't you happy to see me, darling? You don't look very happy."

Lane managed a shaky smile. "Of course I'm happy, Mother. I'm just . . . surprised. Come to think of it, how did you even get here?"

Cynthia began to unbutton her trench coat, scattering raindrops onto the kitchen floor. "Well, I flew, of course. It took three planes to get me here. I finally ended up in Manteo, I think it's called. And then I had to rent a car. I thought I'd never get here. In fact, I was sure the man at the rental place had given me the wrong directions. He didn't tell me I'd be driving to the end of the earth. But then, it's worth it to spend time with my daughter and her young man."

Her . . . *young man?* Lane swallowed a groan. Apparently her mother had been watching reruns of *Father Knows Best* again. Her cheeks were hot as she glanced at Michael, who, rather than showing signs of annoyance, seemed to be enjoying himself—and her predicament—immensely. He had a right, she supposed, since she'd seen fit to make him a part of the drama.

Time to face the music, then, along with her mother's—what? Lane couldn't even come up with a name for what she was about to face. Still, they said it was best to rip the bandage off quickly. They'd just see about that.

"Mother, there's something I need to—"

Before she could get the rest out, Michael extricated himself from Cynthia's arm and came to Lane's side, slipping an arm smoothly about her waist. "Never mind about the dinner, sweetheart. I'll take care of that. Cynthia, I hope you're hungry. Your daughter's an amazing cook." He turned to Lane then, with an adoring smile, and stunned her by dropping a kiss on her cheek. "Now, why don't you pour your mom a glass of wine while I set another place and finish up the pasta?"

Sweetheart?

Lane stood blinking at the two of them. Had he really just agreed to play along with the ridiculous charade for her mother's sake? It was absurd, unthinkable. And yet, to her everlasting shame, she couldn't deny feeling enormously relieved.

Not that her mother was off the hook—not by a long shot. She would deny it, of course, but Lane knew her too well to believe this was anything but a good old-fashioned ambush. When Val had failed to turn up any new information, she'd decided it was time for a little recon mission of her own, carried out under the guise of a holiday visit.

"Mother, where is Robert?" Lane asked as she took her mother's dripping coat and hung it on a peg near the back door. "Please don't tell me you left your husband alone on Thanksgiving to come see me?"

Cynthia quirked one perfectly groomed eyebrow at her daughter, letting the silence stretch just a little long. "It's sweet of you to worry about Robert," she said finally, in the breezy voice she usually reserved for parties. "But I promise you, he'll barely know I'm gone. He's working on some big corruption case that goes to trial in a couple of weeks. It doesn't seem to be going very well, but then, it never does when there are big shots involved. And in Chicago there are always big shots involved. So there you are. I'm all yours."

Lane caught Michael's warning glance and rearranged her grimace into a smile. "Let me get you a glass of wine, Mother. Then I need to help Michael with dinner."

After settling her mother at the kitchen table—now set for three—Lane poured her a glass of merlot, then topped off her own with a heavy hand. To her dismay, Michael had already tossed the pasta and was nearly finished slicing the bread. She'd hoped for a few moments to collect herself before they sat down to eat, to reconcile herself to her mother's sudden and inexplicable presence, and examine the wisdom of maintaining the illusion that she and Michael were lovers.

On one hand, it would be a disaster to continue the charade only to give themselves away with some clumsy slipup, which, given the fact that they'd known each other all of three weeks, wasn't completely out of the realm of possibility. On the other hand, it would only be for a few days. They could pull anything off for a few days. Her mother would fly back to Chicago, happy and none the wiser.

Glancing around the kitchen, Lane tried to see it as her mother must have seen it upon entering: the table set for two, a pair of wineglasses side by side on the counter, the two of them cooking together. It was all very cozy, and apparently convincing, if her mother's pleased expression meant anything. Maybe—just maybe—this could work.

Cynthia beamed as Michael held out a chair for her, then did the same for her daughter. Lane shot him a look that was part gratitude, part confusion. She had no idea why he was doing this, but she certainly planned to find out at the first opportunity. After a deep pull from her wineglass, she began serving up the salad.

"Well, now," Cynthia said, plucking a slice of bread from the basket Michael held out. "Isn't this nice, us being all together like this? Though I hope I didn't interrupt anything . . . private."

Lane cringed at the carefully placed pause. "No, Mother. We were just making dinner. Your timing was perfect, although if you had called I could have met you in Manteo and saved you all that driving."

"Oh, but, Laney, that would have spoiled the surprise. I do wish you could have seen the look on your face when you turned around and saw me standing in your kitchen. I swear, it was like you were looking at a ghost."

"How long are you planning to stay?" Lane asked coolly, ignoring the sharp nudge of Michael's knee beneath the table.

"My return ticket is for the twenty-ninth. That's the Monday after Thanksgiving. I tried for Saturday, and then Sunday, but everything was booked because of the holiday."

Lane did the math in her head. *Sweet Jesus, six days.* Before she could reach for the newly opened wine bottle, Michael grabbed it and topped off Cynthia's glass, then placed it discreetly but pointedly out of reach. She shot him daggers, then fixed her attention on her plate.

"So, Laney tells me you're a writer, Michael," Cynthia said with a broad, beaming smile.

"Actually, I'm a professor who just happens to be writing a book."

"A professor! Well, how very interesting. Where do you teach, if you don't mind me asking?"

"Or even if you do," Lane muttered into her wineglass.

Michael checked her with a sidelong glance before returning Cynthia's smile. "I teach English lit at Middlebury College. That's in Vermont."

"Vermont?" she repeated with another of her pouts. "But that's so far away. Tell me, how in the world did you two ever get together?"

Lane set down her fork with a clatter. She couldn't do this. "Actually, Mother, we—"

Michael's fingers shot out to capture hers in a quick but viselike squeeze. "Actually, we met right here at the inn, Cynthia."

Lane stared at him, astonished as he began heaping pasta on her mother's plate with his free hand. "Your daughter took me in out of the rain one night, like a stray dog, and agreed to put me up. The rest, as they say, is history. Isn't it, sweetie?"

Lane stared at her plate, feeling vaguely queasy. Alternative history, maybe. But what the hell, they were in it up to their ears now. There was nothing to do but keep paddling. Feeling the weight of her mother's expectant gaze, she turned to Michael with what she hoped would pass for a lovesick smile. "Yes, we just . . . hit it right off."

Cynthia was smiling from ear to ear. "Laney, honey, I'm so happy for you. And so glad to know you won't be rattling around this place by yourself anymore."

Lane did her best to return the smile. She could see that her mother meant it. She *was* happy, relieved that her sad and lonely daughter had at long last found a man. Somehow it made the lie that much worse.

Chapter 27

Michael

Michael turned when he heard Lane coming down the back stairs, though he didn't need to see her face to know he had some explaining to do. For instance, what had he been thinking when he decided to assume the role of doting boyfriend? The truth was he honestly didn't know, unless it was the look of abject horror on her face when she turned to find her mother standing in her kitchen.

"Can I see you outside?" she said, not waiting for a response as she swept past him en route to the back door.

Sensing that it probably wasn't a good time to remind her that it had been storming all day, or that it was likely to be freezing, he slid into his jacket and followed her out onto the deck.

For a long time she said nothing, just stood facing the sea, arms folded close to her body. "I can't believe she did this," she hissed at last. "Did she really think I wouldn't see right through this little stunt?"

"She's settled in?"

Lane nodded. "She's on the second floor with you. I swear she brought enough clothes for . . . My God, she's going to be here for six days."

"How long since she visited?"

"Try never. She's never visited. Until today."

"Ah, I guess I see your point. Showing up out of the blue does seem rather suspect."

"Actually, I should have seen it coming the minute Val called."

"Val?"

"My sister," Lane tossed over her shoulder as she pushed through the gate and out onto the boardwalk. "She called the other day on a fishing expedition for my mother. I didn't give her what she wanted, so what does my mother do? Hops on a plane for the Outer Banks."

"Lane, it's freezing out here. Where are you going?"

"Nowhere. Hell, I don't know." She stopped, raking her fingers through her hair. "I just need to put some breathing room between her and me. You don't have to come."

"I know, but I am." Michael shrugged out of his jacket and handed it to her. "Put this on. I won't have your mother blaming me because you caught pneumonia."

"Stop it," Lane snapped, pushing the jacket away. "You don't have to pretend out here."

Michael shrugged, tossing the spurned jacket over his shoulder. "Fine, but anger isn't going to keep you warm, Lane. Neither is being stubborn. I'm not the enemy here. In fact, I'm not sure who is."

Lane said nothing as she moved farther down the rain-slick boards. In the wake of the day's storms, the sky was moonless, the beach blanketed in darkness but for the blue-white sweep of Starry Point Light skimming the dunes at regular intervals. Beyond the stretch of darkened shore, the sea thrummed like a pulse, enduring, insistent.

"Why?" she asked finally, her voice almost lost on the chilly breeze.

"Why what?"

"Why did you do that? The sweetheart thing in front of my mother?"

Michael folded his arms and stared at her, though her face was hidden in the darkness. "Now, that's a funny question coming from you. I did it because your mother thinks we're lovers. And the reason she thinks that is that you told her we were. I remember it all very clearly. We were at the Blue Water when your mother called, and you said—"

"Yes! Yes!" Lane snapped, shooting an anxious glance back at the inn. "I know what I said. I was there."

"Then what? Did we break up, and you forgot to tell me?"

"Look, I know you think this is enormously amusing, but it's never going to work."

"Why? We don't despise each other."

"That's not what I meant. Sooner or later—" She broke off, shoving a handful of wind-tangled hair off her face. "Just tell me why you did it."

Michael's smile slipped away. "Why do you think?"

"Because you felt sorry for me?"

"Not sorry. No. Empathy, maybe."

"It's the same thing."

"No," he said, gravely. "It isn't. Empathy's what you feel when you've walked a mile in someone's shoes. I know what it's like to see disappointment on a parent's face, to know the way you live your life isn't enough for him. I saw the look on your face when you turned around and saw your mother standing there. You were dreading having to tell her the truth. So I decided you wouldn't have to."

Lane closed her eyes, groaning softly. "God, it's so completely ridiculous. I suppose I should say thank you. She thinks we're head over heels, by the way, so nice job there. Maybe you should try your luck on the stage."

"It's not a hard part to play," he said quietly, surprised to find he meant it. He'd never been easy in relationships, a fact Becca would freely admit, but somehow this felt easy, good. Maybe because it wasn't a *real* relationship. There was no chance of getting hurt—or of hurting someone else. He hoped.

He looked at her, so damn pretty with the wind lifting all that fire-colored hair out around her head, but fragile, too, pale and almost breakable. The instinct was there to touch her, but he held it in check.

"I do wonder why you feel the need for the charade in the first place," he said instead. "I understand that she was under your skin the night she called, that you just wanted to get her off the phone, but it seems like there's more to it than that. Earlier, in the kitchen, you looked like you were on the verge of a panic attack, so I'm just wondering what the deal is."

Lane snorted softly. "How long have you got?"

"Actually, I've got all winter."

He followed her gaze to the sky, beginning to clear now as the last vestiges of the storm blew out to sea, the clouds shredding to reveal a smattering of stars and a glimpse of three-quarter moon. He was surprised when she spoke.

"A lot of it has to do with Bruce. He was more her idea than mine."

"Her . . . idea?"

"We met at a party. Bruce was interning, and I was in my third year of undergrad. Eight months later he proposed, if you want to call it that. I don't think the words *will you marry me* ever crossed his lips. Maybe because he was too busy detailing his fifteen-year plan. My mother was ecstatic. She lobbied hard for a yes. The next thing I knew I was walking down the aisle. It was a disaster almost from the beginning. I guess part of me blames her."

"How long were you married?"

"Ten years, but it felt longer."

"No children?"

The question seemed to catch her off guard. She turned away, but not before he caught the shimmer of tears in her eyes. "Almost," she said, barely above a whisper.

Almost. The single word said so much. "I'm so sorry. I didn't know."

"Of course you didn't. It's not the kind of thing you assume, is it? I mean, most women pop out a baby without blinking. I couldn't manage it."

Michael blinked at her in the moonlight. "Lane . . ."

"I was five and a half months. Nothing happened. I just . . . lost it. Afterward, the doctors said I needed to wait before we tried again, but that wasn't part of Bruce's plan. He moved his things out of our room. It was pretty much over after that."

"I'm sorry."

"Don't be. It was never going to work. My mother was the only one who couldn't see it, because she didn't want to. She wanted so badly for me to finally get something right that it didn't matter what I wanted."

"She told you that?"

"Not in so many words, no. But I knew it. My sister knew it. Even Bruce knew it. Nothing I did was ever good enough. The miscarriage was just the last straw, a shortcoming he simply couldn't forgive."

"I'm sorry," Michael murmured again, knowing the words were inadequate but unable to find others.

Lane shrugged. "Don't be. In the end, my mother was the only one disappointed that I left, and I got used to her disappointment a long time ago."

"Your mother loves you, Lane. If she didn't she wouldn't have taken three planes and then driven over an hour in the rain to come see you."

"That's just it. She didn't come to see me. She came to see you."

"You know better than that."

Lane sighed. "I wish I did. But the truth is we've always gotten along better when there was a little distance between us. My sister was the perfect one, cheerleader, prom queen, married to a blue-chip accountant, and gave him two perfect children. Me, I liked books. It drove her crazy. I think I still drive her crazy. I know she does me."

Michael struggled to hold his tongue. She didn't get it. But then, neither had he until it was too late. In the end, none of the petty stuff mattered. What mattered was holding on to family, even if that meant pretending not to see the flaws. Blood mattered. Being there mattered.

"You should try to work it out, Lane," he said finally, sounding gruffer than he meant to. "You'll only ever have one mother, and I can promise that you'll regret it for the rest of your life if you don't fix it and something happens."

Lane cocked her head. "Nothing's going to happen, Michael."

"No. Nothing's ever going to happen—until it does."

"You're being melodramatic."

Uncomfortable beneath her scrutiny, he turned to stare out over the sea, silver now beneath the freshly revealed moon. For a long moment he simply stood there, listening to the pound and pull of the waves. She had no idea what he was talking about. How could she? At any rate, he'd said too much. Her relationship with her mother was none of his business, and even if it was, he was the last person who should be handing out family advice.

"You're right. Forget it."

Her eyes were wide and luminous when he finally faced her again, a mix of confusion and concern. She looked almost ethereal standing there, vulnerable and soft, and shivering just a little, her hair turned gold by the moonlight.

"You're cold," he said, a statement of fact rather than a question.

And yet somehow it never occurred to him to offer the jacket again. Instead, almost before he realized what he was doing, he was pulling her into his arms. She was trembling in earnest now, soft and startlingly yielding as their breaths mingled and his lips closed over hers. She tasted like wine and smelled like the sea. And she felt like heaven.

How long?

The words thundered in his head. How long had he wanted her like this, in his arms, against his body? He had no idea. He only knew, as they drew apart, that whatever had arisen between them hadn't just blown up out of nowhere. At least not for him.

She looked faintly dazed when he released her. "Why did you do that?"

Why seemed to be her favorite word tonight. "I did it for your mother, in case she was looking down at us from her window."

"Her rooms face the street."

"Okay, then, I did it because I wanted to."

Her fingers fluttered to her throat, then to her mouth, still moist and full from their kiss. Something like a smile played there. "Oh. Well, that's all right, then."

"I should get you back," he said, hearing the reluctance in his own voice. "Before you catch your death and your mother decides not to like me anymore."

"Oh, I don't think there's any danger of that. She's pretty well smitten."

"And what about you?" he said, closing the distance between them with a single step. "Are you at all . . . smitten?"

She reached up and touched his face, the back of her fingers icy and featherlight along the stubbled line of his jaw. Her eyes brimmed with uncertainty. "I think I could be . . . if I let myself. I just don't know if I can let myself."

"It's only six days," he murmured, pulling her back for another kiss.

"Six days," she whispered, as her mouth opened to his.

Later, as they drifted back up the boardwalk, fingers loosely linked, Michael couldn't help thinking that if Lane's mother were to peer out the window at that moment she would have no trouble believing that he was head over heels for her daughter.

Chapter 28

Lane

Lane reluctantly dragged her eyes open. Shafts of chilly sunshine spilled through the windows, creeping over the pillows, prodding her awake. Rolling over didn't help. Neither did pulling the covers over her head. She didn't want to think about last night, the thinly concealed look of triumph on her mother's face as she stood in the kitchen with her arm linked through Michael's. The thought left her queasy and more than a little angry.

She'd managed to be civil, but only just, doing what she could between sips of merlot to steer the conversation clear of tricky subjects. She hadn't quite pulled it off. Dinner had been a nerve-racking affair, an awkward and stilted charade, despite Michael's flawless performance as the doting boyfriend.

Michael.

Flawless indeed. Slowly, deliciously, the memory trickled back. He had kissed her. And she had kissed him back. Not for her mother's sake, but because she wanted to, though she hadn't realized just how much until his arms were cinched about her waist. He was the first man she'd kissed since Bruce, a virtual stranger after only three weeks, and yet somehow not a stranger at all. He'd touched something in her last night, awakening things she thought long burned out and gone. It was playing with fire, she knew, flirting with a man who would be gone from her life in a few months, but she almost didn't care. His kiss had left her reeling, had her reeling still.

Or maybe it was only the absurdity of the situation that had her off balance. How could she, for even a moment, believe she could fool the woman who raised her, the woman who had seen through every faked sore throat, every dime of lunch money spent on CDs, every cheerleader tryout ditched in favor of an afternoon at the library? Never in her life had she been able to keep anything from those keen, maternal eyes.

She would have to now, though, and not just about Michael. Her friendship with Mary was just one more detail she'd rather not have to explain to her mother. Throwing off the covers, she pulled on leggings, a baggy sweatshirt, and a pair of warm socks. At the window, she peered down the beach, quiet and cold—and empty. But it was still early. Maybe she'd still come. Perhaps by the time she returned from her walk. Except she wouldn't be walking today.

Her mother's ill-timed arrival made a morning walk unlikely, just as it would make riding over to Hope House unlikely. Something told her when it came to Mary, her mother would almost certainly take Michael's side, and she'd already had more than enough lectures on that score. Best to leave her friendship with Mary out of the equation, especially since she was beginning to doubt that friendship still existed.

Most people can't see past their noses.

Mary had said that once, and maybe it was true. Her mother wanted to see love in Michael's eyes, and she did—even where none existed. There was, however, the small matter of Michael sleeping in his own room on the second floor, and the questions that would surely arise should her mother happen to catch him stumbling out, alone, first thing in the morning.

The thought was enough to send Lane scrambling out of her

room and down the stairs. She had no intention of suggesting they share a room, but they needed to have some sort of story ready. Until then, she needed to head her mother off at the pass.

Outside the door of her mother's room, she caught the creak of floorboards, the opening and shutting of drawers. Gathering her resolve and a lungful of air, she rapped lightly.

"Mother, are you up?"

"Yes, dear. Come in."

Lane stepped into the room, stunned once again by the sheer number of outfits hanging from the backs of doors and draped over every stick of furniture. Beneath the window, lined up like soldiers for inspection, a half dozen pairs of designer shoes hugged the baseboard. Where on earth did she think they'd be going?

"Mother, this is the Outer Banks. We don't have a theater district."

Cynthia was still in her robe and slippers, but her makeup and hair were flawless. She cut her eyes at Lane with a sniff. "I only wanted to make a good impression when I met your young man," she said, her tone somewhere between a sulk and a huff. "And I'm glad I did. He seems quite the catch. Polite, handsome, and apparently very accomplished. What's his book about?"

"It's a biography on Dickens," Lane said, thankful that she actually knew the answer. "It's to do with Dickens's writings as social commentary, and how he used his stories to bring attention to the way Victorian society dealt with the poor."

"Oh. Well, that does sound impressive. Have you met his parents? What are they like?"

Lane felt a flash of panic. "No, I haven't met them. Not yet. His father's an attorney. His brother, too." She was relieved to have at least that bit of information to impart, but she prayed the questions ended there. She hadn't the first clue about their names and knew nothing whatever about Michael's mother.

"Lawyers," Cynthia said gravely, feigning a shudder. "You never see them. They're either in court, preparing for court, or recuperating from a day in court. Thank heavens he didn't follow in his father's footsteps. He's crazy about you, by the way. But I guess you already know that. It's all over his face when he looks at you. He's got forever in his eyes."

Lane bit hard on her lower lip, pretending to be fascinated by the pattern of a nearby houndstooth blazer. In her head she was counting to ten. It didn't help. "Wow," she finally said, not bothering to hide her annoyance. "I believe you've hit a new personal best. It took you less than twenty-four hours to get us down the aisle. But then, after three husbands, I guess you qualify as an expert."

Cynthia stopped fussing with the scarf she was folding and laid it at the foot of the bed. "That was uncalled for, Laney. And you can't blame me. I have no idea what's going on in your life. You shut me out. You always have. You wouldn't talk to me, or your sister, about this man, and I just wanted to make sure—"

"That I was good enough for him?"

Her mother looked as if she'd just been slapped. "Why do you say things like that?"

"Because they're true, Mother. We both know the real reason you're here—the only reason—to make sure I don't blow my last chance."

Sighing, Cynthia closed her suitcase and dropped down beside it on the bed, her eyes focused on her lap and her perfectly manicured nails. "I didn't say a word about you not being good enough. I never have. I also never said anything about this being your last chance. And the reason I know I never said them is that I don't believe either of those things." Eyes the same gray-green as her daughter's lifted slowly. "But you do."

Lane went still, letting the words sink deep. It was absurd, of course, ridiculous—her mother's way of deflecting guilt. Well, it wasn't going to work. How could she believe Michael was her last chance? He wasn't any kind of chance. She hadn't the faintest idea how to respond to such a statement. In fact, she wasn't even going to try. Squaring her shoulders, she headed for the door, pausing briefly as she stepped out into the hall. "I'm going to take a shower, Mother. I'll see you downstairs for breakfast."

The shower helped. She emerged feeling a little more in control of her temper, but only a little. Button pushing, that's all it was. And no one was better at pushing her buttons than her mother. Not even Bruce. In six days it would be over. Her mother would go back to Chicago. Michael would go back to his book. And she would go back to her articles. Until then, she'd simply grit her teeth and do her best to be hospitable.

The delicious aromas of coffee and bacon greeted her as she made her way downstairs. She envisioned Michael already in the kitchen, sipping coffee as he puttered about with the breakfast. It was a pleasant thought, but not an accurate one, she saw as she rounded the corner.

"What on earth are you doing?" The words tumbled out unchecked at the sight of her impeccably dressed mother laying bacon into a skillet.

Damn. Must learn the difference between hospitable and hostile.

"I was making breakfast for everyone," Cynthia said, wearing her best martyr look as she poured a mug of coffee and handed it to Lane. "Call it a peace offering, if you like. I didn't mean to upset you before. I shouldn't have said . . . what I did."

No, you shouldn't have. "Forget it," Lane said instead, just wanting to put the moment behind them. "Need any help?"

Cynthia handed her an open bag of flour. "If you want, you can sift the flour for the pancakes."

Sifting—the secret to her mother's lighter-than-air pancakes. She'd learned it as a girl, along with so many other secrets: how to tell if an egg is fresh, how to slice garlic rather than mincing to keep it from burning, how cold water is the secret to a flaky piecrust. Come to think of it, the kitchen was one place—perhaps the only place—she and her mother had ever gotten along, perhaps because it was the one time they were focused on a common goal. Or maybe it was only because they stayed too busy to find fault with each other.

"You know, I never thought to ask. Does Michael like pancakes?"

Lane took her nose out of her coffee cup. "I'm sorry, what?"

"Pancakes—does he like them?"

"Um ... sure." It was purely a guess, but it felt safe enough. Who didn't like pancakes?

She had just started sifting when a small flash of movement caught her eye just beyond the kitchen window. Breath held, Lane abandoned her bowl of flour and stepped to the window, eagerly scouring the dunes for Mary. Instead, she spotted a father and son emerging from the vacant lot beside the inn. Disappointed, she watched as they turned in the direction of the lighthouse before letting the curtains fall back.

Where are you, Mary?

"Have you finished with— Laney, honey, what is it?" Her mother was beside her now, following her gaze out onto the beach. "Good heavens, is everything all right? You look as though you've seen a ghost."

"No," Lane answered numbly. "I was just ..."

Just what? Looking for the old bag lady who hangs out on the dunes and claims to have killed a child? No, she couldn't say that. She couldn't say anything.

Her mother eyed her skeptically but eventually drifted back to the eggs she'd been cracking. "By the way, where is Michael this morning? I haven't seen him."

The mention of Michael was enough to yank Lane back to the present. One crisis at a time was all she was equipped to handle. "He's

still sleeping," she replied, hoping she sounded casual and not pan-
icked. "He was up late working, so I let him sleep. How about you?
Did you sleep well?"

"I did, surprisingly. I was skeptical about that old four-poster bed
at first, but I was so exhausted I think I could have slept on a bed of
nails. I thought air travel was supposed to be a convenience. I swear,
I feel like I've got jet lag."

"You can't have jet lag, Mother. You crossed one time zone."

Michael suddenly filled the kitchen doorway. "It's all this sea air,
Cynthia. Hits you like a rock if you're not used to it." He made a beeline for Lane, planting a kiss on her temple before dusting a smudge
of flour off her chin. "Why didn't you wake me?"

Lane met his gaze with a mixture of wariness and uncertainty. To
buy time she filled a mug with coffee and pressed it into his hands.
"You looked so peaceful," she said finally, startled by how easily the
lie rolled off her tongue. "I thought after last night you could use the
rest."

Michael smiled, a slow, suggestive curl that made her insides skit-
ter. "Did you?"

Lane felt her cheeks go hot. He had purposely misconstrued her
meaning, leaving the unsaid lingering suggestively in the bacon-
scented air. He really was enjoying himself immensely. And if her
mother's discreetly averted gaze was any indication, she had swallowed the show hook, line, and sinker. And why wouldn't she? As far
as she knew, her daughter was having quite a lot of sex.

Oh, dear God. Turning away, Lane made a beeline for the pantry.
"I'll get the syrup."

Chapter 29

ane snuck a glance at Michael, once again up to his elbows in dishwater. He'd refused help when breakfast mercifully ended, insisting *the girls* enjoy their coffee and make plans for the day. Now, as she stood at the counter waiting for a fresh pot of coffee to brew, dread hit full force. *Six days.* She had no idea how she was going to fill one day, let alone six. She supposed a tour of the inn was as good a place as any to start. Then later, when it was warmer, they could take a walk down to the lighthouse, though her mother had never been much of a beach person.

Starry Point was hardly a cultural mecca, but there were a few trendy boutiques in the village, and neither of them had ever been able to pass up an antiques shop. They'd do a little shopping, then grab a late lunch—anywhere but the Blue Water. And then what? She'd have to think of something. While she didn't relish the idea of spending the next six days gadding all over the Outer Banks, the alternative was hanging around the inn, circling each other like a pair of wet cats, while her mother scrutinized every move she and Michael made.

"Coffee," Lane announced, setting freshly filled mugs on the table and dropping back into her chair.

Cynthia turned from the window and came to join her. She stirred half a spoonful of sugar into her mug, then took a sip. "You picked a lovely spot, Laney. The beach is so quiet."

"That's because it's November and everyone's gone for the season. I thought maybe we'd walk down to the light later on if you're up to it."

Cynthia peered over the rim of her mug. "Was that a crack about my age, young lady?"

"No. I just wasn't sure you'd want to. You said you were tired."

"I came to spend time with you, Laney, to *be* with you. I can be tired when I get home."

Lane felt a tug of something familiar and uneasy. Her father had complained of being tired just before being diagnosed with renal adenocarcinoma. Ten months later he was gone.

"Are you . . ." Lane's voice trailed off, hindered by a sudden thickness in her throat. "Have you been—I mean, are you taking care of yourself?"

Cynthia's gray-green eyes softened with understanding. She set down her cup carefully, stealing a hand toward Lane's. Her fingers were warm and strong as they squeezed. "I'm fine, Laney, and taking excellent care of myself. I'm afraid I'll be around to annoy you for years to come."

"Don't say that, Mother."

"Oh, honey, we both know it's true, so why pretend? You're not exactly thrilled to see me, but I had to come. I had to know if you were happy. And I think you are."

The remark left Lane faintly flabbergasted. Since when had her mother cared if she was happy? Accomplished—naturally. Prominently wed—certainly. But happy? That was news to Lane. And yet there was something earnest flickering in the eyes looking back at her, eyes so much like her own. Regret perhaps? An unspoken apology?

Lane was spared a reply when Dally's signature greeting drifted in from the parlor.

"Hey-howdy! Hey-howdy!"

Cynthia's brows shot up. "What on earth—?"

"Her name is Dally. She helps out a couple days a week," Lane explained hastily, as she pushed back from the table. If Dally started blabbing about Michael before she got the chance to fill her in, the jig would be up for sure. "I forgot she was coming. I better go talk to her."

Dally was still juggling her coffee, keys, and iPod when Lane grabbed her by the sleeve and yanked her into the library, mercifully empty since Michael hadn't settled down to work yet. This was going to be embarrassing enough without him smirking over her shoulder.

"I need your help," Lane hissed close to Dally's ear. "My mother's popped in for a visit."

"Your mother? Cool!"

"Shhh! And no, it is not cool. It's anything *but* cool. She thinks Michael and I are ... involved."

"Involved?" It took a moment for the word to sink in. "Oh, involved." Her dark eyebrows waggled. "And why would she think that?"

Lane wet her lips, not quite believing what she was about to say. "Because I told her we were."

Dally's large brown eyes widened. "Are you?"

"No!" Lane hissed back. "I lied."

"You ..." For a moment Dally stared, openmouthed. "To your mother? Lane, have you lost your mind? Why would you do something like that?"

"She called one night while Michael and I were out to dinner—"

"You two went to dinner?"

"Yes. No. Not like that. Please, Dally, let me finish! She called and started in again about Bruce. She was driving me crazy, so I sort of ... fibbed a little."

"A little?"

"Okay, a lot. And now she's here—in my kitchen."

"Well, well, well. And what does Professor McDreamy have to say about all this?"

"He's loving it, actually. He's quite the actor as it turns out. I was all set to tell her the truth when he stepped in and started calling me sweetheart. I nearly fell over."

Dally lifted the plastic lid off her coffee and took a thoughtful sip. "And now you want me to play along, too."

"Yes. Look, I know this is all very . . . weird. But, Dally, I'm desperate. If she finds out I lied about this—just made up a boyfriend—I'll never hear the end of it."

Dally apparently couldn't hold back her grin another moment. "When I said you should take him on trial, this isn't exactly what I had in mind. But hey, if this is what it's going to take to finally get you—"

"Nothing's changed, Dally. It's all pretend." She tried not to think of the kiss they had shared last night—kisses—tried not to remember how it felt to be held again in a man's arms. In Michael's arms. "It'll all be over in six days."

"Six days, did you say? Do you really think you can pull this off for that long?"

"I don't have a choice. The alternative is to let my mother go back to Chicago thinking I'm even more pathetic than she realized."

"Okay, yeah, I think I see your point."

"Just do me a favor and start upstairs today. It'll give me a chance to get her out onto the beach. With any luck you won't even bump into her. I just wanted you to know—in case."

Dally heaved an affected sigh and shook her dark head dismally. "Far be it from me to point out that all this could have been avoided if you'd just taken my advice and slept with him right out of the gate."

Lane eyed her darkly. "Are you trying to get me to fire you?"

Dally grinned, then stuck out her tongue. "Try it, and I'll go straight to the tabloids with everything I know."

Lane couldn't help scanning the dunes one more time when she and Cynthia finally stepped out the back door and onto the deck. Eleven o'clock and still no sign of Mary. If she were coming she certainly would have appeared by now. Still, it was a relief to be out in the sunshine, where there was space to breathe and room to avoid her mother's keen eyes, which seemed to be everywhere at once when Michael was anywhere in the vicinity.

It was a good day for walking, bright and cloudless, with just a bit of a bite in the air. Lane pushed through the gate and out onto the narrow boardwalk, waiting for her mother to follow.

"That's where we're going," she said, pointing down the beach toward Starry Point Light, stark and almost dizzyingly white against the clear morning sky.

If Cynthia was daunted she gave no sign. She did, however, button her jacket to her throat as she fell in step beside her daughter. "I thought this was the south. It's freezing!"

"Just keep walking, Mother. You'll be unbuttoning that coat before we're halfway there. I brought some bread. We can go out on the jetty and feed the birds."

"Out on the jetty," Cynthia echoed, trying to sound bright but already sounding breathless in her effort to keep up. "That'll be . . . fun."

Lane shortened her stride. It would be no such thing, and they both knew it. Her mother had never been much of an outdoor person, happy to leave things like camping and zoo trips to her father, preferring instead to seek adventure in shopping malls, art boutiques, and smart little cafés. At no time had these differences been more glaring than during family vacations, when she and her father would set out in shorts and sandals for some local point of interest, and her mother and sister, coiffed to perfection, would head for the nearest spa for mother-daughter pedicures.

Lane slowed her pace, then stopped altogether, bending to pluck a small shell from the sand. She turned it over in her palm, ran a thumb over the soft pink striations. "Do you remember the time we all piled in the car and drove to Sanibel Island for vacation?"

Cynthia smiled crookedly. "Your father got sun poisoning."

"And you had to take me to the beach because he couldn't go outdoors."

"Had to take you?" Cynthia shielded her eyes as she regarded Lane. "Is that how you remember it?"

"You and Val were supposed to go souvenir shopping in town. Instead, you were stuck with me."

"We had fun that day," Cynthia said, her tone bordering on defensive. "Don't you remember? We built a sand castle and collected shells."

Lane ran her tongue over her lips, tasting salt. "You made me throw back the chipped ones."

Cynthia's brow scrunched. "What?"

"The shells. You made me throw back the ones that weren't perfect. You said no one wanted something that wasn't perfect, that only the perfect ones were worth keeping."

Something like wariness had crept into Cynthia's expression. "Laney—honey—where are you going with this?"

"Nowhere, really. It's just something that's always stuck with me. Being on the beach with you must've brought it back. Forget it."

"I was talking about shells, sweetheart. About collecting shells."

Lane shrugged and dropped the shell. *If you say so, but it felt like something else.* Dusting the sand from her fingers, she turned back toward the lighthouse and set out again at a brisk pace, leaving her mother to catch up.

As predicted, Cynthia had undone the first two buttons of her coat before they reached the halfway mark. By the time they reached the lighthouse, the coat was unbuttoned completely, flapping in the breeze as they picked their way out onto the rough boulders of the jetty.

Lane couldn't help feeling a pang of admiration. Her mother was almost sixty, and utterly out of her element, but she was doing her best to be a trouper as she moved cautiously toward the end of the jetty, pretending not to mind when the gulls began to screech and swarm. At least the tide was out, no slippery rocks, no spray to dodge.

"You really do this every morning?" she asked when they finally reached the end. "On purpose?"

Lane laughed as she fished a pair of bread-filled baggies from her jacket and handed one to her mother. "I do. It sets the pace for the day. And I think the gulls would be furious if I were to stop."

To demonstrate, Lane tossed up a handful of stale scraps. The gulls swooped greedily, squabbling among themselves for the bread bits as they scattered in the wind. After a few moments Cynthia opened her bag and followed Lane's lead. When the bread was gone Lane took her mother's bag and crumpled it, along with her own, into the pocket of her jacket.

"You belong here, Laney," Cynthia said quietly.

Lane turned to stare. "Where did that come from?"

A smile flitted across Cynthia's face. "When you told me you'd bought this place, way out in the wet wilds, I seriously thought you'd lost your mind, that you were just trying to get back at Bruce for . . . well, for everything. But now, seeing you, I realize you were right. You seem . . . happy. And now with Michael—"

Lane felt her shoulders sag. For a moment she'd actually thought her mother was going to give her credit for something. Instead, it had to do with a man.

"I was happy before Michael, Mother. I had a perfectly good life, all on my own."

"Yes, of course you did, but now—"

Lane closed her eyes, tipped her face to the sun, and counted to ten. *Yes, of course. Now there's Michael—or at least you think there is—so everything's fine. As long as I'm perfect and he doesn't throw me back.*

Chapter 30

L ane checked her reflection in the bathroom mirror. Out of her
T-shirt and sweats, with her eyes made up and her hair blown
out, she looked startlingly like her mother, fine-boned and delicately pale. Val was like their father, with strong, dark features that
bordered on the exotic. Ironic that they should each resemble the
parent with whom they had the least in common, an inexplicable
prank of Mother Nature.

God help her. One day into her mother's visit and already she was
exhausted. Some part of her, the grown-up part, knew she was being
unfair, dissecting every word and look, ready to pounce at the slightest hint of disapproval. But old habits died hard—for both of them,
it seemed. Her mother was trying at least, attempting to bridge the
distance that had always existed between them. But some chasms
were simply too wide to cross.

Sighing, Lane applied a second coat of mascara and girded her
loins for lunch with her mother. On the way downstairs she took a
moment to look for Dally, following the butchered version of "I Feel
Like a Woman" bleeding out into the hall from Michael's room. She
was just putting the finishing touches on the bed when Lane tapped
her on the shoulder.

Dally yanked out her earbuds, eyes wide as she took in Lane's transformation. "You look amazing! Date with Professor McDreamy?"

Lane made a face. "Lunch with my mother."

"You still look great. You should dress up more often."

"For who?" Lane held up a hand before Dally could open her mouth. "Never mind. Don't answer that. Listen, I need you to do me a favor, and I need you to not ask me why. I don't have time to explain right now."

Dally's eyes lit up. "Sounds like more tabloid fodder."

Lane shot a quick look out into the hall to make sure her mother's door was still closed. "You know the old woman who rides around town on that old bike?"

"You mean Dirty Mary?"

"Her name is Mary," Lane replied evenly. "And yes, that's who I mean."

"What about her?"

"Well, she's sort of a friend. Only I haven't seen her for a few days. I'm worried something might have happened to her."

"A friend of . . . yours?"

Lane could already see the wheels turning behind Dally's narrowed gaze. "Look, I know it sounds weird, but I really don't have time to explain. I just need you to keep an eye out for her. Let me know if you see her around town."

Dally shrugged, part agreement, part confusion. "No problem. But don't think I'm letting you off the hook about this. I want to know how you got to be friends with a bag lady."

"Please don't call her that."

Dally shrugged again. "Sure. Sorry. I didn't mean to—"

"Forget it," Lane said, giving her arm a squeeze. "And thanks for not asking questions."

Dally flashed one of her wicked grins as Lane headed for the door. "Oh, you can bet I'll be asking plenty of questions. Just not now."

Downstairs, she found Michael at work in the den, tapping manically on his laptop keyboard. Stepping behind him, she waited for him to finish his current sentence, reading silently over his shoulder. Finally, he turned. His eyes moved over her very slowly.

"Wow, you look...nice."

Lane tried to ignore the pleasant tingle in her cheeks. "I'm taking my mother into the village. I thought we'd hit the Historical Society before lunch, then maybe do some shopping. I just wanted to let you know we'd be out. There's leftover chicken in the fridge if you get hungry."

She was about to step away when Michael took her hand and pulled her back. "What, no kiss?"

Lane took a deep breath and let it out. "I'm sorry about all this. Really. You must think I'm some kind of nut."

Michael's grin warmed into something else, something that made her heart beat faster. "I think nothing of the sort. And even if you were some kind of a nut, what do I care, as long as I get to keep kissing you? It's not exactly a hardship, you know."

Lane stared down at their fingers, loosely twined. "For me, either," she said quietly. When the silence began to stretch, she cleared her throat. "Well, I guess I'd better be off. Oh, I meant to ask, what are your parents' names?"

Michael frowned. "Matthew and Katherine. Why?"

"Because it's likely to come up at lunch."

"Ah, right. Then you'd also better know that my brother is Matt Jr., and my sister is Liz, short for Elizabeth. Matt's an attorney. Liz is an attorney's wife. She and her husband have two children—Brandon and Rhiann—and a pair of springer spaniels. I'm sorry. I don't know the dogs' names."

Lane's shoulders sagged miserably. "God, this really is insane, isn't it?"

"Oh, I don't know," Michael said huskily. "I'm beginning to enjoy playing house."

He kissed her then, without a word of warning, a casual brushing of lips as he pulled her down into his lap. The kiss that followed was more thorough, deep and deliciously slow, turning her bones and her senses to liquid, until she could no longer tell where the lie began and the truth ended. Somewhere in her head a voice warned her that this was a mistake, a charade that could only lead to heartache. And yet—

The delicate clearing of a throat somewhere near the door shattered the moment. Lane slid off Michael's lap, hands darting to her mouth like a teenager caught making out in her mother's basement.

"Oh, excuse me, you two," Cynthia said, smiling conspiratorially. "I didn't mean to interrupt. I just wanted to let Laney know I was ready."

Lane cleared her throat, ran a hand over her hair. "I'm ready, too, Mother. I was just..." Her voice trailed awkwardly.

"Telling your man good-bye. Yes, I recognize it." She shot them both a wink. "I'll be in the parlor. Take your time."

Embarrassed, Lane turned to follow her mother. Before she could take a step, Michael recaptured her hand. "Have fun with your mother this afternoon."

Lane's eyes widened skeptically. "Fun?"

"She loves you, Lane."

Had she imagined the faintly reproving tone? "How do *you* know?"

"Because she's here. That says something. Quite a lot, in fact."

"You don't understand. You couldn't. It's a terrible thing to always be at war with the woman who brought you into the world, to at times wonder if you even...like her."

Michael held her eyes for a long moment. "I understand more than you think," he said finally. "Go on now. And remember what I said."

"Yes, all right. I'll have fun."

She hesitated briefly before turning away, puzzled by the sudden change in his voice, and by the grave, faraway look that now shadowed his eyes. It was on the tip of her tongue to ask what had put it there, but she decided to let it go. Something told her she wasn't likely to get a straight answer.

The scarred honey-pine floorboards creaked noisily as Lane and Cynthia entered the dimly lit anteroom of the Starry Point Historical Society. The attendant, a middle-aged woman in an ill-fitting navy suit, offered them a smile but made no move to get up from her desk at the back of the large, open room. Lane smiled back, then folded a five-dollar bill into the donation box just inside the door.

The atmosphere was somber and sepia-toned, the air heavy with the scent of beeswax. Lane moved to the first exhibit, a tribute to Starry Point Light, finished in 1872, featuring photographs and a sort of time-lapse tableau of the light in various stages of construction. She had seen it before but lingered while her mother read the captions beneath each photo.

"This is where we stood this morning," Cynthia said, pointing to the jetty in one of the earliest photographs. "On these same rocks."

"The very same," Lane said with a nod. "As you can see, we're very proud of our lighthouse. And of our dead whale."

Lane pointed out a rather gruesome black-and-white of a dead whale that had washed up back in 1928 and had made the front page of the *Islander Dispatch*. When she saw her mother's delicate shudder she moved on.

The next exhibit was a wall of images depicting damage done by various hurricanes over the years. The pictures were sobering, dating back to the 1933 Outer Banks hurricane that killed twenty-one people. The collection progressed through more recent storms like Irene and Sandy, all of which had left their mark on the vulnerable Carolina coastline: homes listing into the sea or washed completely off their pilings, fishing boats stranded in backyards, streets waist-deep in water, Highway 12, lifeline to the mainland, warped like a ribbon of shiny black licorice.

Cynthia studied the collection in horrified fascination, a hand pressed to her throat. "Laney, this is terrible. Doesn't it worry you to live in a place where these kinds of things happen all the time?"

"Storms like these don't happen all the time, Mother. These are the worst of the worst, and they span nearly a century. Most of the storms we get are nothing like this. In fact, we just had one, and the damage was pretty minimal, more of a nuisance for most of us than anything."

Cynthia looked dubious as she wandered away from the photographic wreckage, clearly more at ease with images of Starry Point's historical landmarks. "Oh, look," she said, pointing. "Here's your inn, Laney, back when it was still a convent, I think. And isn't this the house just across the street?"

Lane came to stand beside her. "Yes, it is. It's called the Rourke House, after one of the mayors who used to live there."

"It says here that it burned, but you can't tell from the street. Or from this picture, either."

"Most of the damage is to the upper floor, at the back. A little boy died in the fire."

Cynthia's eyes closed briefly. "How awful. No one lives there now, though, do they? It looked abandoned to me."

"It's been empty since the fire."

"Such a shame. It's a beautiful house—or was. I wonder why they don't restore it."

Lane and Cynthia both started when the attendant spoke unexpectedly over their shoulders. "We've been trying to do just that for years. You're absolutely right. It should be restored, but there's always some kind of legal roadblock."

Lane was surprised. "I always assumed it had to do with the expense."

The woman in the navy suit shrugged. "Oh, there's that, too. But we believe we'd recoup that quick enough with a small tour fee. The locals believe it's haunted, you see, so over the years it's gotten quite the reputation. Attracts tourists like crazy."

It was Cynthia's turn to look surprised. "I didn't think anyone believed in ghosts anymore."

"Oh, they do. And this house has two—an old man who hanged himself after the crash, and that poor little boy who died in the fire. I was only a girl when it happened, but it was a sad day in Starry Point, I can tell you. The story's changed a lot over the years, but people claim to see things all the time."

Lane stared at the early image of the house, tidy and well kept in its day, and tried to imagine the parlor beyond its empty, eyelike windows, bright and warm, ringing with boyish laughter, but she couldn't. All she could see was the house as it stood now, hollowed out and gloomy, emptied of any joy that had ever existed within its old plaster walls.

Just thinking about it made her sad, and more than a little uneasy. Suddenly, she couldn't shake Michael's theory about houses having souls and collecting memories. It made sense when you thought about it, emotions leaving imprints on tangible things, scarring them.

All the good and the bad that's ever happened.

Suppressing a shiver, she tapped her mother's shoulder. "We'd better keep moving. It's about time for lunch."

Chapter 31

The Hot Spot was surprisingly busy for a Wednesday afternoon, humming with patrons sipping lattes and munching salads. The owner, Erin Kelley, a pretty blonde in her early thirties, waved to Lane from behind the coffee counter.

"Let me a get a table cleared," she called over the din. "It's been crazy all day."

Lane nodded, giving Erin a *no hurry* wave.

Erin was a transplant from New York. Burned out on city life and disillusioned with corporate America, she'd moved to Starry Point with a savings account and a dream. The locals thought she was crazy to consider opening an Internet café in a sleepy little beach town, but she'd soon proven her detractors wrong. The Hot Spot, with its light lunch fare and decadent coffee concoctions, had become an overnight success.

"Ah," boomed an oily voice from across the crowded café. "Lane Kramer, so good to see you on this fine afternoon."

Lane schooled her face into something like a smile as Harold Landon, Starry Point's three-term mayor, approached. "Hello, Mayor Landon."

"Now, now, I've told you, it's Harold." His car salesman smile was firmly in place, his too-dark hair slicked down to cover an expanding bald spot. "No need for formalities in our little town." He turned to Cynthia. The smile notched up a bit. "And who have we here? A sister visiting?"

Lane fought the urge to roll her eyes. "Actually, this is my mother . . . Cynthia Campbell White." She fumbled a bit over the last names, never sure which to include and which to leave out. "She's visiting from Chicago."

"Chicago," he repeated, pumping her hand. "Well, now, that's a long way off. Tell me, Cynthia, what do you think of our little seaside village?"

Cynthia looked slightly overwhelmed as she withdrew her hand. "I hardly know. I've only just arrived."

"Oh. Well, then. Make sure your daughter gives you the full tour. Starry Point may be small, but we've certainly got our share of local interests. Isn't that right, Chief?"

Lane's careful smile faltered when she saw Donny Breester, Starry Point's chief of police, on his way over. He arrived with his usual cloud of aftershave, tipping back his hat and letting his eyes run the length of her, slow and thorough. When his gaze finally returned to her face, it held the same unspoken question it always did. Lane's unspoken answer was the same, too—not today, not ever.

"Lane," he said coolly.

"Donny."

Landon seemed impervious to the sudden tension in the air. "Say, that reminds me. Donny tells me you called the police a few weeks back, something about a light you thought you saw in the old Rourke House."

Cynthia's head jerked in her daughter's direction. "*The* Rourke House?"

"Yes, *the* Rourke House. And I didn't just *think* I saw a light. I *saw* a light."

Breester was wiping his sunglasses with the tail of his jacket. "We checked the place out good and thorough," he assured the mayor. "No sign of anything."

Lane shot him a look of disbelief. "Good and thorough? Can they *be* good and thorough in five minutes?"

Scowling, Breester shifted his attention back to Landon. "We checked the door and all the lower windows. The top floor was still boarded up in back. No way anyone got inside."

The mayor turned a benign smile on Lane. "Don't feel bad. It's understandable. Everyone's on edge these days with all these break-ins. There was another one just last night, over at the Mott place—a bicycle, a computer, and a coffee can full of quarters."

"Break-ins?" Cynthia echoed, looking alarmed. "Laney, you never said a word about any break-ins."

Landon patted Cynthia's shoulder solicitously. "Your daughter probably didn't want to alarm you. But don't you worry. I feel fairly certain we've pinpointed the source of the problem. With any luck we'll have the entire matter cleaned up in a few weeks. Maybe sooner."

Cleaned up? Lane found the word choice rather odd. "Just what is it you propose to have cleaned up, if you don't mind me asking?"

"There's a halfway house over on the south end of the island, called Hope House. We're pretty sure that's where we'll find our culprit. We don't think it's a coincidence that the incidents have all occurred on the south side of the island."

"You've got witnesses?"

"No witnesses, but—"

"Fingerprints?"

"No, but—"

Lane fought to keep her voice even. "So you're just making assumptions?"

"We've been investigating," Breester put in. "Following up on several leads."

"What kind of leads?" Lane's voice was getting louder now, and she could feel her mother's eyes, bouncing from face to face in confusion.

"This is police business, Lane," Breester answered in his best *CSI* voice. "And at this time we're not prepared to make any statement that might jeopardize our investigation."

Lane pressed her lips together and counted to ten. If the conversation wasn't so disturbing, she'd have laughed in his face. As it was, all she could think about were the mayor's words.

Cleaned up. She was starting to get a very bad feeling.

Offering her back to Breester, she turned to the mayor, doing her best to appear nonconfrontational. "Mayor Landon, when you say you should have the matter *cleaned up* in a few weeks, what exactly are we talking about?"

"Well, it's not official, of course, but with any luck we hope to shut the place down."

Lane was momentarily stunned. "Shut down Hope House? When you just admitted you have no witnesses, no fingerprints, nothing to connect anyone to anything? Have you given any thought to the residents? What they'll do? Where they'll go?"

Breester snorted. "Why do you give a rat's ass about a bunch of schizos and needle freaks, people like that crazy old bag lady with the bike and the pink flag—Dirty Mary?"

"She is—" Lane broke off, aware of several heads turning in her direction. "She is *not* a bag lady." Once again, she felt her mother's eyes, intensely quizzical. She was going to have to explain about Mary. But not until she finished with the mayor. She turned to Cynthia with a tight smile. "Mother, why don't you grab that table by the window and look over the menu? I'll be there in a minute."

Cynthia's gaze slid assessingly from face to face, lingering on Breester. "Maybe I should stay."

Lane shook her head, then nodded toward the empty table,

where Erin stood motioning them over. "Go on. I'm almost finished here."

When Cynthia was out of earshot Lane narrowed in on Breester. "Don't you ever mention that despicable name in my presence again. In fact, I'd rather you didn't mention her at all. But if you must—perhaps in some form of apology—her name is Mary."

Breester opened his mouth to reply, but Landon gave him a subtle nudge before turning his attention to Lane. His smile was gone now, replaced with a distinctly unfriendly resolve. "Ms. Kramer, call the woman whatever you like. I really don't care. My job—my duty—is to keep the taxpayers of Starry Point safe, and I intend to see that duty through."

"Except you haven't got any kind of case against Hope House, or anyone living there."

"Be that as it may, I think we can all agree that a halfway house filled with those sorts of people has no business in this community. God knows where they come from, or what kinds of things they've done in their lives. For all we know some of them may be dangerous."

"I killed a boy once."

Did Landon know? Did Breester? Was that why they were so sure they could do what they wanted? And what about Mary and the other residents? Did they have any idea what Landon was up to? Or were they all about to get blindsided?

"This isn't fair," Lane said, so quietly that for a moment she wasn't certain she'd actually said it aloud. "You can't just shut a place down because you don't like the people who live there. You have to have evidence."

Breester gave her a hard stare. "Don't you worry about the evidence. We're on it."

Another quelling nudge from Landon.

Lane fixed Landon with an accusing stare. "What does that mean?"

All at once the oily smile was back in place, bland and infuriating.

"It means you should stop worrying about things that don't concern you, and leave them to those who are sworn to look out for Starry Point. Now, why don't you go enjoy your lunch? And be sure to tell your mother it was a pleasure meeting her."

Lane was still fuming as she slid into the seat across from her mother. She gulped down half of her ice water, then set the glass down hard.

Cynthia peered at her over the laminated menu. "So, are you ready to tell me what all that was about?"

"Not really, no."

Erin appeared with her order pad and a tentative smile. "Everything okay? You looked like you were ready to slit the mayor's throat with a butter knife."

Lane glanced at the coffee counter, where he and Breester stood waiting for their order, heads bents close. "I wish I'd thought of it," she said darkly. "But yes, everything's fine. Mother, do you know what you want?"

Erin disappeared with their orders, then returned momentarily with a lemonade and a Diet Coke. Cynthia stripped her straw from its wrapper and poked it into her glass. "All right, let's have it. What is Hope House, and who in God's name is . . . Dirty Mary?"

"It's just Mary, Mother. And she's a friend of mine, an old woman I met on the dunes one day. She's . . . eccentric, but harmless."

At least I hope she is. Please, please, let her be.

A pair of lines appeared between Cynthia's perfectly penciled brows. "How eccentric?"

"She's colorful. She rides around town on a rusty old bike and carries an old Crown Royal bag everywhere she goes."

Except now. Because I have it. Along with all her meds.

"And Hope House?"

Lane sighed. It was time to lay it all on the table. "It's the halfway house where she lives. It's for people with mental disorders."

Cynthia paused to sip her Diet Coke. "I see."

"Mother, please. I already know what you're going to say, and I've heard it all from Michael. But she's my friend. She's kind and sweet, and wise in a peculiar sort of way. And I'm afraid she's in trouble."

"Because the mayor wants to close down this halfway house?"

Lane waited for Erin to drop off their salads and retreat before going on. "It's not just that. She's kind of disappeared. We had a bit of a spat the other day—it was my fault—and I haven't seen her since. She's usually on the dunes behind the inn every morning, but it's been three days since I've seen her. And the worst part is I have all her pills."

Cynthia looked up, halted in the act of spearing a cherry tomato. "Pills?"

"She takes a lot of pills, yes. And I have them."

"Are you sure she's harmless?"

Lane toyed with her straw, not sure she should tell the rest of Mary's story. Hard to, really, when she didn't even know all of it. In the end she decided to leave well enough alone. "Yes, Mother. I'm sure."

"But Michael doesn't like Mary?"

"No. Well, actually, he's never even met her. But he's got a problem with people like her, something he won't talk about. He thinks I'm letting myself in for trouble by getting involved with her."

"And are you?"

Lane stared at her lemonade glass, tracing a finger around its rim. "Of course not."

They ate in silence for a while, Lane mostly pushing her food around her plate. The run-in with Landon still had her on edge. Finally, she glanced up, meeting her mother's eyes.

"Thanks for not giving me a hard time about Mary. I expected you to, but you didn't."

Cynthia sighed and pushed back her plate. "You were always your father's daughter, Laney, always softhearted like he was. When you were little you were always collecting strays. Apparently you still are. So I'll tell you the same thing I did when you were little, and trust you to know best—just be careful you don't get scratched."

"Because wild things can hurt you when they're scared," Lane finished for her. "Yes, I know." It was pretty much what Michael had been telling her, but somehow she'd expected worse from her mother, a lecture, even a tirade—certainly not this gentle parental warning. "As I recall, you were never very fond of strays."

Cynthia winced as if she'd suddenly suffered a pain of some sort. "That isn't true, Laney. I just know it can get messy if you let yourself get too close. I saw it happen to your father—all because he got involved with a woman."

Woman?

Her mother must have seen the look on her face. She put down her fork, shaking her head emphatically. "No, no, not like that. She was like your Mary. She just showed up one day, pushing a shopping cart full of junk and talking to herself. She made me uncomfortable, made everyone uncomfortable—but not your father. He'd give her money, buy her food. Once he bought her a coat."

She paused, eyes fluttering closed, as if the pain had suddenly returned. "It was such a cold winter that year. One day your father decided he was going to find her a place to stay. I dug my heels in. I told him he'd done enough, that he wasn't responsible for her. It turned into an argument, an ugly one, but I eventually got him to give up the idea. A few days later he came home from work looking awful and told me she had died. Exposure, the police said. He was devastated. So was I. I talked him into ignoring his conscience, and because of it a woman was dead. How on earth could I lecture you for doing what I failed to?"

Lane stole a hand to her mother's, squeezing gently. For a woman who prided herself on hiding her emotions, it couldn't have been an easy thing to tell. Nor was it an easy thing to respond to.

"I've never heard that story," she said softly. "I'm sorry."

"Well, it's not exactly something I'm proud of. Maybe that's why I like the idea of you befriending this poor woman. Because I didn't and I wish I had. And because it reminds me of your father. Just be careful. That's all I'm saying."

"I'll be careful, Mother." Lane pushed away her barely eaten lunch and forced a smile, eager to change the subject. "If you're through, I thought we could hit some of Starry Point's finer shops and boutiques."

Cynthia closed her eyes, pinching the bridge of her nose in a gesture Lane recognized all too well. Her mother's migraines had been a regular part of life growing up, sometimes lasting for days at a time, forcing her to hibernate in a dark room with hot tea and a cold cloth. Now, at least, she had medications that helped, but they didn't always work if she waited too long.

"Actually, I think I feel one of my headaches coming on. Would you mind very much if we went back to the inn for a bit so I could lie down and close my eyes?"

"Of course I wouldn't mind. Do you have your pills?"

"Yes, but not with me. Oh, I'm sorry to ruin the day. You had it all planned out."

Sliding her purse off her chair, Lane stood. "Don't be silly. There'll be plenty of time to shop tomorrow. Let's get you home before it gets any worse."

Lane had just started the car when her cell went off. When she saw Dally's number pop up she answered immediately. "Hey, what's up?"

"Your friend—the one you asked me to keep an eye out for?"

"Mary," Lane supplied, and felt her mother's eyes shift in her direction.

"I think I found her."

"Found her? Where is she? Is she all right?"

"Not really, no. I'm at the park with Skye and I'm pretty sure I just saw the police take her away in a squad car."

Lane smacked the steering wheel soundly. "Damn it! This has Landon's fingerprints all over it. And Breester's."

"Mayor Landon? What's he got to do with anything?"

"I'll explain later. Right now I've got to go."

"Yeah, I thought you might. Just try not to get yourself arrested while you're doing whatever it is you're about to do, okay?"

"I can't guarantee anything, but thanks."

Lane ended the call and turned to Cynthia, who was eyeing her expectantly. "The police have her. They picked her up in the park."

"She's been arrested? What for?"

"I don't know."

"We'd better get to the police station, then."

"Oh no," Lane said, as she slipped the car into reverse. "I'm taking you home first, to lie down. Besides, I'm pretty sure you won't like the language I'll be using when I get to the station."

Chapter 32

Mary

They've taken me. I suppose I knew they would one day, but it's not like before, not like those other places. There are no White Coats here, no square-jawed nurses lurking with their sharp eyes and soundless shoes, no random screams ringing in the halls. And yet it isn't altogether different.

The room they've put me in is small and stark—all curling linoleum and naked white lights, familiar in a way that makes me queasy. Something to do with the smell of the place, I expect—coffee and anxiety, mixed with disinfectant. I heard the cold scrape of the lock when they left me, an echo of old nightmares. *You're here,* it said mockingly, *for as long as it pleases them to keep you.*

Sweet mother of God, my insides clench to think they might actually keep me here.

Confinement.

It's the nice word for locked up, a pretty word they liked to use at the hospital. But then, there are so many pretty words for the grisly things in life, words meant to sound like something else, sanitized of their awkward, uncomfortable truths. *Melancholia* is another of those words, like music with all its small, fragile syllables, or the name of a flower one might pluck from a country garden. Not a hint of grief in it. No misery. No sorrow. Sorrow and grief are unseemly, you see, and terribly inconvenient for those who must witness the suffering—and we mustn't be inconvenient.

The urge to laugh is suddenly overwhelming, bubbling up into my throat—from where I do not know—until I fear it will choke me. Hysteria, I believe they call it. There, you see, another flowery name; this one meant to pretty up good old-fashioned panic. But there's nothing pretty about it. I see that plainly as I catch a glimpse of my reflection in the small plate-glass window, a blind window that looks out on nothing at all. There are eyes behind it. I feel them watching. Or maybe they're not. Maybe that was before. I can't be sure. Suddenly, terribly, it's as if time has rewound itself, has wrenched me back to where it all began. Or perhaps I should say where it all ended.

I watch the black-and-white clock above the door, the agonizing sweep of its bloodred second hand, and wait for something to happen. I'm aware of a slow, creeping numbness, an insidious blurring of the then and the now, as if my past and present have somehow overlapped. It's how my life is defined, you see, before my confinement and after—then and now. Is this to be a new beginning, then—the start of a new *confinement*? When I've done nothing wrong? I stare a moment at my hands, quiet in my lap, harmless now after so many years of penance and confession. I haven't done anything wrong, have I—nothing new, I mean?

I wish I could be sure.

When the lock turns again I look up. There are two of them staring at me, their eyes full of pity, and something else I don't like the look of. I know what they're like, these hard men with their soft eyes, always dredging up the wreckage and making you look at it, all the bits of your life that have washed up on the rocks, shattered almost beyond recognition. And then they tell you it's your fault, again and again, until you *almost* believe them. Only it isn't true.

It isn't *real*.

But no one will listen. Then, after a while, you stop telling them. You let them believe what they want, and you let them think you believe it, too—even when you don't, and never will.

Chapter 33

Lane

As Lane pulled into the parking lot of the Starry Point Police Department, she found herself almost wishing she'd taken Michael up on his offer to accompany her. Given his feeling about Mary, the offer had both pleased and surprised her, but in the end she'd decided to go alone. As it was, Mary was leery of strangers, and Michael might not be seen as a friendly face. Come to that, she wasn't sure after the way things had ended the other day that Mary would want anything to do with her.

The station was stifling, the air thick with coffee and stale cigarette smoke. The desk sergeant, a stringy young man who couldn't have been more than twenty, glanced at her over his glasses as she moved in his direction, a half-eaten hot dog forgotten at his elbow.

"Afternoon, ma'am. Something I can do for you?"

Lane scanned the lobby, relieved to find it empty. "Mary..." Her voice trailed off as she realized with a pang of shame that she didn't know the woman's last name. "I'm here for Mary."

"The bag lady?"

"Her name is Mary," Lane corrected, for what seemed like the tenth time that day. "And I'd like to know why she's been brought here."

The sergeant peered at her timidly. "Your name, ma'am?"

"Lane Kramer. And I'd like an answer to my question, please."

He clearly had no intention of answering. Instead, he indicated a wall lined with chairs covered in tattered red vinyl. "If you'll just have a seat, Ms. Kramer—"

"Look . . ." She paused long enough to search out his name badge. "Sergeant Matthews, let's not play games. A friend saw you pick her up in one of your squad cars. I know she's here, and I want to know why."

"Are you a family member?"

For a moment she thought about lying but shook her head. "I'm a friend."

"In that case I'm afraid I can't help you."

He sounded polite enough, but there was something in his tone that suggested he was enjoying himself just a little. "You can't or you won't?"

Matthews pushed his glasses back up his nose, his baby-smooth face carefully bland. "The rules state—"

Lane threw up a hand, cutting him off. She didn't care about the rules, except for the one that said you couldn't just drag an old woman in for questioning because you felt like it, especially one with a history of mental illness. "Has she been charged with anything?"

Matthews's eyes slid away.

Lane rapped her knuckles on the desk. "Of course she hasn't. Because she hasn't done anything wrong!"

"Your *friend* is a person of interest, Ms. Kramer."

"Person of interest? In what, exactly?"

"In the recent rash of break-ins."

"That's ridiculous! They haven't got a scrap of evidence."

"They're just asking her some questions."

"And before they started asking questions, I don't suppose she was offered a lawyer, by any chance?"

"No need for a lawyer if she hasn't been arrested. It's just routine."

"It's harassment!" Lane shot back. "Of a woman with a history of mental illness!"

"Ma'am, please. I'm going to have to ask you to lower your voice or leave."

"I want to talk to Donny Breester."

"Chief Breester is tied up at the moment."

"Interrupt him."

"Ma'am, I really can't do that."

Lane leaned over the desk until she was eye-to-eye with Sergeant Matthews. "Get him out here now, or I'll go back there and find him myself."

Matthews scowled back at her but eventually turned away, disappearing down a narrow hallway. A few moments later Breester appeared, looking smug and vaguely annoyed.

"Well, well. Twice in one day. To what do I owe the pleasure?"

"I've come to take Mary home."

"Mary?"

"The woman you picked up in the park, and are holding for no damn reason."

Breester folded his arms. "We've had several reports of her being seen in the general area where the burglaries took place."

Lane's eyes widened at the absurdity of his assertion. "Of course she's been seen in the general area. She *lives* in the general area! Just what did you think you were going to accomplish with this little interrogation of yours?"

"Who said anything about interrogation? We're simply gathering information about her, and her, uh . . . friends."

"Do you intend to charge her with anything?"

Breester's smile was thin and indulgent. "I believe we've already had this conversation, Lane. Police business is police business."

"And harassment is a lawyer's business, Donny. Has she been read her rights? Was she offered an attorney before she started answering your questions? For that matter, does she even know why she's here?"

"I'm not treating her differently than I would any other criminal in my custody."

"Except she's *not* a criminal!" Lane fired back. "And if you haven't arrested her, she isn't actually in your custody. You've got no right to do what you're doing, and you damn well know it. So, either you charge her with something or you let her go." She paused then, lifting her chin a notch. "Unless, of course, you'd rather explain it all to an attorney?"

Breester's smile was lazy, insolent. "You're telling me that woman—that bag lady—has a lawyer?"

Lane fought to keep her voice even. "I'm telling you she has a friend with one. And I'll be only too happy to get him down here."

Breester glared at her while the seconds ticked by, clearly weighing his options. Finally, he glanced at Matthews, who was doing his best to appear invisible. "Tell Deacon I said to turn the old bat loose." He shot Lane a glance before turning away. "For now."

Lane was actually shaking as she and Mary left the station. She filled her lungs with cold air, then exhaled slowly, willing her hands to steady as she helped Mary into the car and fastened her seat belt. She'd never been good with confrontation, especially when she wasn't sure she had a leg to stand on—like today, when she'd bluffed her way out of the police station with a visibly rattled Mary in tow. She knew nothing about the law and, apart from her divorce lawyer back in Chicago, didn't even know the *name* of an attorney, let alone have one on call. Still, she'd pulled it off, winning the battle if not the war. But the worst lay ahead, and it was time Mary knew it.

Rather than starting the engine, Lane reached into her purse and pulled out Mary's purple bag of pills, placing it on the seat between them, a poignant reminder of their quarrel. "Mary, I know you've been through a lot today, and that you're probably still mad at me about the other day, but we need to talk."

Mary's head came around with agonizing slowness. She said nothing, just fixed Lane with a queer, empty-eyed stare.

"Mary... do you know who I am?"

"You're the Inn Lady," she said, with a childlike vacancy in her eyes. "You're Lane."

Lane was relieved to find Mary still tethered to reality, if only loosely. It was clear the day's encounter with the police had left her more than a little rattled. Had they been rough with her? Badgered her into talking about her past—about the boy? Discreetly, she peered down at Mary's hands, searching for traces of ink, but found none. She hadn't been fingerprinted, then. Thank God for that. But if they had, what would they have discovered? A charge of murder? Manslaughter? She shuddered to think what Landon and Breester would do with that sort of information, and how quickly they would use it to their advantage.

"Yes, I'm Lane," she said finally. "And before I say anything else, I want to say I'm sorry about the other day, when I pressed you about... about what you told me. Do you remember that?"

The wide, staring eyes closed briefly. "I remember."

"You don't have to worry. I'm not asking you to talk about that. In fact, after today I promise I won't ever press you to talk about anything you don't want to. But right now there are things you need to know about Hope House... and the police. They want to close it, Mary."

Mary's eyes narrowed, sharp and suddenly lucid. "Why?"

"They think—or they're pretending to think—that the break-ins are connected to someone who lives there."

A long, slow blink. "To me?"

Lane shrugged. "That's the thing. I don't think they care, really. As long as they can pin it on someone, and look good doing it."

"It's the mayor, isn't it? It's Landon?"

"Mostly, yes. How did you know?"

"His wife's been hanging about the last few weeks. Volunteering, she calls it, though I've never seen her peel the first potato. Asks a lot of questions about who's in charge, where the money comes from to run the place, that sort of thing. She hasn't gotten far, I don't think, since no one seems to know. She's been asking about us, too, wanting to know everyone's story. No one tells her anything, of course. It's against house rules."

"I know you said no one seems to know, but, Mary, I've got to speak with whoever oversees Hope House, and let them know what's happening. They can't stop it if they don't know what Landon's up to. Now think hard. Are you certain you've never heard a name mentioned, or a trust maybe?"

Mary shook her head. "There was a Gwen someone or other who set it all up for me. She was just a social worker, though. Nothing to do with Hope House. Can they do it, do you think? Shut it down?"

"I don't know. I just know they're going to try. And the police chief's in on it, too."

"Breester. He's Landon's man, that one. Does as he's told."

Lane was surprised by Mary's keen assessment of the situation, from the hidden agenda of the mayor's nosy wife to the role of Landon's feckless henchman. But there was something else behind those suddenly shrewd eyes, a grim understanding of what Hope House's demise would mean for her, and for her friends.

"I'm sorry, Mary, to be the one to tell you this. But I thought you should know."

Mary's lids slid closed, her head lolling against the headrest as if she'd suddenly grown very tired. "They'll have no place to go. No one to feed them, or make them take their pills. They'll slip back, get sick again. And then they'll be sent back to wherever they came from— back to the White Coats."

She was talking about herself, of course, contemplating the loss of her freedom, perhaps even her sanity, because some small-town mayor and his sidekick had painted a bull's-eye on the place she called home.

"We're not going to let them get away with this, Mary," Lane vowed fiercely as she turned the key in the ignition and slipped the car into reverse. "We're going to fight them—the mayor, Breester, all of them. We'll fight them, and we'll win."

Mary's eyes dragged open slowly, empty again, and so very sad. "How?"

"I haven't figured that part out yet, but I will. In the meantime, I think we should keep this between us until I figure out who I need to talk to. Right now we're going to the park to pick up your bike, and then I'm taking you home."

Michael was waiting at the door when Lane walked in, a pen behind his ear, his face full of questions. He took her keys and the stack of mail she was holding and placed them on the foyer table, then helped her off with her coat.

"Well?" he prompted, when the coat was finally hanging on the rack and she still hadn't volunteered any news.

Lane wasn't sure she was ready to rehash it all, especially with someone who wasn't likely to see her side. Groaning, she kicked off her shoes, crossed the parlor, and sagged onto the couch.

"I just dropped her off at Hope House. They actually had her in a room when I got there, grilling her about the break-ins. I had to threaten to call my lawyer before they'd let her go."

Michael snorted. "They think she's behind the break-ins?"

"No. They just want it to look like they do. I ran into Landon earlier today. He informed me, quite proudly, too, that he plans to close Hope House, and means to use the break-ins to do it, even though they haven't got a shred of evidence against anyone living there."

"You think he hauled Mary in for questioning just to make it look good?"

"Something like that, yes. She also told me the mayor's wife is pretending to volunteer while she pumps everyone for information."

"Sounds like the man means business."

"Yes, it does. And I have to figure out a way to stop him."

"Lane, I know how you feel about this, but have you considered that getting mixed up in a local skirmish like this might be bad for business? We're talking about the mayor and the chief of police. I'm not saying what they want to do is right. It's not. But the deck is sort of stacked against you. These are powerful people you're talking about, at least here in Starry Point."

Lane sighed. She found Michael's advice exasperating, probably because she'd been rolling something similar around in her head since she dropped Mary off at Hope House. It wasn't like her to stick her neck out, to stir the pot and risk any kind of fallout. Yet here she was, ready to take on the world for a woman she barely knew.

No. That wasn't true. She did know Mary, or at least knew her well enough to know she was in desperate need of a friend. Maybe it was the haunted look in those sea-colored eyes of hers, as if she'd lost some part of herself along the way and didn't know how to get it back. Lane had seen that look before—in her own mirror. Broken. Empty. Lost.

She knew what it was like to feel lost in your own skin, to sift through your todays and find no trace of your yesterdays, to know life had shaken you so hard that parts of you had simply fallen away. Mary's circumstances might have been different, but the end result was the same. She was alone and adrift, defenseless in a world bent on mowing her down. Michael didn't understand, but that didn't matter. Mary needed a friend, and she planned on being that friend.

"I hear what you're saying, Michael, but someone's got to fight for her, and at the moment I seem to be all she has. This is a witch hunt, and nothing more. In fact, I'd lay odds that the mayor has plans for the land Hope House is sitting on. I saw it for myself when I dropped Mary off. It's a prime stretch of sound, much too picturesque to waste on a bunch of schizos and needle freaks."

Michael stared at her, clearly stunned by her unsavory description.

Lane waved the look away. "Those are Breester's words, not mine. It's how he characterizes the residents of Hope House. I swear, I nearly smacked him."

Michael eased down beside her, his face somber. "Lane, you need to be very careful about what you're implying. You've got no proof of anything like that."

"Apparently proof doesn't matter. If Landon can imply that Mary's some sort of criminal, why can't I imply that he's using his office for personal gain?"

"Because you could end up in court for slander, or worse."

Lane huffed out a fresh wave of frustration as she let her head sag against the cushions. "God, I'm exhausted. Until today I had no idea how much energy it takes *not* to poke someone in the nose. And poor Mary. You should have seen her, Michael, like she'd just been shaken out of a nightmare. She had no idea why she was even there. And then, when I told her what Landon wanted to do—" Her words dangled when Michael's hand closed over hers.

"You have a great big heart, Lane Kramer. It's my favorite thing about you."

Surprised, Lane lolled her head in his direction. "You have a favorite thing about me?"

"Several, actually."

The words sent a pleasant surge of heat into her cheeks, as did the sparks smoldering in his slate gray eyes. Except none of it was real. He was leaving in a few months. She needed to remember that. She cleared her throat, extricated her hand.

"Yes, well, my great big heart better come up with a plan, and fast. Right now, though, I'm too wrung out to think past grabbing something to eat and falling into bed." Her eyes widened suddenly. "My mother . . . my God, I forgot she was even here."

"Relax," Michael said before she could bolt off the couch. "She's still lying down. I brought her some tea and soup on a tray. She didn't look like she'd be up to having company any time soon. Dare I ask what you did to your mother to bring on a splitting headache?"

"Oh, ha-ha," Lane shot back darkly. "It's a migraine. She gets them all the time. Even when I'm not around."

"Well, then, I suppose you're off the hook. Did you at least have a little fun?"

"I took her to the Historical Society. She seemed to enjoy it, though I'm sure she would have enjoyed bridal shopping more."

"You didn't set a wedding date, by any chance, did you? Because I'll need to let my family know."

Lane grinned, then lowered her voice. "You've got no one but yourself to blame for this little charade, mister. But don't worry. I'll wait a few months, then call her with the teary details of our tragic breakup."

Michael feigned a scowl. "And whose fault will *that* be?"

"Oh, mine, of course. I won't have any trouble selling that. As far as my mother's concerned, it's always my fault. Seriously, though, thanks for looking after her while I dealt with Mary. It really was above and beyond the call of duty."

"Shucks, ma'am. Any boyfriend worth his salt would've done the same. Now, you said something about food. Didn't I see a little pizza joint down the road?"

Lane shot him a grateful look. "Carmine's. There's a magnet on the fridge if you don't mind calling while I hop in the shower. I need to scrub off the police station residue. Anything but anchovies works for me."

Feeling wearier than she had felt in a very long time, she dragged herself up the stairs, dimly aware of Michael's voice in the kitchen as he ordered the pizza. In her sitting room, she scooped a scrap of paper from the floor—a note in Dally's loopy script, scribbled on the back of a grocery store receipt and slipped under her door.

Call me. Dying to know what happened with the police. Enjoy Turkey Day with your mom and Professor McDreamy!

Lane crumpled the note and tossed it in the wastebasket, then stripped out of her clothes. There was no point in denying it. Michael *was* rather dreamy, although admitting it while stripped to the skin and waiting for the shower to warm up was unsettling in the extreme. Almost as unsettling as admitting how comfortable she was becoming with this little game of house they were playing. But then, it had been an unsettling sort of day.

Chapter 34

Michael

Michael balanced the pizza box with one hand and led Lane along the boardwalk with the other, out to the blanket he had scavenged from his room and neatly spread on the sand. Pizza and beer on the beach; he wasn't sure where the idea had come from, or what Lane would think of it, but after the day she'd had, it felt like exactly what she needed.

The fire was crackling nicely now, sending up a plume of fragrant smoke into the evening air. He hadn't built a bonfire since he was a boy, but he'd been surprised at how easily it came back to him—a sandpit and a bit of driftwood, a little crumpled newspaper. It had been legal then. He had no idea what the law said now, but he strongly suspected he was on the wrong side of it. He didn't care.

"When in the world did you do all this?" Lane said, wide-eyed.

Michael knelt with the pizza box and motioned for Lane to do the same with the beer. "While you were in the shower and I was waiting for the pizza. But we need to hurry up and eat it before it gets cold and the cheese congeals."

He divvied up the slices—sausage and mushroom—then opened two beers, handing one to Lane. Lifting his bottle, he offered a toast. "To leaving the day behind."

"Now, *that* I will definitely toast to."

They ate in silence at first, tossing their crusts into the rapidly emptying box. Michael wasn't sure what to talk about but knew to steer clear of Mary and Starry Point's mayor. Finally, it was Lane who broke the ice.

"This is certainly unexpected, sitting out here with a fire, eating pizza."

"When I was a kid we used to roast hot dogs on sticks. Well, charred was more like it. They were usually gritty with sand and raw in the middle, but we thought they were delicious. There was this kid—Smitty Barco was his name—always had a few bucks in his pockets. He was the one who got the hot dogs. He was also the one who taught me to build a decent bonfire. He explained that it was all about the wood. Has to be good and dry or all you'll get is smoke."

Lane grinned as she took a swallow of beer. "Was this at yachting camp?"

Michael tossed another crust into the box, then glanced away. "Yeah, it was while I was at camp."

"It's hard to picture you as a boy, maybe because you're so tall. What about your family?"

"You mean are they tall? Not especially, no."

Lane laughed. "That isn't what I meant. I meant, tell me something about them."

"What do you want to know?"

She shrugged. "I don't know. Anything. Tell me about your brother—Matt, I think you said his name was. You never talk about him. Or your sister, either. Were the three of you close growing up?"

"Close?" Michael shook his head. "No. I wouldn't say we're close. We love each other in our own way, I suppose. We send Christmas cards and call on birthdays, that sort of thing. But we're not part of each other's lives the way most families are. Liz has a fun side, always been a bit of a prankster. My brother, on the other hand, is a carbon copy of our father."

"You don't get along?"

"Let's just say we give each other plenty of space."

"I'm sorry."

"Don't be. We're just different people. We have been since day one. But then, I've never quite fit with any of them. I guess Liz and I are the most alike, but when you scratch the surface she's a Forrester through and through."

"That's an odd thing to say. You're not?"

He glanced at the flames, orange and red against the indigo horizon, and felt his shoulders tighten instinctively. "No," he answered finally, wondering what she would make of that, wondering, too, why he was suddenly feeling so nostalgic. That other time, that other life, was in the past, and that was precisely where it needed to stay. What possible good could come of exhuming it now? Of reliving his failings, rehashing the guilt? Scars were forever, whether they were your fault or not. And his were.

Turning his empty bottle over into the beer bucket, he grabbed another. She'd been poking around in his emotional baggage. Now it was his turn. "Can I ask you something? Something personal?"

There was a flicker of hesitation in her face, but finally she nodded.

"You told me once that you didn't write important things. My question is, why? And let's skip over the stuff about your husband and his professor friend. You're not married to Bruce now. So, what's stopping you?"

Suddenly, her eyes were everywhere but on his. "You know as well as I do that that kind of writing takes time, something I haven't got a lot of most of the year."

"And you know as well as I do that that's just an excuse."

Lane's expression in the firelight was a mix of hurt and surprise. "That's what you think? That I'm just making excuses?"

"Okay, I put that badly. I think what I'm trying to say is that you always seem like you're in retreat mode, like you're—I don't know—hiding."

"Retreat mode?" She bristled visibly now. "And what is it I'm supposed to be retreating from? Enlighten me."

"Life."

"That isn't true."

"Isn't it? You moved all the way to Starry Point, a place with one road in and one road out, just to get away from your husband. Then you bought yourself a castle where you can hide from the real world and live vicariously through your guests."

For a moment she looked as if he'd slapped her. "That isn't fair. The inn is—"

"Lane." He placed a hand on her arm, hoping to soften what he was about to say. "The drawing on your refrigerator was done by someone else's kid. You invented a boyfriend out of thin air rather than tell your mother to stay out of your love life. And instead of following your passion, instead of writing something important, as you call it, you write articles about places you've never been and things you've never done."

Before the words were even out of his mouth, he knew he'd gone too far—again. It was a pattern he'd developed since meeting her, a Jekyll-and-Hyde thing that seemed to bring out his inner jackass. What she chose to write was none of his business. He knew that. Just as he knew it was none of his business how she chose to live her life. And yet he couldn't seem to help himself.

It was the waste that bothered him. She had so much to offer the world. Instead, she chose to hide. But there was more to it than that, he knew, similarities he'd rather not examine at the moment, coupled with feelings he'd also rather not examine. To look at them now, to acknowledge them as real, was pointless, and probably dangerous as well. No, he needed to keep this professional, to focus on her writing potential and nothing more.

Keeping it professional, however, was easier said than done when he glanced over at her, her face lovely in the firelight, despite her anger. "I'm sorry. I didn't mean to sound harsh."

"What about judgmental?" she asked sullenly. "Did you mean to sound judgmental?"

"No. But I did, and I'm sorry. Look, I'm not saying there's anything wrong with the choices you've made. If your life is the way it is because that's how you want it, fine. But if it isn't, if you're making excuses and settling just to stay safe, then maybe you need to rethink things. You've got talent, Lane, real talent, but no one's ever going to know if you keep playing it safe. That's all I meant."

She sighed, a sound full of resignation. "It's too late to start now. I've got the inn."

"That's another excuse. Tell me what you'd write if you knew you'd be successful."

She looked up from the fire, her answer immediate. "I'd write books about women. Real women, with real problems—messy ones—who eventually figure it all out."

"Okay, so you've obviously given this some thought. Why don't you write them?"

Lane drained what was left of her beer and dropped the empty back in the bucket. "Maybe because I'm not qualified to write about *happily ever after*. It doesn't seem right, somehow, writing about women who figure it out, when I can't figure it out for myself."

"Did you ever think that maybe the writing is *how* you figure it out?"

She stared at him for a long time, as if the remark had struck some chord. Finally, she smiled. "You're not going to say something clever now, are you? Like the journey of a thousand miles begins with a single step?"

"I was, in fact, but now you've gone and spoiled it."

"After the day I've had I'm too tired to contemplate Eastern philosophy, or much of anything, really. Can't we just sit here and watch the stars come out?"

Michael gazed up at the indigo sky, silky-dark and flecked with pinpricks of light, at the moon slipping white and lazy from a silvered sea. "I think that could be arranged." Patting the blanket invitingly, he stretched out, fingers laced over his chest. "Sorry. I didn't have time to plan. Next time we'll do s'mores for dessert."

Lane lay back beside him, a smile softening her voice. "Has anyone ever told you you're full of surprises?"

"Oh, once or twice, but I don't think it was meant as a compliment. I hope this time it was." Almost involuntarily, his hand found hers on the blanket, her fingers chilly as he folded them into his. What was he doing? There wasn't room in his life for this—whatever it was. He would be gone in a few months, back to his classroom and his students and his never-ending research. Back behind his walls of solitude and safety. As he watched two new stars wink into view, he realized he wasn't so very different from Lane Kramer.

Chapter 35

Lane

Lane woke the next morning to a flat gray sky and the high thin wail of gulls outside her window. Relieved to find the kitchen empty, she made a pot of coffee and tiptoed back upstairs with her mug, thankful that both her guests appeared to still be sleeping. There were a few things she wanted to check out before breakfast.

At this point, her plan to save Hope House consisted of little beyond locating someone—anyone—connected to the halfway house, and making them aware of the mayor's intentions. She'd poke around a little online, then make a few calls after breakfast. The tricky part would be getting the information without disclosing her reason for wanting it. The last thing she needed was someone tipping off Landon that she was snooping around.

Starting a war wasn't what she was after, but that's exactly what she'd get if word of her interference got back to the mayor. She needed some sort of cover story. Maybe she could say she was looking to interview someone for a piece about the crucial role halfway houses played in the community. All she needed was a name. How hard could that be?

But an hour and dozens of Internet searches later, she found herself grumbling into her coffee cup, baffled as to why she had yet to find anything remotely related to Hope House. Nothing about its founder, or the organization that oversaw its funding. Nothing, period. It was beginning to look as if the halfway house had sprung up out of the sound and simply maintained itself.

It seemed unlikely that public money was involved or there'd be a trail of some sort, and yet Mary had mentioned a social worker. Were social workers involved with privately funded facilities? Lane didn't think so, but then she really had no idea how it all worked. She only knew Hope House had to exist on some radar, somewhere. Perhaps she could call the state hospitals—there were three—or even a few private ones, though she doubted they'd be terribly forthcoming.

After an hour of sleuthing without a single viable lead, she was all but ready to give up. The nearest she'd come was an obscure corporation with an even more obscure name: R&C Limited. There were no names, and no link attached, only a PO box in Raleigh as a point of contact, but at least it was something. After composing a brief note detailing the situation, she addressed the envelope and marked it URGENT, then went down to start the breakfast.

Cynthia looked much improved when she appeared, smiling as she poured herself a cup of coffee and glanced out the window down the beach.

"You look like you're feeling better," Lane said, handing her the morning paper. "Headache gone?"

"Yes, thanks. I'm so glad you and Val don't get them. Are we going for a walk today?"

Lane looked up from a bowl of half-beaten eggs. "You want to go for a walk?"

"Sure. The fresh air will do me good after all that sleep."

"Actually, I was thinking of skipping the walk this morning. I have a few calls to make, and then I thought if you were up to it we'd do a little shopping. There are some nice shops and galleries in the village. And then I need to shop for dinner tomorrow. Dally already ordered the turkey, but I need to pick it up. And then there's all the other stuff. I thought we could bake the pies tonight, if you're up to it."

"Pumpkin and mince?"

Lane nodded, going back to work with her whisk.

"Does Michael like mince pie?"

"I have no idea," Lane answered truthfully. "It's never come up."

"I just asked because unless Michael's fond of it, there's really no need to make the mince." She tipped her mug then, staring into it, a crease appearing between her neatly penciled brows. "We made the mince for Daddy. He was the only one who ever ate it." She lifted the mug stiffly and took a sip, lingering over the rim. "We don't need to make it anymore."

Lane went still, caught off guard by this rare show of emotion. Her mother didn't *do* feelings. Pleasure, sorrow, joy, and even grief, had always been kept carefully at bay, neatly tucked behind a mask of bland propriety. Her mother's poker face, her father had called it. Lane had called it something else, something much less charitable.

Luckily, she was spared having to respond when Michael walked into the kitchen and dropped his customary kiss on the top of her head. It had become something of a ritual, one she was beginning to rather enjoy.

"Morning, Sunshine," he said, flashing a grin that bordered on wicked. "Looks like you managed to get all the sand out of your hair after all."

Lane swallowed her reply, then counted to ten while she waited for the color in her cheeks to recede.

Cynthia frowned up from her paper. "Did you say sand?"

Michael's grin widened. "We had a little picnic, I guess you'd call it, out on the beach last night. I built a bonfire, and your daughter and I watched the moon come up." He paused, offering a languid smile. "It was very romantic."

Cynthia's frown quickly morphed into a smile. "Laney, I believe this one's a keeper."

"Did you hear that, Laney?" Michael prodded, as he reached past her to grab three plates from the cabinet beside the sink. "Your mother thinks I'm a keeper."

Lane shot him a look of exasperation, then dropped her voice to a hiss. "Keep it up, Romeo, and when I make that call about our breakup, I'll make sure it's all your fault."

Michael threw back his head and laughed. "Go ahead. She'll never buy it."

Lane stole a glance at her mother, blissfully sipping her coffee and, in all likelihood, mentally selecting colors for flowers and bridesmaid dresses. "No, you're right. She wouldn't."

Chapter 36

By nine thirty that evening the turkey had been cleaned and was waiting for stuffing, the casseroles were in the fridge, covered with foil and ready for baking, and the pies had just come out of the oven. In the end, she'd gone with apple instead of mince. Not because it was Michael's favorite—she hadn't even remembered to ask—but because she didn't want to risk a glaringly untouched mince pie on her Thanksgiving table. Cynthia had said nothing about her choice, even when she carried the bowl of Granny Smiths to the table for peeling.

Lane was pleasantly surprised at how well they had worked together, slipping into the well-worn rhythm of countless Thanksgivings, the same cranberry relish, green-bean casserole, and candied sweet potatoes they'd been making since she was a girl, the same recipes her mother had made with Nana Jean before that.

It was comforting in a way, the unconscious sameness of it all, the predictable refuge of family tradition, and yet there was something else beneath—the niggling awareness that none of it was real, that they were all moving through some queer kind of pantomime, merely for the sake of appearance. Her father was gone and had been for years, her mother was remarried to yet another man Lane had never met, her sister and the kids were miles away, and the boyfriend with whom she was supposed to be sharing her first Thanksgiving was nothing but a clever ruse that would end the moment her mother's rental car pulled out of the drive. Like Cinderella at midnight, the illusion would vanish.

The thought left an uncomfortable hollow just south of her ribs. Suddenly, she felt weary and a little claustrophobic as she scanned the kitchen, counters dusted with pastry flour and drying scraps of piecrust, sink heaped with every mixing bowl she owned, all waiting to be washed and put away. They'd be lucky to finish before midnight.

Stifling a sigh, she stepped to the sink and began sorting out the mess while her mother moved from counter to counter with a sponge, scraping up bits of piecrust, bread crumbs, and the occasional runaway cranberry.

"You're quiet," she observed with a sidelong glance at Lane. "Everything all right?"

"I'm just tired, Mother. I've got a lot on my mind."

"Are you nervous about tomorrow?"

"Why would I be nervous?"

"Well, it's your first big dinner with Michael. Naturally, you want everything to be perfect."

"I wasn't thinking about Michael," she lied. "I was thinking about Mary, and what's going to happen if they close Hope House."

"Have you learned anything more?"

"No, I mailed the letter to the PO box I told you about, then made a few calls. I spoke with several counselors, but they all claim not to know anything."

"You sound as though you don't believe that."

"Well, it doesn't make sense, does it? Somebody has to know something, but I swear it's as if whoever's behind the place is going out of his or her way to keep it a secret."

"Philanthropists don't always trumpet their good works, Laney."

"I know, but this feels . . . different. Deliberate."

"What does Michael think about you getting involved in this?"

Lane's hands went quiet in the dishwater. It was the kind of thing she would have asked about Bruce. Had she gotten permission? Did her views coincide with the almighty Dr. Bruce?

"I didn't ask," she lied again. "Something has to be done, and I'm the only one who seems to care."

Cynthia stepped to the sink to rinse out her sponge, her mouth pursed thoughtfully. "Laney, honey, I understand that this woman means a great deal to you, but if Michael's going to be your husband—"

Lane spun around to gape at her mother, not caring that she was dripping water down the front of her pants and all over the floor. "Please remind me when I said anything about getting married."

Cynthia's eyes went wide. "Well, I just assumed—"

"That's the problem, Mother. You're always assuming. You assume I need your advice. You assume you know what's best for me. You assume you always know exactly what's going on when you don't have the first damn clue. Why is it that suddenly everyone's an expert on what I'm doing wrong with my life?"

"Laney—"

Lane threw up her hands, taking an abrupt step back. "For once in your life, can't you please just leave me alone?"

Stalking to the back door, she yanked it open, then slammed it behind her with a force that threatened to jar the frame loose. A few minutes later Cynthia followed her out onto the deck wearing Michael's jacket. It swallowed her almost to the knees. She handed Lane a sweater.

"Put that on. It's freezing out here."

Lane took the sweater and slipped it on wordlessly. Obviously the answer was *no*. Her mother couldn't just leave her alone, even when expressly asked.

"So," Cynthia said when the silence began to stretch uncomfortably. "Are you going to tell me what that was all about?"

"I don't want to talk about it."

"Oh, I'm certain of that. You never do. But we're going to talk about it anyway."

Lane folded her arms, fully aware of how petulant she must look. She didn't care. "What is it you want from me, Mother?"

"What do I want?" Cynthia let out a huff of breath that was visible in the briny night air. "I want to know what's behind these show-downs we keep having. I think it's time, don't you?"

"Trust me, Mother. It's really not."

"Fine," Cynthia said, huddling deeper into the ridiculously over-size jacket. "Have it your way. I'll just stand here until I freeze to death."

Dear God, give me strength. "Fine, then. Why did you make me marry Bruce?"

Cynthia's mouth rounded in a little O of surprise. "Make you? Lane, you were twenty-four years old when you married Bruce. And as far as I know, other than his, your name was the only one on the license."

"You know what I mean. You started pushing him down my throat the minute you met him." Lane drummed her fingers impatiently on the railing. "Well? You wanted to have this discussion. Now all of a sudden you've got nothing to say?"

"I'm just trying to figure out why we're talking about this now."

"Why?" Lane stared at her, incredulous. "Because you're here—doing it again!"

"But you and Michael are—"

"Are what? Perfect for each other? I seem to remember you saying the same thing about Bruce, and you couldn't have been more wrong. Not that it mattered, then or now. You wanted your daughter to marry the promising young heart specialist. Too bad he didn't have one of his own."

Cynthia stared at her, stricken. "I didn't know that then, Laney. How could I? You didn't even know."

"No, I didn't. But maybe I could have figured it out if you hadn't been so busy poking wedding invitations in my face and leaving stacks of bridal magazines all over the house. So I could be like Val."

"My wanting you to marry Bruce had nothing to do with your sister."

"Then what did it have to do with?"

"Your father, I think."

"Daddy?" Lane said softly. It wasn't the answer she'd expected.

There was a long stretch of silence, punctuated by the distant thrum of sea, the steady rush of ice-cold wind. When Cynthia spoke again her voice was thready, thinned with some unnameable emotion.

"When your father died—for years after, I was so lonely. We had our ups and downs like everyone else, but through it all he was my rock, the other half of me. When he got sick, when I lost him, my world crumbled. It was all I could do to get out of bed, to put one foot in front of the other, to be a mother to you and your sister. There were times when I wasn't sure I could even remember how to breathe by myself. It was like I didn't have a soul in the world. I know I shouldn't have felt that way. I had you girls. But I couldn't help it. Without your father I was ... adrift."

"You never told us."

"No. But Val knew. She always understood me."

"Is that why you love her more?"

Cynthia looked at Lane, astonished. "Please tell me you don't believe that."

"No, I guess not," Lane said with a halfhearted shrug. "But you can't pretend I ever measured up the way she did."

"It was never a question of measuring up, Laney. It had to do with the differences between the two of you. Being Val's mother was easy. She liked the same things I did. We were comfortable together. But you, you were like your father, smart and serious, and most of the time very closed off. You always had your nose in some book or were scribbling on some pad. And it got worse after your father died. There was no room for me. I was never very good at connecting with you, but all of a sudden I couldn't reach you at all. It was like you were punishing me for something, but I had no idea what. I wasn't mother of the year. I know that. But, Laney, you have to know there were times when you made it very hard to be your mother."

Punishing her?

Lane was so startled she didn't know how to respond. The accusation stirred feelings of guilt and sadness, and she didn't want to feel either of those things right now—probably because she deserved to feel both. It was true. Part of her had blamed her mother for her father's death. If only he'd been diagnosed sooner. If only her mother had paid closer attention when he started complaining about feeling tired. But that wasn't what tonight's blowup was about.

"We were talking about Bruce, Mother. Daddy's death doesn't explain you pushing him at me, or telling me to stay and fight for my marriage."

Cynthia sighed. "In a way it does. I knew Val would find someone to spend her life with, someone who would make her happy, and she did. But you, Laney, I was so scared—scared you'd keep shutting people out, scared you'd be alone like I was. The thought of it broke my heart. So I guess I started pushing. I suppose I didn't want you to be alone because I didn't want to be alone."

"Is that why you married Gary, and then Robert?" Lane asked, feeling the edge starting to wear off her anger. "Because you didn't want to be alone?"

Cynthia looked away and nodded. "I thought someone was better than no one. I learned the hard way just how wrong I was. Gary was a mistake. But now, with Robert, I'm happy. Oh, not like I was with your father, but it's a kind of happy, and at my age that's more than most women can say."

A long silence fell. Finally, Lane broke it. "The other day you said something. You said I thought I wasn't good enough, that I believed Michael was my last chance."

"I shouldn't have said that. Please forget it."

"What did you mean?"

"Laney—"

"What did you mean?"

"What I said, I suppose."

"That I think I'm not good enough? That I—"

Cynthia cut her off. "You should have fought me, Laney."

"What?"

"About Bruce—you should have fought me. Instead you said nothing, and went along with something you never wanted. And then you said nothing to Bruce. You let him bully you into a life you didn't want. You should have fought us both."

At her sides, Lane's hands knotted into fists. "That isn't fair! You don't *let* someone bully you. They just do it. And you weren't saying all this back then. Back then, all you ever talked about was how I needed to learn to compromise."

"I didn't know everything. You never told me how bad it was."

It was true; she hadn't. She'd been ashamed to admit she couldn't pull off something as simple, as basic, as marriage. Val never had any problem. Maybe she was missing something other women seemed to be born with, some wifely gene that had somehow skipped her.

"Maybe it wasn't that bad. Maybe I just thought it was."

"You stopped writing, Lane. Writing. The one thing you've loved all your life, and you just . . . stopped. Because Bruce hated it. That isn't compromise. That's quitting. And you didn't learn that from me."

"No, that's right," Lane fired back. "When it comes to marriage, no one could ever call you a quitter. Your motto has always been *if at first you don't succeed, try, try again.* And I didn't stop writing because of Bruce. I stopped because I was told I wasn't any good."

Cynthia folded her arms, shivering, then shook her head. "No, Laney. You stopped because you believed it."

Speechless, Lane absorbed her mother's words like a slap.

When Cynthia spoke again her voice was weary, but resolved, too. "You want to blame me, fine. Blame me. But maybe it's time you looked in the mirror."

"What's that supposed to mean?"

"It means you've never been one to stand up for what you want. You don't see it, but I do, because I've known you all your life. You've always been content to bury your head in the sand—or in a book, like your father—and let the world have its way. That's what I was trying to say. I told you to fight for your marriage. I didn't mean you should be a doormat. I meant it was time you stood up for the life you wanted, the life you deserved. Instead, you retreated."

Retreat.

There it was again, an unnerving echo of last night's conversation with Michael, but somehow it was harder to ignore when it came from her mother.

"I was miserable, Mother—too miserable and too tired to fight. Especially for something I knew I didn't want. But you could never see that. You didn't want to, and you still don't. After everything, the baby, the women, the bullying as you put it, you still think I should have stayed."

"I don't." Stepping closer, Cynthia laid a hand on her daughter's arm. "All I want, all I've ever wanted, was for you and your sister to be happy. With Val, happiness just seemed to come naturally, but you weren't like that."

"I'm sorry, Mother," Lane said, shrinking from her touch. "At least you had Val, who always did everything right."

Cynthia dropped her arms to her sides with a sigh. "Laney, what I'm saying has nothing to do with Val, or Michael, or anybody. It has to do with going after what you want in life, and to hell with what anyone else thinks. And yes, that includes me."

She paused, drawing a deep, shuddery breath, then squared her shoulders. "I thought—well, I hoped—that over the last few days, we'd gotten past all this. But I see now that we haven't, and probably never will. I wanted you to have someone, a life, a future. I'm sorry you think that was selfish of me, but if you're waiting for an apology, I don't have one to give. I've made mistakes. Lots of them, I suppose. But wanting my daughter to be happy wasn't one of them."

She turned away then and walked back into the kitchen. Lane watched her go, knowing she should go after her, and knowing she couldn't.

Chapter 37

Lane watched the last of the stars wink out as the sky slowly morphed from indigo to pearly pink. It seemed an eternity since she'd ventured out onto the dunes to watch an actual sunrise, but there had been little point in remaining in bed with her mother's words wedged in her head like a pebble in a shoe. Instead, she had pulled on a T-shirt and sweats, foraged a blanket from the chest at the foot of her bed, and slipped out the back door. That had been somewhere around five. Now, nearly two hours later, the sun was up and she was numb in every way possible, chilled to the bone, emotionally drained, and all cried out.

Her mother's words had cut deep, too deep to simply dismiss out of hand. But then, so much of it had needed saying. All these years, she'd been so busy blaming her mother for everything that had gone wrong in her life that she'd never bothered to look in the mirror. If she had, she might have realized that being her mother hadn't exactly been a bowl of roses. Not that that little detail let her mother off the hook for Bruce. It didn't.

A bit of movement caught Lane's eye, a shadow slowly encroaching on the stretch of dune beside her. She stifled a groan, in no shape to resume last night's argument.

"Mother, I really don't—"

"You're up early, my girl."

Lane jerked her head around, surprised and relieved. "Mary."

The woman's keen eyes narrowed. "Something's wrong."

Lane nodded and looked away. "My mother's here," she said, as if that explained everything.

"I've seen her."

"You've seen her? When?"

"Yesterday. You'd just set out for a walk. I made sure to keep out of sight. I didn't think you'd want to explain someone like me."

Lane felt a pang of shame. It was true. The only reason she'd shared Mary's story at all was that Landon and Breester had forced her hand at the Hot Spot. "You knew she was my mother?"

"The minute I saw you together."

"I guess it's not hard to spot. I've always looked like her."

"That's not how I knew."

Something in Mary's tone made Lane glance up. "Then how?"

Mary eased down onto the sand. When she finally spoke, her voice had that faraway quality that Lane was beginning to recognize, a wistful blend of love and loss. "They say blood tells, but it's more than that. We share things. Blood and bone, yes, but memories, too, and ways of being. Small, inconsequential things that are etched into us somehow, without our knowing it, things that can't ever be erased. Not by time or distance—or even death."

Lane wasn't sure how to respond. She was speaking of her sons, of course—her princes, as she called them—the boys she had loved and lost.

"It isn't like that with us," she said at last. "We're not . . . close."

Mary's faint, sagelike smile slid back into place. "It's always like that, my girl. Just because you can't see it doesn't mean it's not so. It's not something you do. It's who you are—both of you—bound by a thousand invisible threads."

Lane propped her chin on her knees, hugging them close as she stared at the shoreline. Coming from anyone else Mary's words might have sounded faintly eccentric, but here, now, they seemed quite sensible, one more example of her unique brand of wisdom.

"I suppose it's like that with my sister. They're close, and always have been. As far back as I can remember she just had a knack for making my mother love her. I, on the other hand, was never very good at that."

Mary shot her a look of reproach. "That's a little girl's hurt."

"You don't understand. You don't . . . know her."

"I do know her!" Mary barked back. "I know a mother's heart—what breathes, and beats, and bleeds there. Never think I don't, no matter what you ever hear of me. Whatever your mother did—or didn't do—was because she loved you and wanted you to be happy. It's all we ever want for our children—all of them."

"It isn't that simple. We had a terrible fight last night. We said things—hurtful things."

"My girl," she said, taking hold of Lane's hands. "To live and to live well are two very different things. The former, it seems, cannot be escaped, while the latter is rarely obtained, and never for long. Most people live in between."

"I don't understand. What's that got to do—"

"Purgatory is the in-between, my girl, the earthly here and now where we take our lashes and pay for our frailties. If you'd lived through what I have, lost what I have, you'd know that words are only flesh wounds. They can't leave scars unless you let them."

Lane eyed Mary warily, wondering if she had lost her grip on the conversation. "Why are you telling me this, Mary? We were talking about my mother."

"And we still are. I don't know what's been festering between the two of you, but whatever it is, you mustn't let it leave scars. She's your mother, the only one you'll ever have, no matter how many harsh words pass between you. Never let the thread snap."

"And how do I do that?"

"You're a woman. So is she. Meet her there—woman's heart to woman's heart."

Lane stuck out her chin. "I don't see that happening. I'm thirty-nine, and she still treats me like a child."

"Come, now, don't be petulant. It doesn't suit you."

"I left my husband because I was miserable. Now she can't stop reminding me that if I'm not careful I'll be alone for the rest of my life." Lane looked away and dropped her voice. "So a few weeks ago I did something stupid."

"This stupid thing you did—it's a man?"

Lane nearly smiled. How was it this woman saw through her so easily? "Yes, it's a man. I'll tell you about him one day, but not now. Right now I think I need to be alone for a while. Then I suppose I'll have to go in and straighten out the mess I've made."

Mary gave Lane's hands a final squeeze before getting to her feet. "You'll find the way, my girl. Just remember—woman's heart to woman's heart."

"I haven't forgotten my promise, you know, about Hope House."

"Of course you haven't. We'll talk about it when you're feeling better."

Lane smiled up at her. "Thank you, Mary. I'm glad you came into my life."

The remark seemed to take Mary by surprise. Something like a smile flickered briefly about her mouth before she turned and headed down the dunes. Lane watched as she made her way up the sandy, vine-tangled rise, then disappeared down the other side, and wondered why it was so much easier to talk to a virtual stranger than to her own mother.

Woman's heart to woman's heart.

Was it possible, after all the hurtful words and finger-pointing, to see past the mother who had raised her—the mother she always seemed to disappoint—and find the woman beneath? To be seen as more than just the daughter who needed saving? She honestly didn't know. It wasn't their first argument, nor was it likely to be their last. They were different women, with vastly different views of the world, but they were family, mother and child bound by blood and years—and yes, by love. Maybe Mary was right. When it came down to it, maybe words *were* only flesh wounds.

After the chilly wind out on the dunes the kitchen felt almost stifling. Lane peeled out of the blanket, letting it puddle on the floor just inside the door. Cynthia looked up briefly from the table, a mug of coffee pressed between her palms, her eyes puffy and red-rimmed.

"Mother—"

"There's coffee," she said thickly into her mug.

Lane scanned the counters, spick-and-span now, neatly stacked with pots and pans, washed and waiting to be returned to their proper places. She'd left a mess last night when she stalked out. At some point Cynthia had cleaned it up, by herself. She tried not to envision it—her mother up to her elbows in dishwater, crying quietly over the sink.

God.

The clock ticked heavily as she filled a mug with coffee, then added a splash of cream. Lingering over the first sip, she cast about for something to say, for how and where to begin. But the words seemed to stick in her throat, mingled with the ache of last night's tears. When nothing came, she set down her mug, crossed to the table, and wrapped her arms around her mother's shoulders.

"I'm sorry about last night, about everything."

Cynthia stiffened briefly, before melting into her daughter's embrace. "I never meant to hurt you, Laney. Not with Bruce, and not last night."

Lane dropped into the nearest chair, quiet for a time as she again searched for the right words. "I don't think I ever realized how well you know me."

Cynthia was clearly surprised. "I'm your mother, Laney. Of course I know you. You're part of me."

"I guess I thought you never paid enough attention to know me. Now I'm starting to think maybe I was the one not paying attention." She laid a hand on her mother's arm. "I'm sorry I was difficult after Daddy died . . . and that I never noticed you were sad."

"It wasn't your job to worry about me. It was my job to worry about you."

"And it seems I gave you plenty to worry about."

Cynthia searched her daughter's face with eyes that missed nothing. Finally, she reached up to brush a strand of bangs from Lane's eyes. "I only want you to be—"

"Happy. Yes, I know."

Cynthia averted her gaze. A single, shiny tear tracked down her cheek. She brushed it away. "I'm sorry I pushed you about Bruce. It was wrong of me, and selfish."

Lane drew a long breath and held it as she digested the apology, savoring the balm of finally, finally, being heard. "You didn't mean it to be. I know that now. Besides, it was me walking down that aisle, me standing beside Bruce, me saying I do. You said last night that I should have fought you, and you were right. I've just never known how."

"Oh, I don't know. You seemed to do a pretty good job last night."

"I'm sorry about that."

"Don't ever stop fighting, Laney. I should have taught you that."

"I love you, Mother. And you taught me plenty."

Cynthia managed a shaky smile. In the remnants of yesterday's makeup she looked pale and suddenly fragile, as if she hadn't slept at all. She glanced about the kitchen, looking slightly overwhelmed. "It's Thanksgiving. I almost forgot. We've got the turkey, and all that food..."

Lane smiled through an unexpected sheen of tears. Yes, it was Thanksgiving. And today they would cook. Side by side. Woman to woman.

They gathered in the dining room just after five. Lane ran a critical eye over the table, set with her best crystal and silver, but could find no fault. When she was a child, her mother had taken great pains with her table at the holidays, and Lane had gone out of her way to duplicate her results, right down to the precisely placed water glasses and carefully folded napkins.

"Oh, Laney, your table is lovely. And that bird is an absolute picture."

Michael made the appropriate appreciative murmurs as he slid around to hold out Cynthia's chair, then settled into his own. Lane went to work with a corkscrew and a bottle of Gewürztraminer she had chosen especially for the meal. Now that the work was done and they were seated, she actually felt a little nervous, which was silly since she and her mother had been preparing Thanksgiving dinners together for years. Maybe it had to do with being reminded almost hourly that this was her first Thanksgiving with Michael, and everything needed to be perfect.

"Shall we say grace?" Cynthia asked, holding a hand out to Michael.

Lane flicked an anxious glance at Michael—they'd never spoken about religion—but he seemed fine as he accepted Cynthia's hand. "Go ahead, Mother. You've always done the blessing."

She beamed as she took her daughter's hand, and for a moment Lane thought she saw tears sparkling in her mother's eyes as she bowed her head. "Heavenly Father, we gather together today to offer thanks for your bounty, for this wonderful meal, and for the gift of family and friends. May we never forget their place in our hearts and our lives. And thank you especially for bringing Michael to our table, and into my Laney's life. May this be the first of many holidays together. For these things and more, we humbly thank you. Amen."

Lane's cheeks were flaming by the time the prayer ended. Lying to her mother was one thing. Now they were lying to God as well. Surely there would be some retribution for that, some plague visited upon her house—boils perhaps, or locusts. And it certainly couldn't have been a very comfortable thing for Michael to sit through. She could barely look at him as she passed him the wine bottle, though when she managed to sneak a glance in his direction, his face gave nothing away.

"Michael," Cynthia said, oblivious of any tension as she picked up the carving knife and handed it to him. "Will you do the honors?"

"Me?"

"Well, you *are* the man of the house at the moment."

Michael threw Lane a helpless look. "I have no experience with turkeys. My father was always in charge of that."

Lane grinned, enjoying the sight of him outside his comfort zone. "Oh, go ahead. Take a whack at it. If you make a bad job of it we'll just call it hash."

Michael managed without making too big a mess. When he finished, he relinquished the knife and bowed with a flourish, though he was clearly relieved to be back in his chair and out of the spotlight.

Plates filled as potatoes and stuffing and glazed carrots were passed around. Lane watched her mother spoon a bit of cranberry relish onto her plate. The day had begun on shaky ground, but somehow they had talked it out, struck a truce, and come together to make something lovely. She was about to take her first bite of turkey when Cynthia turned to her, peering pointedly over her wineglass.

"So, have you two lovebirds given any thought as to how you'll spend Christmas? It's your first, after all, so you'll want to make it special. You could always come to us. Valerie would love to see you, and so would the kids. It would be great to have everyone together, and we've got plenty of room."

Lane's fingers tightened around the stem of her wineglass. Suddenly, she knew exactly how a deer felt the moment it was snagged in oncoming headlights. "Christmas?"

"Yes, dear," Cynthia said sweetly. "It's the holiday after this one. There's usually a tree involved, presents, that sort of thing?"

Lane held back a sigh. It wasn't really an out-of-the-way question, after all. Michael was living with her, ostensibly, and would be for the entire off-season. What made it awkward was the lie, and she had no one to blame but herself for that. She took a sip of wine, briefly toying with the idea of blurting out that Michael was Jewish—or perhaps a Buddhist—and didn't celebrate Christmas. Instead, she settled for a half-truth.

"To be honest, Mother, we haven't really thought about it. Michael's so busy with his research right now, and I've got several articles coming due. I don't really think—"

"Actually, Cynthia, we would love to come to Chicago," Michael interrupted, causing Lane's head to whip around sharply. "But the truth is—and I was really going to try to surprise Lane with this—I was sort of planning a romantic Christmas for two. I thought we'd go pick out a tree, decorate it up, maybe light a fire and put on a little Bing Crosby."

Cynthia smiled conspiratorially. "Well, now, what mother could argue with that? Even if it does mean not having my baby and her young man with us for the holidays, I think it sounds perfectly lovely."

Lane clenched her teeth to keep her jaw from dropping, and prayed the gesture would pass for a smile. He hadn't batted an eye as he painted the scene, knowing full well that nothing would make

Cynthia relinquish the idea of a family Christmas faster than the thought of the two of them snuggled up in front of a roaring fire—perhaps with a tiny box beneath the tree.

She had barely finished the thought when Michael reached for her hand and raised it to his lips. It was a quick touch, the barest brush of warmth against her knuckles. Their eyes met briefly, and she saw the teasing smile there. God, they were getting in deeper by the minute. Her mother was never going to forgive her when the bogus but inevitable breakup occurred and she learned her daughter had let this amazing man slip through her fingers.

Chapter 38

L ane stood by while Michael helped Cynthia load her bags into the trunk of the rented Buick. The weather was good and her flight wasn't until one thirty, so they'd have plenty of time to grab breakfast before she needed to head to the airport. Getting to Starry Point from Chicago had been no small feat for a woman unaccustomed to traveling alone—three planes, a rental car, and an hour and a half of partially flooded highway—but Lane had to admit she was glad her mother had taken the trouble.

They'd spent the final days of her visit paging through imaginary scrapbooks, recalling birthday parties, Christmas Eves, and summer vacations. Their relationship would never be as close as the one her mother shared with Val, but thanks to Mary, they had become more than just a mother and daughter who shared a bumpy past—they had become friends.

It was a Monday and the breakfast crowd at the Patty Cake Diner was thin, Old Pointers mostly, in gaggles of three or four, washing down the latest gossip with bottomless cups of coffee. Lane nodded and waved to several familiar faces as she threaded past the PLEASE SEAT YOURSELF sign toward an empty corner booth.

Cynthia scooted in next to the window. Lane slid in beside her.

Michael took his place opposite and plucked three syrup-sticky menus from between the napkin dispenser and the salt and pepper. Cynthia stared at the laminated cover, fascinated by the depiction of the house specialty—the Patty Cake Platter—which consisted of three pancakes, three eggs, three sausage patties, and a biscuit the size of a lumberjack's fist smothered in sawmill gravy.

"Who on earth could eat all that? And what is it they've poured all over that biscuit?"

"This is the South, Mother," Lane said with a chuckle. "We take our breakfast very seriously. And that's sausage gravy. I'd stick to the short stack if I were you. Pat's pancakes are legendary around—"

The rest was left dangling when Lane noticed a man in an orange Windbreaker taping a notice of some sort to the front door. Beneath his arm were several more of the pale blue sheets. When he was sure the notice was secure, he slipped out the door with a wink and a wave for the pink-cheeked blonde behind the counter.

It took only moments for the first patron to leave his seat and investigate, a grizzled man in baggy overalls and a green corduroy jacket. His lips moved as he squinted to read the printed words. When he was finished, he peered over his glasses at the members of his party, then strode back, lips pursed thoughtfully.

Lane watched, amused by how quickly the news—whatever it was—fanned out from his table at the back of the diner, heads bending from table to table, until it seemed everyone in the place was talking about whatever was taped to the door.

"Mornin', guys." Their waitress had arrived, plump and cheerful, as she plucked the pen from behind her ear, ready to jot down their order. "Can I bring y'all some coffee or juice to start?"

Lane ignored the question. "Mindy," she said after a quick glance at the woman's name tag. "Can you tell me what all the buzz is about? What did that man just post on your door?"

"Oh, just a notice about the meeting tonight."

"Meeting?"

"Seven thirty, at the town hall. Mayor called it this morning, apparently."

Lane nodded, a cold knowing already settling in her belly. Landon wasn't wasting any time, and she was no closer to blocking him than she'd been the day he made his intentions known. Michael had obviously drawn the same conclusion. He covered her hand and squeezed gently, the look he shot her a blend of caution and concern.

Mindy, unaware of the sudden tension at the table, stood smiling with her pen poised. When she retreated with their orders and a promise to return with water and coffee, Cynthia was the first to speak.

"It's about the halfway house, isn't it? The meeting?"

Lane huffed, then nodded. "What else could it be? It's just like him to call a meeting on such short notice."

Michael gathered up the menus, returning them to their rightful place. "He hopes no one actually shows up. That way he can ram his plans through and still be able to claim he kept the community informed."

Cynthia bristled visibly. "Can he actually do that?"

Michael shrugged. "It would seem so."

"But there must be laws about how these things have to be handled. A man can't just decide he wants to kick people out into the street, even if he is the mayor."

"Ah," Michael said with a fleeting smile. "You sounded just like your daughter then. She's been saying the same thing for days now."

"Because she's right. That man is picking on people who can't defend themselves, and it's because he doesn't believe anyone will stop him." Cynthia quieted as Mindy appeared with a pot of coffee, but she picked up the thread of the conversation the minute they were alone again. "I'll bet you everything in Robert's bank account that he's got his own reasons for wanting that place closed. I'm telling you, someone needs to put a stop to it before it's too late. Laney, have you had any luck with your searches?"

Lane stifled a smile, wishing she'd seen this side of her mother sooner. "Not really. So far, it's just the PO box I told you about. And with it being Thanksgiving week, I doubt they've received the letter yet."

"It's all a bit mysterious, don't you think? How would you feel about me asking Robert to do a little poking around? He's got people working for him who can find out anything. And, Laney, if it gets ugly, I want you to know you can count on him for legal advice."

Lane didn't bother to hide her surprise. "I've never met the man. Why would he do that?"

"Because he loves me, and he knows I love you. I'll talk to him the minute I get in tonight."

Lane reached for her mother's hand, an unspoken thanks. At the same time, she caught the look of trepidation on Michael's face.

"You'll be attending this meeting, I suppose?" he asked drily.

Cynthia chimed in before Lane could answer. "Well, of course she will. And you'll be there with her, I hope, to lend support. Your mayor likes to wear a great big smile, but I know a bully when I see one, and that man is definitely a bully."

Lane felt a stab of guilt as Michael nodded his grudging assent. She'd let him off the hook once her mother was gone, though deep down she would feel better with him there. Her mother was right. Landon was a bully, and she'd never had much luck with bullies.

Cynthia had produced a small notebook from her purse and was still scribbling furiously when breakfast arrived. Tucking it away, she checked her watch, then patted Lane's hand again before picking up her fork. "Eat up now, both of you. I need to get to the airport so I can get home to Robert and get him to work on this."

Later, in the parking lot, Lane and Cynthia said their good-byes, each fighting tears and failing miserably. Michael gave Cynthia a refresher on the route back to Manteo, then submitted to a lavish farewell hug.

"Take care of my little girl," she said with a watery smile.

Michael's expression never faltered. "You know I will."

She turned then, for one last farewell from Lane. For a moment their eyes met and held, unspoken words passing between them until Cynthia finally dragged her daughter into her arms. "Marry him; don't marry him," she whispered against Lane's cheek. "Hell, don't marry anyone if that's what you want. I just want you to be happy. I swear that's all I want, Laney."

"I know that, Mother," Lane whispered back.

For just a moment, she found herself fighting the urge to blurt out the truth about her relationship with Michael. It felt wrong somehow to let her mother return to Chicago nursing hopes that were completely false, especially after they had managed to find some sort of common ground. But was the truth really the wisest course? After years of emotional distance, they had finally pulled down their fences. Why risk this new and fragile détente with an awkward confession just as her mother was leaving?

The decision was made for her when Cynthia slid behind the wheel of the silver Buick and started the engine. She blew Lane a kiss, then with one final wave pulled out of the parking lot. Lane wiped her eyes on her sleeve as she watched the car disappear from sight, dimly registering the comfort of Michael's arm as it slipped about her waist. It was a gesture of kindness, she reminded herself, kindness and nothing more. And yet it felt strangely intimate—and far too comfortable.

Slipping free, she turned and headed for the car, wondering if the real reason she hadn't told her mother the truth about Michael was that she didn't want to admit it to herself.

Back home, she didn't bother removing her jacket. Instead, she told Michael she was going out to the dunes to look for Mary, to tell her about the meeting.

Michael eyed her dubiously. "Surely, you're not thinking of asking her to tag along, because if you are, you should know you'll be playing right into Landon's hands."

"How?"

"By giving him a poster child for his scare campaign, for starters. Not everyone sees what you do when they look at Mary. They see a crazy old woman who rides around town on a rickety old bike and mumbles to herself. They see Dirty Mary."

Lane cringed at his use of the moniker. "She's not dirty. And she doesn't mumble."

"I noticed you didn't say she wasn't crazy."

Her mouth worked silently for a moment, groping for a way around what she knew of Mary's past. "Scarred doesn't always mean crazy," she said finally.

"No? Then what does it mean?"

"I don't know . . . confused . . . sad."

"Maybe. But that's not what people are going to see, Lane. They'll take one look at her and swallow every nasty insinuation Landon's going to make about the people living at Hope House. It'll be over before it starts. And don't look at me like that. You know I'm right."

The sad part was he likely was right. "I still want her to hear about what's happening. And who knows, maybe she's found out something that could help us."

"Us?"

"Okay, me. Will you go tonight?"

Michael glanced down at his shoes, shifting his weight from foot to foot.

"You did promise my mother."

"Yes, I did. And I suppose a promise is a promise."

The tentative morning sun had given way to a threatening pewter sky by the time Lane stepped out onto the boardwalk. Mary had perched herself on a dune about ten yards down the beach, no doubt in deference to Cynthia. But Cynthia was halfway to Manteo by now, on her way back to Chicago to enlist the aid of a stepfather Lane had never met, to help a woman she barely knew.

Mary raised a hand in greeting as Lane approached, her pale hair standing out around her head like a dirty storm cloud, tattered orange scarf flailing in the wind, an unfortunate parody of the neon bike flag. Michael was right. They would only see Dirty Mary. Landon would win the war without ever firing a shot.

"My mother left this morning," Lane announced as she dropped down beside Mary. "You don't have to stay away anymore. Not that you ever did."

"Easier for everyone," Mary answered without taking her eyes from the sea. "How did the two of you leave it?"

"I did what you said, and it's . . . better. She's even offered to ask her husband—" She broke off abruptly, realizing she needed to back up. "Mary, the mayor has called an emergency meeting of the town council tonight. I'm pretty sure it's about Hope House."

Mary stiffened but said nothing.

"I haven't been able to get in touch with anyone yet, but I've written a letter to a corporation that might be tied to Hope House. Have you ever heard of R&C Limited?"

Mary shook her head.

"It's all I've been able to find so far, but my mother's husband has people who do this sort of investigating for a living, and she thinks he might be able to help us."

Mary remained silent, rigid as a pillar.

"I promise you, Mary, I'm not giving up. I'll be there tonight, at the meeting. And the minute I know who it is I need to talk to, we're going to put together some sort of plan to stop this. Michael's coming, too."

Mary surprised her by turning her head. "Michael?"

"The man . . . I mean the guest . . . who's staying with me through the winter. I sort of mentioned him to you the other day."

"He's the stupid thing you did?"

"Not exactly, but it has to do with him. I sort of lied to my mother about our relationship."

"Lied how?"

"I told her we had one."

"And you don't?"

"Not a real one. No."

Mary's pale brows lifted. "You have a pretend relationship?"

Lane stifled a groan. Put like that, it sounded even more pathetic. "I guess that's what you'd call it. It started with something stupid I said one night when we were on the phone. She was pushing my buttons and I just blurted it out. But then she flew halfway across the country to check him out. I meant to tell her the truth, I really did, but Michael stepped into the role of boyfriend before I could get it out. After that, it just never seemed to be the right time. She fell in love with him, but then, of course she would. He's handsome and brooding in a Heathcliff sort of way, and polite, and smart—he's a literature professor at a small college in Vermont and he's writing a book."

"I see," Mary said, in that quiet way she had. "And you're sure it's just pretend?"

Lane looked away, feigning interest in the darkening sky. "Yes, I'm sure."

"But you don't want it to be, do you? This Michael—he means something to you?"

"I'm afraid he's beginning to, yes." With her usual acuity, Mary had seen straight to the heart of things. "The problem is I don't know what to do about it. My mother's gone, which means there's no need to go on pretending. Except deep down I want to."

Mary's gaze slid toward the sea. "Be careful, my girl. Pretending is a dangerous thing. One day you spin a pretty web, a fairy tale to cling to, and the next you're caught in it, because somehow, without meaning to, you've begun to believe it. And the day after that they start calling you crazy."

They were no longer talking about Michael. Mary had slipped away again, into some deeply worn groove of her past, where the view was meant only for her. Lane swallowed the urge to delve deeper. She remembered only too well what had happened the last time she pressed for answers. She'd have her answers when Mary was ready to give them. For now it was enough to sit quietly together and simply share the view.

Chapter 39

Mary

I watch her as she goes, her head ducked low against the wind as she makes her way along the dunes, back to her inn, and her Michael. She's in love, poor thing, though I don't believe she's ready to admit just how deeply. How I wish I could be happy for her, this lovely woman with the sad eyes and the heart that's so much bigger than she knows.

But I cannot.

A woman's heart is like a bit of porcelain, you see, a fragile thing, not to be handled roughly. But men are so careless, so clumsy. They cannot be trusted with delicate things. Like fine lace or a bird's wing, wounds of the heart are rarely mended. But then, perhaps this Michael is one of the rare ones, a man who will stand firm when the ground beneath him begins to shift, and not let himself be swept away—a man who will stay. I used to believe in such men, long ago, in my own fairy-tale days.

Now as I watch her move away, my heart is heavy with the warnings I should have given but did not, about the dangers of being reckless with one's heart, and what can happen when you make room for the ones who can't stay. But it's not really my place. I'm not her mother. I'm no one's mother now, and no one's wife. I'm no one's anything. I was once, though, before the tide came in and the wreck-age washed up.

We never dream we might lose those we love, because it's too terrible, too inconceivable. They are simply the furniture of our lives, to be sidestepped, rearranged, and even stumbled over. Then one day they are simply gone, erased, and you're left with only empty rooms and the echo of what once belonged to you. In that moment, that fraction of a second when your slate is wiped clean, there is the ab-solute certainty that none of it is true, that some error has been made, some hideous lie told, and that someday, somehow, it will all come right again. If you can only make them listen to the truth, the truth that you—and only you—know with your whole heart. But they don't listen, and the rooms remain empty. And after a while your heart grinds to a halt, and you're almost glad.

It's a strange thing to know that you're finally undone, to feel yourself at long last spooling free, that moment of terrible, wonderful freedom that comes when there's nothing left to cling to, and you nearly weep with the relief of it.

And yet, beneath it all, the emptiness remains; the jagged place where love used to reside, where my princes reside still, has never fully closed. To lose one was a tragedy; to lose both was unspeakable. But no human frailty goes unpunished, or so the good nuns always told me, and my frailties are legion. And so I suppose my lost princes are my cross to bear, my bloodied crown of thorns, crucifixion with-out resurrection, sin without hope of redemption.

Through my fault.

Through my fault.

Through my most grievous fault.

Chapter 40

Lane

Lane felt her stomach clench as Michael pulled into the parking lot of Starry Point Town Hall. If Landon hoped waiting until the last minute to post the meeting notice would keep people away, he was going to be disappointed. The parking lot was jammed. She wasn't sure if that was a good thing or a bad thing. She only prayed that at least one car belonged to someone affiliated with Hope House, someone prepared to stand against Landon and Breester.

Heads turned as they entered the hall. The room was overwarm, and humming like a beehive, a blended rumble of curiosity and impatience. Lane scanned the crowd for allies. Erin from the Hot Spot sat in one of the blue plastic chairs near the front, Dally and her mother were somewhere in the middle rows with Skye sandwiched in between, and Sam, her handyman, stood near the back with his arms folded and his grizzled chin stuck out. She had lived in Starry Point for more than five years. She ran a business here, was a member of the community—and she barely knew a soul. How was that possible?

Row by row, she studied the unfamiliar faces, wondering how many of them would ultimately side with Landon. Most had no idea what he was about to propose. Neither did she, really. But she had a pretty good hunch. She only hoped they had the good sense to see it for what it was, and would refuse to let him get away with it.

Up on the dais, a long table had been set up and covered with a starched white cloth, its pristine surface neatly lined with eight pads and pens, one each for Mayor Landon and the six members of the council, the eighth almost certainly for Donny Breester.

Breester and Landon were holding a private powwow in the corner, their heads bent close. As if sensing her gaze, Landon glanced up, following her with keen eyes as she and Michael found a place along the back wall. Breester's gaze came next, dull and hungry as he looked her over, then going flinty when he spotted Michael at her side.

Lane looked away in time to catch Landon's wife, Anne, give her husband a brisk nod. The room quieted as Mayor Landon peeled away from Breester and took his place at the table, calling the meeting to order. Briefly, he found her again, the unyielding set of his jaw a warning that she'd best keep her nose out of this.

"Friends and fellow residents," he began in a booming voice. "I have called this meeting to discuss the recent crime wave that has infected our once-peaceful community, to update you on the progress of our investigation, and finally to propose a solution I believe will eradicate the dangerous elements we have reason to believe are at the root of the problem, before we see it escalate—as it most certainly will if allowed to go unchecked—into violence."

Lane glanced from face to face, not liking what she saw in their expressions, fear in the women, brashness and anger in the men. It was already working.

"I can't stand here and listen to this," she hissed at Michael. "Dangerous elements? Violence? It's nothing but a pack of lies meant to frighten people into doing what he wants."

Michael cut his eyes at her. "You expected different?"

"I didn't expect this. I hoped—" But he shushed her before she could finish, pointing up at the dais as the mayor went on.

"I'm going to let Chief Breester say a few words now, to fill every-one in on the current state of our investigation, what we already know, and what we soon expect to learn."

There was a smattering of applause, a brace of bland smiles from the members of the council. Breester squared his shoulders and stood very still beside the mayor, waiting with an air of self-importance until the crowd fell silent and all eyes were trained on him.

"As Mayor Landon has just said, Starry Point currently finds itself in the grip of an unprecedented crime wave, something that as chief of police I take very seriously, and very personally. To date, there have been a total of sixteen reported break-ins, all of which have occurred on the sound side of the island, each resulting in material loss as well as property damage, not to mention the damage done to the peace of mind of our friends and neighbors."

"They cut the screen out of my back door and stole my son's bike off the porch," a woman in the front hollered up at the dais. "That was almost three months ago, and so far no one's been caught. We moved here from Richmond because we thought it was safe, and then this happens."

Breester nodded gravely in her direction. "We understand your concerns, Mrs. Bridges, which is precisely why the mayor and I have called this meeting. We have reason to believe we've zeroed in on the perpetrators who broke into your home, and we need your help to . . . remove them from our midst."

"Let's hear it, then!" someone belted from the back row. "Or are we just going to sit here all night?"

Breester managed a tight smile and cleared his throat. "No, George, as a matter of fact we're not. Over the last few weeks we've received several tips, each leading us in the same direction." He paused for effect, scanning the crowd, like a revival preacher preparing to deliver his brimstone. "There is a certain element being housed in a certain facility over on the sound side of the island, the same side,

I might add, where all of the burglaries have occurred. It's this element we've been investigating, and this element we believe responsible for all our problems."

Lane felt her blood boil as she watched the council members scribbling furiously on their pads. "What tips?" she fumed near Michael's ear. "He didn't say a word about any tips the other day. This is nothing but a farce!"

A man in a John Deere ball cap shot to his feet. "Sounds like you're talking about that halfway house."

"Hope House," Breester supplied curtly. "And yes, I am. We've interviewed several of the inmates and have reason—"

"They're not inmates!" Lane shouted when she could stand it no longer. "And to suggest otherwise is a lie! They're there of their own free will. They're free to leave anytime they wish."

Landon locked eyes with her briefly, his warning unmistakable, before nodding for Breester to continue.

"As I was saying, we've interviewed several of the, uh . . . residents . . . of Hope House, and have good reason to believe there is a theft ring operating out of that facility. We also have reason to believe they've been working with a local pawnbroker to sell what they steal . . . in order to finance their drug habits."

A collective gasp went up. Lane stood silent, fists clenched at her sides as the mood in the room turned ugly. But none of it was true. Breester had as much as admitted it the other day. No witnesses. No evidence of any kind. And yet here he stood, laying it all out, one falsehood at a time—and the crowd was lapping it up.

"Will arrests be made?" the woman in the front row demanded. "Is someone going to be made to pay for my screen door? And will my son get his bike back?"

As if on cue, Breester backed away and Mayor Landon pushed back his chair, reclaiming the room's attention. "Unfortunately, Mrs. Bridges, despite Chief Breester's strenuous efforts, we have been unable to secure the kind of evidence that would be needed to make any kind of arrest or demand for reparation."

"Then what the hell are we doing sitting here?" a new voice fired up at the dais. "I didn't come here to listen to you brag about knowing who's breaking into our houses and stealing our stuff. I came to hear what you plan to do about it!"

The clamor rose steadily as more and more residents joined in the shouting. Breester stepped back from the table, a slim smile playing about his mouth as the seeds of anger he'd planted fanned to life and caught fire.

"Shut it down! There's your answer!" someone finally shouted. "We don't need a bunch of schizos and needle freaks living in Starry Point, stealing our things and sniffing around our children, thinking God knows what! I say, shut it down."

There it was, then, Landon's trump card at last, dramatically dealt by a man of his own careful choosing. *Schizos and needle freaks.* The same words Breester had used the other day at the Hot Spot, and surely no coincidence.

Several more shouts of "Shut it down!" rose. The council members looked out over the crowd. Several looked ready to bolt. Eventually Landon stepped up to quiet the crowd. For a split second, he found her at the back of the room, a flicker of triumph in his small dark eyes as he made his next statement.

"It seems we have a consensus among our residents that the facility in question be closed and the land put to some better, and dare I say, safer, purpose."

His triumphant expression was short-lived, however, vanishing as Lane stepped forward and the room quieted again. "And where will the people living there now go, Mayor Landon, if Hope House is shut down?"

Landon had just opened his mouth to reply when Breester chimed in. "I don't really care where they go, as long as they get the hell out of Starry Point."

The mayor shot a sidelong glance at Breester, who finally settled back into his chair.

"Mayor Landon, the question was for you," Lane reminded him curtly. "And I'd like an answer."

Landon donned the smooth smile again, a blend of impatience and condescension. "Ms. Kramer, may I remind you that it was I who took up your cause when you came to Starry Point, wanting to turn one of our most historic buildings into a bed-and-breakfast? I did so because I was convinced the proposition would prove a good thing for Starry Point, just as I'm convinced that closing this halfway house and ridding our community of its potentially dangerous element will prove a good thing for Starry Point. Perhaps, coming from Chicago, where crime and bad elements are tolerated, you can't understand our desire for safety."

"Safety?" she shot back, furious at this unfounded implication. "We're talking about television sets here, bicycles and coffee cans full of change. No one's been hurt."

"Yet."

The word hung in charged air while Lane searched for a response that would settle the room. "Hope House has been in existence for several years now, Mayor Landon," she said at last, over the din. "Can you tell me, please, if there's ever been an arrest of any kind associated with its residents?"

Landon's eyes slid to Breester, who was sitting with his arms mutinously folded.

"No, there has not, Ms. Kramer," Breester said flatly. "But, as I'm sure you know, the population of Hope House isn't a stable one. They're drifters and transients, there one day, gone the next. Consequently, we have no idea on any given day what sort of element might be housed there—or what they might be capable of."

More murmurs, more eyes turning in her direction. He was playing on their prejudices, shamelessly stoking their fears, and it was working.

"Of course they're transient!" she shot back in total frustration. "They're there to get back on their feet so they can reenter society. The fact that they do eventually leave is proof that Hope House is helping people. And now you want to pull the plug based on zero evidence!"

Landon smiled at Breester, an icy curl that signaled he was ready to step in. "Tell me, Ms. Kramer," he said, the warning plain in both tone and expression. "How do you think it would affect your business if it were known that you encourage people like Dirty Mary to hang about your inn?"

The threat hadn't been a subtle one. Michael cleared his throat and stepped forward. "I don't believe you've answered Ms. Kramer's question, Mr. Landon."

Something dark flitted across Landon's face. He produced a handkerchief from his suit pocket, dabbed briefly at his upper lip, then tucked it away. The condescending smile slid back into place, a bit tighter than before.

"You're a friend of Ms. Kramer's, I take it, Mr.—?"

"Forrester. And I'm currently a guest at the Cloister."

"A guest. Well, then, this really doesn't concern you, although I suppose I don't mind answering the question. It's very simple, really. Here in Starry Point, we're not used to having our homes plundered, and our women afraid to go out after dark. In fact, before this nonsense started, very few of our residents even bothered to lock their doors. They do now, though, because they feel threatened by the dangerous element in our midst. That doesn't make me happy, Mr. Forrester. My first concern—my only concern—is the safety of our citizens. Where the residents of Hope House ultimately end up isn't my problem."

"Dangerous element," Lane spat. "Who told you anyone at Hope House was a dangerous element? Have you spoken to the people who run the place? Have you spoken to a single doctor? Or is this just a convenient conclusion?"

"Ms. Kramer, you seem to have a short memory. I seem to recall you feeling compelled to call the police yourself several weeks ago because of a light you thought you saw?"

"A light Donny Breester assured me was only a figment of my imagination."

"Sit down, lady, and let's get on with this!" someone shouted near the front. But Lane wasn't finished.

"You haven't got a shred of evidence, and you're tossing around words like *transient* and *dangerous* because you want people to be afraid. But what happens when you get your way? What happens when Hope House closes and the break-ins keep happening? Because they *will* keep happening."

Landon gave the knot of his tie a yank, then cleared his throat. "Ms. Kramer, it seems you've allowed your personal feelings for these . . . *people* . . . to cloud your judgment. But what you need to keep in mind is that it only takes one unbalanced individual to put this community at risk, something our Old Pointers know only too well. They've seen what can happen when an unstable individual is allowed to walk free rather than being kept under lock and key. The result is very often tragic, as it was in this case. And it didn't have to happen. The party in question was confined for a time, but ended up being released. Because of that, someone died. I'm not going to end up with something like that on my hands."

Lane had no idea what he was referring to, but the older members of the crowd apparently did. A rumble went up. Grim faces. Heads nodding in shared recollection. Landon seemed to sense his moment and took it, his voice suddenly thundering above the din.

"Which is why I'm asking the council to take up the matter and schedule a vote for the immediate closure of Hope House, as well as exploring the possibility of eminent domain of the property for auction at some future date."

Lane felt a sick hollow in the pit of her stomach as one by one the council members nodded their assent. And with that, Mayor Landon announced the date of the vote, two weeks hence, and quickly concluded the meeting.

Scattered applause gradually gained momentum, a wave that seemed to roll from the front of the room to the back, where she and Michael were standing. Lane couldn't say she was shocked; numb was a better description for what she felt. One look at Michael, however, was enough to tell her he was anything but numb. His hands were fisted at his sides, his shoulders bunched up toward his ears, an enigmatic gesture that had become strangely familiar.

"Michael?"

He didn't answer, just stared at the dais where the council members had begun to collect their things and move toward the steps.

"Michael," she said again. "The meeting's over."

He turned finally, blinking hard, as if he'd forgotten she was there at all. "Let's go," he said thickly, and headed for the door.

Lane trailed him to the car, saying nothing as they waited their turn to pull out of the rapidly emptying lot. She was caught between seething over Landon's false accusations, and an uneasy curiosity about the black mood that had suddenly come over Michael. While she would dearly love to think he'd suffered a change of heart about Mary, it hardly seemed likely.

It was far more probable that he was miffed with her for ignoring his advice and publicly crossing swords with the mayor. Well, maybe she had, but someone had to stand up for what was right. Not that it had made any difference. If she didn't connect with someone from Hope House soon—someone with the resources to fight Harold Landon—there'd be no hope for Hope House.

Chapter 41

The parlor felt too quiet after the crowded buzz of the meeting hall, the clock in the hall hollow and gloomy as it began to strike nine. Michael pocketed his car keys and headed for the stairs without so much as a word. Lane watched him go, his feet slow and heavy as they negotiated the steps. He hadn't even bothered to remove his jacket.

He hadn't said a word on the ride home, his eyes intent on the road, hands locked on the wheel, as if driving through a storm only he could see. She had wanted to go for coffee, or maybe grab some dinner, since neither of them had eaten, to talk about the meeting and ask what he thought she should do next. Instead, she had decided to leave him to his mood. This was her fight, after all. He'd made that plain from the start.

Her head was throbbing, and had been since about halfway through the meeting. In the kitchen, she scared up a couple of Advil, washed them down with a glass of milk, made a peanut butter sandwich, then climbed the two flights of stairs to her rooms. She hadn't done much work of late, almost none, in fact, and she had an article due next week. It was only nine. Maybe she could get the thing started, scribble down an outline, a few bullet points. Except she didn't feel like working. Her thoughts were too jumbled, outrage and impotence and disgust all roiling together like water behind a dam, bottled up with no outlet.

Tomorrow she'd have to tell Mary how things stood, that they had two weeks to find a way to block the mayor's plans or Hope House would be shuttered, its residents scattered who knew where. Two weeks. She dreaded being the bearer of such news. But what of the recipient? What would it be like for someone like Mary to hear such a thing, to know the one safe thing in her life was about to be yanked away?

After changing into her sweats, she wandered into her writing room and flipped open her laptop, hoping the muse would descend. Instead, she checked her e-mail. Her mother had arrived home safely. Robert promised to have his people on Hope House's funding trail first thing in the morning. Well, it was something at least. And maybe she'd hear something back from R&C Limited in the next few days.

It took only a few minutes of staring at her notes to realize she was wasting her time trying to work in her present mood. Instead, she shut down the computer, removed the battered sketchbook from the desk drawer, and padded back to the bed to prop herself up against a bank of pillows.

As always, the fairy-tale images spoke to her, a beautiful queen and handsome young knights, castles twined with flowers like small white moons. But tonight there was something new—or rather, something she'd missed—tiny, almost imperceptible differences between one page and the next that she now realized created a kind of visual timeline. Suddenly, it was clear, in the gradual but steady climb of vines up castle walls, the subtle leaching of color from the queen's golden hair, the growing gloom of a darkening sky and mounting gray waves, all of which seemed to culminate on the book's final page, with the red-haired siren calling across the waves to a beached and broken boat. It was an ominous chronology, a cautionary tale woven from page to page—but a caution against what?

Not liking the dark direction of her thoughts, Lane closed the book and slid it into the nightstand. She had enough on her mind without worrying about a collection of old drawings. Flicking off the lamp, she rolled onto her back, praying that sleep would come quickly, and without dreams. Instead, she lay awake, counting the seconds between the rhythmic blue-white strokes of Starry Point Light.

She had just dozed off when something, a creak or a thud, brought her up with a start. Propped on one elbow, she trained her ears to the silence. There was nothing. Convinced that she'd imagined the whole thing, she lay back down, then heard it again, though perhaps sensed was a more apt description. She was used to the inn's arthritic moans and groans, the creaking of walls and floors, like century-old bones settling at the end of a long day, but this was different. This was man-made and furtive somehow—the kind of sound a person made when trying to make no sound at all.

Breath held, she padded to the door, peered out into the empty corridor, then tiptoed down the first flight of stairs. Michael's door was closed, no sign of light leaking from the narrow chink beneath. At least someone could sleep.

Downstairs, she moved from room to room, bumping about in the dark as she checked doors and windows, but nothing seemed amiss. She had just placed a hand on the newel post, preparing to return to her rooms, when she caught the muffled but unmistakable crack of breaking glass, shards ringing in the quiet night air as they tinkled to the ground.

It came again, from outside, from somewhere near the front of the house. Lane hurried to the parlor and pushed back the curtains, peering across the street at the Rourke House, bone white now, and bled of color beneath the waning half-moon. She saw nothing at first, just vacant windows and the stark silhouette of its long-forsaken tower. Then her heart squeezed against her ribs as a light appeared, not inside the house this time, but moving stealthily through the greenhouse. A prickle coursed the length of her spine as she stared at the hollowed-out structure, eerily skeletal with half its panes gone.

With hands gone suddenly clammy, she eased open the window, wondering how she'd ended up in a bad episode of *Scooby-Doo*. The sound came again, jarring in the icy stillness, but this time it was punctuated by a wild arc of thin white light. Again and again, the brittle shattering repeated, each blow synchronized with a similar blade of light.

It took a moment to make sense of what she was seeing, but eventually she realized the intruder must be using a flashlight to smash out the greenhouse's few remaining panes. She shivered as it came again, a stark and chilling sound, of long-held anger finally being unleashed—of someone gone mad.

She should wake Michael, she knew, but she was shaking all over, and her legs seemed to have grown roots to the floor. And then, as suddenly as it had appeared, the light was gone, the night dead still. She was about to head for the phone when she was struck with the uneasy notion that she was being watched, that whoever was in the greenhouse not only knew she was at the window but was staring right back at her.

The thought sent a shot of adrenaline through her. Finally, she was able to move, to think. Should she phone the police, or would it only fuel Landon's plans when the story hit the *Islander Dispatch* the next morning, as it almost certainly would, complete with quotes from Starry Point's illustrious police chief? On the other hand, if she did call and they managed to catch the real perpetrator, the mayor's accusations would be exposed as the utter nonsense they were. Hope House would be spared.

Easing the window closed, she flipped the latch to the locked position, double-checked it, and made a beeline for the phone. She no longer cared about being quiet. Michael would be up soon enough when the police arrived. She had just picked up the handset when she noticed a pale spill of light from the kitchen, a light that hadn't been on when she came down. Had she been so distracted that she'd left the back door unlocked?

The phone felt slippery against her palm as she crept toward the kitchen. She was still trying to decide whether to use it to dial 911 or wield it as a weapon when she heard what sounded like the refrigerator door opening and closing. She let her breath out. Unless the intruder had worked up a thirst and rushed across the street for a cold beverage, she was probably safe.

Michael tossed her a look as she peered tentatively into the kitchen, his face in shadow from the small fluorescent over the sink. The sight of him, standing there with a carton of orange juice in his hand, nearly made her legs buckle with relief.

"God, Michael," she said breathlessly, moving to check the bolt on the back door. "I thought you were asleep. Actually, I'm glad you're not. I was about to call the police. There's someone over at the Rourke House again, in the greenhouse this time."

"You saw them?"

"No, but I saw a flashlight and heard glass breaking. Breester won't be able to pretend it was all a figment of my imagination when there's glass everywhere."

Michael made no reply, just stood there, looking at her, his glass of juice untouched, a faint sheen of sweat slicking his forehead.

"Michael, are you—"

She saw it then, his jacket draped on the peg beside the door, the collar glistening with splinters of broken glass. She reached out to touch the sleeve—still cool—and bumped against something protruding from the pocket. With a dawning sense of dread, she pulled it free—a heavy black flashlight, its lens shattered.

She took a step back, and then another, until her spine was against the door and there was nowhere to go, nothing to do but stand there, a flashlight in one hand, a phone in the other, as she put the pieces together, remembering another night, another mysterious beam of light.

"It was you?"

Michael said nothing. He was breathing heavily, she saw now, his nostrils flared with the effort to appear composed. But his eyes were somewhere else, vacant and filled with something that made her mouth go dry.

"What were you doing at the Rourke House tonight?" she demanded, holding up the phone. "Tell me now, or I'm dialing 911."

Michael set down his juice and met her eyes without flinching. "I grew up in that house."

Chapter 42

Michael

There was a flood of relief as the words left his mouth, relief and horror that for the first time in thirty years he'd actually said them aloud. And yet deep down, he'd wanted to say them, had perhaps even needed to. A bead of sweat traced along his temple as the clock ticked and the silence yawned. Before him, Lane stood pale and disbelieving, back against the door, knuckles white around the damning flashlight.

"I don't understand. Tell me why you were there."

He couldn't help it. He found himself grinning at her, a slow-spreading rictus that had nothing to do with humor and everything to do with the quiet rage still thrumming in his veins. It wasn't new, this rage; he'd been living with it for thirty years, quietly ignoring it, carefully controlling it—or so he'd thought until tonight. Landon had been the touch paper, the bastard's thinly veiled reference to his mother and the fire that had taken his brother's life, tossed to the crowd like so much red meat, as if he actually gave a damn about the Rourkes, or the events that had torn them apart.

He hadn't planned on losing it when he slipped out the back door and across the street with his flashlight. He'd gone there to be with his anger, to prove to himself that he could still live with it, control it. But that's not what happened.

"Michael?"

She said his name as if she were calling him back from somewhere very far away, leery, tentative. He was scaring the hell out of her, he knew, but he was eager to have it all out now. The words kept coming, like water from a hose that had been clamped for years.

"I was born Evan Michael Rourke, son of the Honorable Samuel R. Rourke, Starry Point's once-beloved mayor, and his mad wife, Hannah. The little ghost everyone's so fond of talking about was my brother, Peter. Tonight, at the meeting, the crazy person Landon was talking about was my mother."

A series of emotions played over her face: shock, pity, fear. She was shaking her head back and forth, slowly, as if trying to get the words to settle into some space in her brain where they might make sense. He wanted to tell her not to bother. He'd long since given up trying to figure out life's brutal sense of humor.

"There's more," he said, and saw her go a shade paler. "Showing up here wasn't an accident. I didn't need a place to do research." Was it possible she'd pressed herself even more closely against the door? "The truth is that for nearly two years I slept under this roof with a lot of other boys in what you now call the Tower Suite, and I needed to come back."

"Why?"

Why indeed? He felt a wave of nausea as he flashed back to that night, to the mingled reek of vomit and whiskey and smoke, his mother clinging to him, wild-eyed with panic. How could he make her understand the shame of it, the guilt of an eight-year-old boy, carried with him still, not for some hideous thing he'd done—but for something he hadn't? How telling it, even now, brought the terror of that night screaming back, until he could taste the ashes at the back of his throat, hear the terrified screams of the brother he couldn't save.

"I needed to find something."

She tilted her head, eyeing him warily. "What?"

"Something I left behind when I was a boy. I thought it might . . ." He let the words dangle. "It doesn't matter." But it did matter. It mattered a great deal, though even now he couldn't say why. So he lied. Because it was easier, and because he wanted to believe it. "It was a lifetime ago, three lifetimes, actually. Hannah and Peter Rourke are dead, and I'm someone else now."

Lane took a step forward, then checked herself. "Your mother was . . . sick?"

He nodded. She was putting it all together now. He could see it in her eyes. "For almost as long as I can remember."

"And you blame her for Peter?"

"I blame myself."

"But that's—" She stopped midsentence and blinked at him. "Why?"

"I wasn't there. When the fire started, I wasn't there."

"Where were you?"

He hated the gentleness of her voice, the carefulness of it, as if he were as mad as his mother and might suddenly snap. "I was in the greenhouse. I would go there sometimes. Hannah used to grow these flowers that only bloomed at night. Moonflowers, she called them. They were her favorite. She said if you waited for one to bloom and then made a wish, whatever you asked for would come true. So I was out there waiting to make a wish."

Her face softened. "What were you wishing for?"

It was an absurd question, but one he had known she would ask. "For my mother to not be crazy anymore. It didn't come true. I fell asleep instead, listening to the rain against the glass. When I woke up I saw the flames shooting from our bedroom window."

She laid a hand on his arm. At some point she had put down the phone and the flashlight; he didn't know when or where. Her eyes were wide and full of feeling when they met his. "That's why you went there, why you smashed the windows."

"I think I must have been waiting thirty years to do that."

"Do you feel better?"

"No."

"Michael, you can't blame yourself for what happened that night."

"I was supposed to be the man of the house. That's what Hannah said when my father died, that it was up to me to look after her and Peter."

"Yes. It's what mothers say when they need their sons to be brave. But you were a child. She didn't mean it literally. She couldn't have."

"You don't understand. Hannah Rourke wasn't like other mothers. There was talk, after my father died, and even before, about putting her away. 'All those pills she takes, and who's going to make sure the children are fed, and what if she finally snaps and hurts one of those poor boys?' They never said any of it in front of me, of course, but even as a kid you hear things. They could have done it, too—she was that crazy. But she was married to the mayor. So they left her alone— or mostly alone. But things got bad after my father died. Hannah wouldn't believe he was dead. She wouldn't even go to his funeral."

"I'm so sorry," Lane said, and he could see that she was. She bit her lip, as if reluctant to say what would come next. "People say . . . I mean . . . I'd always heard that Hannah survived the fire. But just now you said she was dead. How did she die?"

"No idea. I didn't ask for details. My mother—my adopted mother, I mean—told me she heard it from her attorney a few years ago. I think she was relieved. I've always had a hunch she was afraid Hannah would pop up one day to claim me, and there'd be a terrible scene."

"She never did, though?"

"No."

"Did you want her to?"

Michael turned away, splashing his untouched juice into the sink. "No."

"It must have been hard on you."

He heard her come up behind him, felt her hand on his shoulder. "It was harder on Peter," he said bitterly, shrugging free of her touch. He didn't want her pity, didn't want to be consoled.

"Were you very close?"

"Of course we were close. He was my brother."

"No," she said softly. "I meant you and Hannah."

"I don't want to talk about her anymore."

"It might help."

"It won't."

"Sometimes if you talk things through you realize you've been remembering them wrong."

He rounded on her then, feeling the memories like brands, as sharp and searing as fire across his right shoulder and down his back. "What do you want to hear, Lane? That I got there too late? That by the time I dragged my drunken mother out of her room the fire had spread too far? That the stairs collapsed while I was trying to get to Peter? That he died because I was out making a wish on a goddamn flower?"

"I'm sorry. I didn't mean—"

"Forget it."

Lane wound her arms tight to her body, shuddering visibly. "I don't think I can. I don't think you can either, though you've certainly been trying. Can I ask you something?"

He studied her face a moment, wondering what was coming, then decided the harm had already been done. "What?"

"That thing you do with your shoulders, the way you hunch them sometimes, like you're doing now—I've noticed that it happens when you talk about the past."

Michael went very still, taking careful inventory of his body. He wasn't aware that he'd been doing *that thing*. In fact, he'd been doing his best to control the annoying and largely unconscious impulse that had plagued him most of his life. He hated that she'd noticed.

"I'm sorry. Was there a question in there?"

"I was wondering why you do it."

Michael said nothing. No words could describe the reminder he carried on his shoulders, the thing that marked him with the horror of that night, that would never let him forget. His fingers went to the collar of his shirt, numbly working one button at a time, until he was able to slide the blue oxford down his arms. Shifting slightly, he turned his right shoulder to the light.

It was Lane's turn to be silent, though her lips parted in a slow dawning of—what? Pity? Revulsion? He wasn't sure. Becca had simply pretended not to see them, her fingers always careful to skirt the shiny patches of puckered flesh. To this day he couldn't say for certain that she'd ever touched them.

There were tears in her eyes now, clinging to her lower lashes, making tiny spokes of them. "From that night?" she whispered. "From the fire?"

He nodded, about to pull his shirt back on when she reached for him. Her fingers were soft and cool, featherlight as they lit on his ruined flesh, a gesture of sympathy—and startling sensuality.

"Don't," he said, flinching, but made no move to avoid her touch. "Please."

The softest of pleas, little more than a whisper. Standing rigid, he closed his eyes, scarcely breathing as her fingers traced the shiny stretch of tissue, forcing himself to absorb all that was in the touch: recognition, acceptance—wanting. She wanted him. The realization was like a jolt of electricity through his limbs, undeniable and nearly crippling. Suddenly, he was shaking.

"Was it very bad?" she asked quietly.

"Yes." It was all he could do to form the word, to deny the fever

suddenly thundering in his blood. "They kept me in the hospital..."
His words trailed off in a gasp as he felt the moist warmth of her
mouth graze his shoulder, the caress of her cheek, pressed damply
there and held.

"I'm sorry," she breathed against his skin. "About all of it."

Her arms came around him then, circling from behind, the thrum
of her heart pounding against him and through him, matching the
beat of his own. At his core, something feral breathed to life, uncoil-
ing like a live thing: primitive, reckless, hungry. How had they come
to this place, this blinding flashpoint of rawness and need? He didn't
know, and he didn't care. Turning, he met her gaze and found the
only answer he needed.

Yes.

Chapter 43

Lane

Lane lay very still, afraid to break the spell. It was strange having a man in her bed, to lie naked and sated in this room she had never shared with anyone. She'd almost forgotten how good it could be, and how frightening—the yielding of secret places, of the self. There'd been no one since Bruce, and for the last year of their marriage, there hadn't even been him.

In the dark, she blushed as she relived the memory of Michael's mouth, his hands, everywhere at once, burning without consuming, taking without emptying, and she, in those deep, delicious moments, willing to give everything.

She hadn't meant for it to happen. It began with a touch, a simple gesture of compassion, but like Michael's brutal reaction in the greenhouse, emotions she thought under careful control had suddenly ignited without warning. She had gone out of her way to keep her feelings tightly reined, buttoned up, and out of sight—and for good reason. The last time she let a man into her life, she had allowed herself to be systematically dismantled, her pieces rearranged into an almost unrecognizable version of herself, until even now, five years later, she wasn't sure she had relocated all the fragments.

He was sleeping, one long bare leg draped casually over hers, his breathing smooth and rhythmic, keeping time with the milky beam of light that swept through the room at regular intervals. The tortured look was gone from his face, but for how long? They had talked after, about the horrors of that night, the blank horror in his mother's eyes when he found her frozen on the stairs, the weightless terror he felt as he plunged through a burning staircase—the terrible moment he realized Peter had stopped screaming.

The bleak unfairness of it was almost inconceivable. The boy—Evan then—who by the age of eight had already suffered a lifetime of tragedy, and the man asleep beside her now, who still carried those tragedies on his scarred shoulders, and probably always would. Because there was no way to reconcile with the dead, no way to forgive and no way to be forgiven.

Now, in retrospect, so many things made sense, like puzzle pieces shifting into place, the picture finally coming clear: his aversion to *Great Expectations* with its madwoman and its burning house, the warning to mend the rift with her mother before it was too late, his unapologetic revulsion of Mary and others like her, too poignant a reminder of the mother whose gradual unraveling had ultimately torn his family apart. Even his theory about houses having souls made sense now, in light of what the walls of the Rourke House must have witnessed in Hannah Rourke's day.

The rest of the story was only slightly better. Michael had lived at the Cloister, in the not-so-tender care of the nuns, until a suitable family could be found. It took almost two years before he was whisked away to Boston to meet his new parents, who apparently had no shortage of money, but fell rather short when it came to demonstrations of affection. Having his name changed the minute he arrived certainly couldn't have helped matters, though he'd claimed with a shrug against the pillows not to have cared one way or the other. She suspected he'd probably stopped caring about a lot of things by then.

It would be light soon; she should try to sleep. Beside her, Michael sighed and turned away, taking his warmth with him. The loss was startling. Rolling onto her side, she scooted closer, fitting her hips with his until the tips of her breasts grazed the scars along his back. He stirred, groaning sleepily, then went still again. Yes, Lane thought, closing her eyes, it was good to have a man in her bed—this man. Michael Forrester or Evan Rourke—she didn't care which he was, so long as he was beside her when she woke in the morning.

He wasn't, though.

Instead, she woke to a tangle of cold sheets and a dent where his head had rested only a few hours before. It was early, a little past six, the room bathed in flat gray light. Lane surveyed the telling trail of clothing strewn across the carpet—sweatpants, T-shirt, socks, panties—precisely where they'd been shed in a feverish route to the bed. But nothing of Michael's, she noted, as if he'd gone out of his way to erase all traces of his presence.

Listening for signs of life, she was greeted with only silence. No creak of floorboards, no rush of water through old pipes. Had he packed up and slunk away during the night, convinced what had happened between them was a mistake? The thought left a hollow place in her belly.

After dragging on fresh sweats, she padded down the back stairs, relieved to catch the smell of coffee drifting up from the kitchen. Not gone, then. Her knees actually wobbled with relief as they cleared the last few steps. But Michael wasn't in the kitchen, and the jacket he'd hastily draped on a peg near the door last night was gone. Beside the coffeepot stood a clean mug and spoon, along with a curtly penned note.

Gone for a walk to clear my head. Made coffee.

Lane blinked at the note briefly, then crumpled it in her fist. Of course he'd made coffee. She could see he'd made coffee. What he hadn't done was explain why he had slipped out of her bed before dawn, and out the back door like a thief.

Filling the mug Michael had set out for her, she slumped into the nearest chair. She had imagined a breakfast prepared together, a newspaper shared between shy, furtive smiles, fingers stealing across the table to touch, and linger. Instead, here she sat with a mug of coffee—alone.

The clock above the sink ticked steadily against the silence, a grim reminder of other empty mornings, and the stretch of others like it that seemed to await her. How had she come to live this life of near misses? A marriage that had never quite gotten off the ground. A pregnancy that had suffered the same fate. Even her novel had been stillborn.

She thought of the half-finished manuscript. Had Bruce thrown it away? Or was it still there in the bottom drawer of her nightstand, covered with Professor Bingham's scathing red notes—one more failure, one more loose end? She had her articles, a kind of consolation prize, she supposed, for the life she wanted but had failed to create— a year's supply of Turtle Wax instead of a novel with her name on the cover.

Her eyes wandered to the refrigerator with its crayon-bright stick girl and grinning stick dog. The scoopy blue waves and orange-slice sun were unbearably happy, stirring an ache that suddenly made it hard to breathe. She had wanted all that once, the crayons and the peanut butter sandwiches, the school supplies and field trips to the zoo.

She had wanted so much once. When had she stopped? When had she resigned herself to solitary mugs of coffee drunk in a solitary kitchen? Michael was right. Somewhere along the way, by small, insidious degrees, she had decided it was safer to hide behind the Cloister's thick stone walls than to risk another failure—to risk being unloved.

Until last night, when in a moment of weakness, she had let Michael inside those walls, had let him see and touch the fragile parts of herself, parts she'd hidden away for safekeeping. The result had been so primal, so wholly and blindingly unexpected, that it almost frightened her. Could she come out of hiding, open her heart again? Risk loving—and losing? And with Michael off somewhere clearing his head, did it really matter?

Come to think of it, her head could do with a bit of clearing, too. Stretching up out of her chair, she grabbed her jacket from the peg near the door, wedged her feet into her duck boots, and stepped out onto the deck. The weather fit her mood as she crossed the dunes and made her way toward the shore, blustery and cold with no sign of clearing.

She loved blustery days, when she had the beach to herself, the wild thrash of the sea, the wind raking through her hair, Starry Point Light looming chalk white against a dull metal sky. She was just beginning to leave her thoughts behind, to lose herself in the rhythm of her heels against the hard-packed sand, when a splash of green out on the jetty caught her eye.

If she was quick about it, maybe she could turn around and slink back to the inn before he spotted her. And yet her legs refused to move. Instead, she studied him in the distance, perched on a sharp jut of rock, shoulders hunched, gaze trained out to sea.

He had to be freezing out there in all that wind and blowing spray, and yet he found it preferable to facing her and dealing with what had happened last night. The thought was vexing enough to start her feet moving again. Out on the jetty, he couldn't run.

She had closed the distance by half when she saw his posture change. Even at a distance she could feel his eyes, feel the tension stretch between them across the length of wind-whipped beach. He stood when she reached the base of the light, hands shoved deep into the pockets of his jeans as he watched her navigate her way out onto the craggy boulders. For one yawning, interminable moment they stood staring at each other over the steadily drumming waves.

"You were gone when I woke up," Lane said finally.

Michael ducked his head sheepishly. "That probably didn't look good."

"Not very good. No."

"I made coffee."

"I know. I read your note. The head-clearing thing...did that happen?"

"Lane—"

"Please," she said, cutting him off. "Let me go first."

Michael nodded, but the steady tic along his jaw told her he already knew what he was going to say, and was clearly impatient to be done with it. For a moment, she wondered if she should bother saying anything at all. Then she heard her mother's voice, telling her to stand up for what she wanted. Squaring her shoulders, she cleared her throat.

"Last night we connected. And I don't just mean between the sheets. You told me things—things I suspect you've never told anyone, things I think you've always been afraid to say out loud. I don't know what that means, but it has to mean something. So before you say what I think you're about to—"

"Lane—"

"Am I wrong?"

"No. You're right. I've never told those things to anyone. But then, you didn't leave me much choice. You were about to call the police."

Lane's eyes widened at his cavalier tone. "And afterward, when you were lying in my bed—all those memories, about Peter and your mother—I wasn't holding the phone then."

"You don't understand. I don't expect you to, but I...needed someone."

Lane flinched, absorbing the words like a well-aimed slap. "You're saying I was handy?"

"I didn't mean it like that." He paused, raking his hair off his forehead. "Or maybe I did. I don't know. I wasn't exactly thinking straight, as you'll no doubt recall."

"Well, lucky for you, then, that I happened to be around."

"It was more than that, and you know it. I'm just . . . I'm not good with intimacy."

"Oh, on the contrary, you're very good at it. It's the aftermath you suck at."

Michael grimaced. "Lane, please. I don't want it to be like this. I never meant to take things where they went. I care for you, but—"

"But what?" A gust of wind sent her bangs into her eyes. She shoved them back. "This past week, while my mother was here, you . . . we . . . I thought—"

"I know what you thought, Lane. I'd be lying if I said I hadn't thought about it, too, but the kind of life I've had, the things I told you last night, don't exactly make for happy endings. Marital bliss and happily ever after weren't part of any world I grew up in. Which is how I know they can't ever be part of my future. And that's why I'm out here, making my peace with what my gut knows is the right thing to do."

Lane felt dread, hot and salty, clutching at her throat. "The right thing?"

"Leaving Starry Point. Forgetting last night. Forgetting you."

She blinked back the beginning of tears now, determined not to let him see. "And that's what you want—to just forget?"

For a long time he was silent, as if choosing his words carefully. "I should never have come back," he said at last. "I came back to find something, or at least look for it—something silly, I realize now. I thought if I could hold it, face it, the dreams would stop and I could get on with my life. I was wrong."

"You haven't answered the question."

"You mean is leaving what I want?" He paused, craning his head back to eye a pair of gulls circling against the cold gray sky. When his gaze returned to hers, his eyes were empty, flat. "I wish I had a better answer, Lane, but I won't lie. Even if leaving isn't what I want, it's what I need. And if you listen to what I'm telling you, you'll realize it's what you need, too. I wouldn't be any good for you. What you need from a man—what you deserve—I just don't have to give."

"How do you know?"

"Because it died. Years ago, along with my father, and Peter, and my crazy mother. The night of the fire ... before ... after. That's too many nightmares to share with another person. I won't make promises I know I can't keep."

"So that's it?" She blinked at him, her eyes watering in the wind. "You're going?"

"It's best. And not just for me. I know that's not what you want to hear. It's not what I want to say, but it's what has to happen—before I hurt you."

"You wouldn't hurt me."

He looked at her then, long and steady. "I would, Lane. Not on purpose, but I would. And I'd rather hurt you a little now than hurt you a lot later. You don't need another man who can't love you the way you should be loved. And that's who I'd be."

Lane fought to keep her voice under control, though everything in her ached to ask him to stay. "How soon will you go?"

"There's a nor'easter heading for the coast. As soon as it clears I'll get on the road."

That was it, then? A slightly more eloquent version of *It's not you; it's me*? And he'd already checked the weather. How efficient.

She managed a nod but kept her eyes on the sea. She didn't trust herself to look at him, not when her emotions were still so raw, her heart so exposed. Apparently she'd wasted her time worrying about whether she was ready to risk her heart. The choice had been made for her, before the memory of his touch had even been allowed to fade.

"You're freezing," Michael said, taking a step toward her. "We should get back."

Lane stepped out of his reach, certain she would come undone if he touched her now. "I'm fine," she lied, wrapping her arms close to her body. "You go. It's my turn to clear my head."

Chapter 44

Dally was unloading a bag of supplies in the kitchen when Lane returned. She'd forgotten it was Thursday, Dally's usual day, and that she'd asked her to pick up a few things Sam needed from Sewell's Hardware to finish repairing the shed roof. She finished checking off the items in the box—nails, caulk, paintbrushes—then handed off the receipt.

"It's all here. Where do you—hey, you look like crap on a cracker."

"Thanks. Bit of a bumpy night. Have you . . . uh . . . seen Michael?"

"Professor McDreamy?" Dally jerked her chin at the ceiling. "Been banging around upstairs since I got here. I think he's rearranging the furniture."

No, he was steering clear of her, hoping to avoid a sequel to their earlier conversation. And probably packing. He'd said what he needed to. All that was left was the leaving. Part of her—the rational part, at least—understood. He'd been hurt, scarred in every way it was possible for a man to be scarred, and he needed to protect himself. But the other part, the part that had let down its guard long enough to fall in love, needed him to fight through those scars, to risk new wounds in order to heal the old ones.

Was it fair to want such a thing? To ask him to lay himself open, to trust, when, given their track records, it was very possible they'd both end up hurt? Probably not, but right or wrong, she did want it. If she knew more about those terrible years, about the boy who had endured such loss, the man who, even now, suffered such guilt, perhaps she could—what? He was leaving in a few days. There was no time.

"You left the coffeepot on," Dally scolded.

Lane blinked at her. "What?"

"I said you left the pot on. Are you sure you're okay? You don't look so good."

"We just didn't get much sleep, that's all."

Dally instantly seized on the gaffe. "We?"

"I meant I didn't get much sleep."

"You said *we*."

Lane groaned, too weary to wriggle out of the noose. "Okay, fine—we."

"You and the professor? I knew it! Hey, the Christmas trees are in at Sewell's. They were unloading them this morning. You should get one this year. You and the professor could decorate it together."

"The professor will be gone by Christmas," Lane said evenly.

"Gone?"

"In a few days, as a matter of fact."

"I thought he was staying through the winter."

"Something . . . came up."

Dally stared at her. "And you're not going to tell me what it is, are you?"

"Not now, no."

"You don't want him to go. That's why you're upset. You're falling for him."

Lane shifted her gaze to the window. "Fell," she said softly. "But it doesn't matter. He's going back to Vermont."

"But why?"

"He says he can't be the man I deserve."

Dally's mouth rounded. "He actually said that? Jesus, he's a player! A lousy, two-faced player! And not even an original one if he's using lines like that."

Lane shook her head. "There's more to it, Dally. I can't say what, but there is. He has his reasons. Or thinks he does."

"Don't defend him! How do you think the bastards always get away with the stuff they do? No one calls them on it, that's how. I've had experience with his type. I've got Skye to prove it. I say you toss him out on his ear. Today. Now."

Lane winced. She couldn't say the idea hadn't crossed her mind. It had. But some tiny, shameful part of her still hoped Michael might change his mind, might be willing to take a leap of faith, to reach for happily ever after.

"Oh, honey, I'm sorry," Dally said, her voice soft now. "You're upset, and here I stand, telling you how to live your life because five years ago I let myself get knocked up by a bastard. Don't listen to me. Your lips are blue. You must be freezing. Why don't you go have a nice long soak? Everything looks better after a bath."

Upstairs, Lane hovered in the doorway of her room, staring at the discarded bits of clothing strewn haphazardly across the floor, recalling the storm of passion that had erupted in the kitchen and continued all the way up the stairs. She hadn't bothered to think about the fallout. Neither of them had. At the time, in that breathless, mindless moment, it had seemed right, inevitable somehow. But now, with the breathlessness gone, she saw it for exactly what Michael admitted it was—a night of convenience.

Snatching up the clothes, she dumped them into the hamper, then tidied the bed. Not for Dally's sake, but for her own. She couldn't undo what had happened last night, but she could at least hide the evidence.

In the end, she opted for a shower rather than a bath. The last thing she wanted was to languish in the tub, wallowing in self-pity and recrimination. She needed to do something, occupy her mind with something besides Michael. In fresh sweats, she padded back down to the kitchen for a much-needed jolt of caffeine. Less than two hours' sleep, compounded by this morning's rather unpleasant scene on the jetty, was beginning to take its toll. Her head ached dully and she was starting to bump into things, a sure sign that she was heading for a crash, and probably not a pretty one.

The kitchen smelled faintly of scorched coffee, the remnants of Michael's good deed nearly boiled dry now. Dumping the syrupy dregs into the sink, she scrubbed the pot clean, then measured several scoops of dark roast into the basket. She was relieved to find that Dally had gone up to start her work. She absolutely adored the girl, but she really didn't feel like being the object of anyone's pity.

She'd planned to get some work done, to hide out in her writing room as long as she could before having to face Michael again. Now she seriously doubted she'd be able to string two sentences together. She had never been one for naps but was contemplating one when she saw Mary crabbing her way around the corner and up the dune.

The vote.

She'd nearly forgotten about last night's town council meeting— and the bad news she was going to have to deliver. A sense of dread settled over her as she pulled out the thermos and turned the gas on under the kettle. She was too wrung out to have this conversation now. And yet Mary deserved to know. How exactly was she supposed to say it? *In two weeks the town council is going to vote on whether you have a place to live?*

Maybe it could wait a bit, until she received a response to her letter, or heard something from her mother. The news would go down better with a little dash of hope. She could just leave out the part about the mayor calling for a vote, say the meeting had been about Hope House, but only to take the pulse of the community. Would that be wrong? The thought of lying made her squeamish, but not as squeamish as telling the truth. And it wasn't as if Mary's knowing would affect the outcome. Yes, it could wait.

Mary glanced up as she approached, shielding her eyes with one hand. "What's wrong?" she said instantly. "Something's happened."

"No, I just—"

"It's to do with the meeting, isn't it? It's bad?"

Damn. She should have known better. "It isn't good," she said, taking a seat on the sand. "The mayor wants everyone to think the break-ins have to do with someone from Hope House."

"It's a lie!"

"I know that, Mary. Lots of people do. But there are some who . . ." She let the words dangle, not wanting to go on but knowing she needed to. "He's trying to scare people, hinting that you and the others are . . . dangerous."

Mary's lower lip jutted angrily. "No one there is dangerous. You can't go to a place like Hope House if you pose any kind of threat. They're careful about that."

"I know that, too, but there are some who don't, and at the moment, that's playing right into the mayor's hands." Lane unscrewed the thermos, filled a paper cup with tea, and handed it to Mary.

Mary sipped thoughtfully, then surprised Lane by reaching out to take her hand. "You're a good one, my girl. A very good one. No matter what happens."

Lane glanced at the hand resting on hers, thin and slightly papery, the knuckles blue with cold. "We'll hear something soon. I promise. And then we'll be able to fight."

It was a promise she knew she had no business making. What if no one came forward with the resources to stand against Landon? She could still see the faces at last night's meeting when he'd hinted that the tragedy that had taken the life of Peter Rourke could happen again if they failed to heed his warning. Fearmongering at its most shameless, and yet it had worked. No wonder Michael had gone a little crazy. It couldn't have been easy listening to that, knowing full well it was his mother Landon was talking about.

"Mary," Lane ventured cautiously. "You seem to know a lot about Starry Point. Can I ask you something?"

Mary withdrew her hand and sat waiting.

"Last night, at the meeting, Landon hinted around about something that happened here a long time ago in the house across the street, about the boy who died there in the fire. I was wondering if you could tell me anything about his mother. Her name was Hannah Rourke."

Mary stiffened. "I can tell you she's dead. Dead and gone."

"Yes, but when she was alive, was she—"

Mary raised her eyes to Lane's, the beginnings of a storm quietly churning in their depths. "Crazy?"

Lane bit her lip, wondering suddenly if this was a good idea. "I was going to say ill. But yes, I suppose that's what I mean."

Mary was quiet for a time, her attention pinned on the horizon. When she finally spoke her voice was strangely flat, devoid of anything like sympathy.

"She cracked up. They put her somewhere, locked her up good and tight. But then, they had no choice, you see. She kept making noise, going on about her husband, how he wasn't really dead, just holed up somewhere with his money and a woman. If she was smart she would have gone along nice and quiet and not tried to spoil the man's plans. But she wasn't smart."

Lane pulled her knees to her chest, hugging them tight. It was exactly what Michael had told her. "Do you know how she died?"

Quietly, almost imperceptibly, Mary began to rock. "Does it matter? Does anyone really care how people like that—people like me—die, so long as we do it cleanly and quietly? And why ask me? After so many years, why ask at all?"

Lane sipped her tea, toying briefly with the idea of sharing Michael's story. That was the real reason she'd brought all this up, after all, to dig for something, anything, that might give her some insight into what Michael had gone through, something that might make him stay. But it was too personal, and not really her story to tell. Instead, she settled for a half-truth.

"Last night, Landon was trying to scare people into agreeing with him about closing Hope House. He brought up the fire, and Peter. He wants to connect Hope House with the kind of people who could hurt a child."

"The boy," Mary whispered, rocking in earnest now. "They've found out about the boy."

"I killed a boy once."

A sudden chill prickled up Lane's spine. She'd been so desperate for answers that she hadn't bothered to consider what bringing up Peter Rourke's fate might mean to Mary's already precarious psyche, the dark association she might make to her own tragic past—and the ghost of another dead boy?

"Oh, Mary, no. I didn't mean—"

"My fault," she muttered. "My fault. My fault. All my fault."

"Mary, look at me. Listen to me. We weren't talking about you. We were talking about Hannah, about the fire."

"Burned," she wailed mournfully. "All burned."

"Yes, the upstairs burned in the house across the street. Do you remember now?"

Mary shook her head miserably from side to side. "I was careful. Always careful. But someone must have told about that poor dead boy." Her head came up, her face crumpled with misery. "Did you tell?"

"Mary, please. You're just mixed up. What I asked has nothing to do with you, nothing to do with the boy. I want you to forget about it."

"They'll close Hope House because of me. Because I'm the dangerous one. I'll have nowhere to go."

Lane reached for her. "Mary, please—"

Mary jerked back as if she'd been burned. "I won't go back! I won't!"

Before Lane could stop her, Mary was on her feet, scrambling away, up and over the dune. It took a moment to register what was happening, but finally Lane got her legs under her and gave chase, stumbling as she crossed the boardwalk and headed at a run for the empty lot. By the time she reached the road, Mary was already out of reach, on her bike and pedaling away, her neon pink flag bobbing in the wind.

Lane felt a sickening sense of déjà vu creep in as she watched the bicycle disappear from view. She had promised not to pry. And she hadn't, exactly. Instead, she had raised questions about another woman with mental illness. And another dead boy. It didn't matter that their pasts were unconnected. The similarities had been too much for Mary. She had melted down—again. And it had been her fault.

Chapter 45

Michael

Michael surveyed the library wearily. There were books everywhere—spread open on the large mahogany table he had converted to a desk, arranged in untidy stacks on the floor, relevant pages carefully marked with yellow sticky notes—all needing to be packed and loaded for the drive back to Middlebury. He eyed the pile of scribble-filled legal pads on his chair, thought of the dozens of research files he'd filled. He'd done a lot of work here, good work by both literary and academic standards, and yet he couldn't muster a sense of anything resembling satisfaction.

How was it possible that he'd spent so much time and energy on a thing he no longer gave a damn about, or more accurately, had never really given a damn about? And how in God's name was he supposed to go back and finish the thing?

He had purposely waited until Lane went out to the dunes to begin packing up. She was angry, hurt. He didn't blame her. In Dickens's day his actions would have earned him the reputation of a cad or bounder. Fair enough. Except he'd never set out to hurt her. What happened between them had simply erupted in the heat of the moment. But even as he formed the thought, he knew it wasn't true. Their lovemaking might have been spontaneous, but he sure as hell couldn't say it was unexpected. Not when he'd so thoroughly enjoyed playing house with her, kissing and touching until the lines had blurred and he'd forgotten it was all just a charade. Last night might have been a mistake, but he sure as hell couldn't call it an accident.

Restless, and not at all motivated to start boxing up his mess, he set down the borrowed volumes of Dickens he'd been about to reshelve. He needed some air, a distraction, maybe another trip down to the lighthouse—alone this time.

He had no desire to run into Lane, or to renew this morning's discussion, especially when he didn't trust himself to stand firm. He'd expected her to try to change his mind, to ask him to stay, to give them a chance—but she hadn't. Maybe he had misjudged her feelings. Or maybe she knew he was right.

Wandering to the kitchen, he considered making coffee, then thought better of it. He was jumpy enough without adding caffeine to the mix. From the window over the sink, he scanned the dunes. No sign of Lane, or of Mary, either, thank heaven. It wasn't nice, he knew, but the mere thought of the woman, her mismatched clothes and pale, roughly cropped hair, filled him with revulsion, with recognition that wasn't really recognition but felt too much like it.

His mother had looked like that near the end, medicated to the point of numbness, unkempt and uncaring, so divorced from reality that days often passed without her leaving her room. He'd done his best to look after her, and Peter, too, heating up the casseroles the neighbor women brought by, making her eat when he could, bringing her pills at the appointed times—retrieving them from her various hiding places later on.

The memory still made him shudder, too vivid, too raw. He'd always believed that if he ever managed to spill his guts about the night of the fire, he would somehow feel relieved, released, but he'd been wrong. He'd also believed coming back to Starry Point, seeing the old house, standing in it, would free him from the dreams that had been plaguing him for months. He'd been wrong about that, too. Then again, maybe he simply hadn't stood in the fire long enough, hadn't confronted the darkest of his demons, felt what he needed to feel.

Not bothering to grab his coat, he marched through the parlor and stepped out onto the Cloister's stone porch. He wavered briefly as he eyed his childhood home, staring back at him now with its frowning front porch and blank dark windows, more daunting, somehow, in the cold gray light of day than it had seemed last night in the pitch-dark. He wasn't a boy anymore, he reminded himself, and forced his feet to move. He needed to do this.

Crossing the street, he slipped around the sagging side porch, then disappeared between the line of overgrown hedges that ran along the north side of the house. Groping blindly along the stone foundation, he located the small wooden door he'd often used as a boy, the one he'd slipped through to visit the greenhouse the night of the fire.

He had expected to find it boarded that first night, then realized it was doubtful anyone even knew the door existed. The latch had rusted through, leaving only a dangling bit of metal that fell away the moment he gave it a tug. The door itself was bowed and swollen, stubbornly refusing to yield to the pressure of his shoulder. Leaning back on his haunches, he aimed his feet squarely and gave the door a solid kick.

The crawl space was tighter than he remembered, but eventually he made his way through the passage and up the narrow flight of steps to the room off the kitchen his mother had used as a pantry. It was bare now, as was the kitchen, the glass-front cabinets emptied of everything but cobwebs and the faded contact paper that still lined the shelves. As he passed through the vacant dining room, he found himself wondering what had happened to his family's belongings after the fire. Had they gone to neighbors, to auction, to charity? Or had the smoke ruined it all?

He could smell it suddenly, acrid and thick at the back of his throat, boiling down the stairs, filling the parlor. And then, weeks later, when he'd managed to sneak back inside, the sickening stench of cold, wet ash. The damage was still visible, in the water-stained floors and soot-smeared walls, the blackened staircase with its charred and tortured woodwork. That was the physical damage. The other damage—the real damage—was invisible, but much, much too real.

As a boy he had known instinctively that his mother wasn't like other mothers, that his home life was nothing like that of his friends, where birthday cakes and Christmas trees—the normal childhood things—were taken for granted. It was inevitable, he supposed, the implosion of his family, a thing he now realized on some gut level he'd always been waiting for, some vivid and violent unraveling that seemed always to be looming. And yet when it came, it had still knocked him for a loop.

In the front parlor a feeble, dun-colored light filtered through the grimy windows, lending the room a strange, underwater gloom, de-cades of ash and dust hazing the quiet air, mingling with the pong of mildew and old smoke. Steeling himself for the worst of it, he forced his eyes to the staircase. It was why he'd come, after all. To face all of this, to stand in the metaphorical fire and make himself remember.

The images came more quickly than he'd expected: his mother on the second-floor landing, eyes wide with panic as the flames licked down the railing, the reek of scotch as he grappled with her, the slow-motion shower of buttons raining onto the carpet as he clutched the front of her robe and dragged her forcibly down the stairs.

He'd found one of the buttons the day he left the burn unit—tiny and pink, like the mints she used to have on the table at luncheons—tucked into the cuff of the pants he'd been wearing the night of the fire. He couldn't say why he'd never thrown it away, a warped sense of nostalgia perhaps, a twisted need to cling to who he'd been before the Forresters changed his name and made him over into some other boy.

They'd meant well, trying to make him forget. What they never understood was that it hadn't all been bad, not early on, not before his father died, and that some small part of him needed to remember the mother who told him stories and made wishes on flowers. At the end she'd been an ungodly mess, sick and unhappy and overmedicated, but once, long before that, she had loved him.

Unbidden, thoughts of Mary filled his head. It shamed him to feel revulsion for a woman he'd never actually met. It wasn't a conscious decision, but a visceral one, carved into his heart at an early age and breathing there still, a shameful echo of what he'd felt for his mother toward the end.

Even now he found it difficult to forgive her for being what she was, though the rational part of him knew she'd had little or no control over her condition. If only he'd realized it then, he might have helped her, reached her somehow. With a fresh pang of shame he thought of Lane and the way she was with Mary. It was hard not to wonder how different his mother's life might have been if she'd had such a champion.

His father had certainly never been a champion, too busy moving his money around, or seeing to his duties as Starry Point's mayor. Hannah Rourke had been just one more thing to manage, or rather, to delegate to the doctors, who despite a merry-go-round of prescriptions had failed miserably. She had teetered for a while, hovering on the brink of disaster, reclusive and paranoid, until one day something snapped and she hurtled over the precipice.

She'd *gone away* after that—to heal, his father explained. The neighbors never knew all the details, but they knew enough to realize the story about a sick aunt didn't quite pass muster. She was better when she came home, or at least more docile, with a new set of pill bottles to manage her moods. His father didn't seem to mind, as long as his wife didn't embarrass him in front of his constituents. So much for happily ever after.

Not that he'd ever really bought in to all of that. His mother had, and look where it got her. And what of his adoptive parents? They were content, comfortable, which he supposed was a kind of happy, though not in any fairy-tale sense. But then, maybe that's when it worked, when expectations were low and duty took the place of passion, when neither partner was looking for the happy ending.

Lane was, though. Even if she didn't know it.

She liked to pretend she was battle hardened, her armor free of chinks, but the way she'd looked at him this morning when he told her he was leaving said otherwise. She wouldn't be happy with scraps, nor did she deserve them. It had sounded cliché, the kind of thing guys say just before they beat a hasty retreat, but he really *would* end up disappointing her, and he had no intention of letting that happen.

Stepping to the window, he scrubbed a small circle in the grit and peered across the street at the Cloister, enduring and stoic, its stone towers thrusting against the heavy sky. It had been a kind of prison for him once, its upper rooms lined with narrow iron cots, where homeless, loveless boys dreamed each night of belonging somewhere— anywhere. Now, years later, Lane had made it into a kind of fortress, a place to hide from the world, to insulate herself from her memories and her dreams. Because pretending not to want anything felt safer than wanting something you couldn't have. He got that, and it wasn't a bad strategy. It was just a damn lonely one.

He lingered awhile at the window, until the shadows began to stretch and a light came on in one of the towers. Lane's silhouette drifted past, a glimpse of pale blue sweats, a flash of auburn ponytail. He should step away before he was seen, and yet he found himself rooted to the spot, caught unaware by a homing instinct so sudden, so primal, it almost made him forget to breathe. Suddenly, almost desperately, he wanted to be there, near her, with her, where it felt good and right, and where, he realized now, he'd been happier over the last few weeks than he'd been in a very long time.

All the more reason to get out while he could—while they both could.

Chapter 46

Lane

"**I** won't go back. I'd rather die first."

The words rang in Lane's head as she opened her eyes. Mary's words, delivered in the throes of hysteria, perhaps, but what if she meant them? Given her past—the wrists webbed with scars—it was a question worth asking.

It was raining again, Lane saw as she padded to the window and peered out: a steady drizzle and a sky the color of steel. No sign of Mary, nor was there likely to be. Not in this weather. At least she wanted to believe it was the weather that was keeping her away. Deep down, though, she knew better. She had stepped over the line yesterday, way over, in fact. That it had been unintentional didn't matter. She needed to make it right. The sooner the better.

After a quick shower, she booted up the laptop to check her e-mail. Nothing from R&C Limited, and not much more from her mother, just a few lines saying Robert had drafted a very official-looking letter on his firm's stationery and hoped to receive a response soon. *Damn.* She could do with a bit of good news. Time was slipping away, and she was no closer to finding an ally in her quest to save Hope House.

Downstairs, Lane found a freshly brewed pot of coffee but no sign of Michael. That he was keeping his distance didn't surprise her. If she weren't obligated to play hostess, she'd be doing precisely the same thing. As it was, seclusion wasn't an option. After filling a mug with coffee, she started breakfast, popping a batch of orange-cranberry muffins into the oven, then scrambling eggs for an omelet.

She found him in the library. He glanced up when she entered with the breakfast tray, offered an awkward, fleeting smile. "You didn't have to."

"Ah, but I did," she answered lightly, as if he were just another guest, and not someone she'd made love to twenty-four hours ago. "The Cloister's a bed-and-breakfast. Take away the breakfast and all I'd have to offer is—"

A bed.

The word dangled unspoken in the charged air. Lane looked away. Michael shifted uncomfortably. Finally, she found her voice. "I didn't . . . I wasn't—" Whatever she meant to say evaporated when she spotted the carton of books on the desk. He was packing, so he'd be ready to go the minute the weather cleared. She set down the breakfast tray and turned to go.

Capturing her hand, he pulled her back to face him. "Is something wrong?"

Lane blinked at him, mildly stunned. *Is something wrong?* Was he really that dense, or was it just easier to pretend he hadn't hurt her? "It's nothing," she answered stiffly. "Mary had a sort of episode yesterday, a pretty bad one, and this morning she didn't show. It's got me worried."

"Did it have to do with the meeting?"

"No. Something else. I need to talk to her."

"You can't go running after the woman every time she throws a tantrum. She'll get over it. And when she does, she'll be back."

Lane tilted her chin up at him. "You don't know anything about her."

It seemed it was Michael's turn to look stunned. "Were you not paying attention last night? I know how this works, Lane. This isn't the first time she's pulled a disappearing act, and if you go chasing after her I can promise you it won't be the last. She needs to learn to cope with things instead of running away. That'll never happen if you keep rewarding her."

"Rewarding her?" Astonished, Lane glared at him. "She's not a springer spaniel, Michael. She's a woman, with feelings. And you have no idea what this is about."

"Fine. What's it about?"

Lane opened her mouth, then closed it again, realizing there was no way to explain what had set Mary off without admitting that she'd been prying into his past. "Never mind," she said, turning to go. "Your omelet's getting cold."

"Lane."

He reached for her again but missed this time, his fingers just grazing her elbow as she moved away. She glanced back when she reached the door, her face a cool, careful blank.

"Yes?"

"I hope she's okay."

"Thank you," she said, because she could see that he meant it.

The rain had picked up by the time she climbed into her car and headed for the south side of the point. As she drove she mentally rehearsed her apology, her thoughts competing with the squeaky-wet slap of wipers. Just past the marina, she turned onto a narrow dirt road that wound back into a scrubby wood of beech, holly, and pine. A mile later, a red metal roof appeared through the trees.

Lane pulled into the crushed-shell lot and cut the engine. She'd been to Hope House once before, the day of the police station fiasco, but it had been dark by the time she dropped Mary off. Now, in the light of day, she saw that it wasn't at all what she'd expected, more country retreat than halfway house, with rough-hewn siding and a fieldstone chimney, a wide front porch and a handful of rockers.

A pair of men paused in their rocking to eye her as she stepped out of the car and into the rain. She nodded in greeting. The men nodded in return, expressions shifting from curious to leery as she made a beeline for the door. Was she allowed to be here? She had no idea. Nor did she know how to go about locating Mary once she was inside.

She was surprised when she was able to walk right in; no checkpoint, no third degree, just the turn of a knob. A kind of great room opened up off the entryway, with high timbered ceilings and a large stone fireplace. Every inch of space appeared to have been put to use. Well-stocked bookshelves lined two of the walls. There was a long leather couch, several reading chairs with good lamps nearby, and a handful of game tables offering Scrabble, chess, and checkers.

A woman wearing bedroom slippers and a lavender cardigan stood watching her from across the room, the only person in sight. Lane approached, hand extended. The woman, who carried what looked to be a knitting bag beneath her arm, eyed it with a blend of caution and hostility but made no move to take it. Understandable, Lane supposed, withdrawing the hand.

"My name is Lane Kramer. I'm a friend of Mary's."

The woman looked her up and down with narrowed eyes. "What kind of friend?"

"The good kind. I promise. We have tea together some mornings."

The woman's posture changed instantly. "You're the Inn Lady."

"Yes. I'm the Inn Lady. Do you know where I might find her?"

A shrug. A shake of the head. "Haven't seen her today. Missed dinner last night, too. But her room's at the end of that hall if you want to check. Tell her Dana sent you."

Lane summoned a smile. "Thank you, Dana. I will."

Hadn't been seen all day. Lane tried not to contemplate what that might mean as she moved down the door-lined corridor, the soles of her duck boots squelching damply on the laminate-wood floor. With every step, she expected to be stopped, questioned, but no one seemed to care that she was there.

The indicated door was closed when she reached it. Pausing, she pressed an ear to the panel—nothing. Perhaps she was sleeping.

Please, God, let her be sleeping.

"Mary?" She tapped softly, three times. "It's Lane. Can we talk?" When she got no response she tapped again, waited a few seconds, then took hold of the knob.

The room was empty.

Feeling every bit the intruder she was, Lane stepped inside, then paused, letting her eyes adjust to the dim interior. It was a small room, sparsely appointed: a single bed, a small table and lamp, a plain, serviceable dresser, and a single window with curtains still drawn. No frills of any kind, unless you counted the shabby, half-peeling wallpaper.

Curious, Lane held aside the curtain to try to make out the pattern, then realized she wasn't looking at wallpaper at all but sheets of paper neatly taped to every square inch of wall. When she reached for the lamp switch and flicked it on, what she saw made her legs go weak.

A shiver tripped along her spine as she tipped her head back and pivoted in a slow circle, an ice-cold prickle of recognition, of absolute certainty. Sinking down onto the edge of the bed, she tried to wrap her head around what she was seeing—tried to comprehend the incomprehensible. Some of the drawings were in pencil, others in chalk, but there was no denying what she was looking at, the images so familiar she could see them with her eyes closed, on the pages of the sketchbook found in her basement: a golden-haired damsel in her castle tower, a two-masted schooner foundering in a storm, a flame-haired siren luring a boat to its doom.

The shock of it nearly took Lane's breath away. But how was she seeing them now, here? Sweet Jesus, was it possible? For a moment, she let herself play with the possibility, cobbling bits of story together, trying to make them fit, until she realized she was being absurd. Hannah Rourke was dead, and had been for years.

Hadn't she?

Michael had gotten the news secondhand, but it was hardly the kind of thing lawyers got wrong. Still, something nagged at her, some nebulous detail she couldn't quite put a finger on. And then suddenly she knew what it was. She'd noticed them before, in the sketchbook: white trumpetlike flowers winding around page borders and up castle walls, inserted in some fashion into every sketch. And they were here, too. Moonflowers. Hannah's favorite, and the ones Michael had gone to the greenhouse to make a wish on the night of the fire.

It was true, then.

"I killed a boy once."

The words filled her head suddenly, unbidden and terrible. All that time. All that time, she'd been talking about Peter, about the fire. No wonder she'd come apart at the mention of Hannah. Her questions hadn't just hit too close to home; they'd struck a bull's-eye.

Mary's story. Hannah's story. The same.

And it was Michael's story, too.

Almost before thinking it through, Lane yanked one of the sketches from the wall and folded it into the pocket of her jacket. She had to find Mary, to confirm what she already knew, and decide what to do about it. At some point, someone was going to have to tell Michael his mother was still alive.

Dana was still in the great room when Lane emerged, seated snugly by the fire with her knitting. She glanced up, iron gray brows arched inquisitively. "You find her?"

"No. I didn't. Do you know where else she might be? Where she goes?"

"You mean aside from your place? You could try the library. They let us stay there sometimes when it's raining, but only when old Mrs. Tilden isn't on duty. She chases us off. You could check the park, but I don't think she goes there much anymore since that time with the police. Oh, and there's St. Mark's. She goes there when she's sad."

Lane frowned. "The church?"

Dana nodded, fingers busy.

Mary had never expressed any kind of religious leanings—quite the opposite, in fact—but there was no accounting for what people did when they were in pain. She'd drive by, just in case. But first she'd try the library.

As she flicked on her wipers and pulled back onto the road, she tried not to dwell on the fact that Dana and the rest of the residents of Hope House might not have a place to live in two weeks. There wasn't space in her head right now for Landon's schemes or R&C Limited. There was only space for Mary, and the inexplicable truth she seemed to have stumbled upon, a truth that in retrospect should have been obvious almost from the start.

Now, as she drove through the blowing drizzle, it was all beginning to make sense, thread by inconceivable thread, Mary's story unraveling, reweaving itself as Hannah's—the wall plastered with drawings, nearly identical to the ones in the sketchbook, each one a page from Hannah Rourke's past, told in the only way she could bear to tell it.

It was the book, of course—the thing Michael had come back to Starry Point for, the book of images his mother had created all those years ago. They'd been important to him, were important to him still. And she'd had them all the time.

Her stomach clenched when she thought about what would come next. If her suspicions about Mary proved true—as they almost certainly would—how would he handle the news? He'd never made any bones about his feelings for his mother.

And what of Mary? She had her reasons for burying Hannah, and for wishing her to remain buried. She had lived two lives, Hannah's and Mary's, and neither had been happy. What happened when those lives intersected, when fresh grief was suddenly layered upon old?

In her rush to make things right, she hadn't stopped to think about the potential fallout, of the wounds that would be torn open, the hearts that might bleed in the process. Perhaps she was making a mistake. Perhaps the right thing, the safe thing, was to do nothing at all, to let Mary go on pretending, to the world and herself, that Hannah Rourke was dead, to leave Michael blissfully unaware that his mother was actually alive. But no, that couldn't be right. Not when there was even the slimmest hope of reconciliation. And there was. He had come back for the book. That meant something.

The trip to the library had proven futile; no one had seen Mary in over a week. The park, too, had been a waste of time. Now, as she reached St. Mark's, the rain had eased off slightly, though the wind had picked up and the temperature was beginning to drop. Michael's nor'easter was blowing in right on schedule.

The lot was empty as she turned in, the heavily pocked pavement already beginning to puddle. Not a soul in sight. With any luck they had just missed each other, and Mary was back at Hope House, warm and dry and—*please, God*—safe. But from the corner of her eye, she caught a flutter of neon pink: Mary's bike propped against a tree along the front walk. Thank God. Leaving the car in the middle of the lot, lights on, wipers going, she cut across the lawn to the front steps of the church, only to find the large double doors locked.

"She goes there when she's sad."

Suddenly, Lane knew where to find Mary. Circling around to the back of the church, past uneven rows of cold gray stone, she finally found her, kneeling on the wet ground, shoulders hunched, head bowed, her grief a palpable thing as she mourned at the grave of her son—of little Peter Rourke.

Emotions, hot and salty, caught in Lane's throat. She began to second-guess what she'd come to do, thinking of all the ways her good intentions could go terribly wrong. And then she recalled the folded bit of paper in her pocket and knew what she had to do.

Before she could take a step, Mary seemed to sense her presence. Her head snapped up, eyes wide and fixed. For a moment, Lane thought she would bolt. Instead, she came up off her knees and simply stood there, her cropped white hair dripping rain into her eyes.

"Leave me alone."

Her voice, so ragged and so very grieved, made Lane flinch. "I can't do that, Mary. You know I can't. There are things I need to say . . . things you need to know. Please, let me take you back to Hope House where we can talk."

"There's nothing either of us needs to say."

"But there is, Mary. I think you know there is."

Dread flickered briefly in her pale eyes. "No," she said, and turned to go.

"Hannah . . ."

Mary turned back stiffly, her face pale as bone. "Hannah is dead."

"We both know that isn't true."

"It is true! I made it true. There's only Mary now."

"Please, listen to me."

Lane moved to close the distance between them but stopped when Mary began to back away. This wasn't how she'd intended things to go. She meant to ease into it, not ambush the poor woman with the truth, and certainly not while standing beside the grave of her dead son.

"Please," she said again. "You're wet and you're freezing. Let me take you back to Hope House. You can get warm, and then we'll talk all this through."

"There's nothing to talk through."

"There is. You know there is. When you didn't show up this

morning, I went to Hope House. I've been to your room. I've seen the drawings."

Mary lifted her chin. "They're nothing. A crazy woman's scribbling."

"And the sketchbook you filled all those years ago, with the very same drawings? The one with the green leather cover—was that nothing, too?"

"How do you . . . How do you know about that book?"

The question dangled while Lane scrambled for an answer. She needed to tread carefully. "I know about the book because I have it," she finally answered. "Some workmen found it while they were rummaging around in the basement. I had no idea what it was then. But I do now. The ship. The storm. It's your husband. It's how he died."

Something in Mary seemed to break then, the pieces of her careful mask crumpling and falling away. Tears welled in her eyes, trembling unspilled. "Hannah Rourke is in her grave. Can you not—any of you—just leave her there?"

"I'm sorry, Mary. I hate upsetting you, but there are things you need to know. If you still want Hannah dead after you've listened to what I have to say, I'll respect that."

"I should never have come back," she whispered, shaking her head miserably. "I should have stayed away, but I couldn't."

"Because you needed to be near Peter," Lane supplied quietly. "Because you needed to be near your son."

Mary turned to stare at the small gray stone, her tears finally spilling over. "I wasn't there when they buried him. They wouldn't let me. I killed him, you see. Did I ever tell you that?"

The grief in her voice, the sorrow in her eyes, broke Lane's heart. She couldn't be allowed to remember it that way, to blame herself for something that wasn't her fault.

"No, Mary. Peter died in a fire. It was an accident."

"So many pills," she whispered, her eyes waxing vacant. "I swallowed them—all of them—with half a bottle of scotch. I wanted it to stop—for the pain to stop, and the shame. Instead, I killed him. When the fire started I couldn't do anything. I couldn't help my boy!"

Lane closed her eyes, shuddering against the image. The guilt of it, the daily, heart-wrenching horror of living with such a thing, would be enough to push anyone over the edge.

"It was an accident, Mary, a terrible accident. You never meant for Peter to be hurt."

Mary wasn't listening. Her eyes darted anxiously to her bike out near the road. *Please, God, don't let her run again.* But the thought came too late.

Without a word, Mary darted past the gravestones and made a break for the road. Lane followed, struggling to see through rain-soaked bangs. She couldn't let Mary get on that bike. Not in her current state. Taking the angle, she cut across the churchyard, reaching the bike just as Mary was scrambling onto the seat. She took hold of the handlebars, but Mary was too quick, wheeling around in the opposite direction and out into the street.

Lane heard herself scream, but the warning came too late, the white four-door Nissan too fast. There was a slick, wet skid of tires, a stomach-lurching thud, then the crunch and clatter of metal as Mary's bike went catapulting over the asphalt.

Time slowed hideously, so that an eternity seemed to pass before Lane was able to make her legs move, but finally she was kneeling beside Mary. She was breathing, thank God, but she was still and so very pale, her left arm splayed at an awkward angle, an ugly gash on her forehead weeping blood down her temple and into her dripping wet hair.

On the sidewalk, the Nissan driver was screaming at 911 dispatch to send an ambulance. She might have just killed a bag lady, the one that rides around on the bike with the pink flag.

Chapter 47

Lane told them what she could at the ER desk, which wasn't
much, other than that Mary had some *problems* and was on
medication for her mental state. "She usually keeps them with
her, in a purple bag, but I didn't see her carrying it today. Is she going
to be all right?"

The desk nurse glanced up over her clipboard but seemed not to
have heard the question. "Has she taken her meds today?"

"I don't really know. I don't live with her. I'm just . . . a friend. I was
there when it happened. Please, can you at least tell me if she's conscious?"

"The doctor's looking at her now. In the meantime, we'll need
more information about her meds. Does Mary have a local physician?
Someone we can call for patient records?"

Lane felt utterly helpless. "I have no idea. She's . . . I have no idea.
You could call Hope House. Maybe someone there knows."

A second nurse, petite with a salt-and-pepper pixie cut, glanced
up from the frilly strand of silver garland she was taping along the
edge of the desk. "Did you say Hope House?"

"Yes. She lives there."

"And her name is Mary?"

Lane nodded, vaguely aware that something had shifted in the conversation.

Before she could say another word the woman was on the phone, requesting that a Dr. Stephen Ashton be paged immediately. When she hung up, she gave Lane a blank smile and directed her to the ER's waiting area.

Shivering and soaked to the skin, Lane fumbled in her purse for a few coins and dropped them into the vending machine, then waited numbly for the paper cup to fill. The thin brown liquid could only loosely be called coffee, but at least it was hot. Sagging into one of the hard plastic chairs, she considered calling Michael and asking him to bring some dry clothes but ultimately decided against it. She wasn't ready to explain any of this to him yet.

She'd spent the drive to the hospital trying to think of some gentle way to break the news that his dead mother was actually alive, but she'd come up empty. How, exactly, did one begin such a conversation? The thought made her queasy. And yet, sooner or later, he would have to know the truth—and decide what to do with it. She only prayed he would somehow find it in his heart to forgive.

It was nearly dark when she jerked awake to the sound of rain pelting the ER's glass double doors. Stiff, and slightly numb, she shifted in the torturous chair and tried to get her bearings. At some point, the nurse with the pixie cut had stopped by with a blanket and the news that while Mary was pretty banged up, she was expected to make a full recovery. Relieved, exhausted, and warm for the first time in hours, she had dropped off instantly. Now she wanted more information, and to see Mary for herself. No, not Mary, she reminded herself—Hannah. She needed to start thinking of her as Hannah now.

"You're awake." It was the nurse with the pixie cut. "I just spoke with Mary's doctor. He'll be out in a few minutes to speak with you."

Lane felt a frisson of dread. She let the blanket slide off her shoulders as she stretched stiffly to her feet. "Is everything all right?"

"Everything's fine. He just wants to have a word. Mary's . . . sort of a special case."

On cue, a man in a well-cut suit and shiny black shoes came through the swinging doors. "Dr. Stephen Ashton," he said, extending a hand. His hair was graying and impeccably combed, his face shiny-smooth from a recent shave.

"Lane Kramer. I'm a friend of Mary's."

"Can we take a walk, Ms. Kramer?"

Lane nodded, falling into step beside him.

"The attending tells me you were with Mary when the accident occurred."

"I was. It was . . . God, it was awful. Is she hurt very badly?"

Ashton frowned, tugging thoughtfully at his chin. "She sustained some injuries, a fractured skull and a concussion, but all in all, she appears to have been very lucky. We're keeping her in ICU as a precaution, though it's not her physical condition we're worried about so much as . . . other things."

Other things.

Lane heard the warning bells go off. "May I see her?"

"Yes, in a moment, but first there are a few things I'd like to discuss with you . . . about Mary's mental state. As you probably know, she has no family to speak of, which means she's going to have to depend on friends as she recuperates. You may not be aware that Mary has had a somewhat difficult past, and that from time to time she suffers from . . . episodes."

Lane held up a hand. There was no sense tiptoeing around it. "I'm aware of Mary's . . . condition, Dr. Ashton. And I know something of her past."

He seemed surprised but nodded. "Good. I'll speak freely, then.

This afternoon, at the time of the accident, how would you describe Mary's emotional state? I'm asking because it feels a little odd, riding her bike out in front of an oncoming car."

"You're asking if I think she did it on purpose, if she was trying to . . . hurt herself?"

"I am."

"Oh God . . ."

Lane felt the blood drain from her face. It had never occurred to her that Mary might have been trying to end her life. It wasn't really out of the realm of possibility, though, was it? That she'd rather die than face her past? And if she now told Dr. Ashton the truth—that Mary had been upset, and why—what then? They might lock her up again, send her back to the White Coats.

"I'm sorry, Ms. Kramer. It's a terrible thing to suggest, I know. But I have to ask. There's some history there, you see."

Lane nodded numbly. "I know her history. I've seen the scars. But what happened today was an accident. I'm sure of it."

"She was in good spirits, then? Nothing going on that might have upset her?"

"She wasn't trying to hurt herself," Lane said firmly, sidestepping the question. "It was an accident."

Ashton pretended to accept her answer, though he was clearly skeptical. "I'm asking because she seemed rather agitated when she came into the ER." He paused then and looked at Lane pointedly. "You understand, Ms. Kramer, that for Mary, agitation can be a rather dangerous state?"

Lane took a deep breath and let it out slowly. Time to stop dancing around it. "We'd been talking about the past— about Hannah's past."

"I see." Ashton did a remarkable job of hiding his surprise. "Then you'll understand what I'm about to tell you. Mrs. Rourke has been through a very traumatic injury, one that could just as easily have killed her. We've given her something to keep her calm and help her rest, but we really don't know what to expect when we withdraw the sedation. Do you understand?"

Lane nodded. It seemed strange to hear Mary referred to as Mrs. Rourke. "Have you any idea how long she'll need to be hospitalized, Dr. Ashton? I'll need to let her son know what's happened, and I'm sure he'll ask." She was actually sure of no such thing but liked to think it was true.

This time Ashton didn't hide his surprise. "I haven't seen Hannah in almost a year. I wasn't aware that she was in contact with her son."

"She isn't yet, but there's been . . . a development."

Ashton eyed her warily. "What kind of development?"

"Evan is here, in Starry Point. He doesn't know about Hannah yet, but I'm hoping . . ."

"For a reunion?"

"Something like that, yes. I know it'll be a bit of a shock when he learns she's alive, and that it's going to take some time before he's ready to let her back into his life. But eventually . . ."

Ashton placed a hand on her arm. "Ms. Kramer, I want to caution you in the strongest terms possible against what you're planning. If Evan isn't ready to accept Hannah back into his life, if he isn't ready to forgive the past, bringing the two of them together may well prove catastrophic. That kind of emotional shock, a reminder of that terrible time in her life, the loss of her husband and her son, could easily reverse whatever progress we've managed to make over the years, and ruin any hope of further recovery."

Lane blinked at him. "You call the way she is now *progress*? Still believing, after all these years, that Peter's death was her fault? Pretending to be someone else because she can't forgive herself for an accident that happened thirty years ago?"

"If you had seen her right after the fire you'd understand the kind of demons she's had to overcome. It's been a long road back, a hard road, and I'm committed to keeping her on it. Hannah's condition is manageable—as long as her environment remains safe and stable."

"I thought if she could see her son again, and know that he doesn't blame her for what happened, maybe she could finally learn to forgive herself."

"Are you saying he doesn't blame her?"

Lane met the doctor's gaze and for a moment she felt her chin wobble. "No," she whispered. "I can't say that. I can't say that at all."

The hand he placed on her shoulder was reassuring but unmistakably firm. "What you're trying to do is laudable, Ms. Kramer, and under the right circumstances, might actually have merit. But as things stand now, a reunion that isn't welcome equally by both parties could cause untold harm. If you're hell-bent on doing this, and I suspect you are, I strongly advise you to be sure her son is fully on board before attempting any kind of reunion."

Lane felt a flutter of hope. "So you're not saying no?"

"I'm saying her son has to be ready to forgive before you attempt anything of the sort, and the sooner that conversation takes place the better. Remember what's at stake."

There was no mistaking the gravity of his words, or their meaning. Lane nodded, then forced herself to ask the hard question. "Do you think ... would she still be capable of ... something like that?"

Ashton gentled his expression, though his tone was no less grave. "Ms. Kramer, under the right circumstances, we're all capable of something like that. But I won't lie to you. Given Hannah's history, she's a bit more prone than most. What happened today is an example of what can occur when the balance is upset. It could have been much, much worse."

Lane nodded. "I understand. Can I see her now?"

"Briefly, yes. But you need to prepare yourself; she's pretty banged up. Nothing that won't heal, but it's pretty dramatic-looking stuff."

"Is she conscious?"

"We've got her sedated, which at this point is as much for her mental state as for the pain. We'll start weaning her off tomorrow and see how it goes."

Chapter 48

Lane's breath caught painfully as she entered Hannah's room. The doctor had prepared her, or had tried to, but actually seeing her, so pale and still against the pillows, brought tears scorching up into her throat. The gash on her forehead was bandaged now, the eye beneath shiny and swollen, already turning a livid shade of purple. Lane brushed her fingers over the back of Hannah's hand, carefully avoiding the tape that held her IV in place.

"She looks so . . . frail."

Ashton smiled. "If there's one thing Hannah Rourke isn't, it's frail. What happened today would have—well, let's just say most women her age wouldn't have fared nearly as well. She's a fighter. She's had to be."

For the first time, Lane noticed the heavy black sling just visible above the sheet. "She broke her arm?"

"Her right shoulder and elbow were both dislocated. They're back in place for now, but more may be required down the road. At the very least she's going to need some physical therapy. Unfortunately, I believe she's left-handed, which means she's going to need a significant amount of help when she gets out. Bathing, dressing, meals, that sort of thing."

"That won't be a problem. Can you give me any idea when that might be so I can make arrangements?"

Ashton pursed his lips. "It's hard to say just now. We'll need to assess her again when we withdraw the sedation, keep an eye on the head injury, and possibly adjust her current meds. If all goes well, it might be as little as a week. But again, given her history..."

Lane nodded when he let his words trail. There was no need to finish the sentence. As she turned back to the bed, the floor seemed to shift, the entire room to wobble. Grabbing the bedrail, she closed her eyes and waited for the world to right itself, dimly aware of Ashton's hand on her elbow.

"Right now I think I'm more worried about you than I am Hannah. When was the last time you ate, Ms. Kramer?"

Lane shook her head vaguely. "I had some coffee from the vending machine."

"I thought as much. Look, there's nothing more you can do here tonight. Why don't you go home, eat something, and get some sleep? You can leave your number with the desk. Someone will call if there's any change."

"But if she wakes up—"

"She won't. I promise. Not with what we've given her. My suggestion is that you rest up. She'll need you down the road, and she'll need you at your best. Go on, now. Get some rest."

Lane looked down at Hannah, apparently resting peacefully. It had been an exhausting day, and an even longer night. Sleep wasn't likely, but a shower and food weren't half-bad ideas.

"All right," she agreed reluctantly. "But I'll be back first thing in the morning."

Dragging her purse onto her shoulder, she headed for the door and the nurses' station to leave her number. There was nothing to do now but go home and face Michael with the truth, to tell him the woman he'd spent years hating and blaming for the death of his brother was very much alive, and very much in need of her son.

The lights in the library were still on when Lane pulled into the drive. She had hoped they wouldn't be, that he would be upstairs in his room, sound asleep. No such luck. Her legs felt like lead as she stepped up onto the front porch and fumbled her key into the lock.

Michael was in the foyer when she walked through the door. "Where have you been all— Jesus, is that blood?"

Lane felt strangely detached as she blinked down at the front of her pale blue hoodie. She hadn't realized she was covered with blood. "It's not mine," she said thickly.

"I've been calling your cell for hours. What happened? The last thing I knew you were on your way to Hope House. That was this morning."

She dropped her keys and purse, unzipped the hoodie slowly, stalling. "They make you shut them off at the hospital."

Michael took a step forward. "You were at the hospital? Are you hurt?"

"No. There was an accident. I was...We were..." Her words trailed away as the room began to tilt. She pressed a hand to her eyes, steadied herself. "Sorry. It's been a long day."

He touched her then, a hand on her elbow. "You're pale, and you look exhausted. Have you eaten?"

Lane ignored the question as she dropped onto the sofa and patted the cushion beside her. "Michael, I need to tell you what's happened, and I think you should sit down while I do it."

Frowning, he eased down beside her. "All right, you have my attention."

"I didn't tell you this morning, but the reason Mary was upset was that I was asking her some questions—about Hannah Rourke. That's when she started to unravel. I didn't understand then, but I do now."

Michael stared at her, clearly annoyed. "You were asking her about my mother?"

"Michael, there's something you need to know—"

"We're talking about Mary."

"Her name isn't Mary."

The words had tumbled out before she had time to think about them, before she'd given any thought to how she would finish them. Now there was no going back, no closing the door she had dragged open.

"I couldn't find her when I got to Hope House. A woman named Dana pointed out her room, so I went to look for her." She paused briefly, letting the words settle. "The walls were covered with drawings."

Reaching into the pocket of her hoodie, she produced the damp and rumpled sketch, unfolding it before she handed it off. Michael's face went through a parade of emotions as he stared at the sketch—recognition, shock, denial.

"This is ... from Mary's room?"

"Yes. But she isn't really Mary."

He looked up then, shaking his head slowly. "No. This can't be—"

"It is, Michael," Lane said softly. "She's Hannah. She's your mother. I should have seen it sooner, put two and two together. But she was always so careful not to give herself away, to steer away from details. It wasn't until I saw the sketches that it hit me. After that, everything started to fit—the princes, and the wrecked ship. It was her story."

Michael was on his feet now, stalking the parlor with the sketch still in his hand. "It's a scam—some kind of bullshit scam. It's obvious when you think about it. You live across the street from the house. You presumably know the history. You're the perfect mark."

"I'm not a mark, and there's no scam. Look at the drawing, Michael. She's Hannah."

"I don't have to look at it."

"You're saying you don't recognize it? That it isn't almost identical to the sketches your mother used to do?"

"I never told you Hannah drew. How—"

Lane pushed to her feet. "Wait here."

A few moments later, she returned with the old leather sketchbook. "I think you've been looking for this."

Michael eyed the green leather cover and took a deliberate step back. "Where did you get that?"

"Some workmen found it in the basement. It was under the stairs—where you left it."

Michael took the book, sinking into the nearest chair. After flipping a few pages he glanced up. "Why didn't you tell me you had this?"

The unspoken accusation raised Lane's hackles. "Tell you? I didn't know what it was, or that it meant anything to you. How could I? Until a few days ago I didn't know who you were."

Michael nodded, grudgingly conceding her point, then turned his attention to the sketchbook, open now to a pair of colorful young knights—Hannah's princes, Lane now realized.

"It's what you came back for, isn't it?"

Michael cleared his throat and closed the book. "I thought they were just pictures. I didn't realize what they meant, that they were about her life—and my father. I hated her so much after Peter died, couldn't bear to think of her. And yet I had to know if the damn thing had survived the fire. So one night after they brought me here, I snuck out to look for it."

"And you found it."

He nodded. "Yes, and brought it back here. I kept it hidden under the stairs so the other boys couldn't get at it. There wasn't time to go after it when they came for me." Smoothing his palm over the worn leather cover, he smiled almost sadly. "For thirty years I've been wondering if it was still there, and so I came. When I didn't find it I tried to convince myself it didn't matter."

"But it did."

"Yes."

Lane waited while the silence yawned, hoping he'd say more. Finally, she laid a hand on his shoulder. "You believe me, then, about Hannah?"

He shrugged. "I've no choice but to believe you."

"What are you going to do?"

"Do?"

"About Hannah, now that you know she's alive."

He glanced away, the muscles in his jaw clenched. "I'm not going to do anything. I know you're hoping for some happy ending here, but this doesn't change anything. Alive or dead, Hannah Rourke isn't a part of my life, and that's how I intend to keep it."

The anger in his voice was so raw, so brutal, that it set something off in her. Sliding off the arm of the chair, she stared down at him, her hands on her hips. "She was hurt today, Michael—badly. That's where I've been all this time, in the emergency room. She was hit by a car. She was upset and she . . ." She paused, ran a hand over her eyes, pushed her bangs off her face. "It was my fault."

He stood then, stretching to his full height to glare down at her. "Don't ever say that again. I'm not letting you blame yourself for something that woman did. If you want to blame yourself for something, blame yourself for getting involved with her in the first place, for letting her into your life—and back into mine. The woman was dead, Lane. Dead! But you just couldn't leave it alone. You had to dig her up, shove her under my nose. I warned you, didn't I? That this would turn into something else? That sooner or later she'd suck you in? Well—welcome to the club. You've just earned your Hannah Rourke merit badge."

Lane held her ground. "She needs you, Michael. You're her son—the only one she has left."

"And whose fault is that?" The words seemed to explode out of him. "I'm her only son because she couldn't be bothered keeping the other one safe. Does she remember that part? Or was that someone else's fault, too?"

"Do you know where I found your mother yesterday?"

"Stop calling her that! My mother's name is Katherine."

Lane pretended not to hear, raising her voice to match his. "She was kneeling in the rain, in front of Peter's grave. She blames herself—no one else. It's time to forgive her, Michael, so she'll finally stop torturing herself."

"Sorry, I can't help with that. I won't get sucked in again. The sooner I see Starry Point in my rearview mirror, the better. And if you're smart, you'll see that I'm right. You do what you want. It's your life, which is certainly none of my business, but I'm telling you, the best thing you can do is stay away from that hospital and forget you ever met Hannah Rourke—or me."

Lane felt the words like a knife, cool and true to their target. Lifting her chin, she blinked back the sting of tears. "My life isn't your business. Fine. But I can't do what you're asking. And if you can, you're not the man I thought you were."

"I believe I tried to tell you that."

Lane winced, then turned her face away. "So you did."

Michael shifted his weight, scraped a hand through his hair. "Look, I don't need a lecture, and I sure as hell don't need a guilt trip. Have you forgotten that I was the one who dragged her out of the house the night my brother died? Or do you need to see the scars again?"

"She isn't that woman anymore. She's . . . better. And she needs you."

"Needs me?" He blinked at her a moment, then laughed, a hollow sound that rang sharply around the room. "Well, now, that is rich. You'll pardon my skepticism if I find it hard to believe she's given up the pills and the booze long enough to care about someone besides herself. That's how the fire started, by the way. Or didn't she tell you that part? The night Peter died she was so blind drunk she could barely stand up."

The words made Lane go stock-still. "That's what you think? That Peter died because your mother was drunk?"

"I was there."

"No, Michael, you weren't. You were in the greenhouse."

"You're saying it was my fault?"

"No. I'm saying you're remembering it wrong, that there are things you don't know about that night."

"Really?" he fired back coldly. "By all means, enlighten me."

Lane bit her lip, not at all sure what she was about to tell him would help her case. And yet she couldn't let him go on remembering it as he did. "Michael, the night Peter died your mother had washed down a handful of pills with a bottle of scotch. She wasn't drunk. She was trying to die."

Michael's face darkened with a mix of anger and disbelief. "Who told you that?"

"She did. And her doctor pretty much confirmed it."

For an instant, he looked dazed, as if he'd just been sucker punched. "Well, then, that's much better. Not boozy, just suicidal."

"She was sick, Michael—and ashamed. She thought you and your brother would be better off with no mother at all than with her."

"Don't!" he barked the second the words were out of her mouth. "Don't you dare stand there and try to make me feel sorry for her. This is how she does it, how she sucks you in, makes you care. And I guess it all comes back to me, then, doesn't it? Because I wasn't there when Peter needed me."

"Michael, no one believes that but you. And maybe if you could see that, you'd stop hating her for things that were beyond her control."

"That's right, stand up for her. Hell, canonize her, if you want to.

But I'm not sticking around to see it, or to pick up the pieces when it all goes to hell again. And it will. Only this time it's you she'll be taking with her. Just remember, I tried to warn you." With that, he turned and headed for the stairs, taking them two at a time.

"Where are you going?"

"To pack up the rest of my things. Storm or no storm, I'll be leaving first thing in the morning."

Lane closed her eyes, trying to channel the urge to cry into something more like anger. It was easier to be angry than to feel what she was really feeling. She waited until she heard his door slam to pick up Hannah's sketchbook. Perhaps she'd try again in the morning, after he'd had a little time to digest the news. But then, what was there to say that hadn't already been said—by both of them?

Chapter 49

Lane was dazed when she woke the next morning, aware of a vague sense that something was wrong, but unable to put her finger on what. Then she saw the hoodie tossed on the chair, smeared with a combination of mud and blood.

Mary—no, Hannah—was in the hospital.

And Michael was leaving.

She hadn't expected him to be happy about the news, but she hadn't expected rage, either. There had been a moment, as he opened the sketchbook, when his face had softened and some of the anger had drained away, a moment when she thought there might be reason to hope, but it hadn't lasted. Instead, he had turned on her, lashing out like a wounded animal, accusing, blaming, and ultimately shutting her out. How could something she believed so right have turned out so wrong?

She showered and dressed for the hospital, frowning at the pale face and darkly smudged eyes staring back at her from the mirror. She scraped her damp hair into a ponytail, thought about dabbing on some concealer, a little lip gloss, anything to make her look less undead, then decided coffee would have to do.

With Hannah's sketchbook in hand, she ventured down to the

kitchen, trying to ignore the hitch in the pit of her stomach when she found it empty, the coffee machine conspicuously untouched. It shouldn't come as a surprise. He'd made his intentions clear last night, and she couldn't help noticing as she came down that the door to his room had been left open, the drawers of the bureau not quite closed, all the signs of a guest preparing to check out.

She found him in the den, packing the last of his books. He didn't look up when she entered, though the subtle tensing of his shoulders told her he knew she was there. She took a deep breath, opened her mouth, then closed it again, wanting to find the words that would make him rethink his decision to shut Starry Point and his mother out of his life. In the end, she said nothing, just laid the sketchbook on the smooth mahogany table.

Michael glanced at it, then looked away. "I don't want it."

"You did—enough to come back and look for it. You should take it so you'll at least have something of hers. I think she'd like to know you had it."

His eyes, cold and steely, locked with hers as he leaned across the table and pushed the book back at her. "I need you to promise me— to swear to me—that you will never bring up my name to her. Never. Do you understand?"

Lane stiffened. "I have absolutely no intention of bringing up your name, not after everything she's been through. Her doctor was ada-mant about not exposing her to any emotional upheaval. And if learning your last living son is within your reach but wants nothing to do with you doesn't qualify as emotional upheaval, I don't know what does."

"Everything *she's* been through?"

Lane fought to rein in her emotions. He needed clarity, not a lecture. "Michael, I know this is hard for you, that it brings up a lot of painful memories, but Hannah's life hasn't exactly been a picnic, either. She lost her husband, and then Peter, both in such awful ways.

Then to be locked up for years, put through God knows what. It's a miracle she survived at all. That's all I'm saying. I'm not asking you to forget everything, but a little compassion would be a good thing for her right now. And for you."

Michael wasn't having it. He thrust his chin out, eyes flashing. "Whatever she survived, she created. Do you know why my father left that day? Why he headed out on the *Windseeker* when he knew full well there was a storm coming? It was because he couldn't take anymore. He wanted a little peace and it killed him. She killed him."

"That's not fair."

"Maybe, but it's true. It's what she does. She hurts the people in her life—my father, my brother, me. And now she's dragged you in. I'm telling you, you need to stay as far away from that woman as you can get, which is exactly what I plan to do."

Lane fought the tightening of her throat. He was staring at her, waiting for her to say something—good-bye probably. She let her eyes slide to the box of notebooks and legal pads near the door, the only proof that, for a time at least, he'd been a part of her life. Soon even that would be gone. She squared her shoulders.

"You do what you have to, Michael. I wish you'd stay, but I understand why you think you can't. I won't turn my back on her, though. Maybe because I didn't go through what you did. Anyway, I have to leave for the hospital now. They're weaning her off the sedation today, and I want to be there when she comes to. You can leave your key under the mat when you finish packing up. I'll settle your bill to your card and mail you a copy of your receipt."

Michael shoved his hands in his pockets and stared at his feet. "I'll be happy to pay for the whole winter."

So this was what it was now. Innkeeper and guest. Polite. Businesslike. "No," she said with an evenness that surprised her. "Just for the time you were here."

He cleared his throat, shuffled from foot to foot. "Lane, I know you think I'm some kind of monster for running out, but I just can't stay. I thought maybe I could, that I could learn to deal with the memories, maybe even put them behind me. But I can't now, not with her here. This is what I have to do."

"I get that you think it is. But you told me once that I only had one mother, that I'd be sorry if anything ever happened to her. Do you remember that?"

"This is different."

"No, I don't think it is," she said evenly. Getting self-righteous wouldn't solve anything, and it certainly wouldn't change his mind. "Hannah's your mother, the woman who brought you into this world, and loved you in the only way she knew how. And I'm afraid that one day you're going to regret this, and that you'll have to live with it for a very long time."

He shocked her by smiling, a slow, hard, bitter curl of his lips. "You think that's the worst thing I'll have to live with?"

"That's a question only you can answer, Michael." She turned away then, before he could see the tears pooling in her eyes, realizing too late that they'd never gotten around to saying good-bye.

Chapter 50

Mary

It seems at long last that I have finally come unmoored, detached from arms and legs, hovering in some underwater twilight, my only awareness the dark slippery walls of my own mind. Is this death, then? The wispy shift between the world and what comes after? I think not. Hell wouldn't be so quiet—or so cold. And there's a pain slowly coming to life behind my left eye, a knife slicing through my skull that tells me I'm alive.

The restraints again, then, pinning my limbs to the bed. Yes, that must be it. They've sent me back, found out who I am and what I did. The smells are familiar, too, Pine-Sol and misery. I try to open my eyes, to see where they've put me, but my lids are so heavy, so gritty, that I can only lie here and force my brain to take inventory of my body, of its throbs and aches, and wonder what they plan to do with me.

And then I see it all, playing out on the backs of my lids, like a movie running the wrong way. A crushing pain as my head smacks the pavement. The crunch and give of something in my shoulder. A kind of lurching, disembodied tumbling as I sail, sail, sail through the air. Running with the rain in my eyes. Running from the truth, from the shame—from the name Hannah Rourke.

The memory grabs hold, dragging me toward some shiny surface

I have no wish to break. I struggle against it, wanting only to sink back into the darkness, to linger in the blissful depths, where all is safe and unknown, where Hannah is still dead and no one knows the truth. But the pain is stronger now, nudging me toward awareness, until I have no choice but to open my eyes.

The room is dim: a window with curtains drawn, but not my window. Not my room. Not Hope House. There's a railing on both sides of the bed, but no restraints, I realize now. My feet and legs are free, but one of my arms, the left one, will not move at all. It's strapped against my body—and it hurts. I gaze about, bleary but comprehending, at the clear white tube snaking into my hand, the pole and bag hung beside the bed, at the steel panel of knobs and dials on the wall.

Yes, of course—the car.

But before the car there was Lane, standing with me at Peter's grave, listening while I blathered about the night my poor boy died. We have no secrets now, she and I. She knows it all, my name and my sins. But then, it was foolish of me, wasn't it, to ever think I could outrun them? I see now that when I buried Hannah Rourke I should have dug the hole much deeper.

Chapter 51

Lane

Lane hovered in the doorway of Hannah's hospital room, clutching the vase of flowers she'd just purchased at the gift shop. She hated hospitals. She'd been too preoccupied last night to register it, too worried about her friend to connect the dots back to the day she'd opened her eyes in a room like this one, cold and dim and unnaturally quiet, but today the reminders were everywhere. Every smell seemed to hold a memory, every memory to hold a knife. Time might have blunted the loss of her unborn child, but it hadn't erased the days and weeks that came after, when the loss and the emptiness had threatened to swallow her.

There was always an aftermath after an accident, a putting-back-together of lost and broken pieces, the physical ones, and the not so physical. Hannah would have her own aftermath soon, when the bruises faded and the stitches came out, the uncomfortable reckoning of past and present, the unwelcome reentry into the life she had tried so desperately to leave behind.

And she was to blame. Michael was right about that, at least.

None of this would be happening if she hadn't poked her nose where it didn't belong. Hannah wouldn't be lying on a hospital bed with a black eye, a dislocated shoulder, and a three-inch gash across her forehead. She'd still be Mary, Starry Point's harmless old bag lady. Now, thanks to Lane, she could never go back. She had pushed so hard for a happy ending that she had endangered Hannah, and had driven Michael away in the process.

So much for fairy tales.

Forcing her feet to move, she stepped into the room's gloomy interior, looking for somewhere to deposit her gift shop flowers, settling finally on the empty meal tray against the wall. She was rearranging a few bedraggled blooms when she heard a faint rustle behind her.

She was startled to find Hannah's eyes on her when she turned, dazed and full of questions. She'd been hoping for more time to prepare, to school herself on what she should and shouldn't say. Instead, she pasted on a smile and stepped to Hannah's bedside.

It was all she could do to keep her face from betraying her as she surveyed the damage. She looked so vulnerable, so broken and pale, her lower lip split and swollen, the bruise on her cheek now the color of a ripe eggplant.

"You're awake," Lane said thickly. "Does it hurt very much?"

Hannah's head moved back and forth on the pillow, but her wince gave her away. "Headache," she mumbled. "And I can't . . . move my arm."

"You dislocated it in the accident," Lane explained, realizing sheepishly that she was speaking rather loudly, which might prove helpful for a patient who'd lost her hearing, but was probably less so for one suffering from a concussion and a fractured skull. Lowering her voice, she tried again. "Do you need anything? Would you like me to buzz for a nurse?"

Hannah shook her head again, then lifted a hand to her forehead, prodding at the bandage there. Her eyes met Lane's questioningly.

"They had to stitch you up. The doctor says you were very lucky. Do you . . . can you remember what happened?"

"The car," Hannah said haltingly. "I didn't see it."

Lane's throat tightened with a combination of guilt and relief. Not on purpose, then. "It was my fault. I should never have...I only meant...I'm so sorry."

Hannah patted the sheets in protest. "Here, now. Stop that. I was the one running away, wasn't I?"

"But I was the one who made you run, the one who made you remember Hannah."

"Come, my girl. Surely you know I've never forgotten her. No matter...how I pretended, she's been here all along." There were tears in her eyes now, spilling past her pale lashes and onto her cheeks. "I need you to know what happened that night. I need someone...to know."

"We can talk about that later. Right now you need to rest, and heal."

"No!" Hannah said with surprising heat. "Someone has to know that I never meant to harm my boy...that I loved him."

Lane briefly contemplated slipping down to the nurses' station, asking them to give her something, but the ache in Hannah's eyes told her it wouldn't matter how many times they sedated her. She would come to, still needing to tell her story.

"Hannah, please. The doctor says you need to stay calm. If I promise to listen, will you promise to stay calm?"

Hannah nodded with visible relief. "Pull the chair close."

Lane did as she was told, dragging the blue vinyl armchair up beside the bed. She was barely seated when Hannah began to speak.

"The night of the fire...I had taken some pills."

"Yes," Lane said. "And washed them down with a lot of scotch."

"I thought that would do it. Neat and quiet this time. No blood."

Lane suppressed a shudder but let her go on.

"Something woke me. The pills—I couldn't get my bearings. I smelled smoke, could even taste it. Then I remembered the candle. There was a storm that night. I never would have taken the pills if I'd known a storm was coming. Peter was afraid of storms. He begged me to stay with him, to read to him. I went down and made some chocolate to help him sleep." She paused, smiling sadly. "I used to float animal crackers on top instead of marshmallows. Evan liked the lions best, but Peter liked the elephants."

Lane stared down at her hands, not sure whether to smile or cry. It all sounded so normal, so mother of the year. How could such a lovely scene have gone so terribly wrong?

Hannah's eyes were clearer now, though strangely lit, and not focused on Lane at all. Her voice was chillingly detached. "I had only gone two pages when the lights went out. Poor Peter. He was so scared. I lit a candle and kept going, but it was hard. The pills were starting to work, and the words were sliding all over the page. I opened the window next to the bed to let in some air to keep me awake... until I could get Peter to sleep. I don't remember leaving his room, but when I woke I was on the bathroom floor... covered with vomit. I could hardly see for the smoke."

Instinctively, Lane reached for her hand. Hannah seemed not to notice.

"I had forgotten the candle." The tears were coming faster now, her words sticking in her throat. "They say the drapes caught. By the time I realized Peter was crying for me, it was too late. I tried... I couldn't... the smoke was everywhere, but I couldn't stay on my feet." Her eyes froze open then, glazed with the horror of what she had seen that night. "I was trying to get to him when Evan came... I don't know where he came from. He was always running off, always hiding somewhere."

The greenhouse. He was out in the greenhouse, wishing on a flower.

Lane closed her eyes, waiting. There was nothing to do now but let her finish.

"The stairs were already burning. He wouldn't let me go to Peter. He grabbed me and... dragged me down the stairs. He was on his way back up again when the stairs gave way. It was days before anyone would tell me if he was alive or dead. I... never saw him again."

Lane stood abruptly. Knowing what she did, she found it impossible to endure another word while sitting down. A son lost, another burned, scarred because their mother had tried to take her own life. The surviving son racked with guilt, for the brother he couldn't save, and the mother he couldn't forgive. She'd seen the scars with her own eyes, even had a vague idea of how he'd earned them, but until now she hadn't truly grasped just how deep those scars ran. Not just for the son, but for the mother as well.

"You must miss him terribly," was all Lane could trust herself to say.

Hannah's eyes fluttered closed, her breath coming in short, hiccupping bursts. "They took him . . . the gray birds and that judge. And they put him up in your tower, way up high where no one could get at him. And then they . . . gave him away."

Lane looked away, but there was nothing else to focus on, no way to sidestep Hannah's anguish. She thought about the brand of desperation required to wash down a handful of pills while your children slept in the next room. She was beginning to see why Hannah had chosen to become someone else.

"I didn't know," Hannah choked out. "If I had I never would have . . ." Her voice trailed away as she reached for Lane's hand. "Can you forgive me?"

Startled, Lane sank back into her chair. "It isn't my place to forgive you, Hannah. It's yours. And it's time."

Hannah sighed, letting her head loll against the pillows. "You're all I have, my girl. Please, just once, before I leave this world . . . I need to hear someone say it."

Lane hesitated. She was neither eager nor qualified to grant this woman absolution, especially for something that had clearly been beyond her control. And yet her eyes were so desperate, so full of tears and grief.

"Yes, Hannah. I forgive you."

Hannah's face softened as she relaxed against her pillows, but the moment was broken when a slender brunette in purple scrubs bustled in with a plastic rack lined with collection vials.

"She's awake," the woman said brightly, aiming the observation at Lane. "How is she?"

"I think she's in some pain, but she's been talking."

"I'll stop by the nurses' station and let them know. It's probably time for some more good stuff. But first I need to take a few vials of blood. Won't take me a minute. Hannah, honey, can I borrow your arm?"

Lane stood, sidling discreetly toward the door. "I'm just going to slip out for some coffee while you do your thing."

"Sure. No prob. I'll be out of your hair in two shakes."

In the cafeteria, Lane bought a cup of coffee and a bagel, then headed back to the gift shop, where she selected an armload of magazines and the only two paperbacks whose covers didn't boast an expanse of rippling abs.

Leaving the shop, she paused to dig her cell out of her purse. Against her better judgment, she dialed the inn. She didn't expect him to answer—he was probably already gone—but she had to at least try. After eight rings she gave up and tried his cell. It went straight to voice mail. She imagined him recognizing her and hitting IGNORE CALL, and felt her throat tighten.

She really was pathetic.

Hannah was dozing when she stepped back into the room. Lane stacked the books and magazines within arm's reach on the bedside table, chose one for herself, then tiptoed back to her chair. After a few minutes she closed the Christmas issue of *Coastal Living*, opting for a catnap instead.

She had just begun to drift off when something made her open her eyes, not a sound exactly, as much as an awareness that she was no longer alone with Hannah. She was expecting to see a nurse when she opened her eyes, or even Dr. Ashton. Instead, Michael hovered in the doorway, shoulders squared, legs wide apart—a man prepared to do battle.

Chapter 52

Michael

Michael felt vaguely nauseated as he stood in the doorway of Hannah Rourke's hospital room, palms slick, legs turned to stone at the memory of his days in Starry Point General's burn unit: waking up with his back on fire, the burns too fresh to allow him to do anything but lie facedown and sob onto the sterile white sheets.

No one had to tell him Peter was dead. He'd known it when they loaded him into the ambulance—alone. Hannah was a different story. He had begged to know where they'd taken her, though he had a pretty good idea. He'd heard the screams as they strapped her down and took her away, the wild keening of an animal in pain. It was weeks before they finally told him the truth—that his mother wouldn't be coming back. And now the woman who'd caused it all was lying just inside the door.

He was dimly aware of Lane getting to her feet, of her eyes following him as he stepped into the room. He could feel the anxiety radiating from her, an almost palpable dread that he was about to make a scene. And an hour ago she would have been right, since that was precisely what he'd intended when he turned around on Highway 12 and headed back to Starry Point. But now, as he stared at the woman asleep on the narrow hospital bed, so fragile and battered, the words he'd rehearsed all the way back suddenly died in his throat.

He would have known her anywhere, this woman who had once spun stories and drawn pictures, who believed in fairy tales and made wishes on flowers. He had forgotten those times, had made himself forget them. Now they came rushing at him on a tide of emotion that nearly choked him. Her beauty had faded, victim to the ravages of guilt and loss. An unexpected knot constricted in his throat as he took in her bruises and abrasions, the bandage on her forehead, the sling that bound her shoulder.

He wasn't prepared when her eyes fluttered open. Startled, he took a step back. Those eyes had been filled with terror the last time he saw them. Now they were glassy and dazed, confused by the stranger standing over her bed.

The silence spun out as he fumbled for something to say. How was it possible that after thirty years and more than a thousand imagined rants, he couldn't manage to spit out a single word? Perhaps it was the quiet chaos brewing behind his mother's eyes, the troubled questions that must be flitting through her head at that moment. Or maybe it was because he hadn't remembered to take a breath since he entered the room.

He took one now, forcing air into his lungs, forcing it back out. And then, almost before he could register it, it was there—a kind of quickening in Hannah's expression, when confusion became recognition, and then, finally, a heartrending knowing. She reached for him, her small, slender hand imploring.

"My prince."

In that moment, Michael found himself trapped, caught in the dizzying space between anger and need, resentment and relief. From the corner of his eye, he saw Lane take a quick step forward. He stayed her with a look and, taking Hannah's outstretched hand, finally found his voice.

"My lady," he whispered hoarsely, the words strange on his tongue after so many years.

Lane's eyes slid to his, shiny with tears. He looked away. For better or worse, he had her to thank for this. She had guilted him into coming back, into doing the right thing, because she believed in happy endings, and because, for reasons that completely escaped him, she seemed to believe in him, too.

"Evan?" Hannah choked tearfully. "Why are you here?"

Michael shot Lane a helpless look. He had no idea where to begin, no idea what she knew and what she didn't. He was relieved when Lane stepped in.

"Michael, the man who's been staying with me, is really Evan—your Evan. I only found out myself a day ago. I wanted to tell you, but the doctors were afraid . . ."

Hannah's eyes closed briefly. "I know what they were afraid of." Her gaze narrowed then as a new light gradually began to kindle. "This was . . . the mistake?"

The mistake?

Michael caught Lane's almost imperceptible nod but decided to let it pass—for now. It never occurred to him that he might have come up in conversation. Now he found himself wondering exactly what had been said. Had she painted him as the type of guy who got a woman into bed and then promptly skipped town? Jesus, Hannah Rourke had been back in his life for all of ten minutes, and already there were complications. But then, she wasn't really back in his life. He'd come back to close a door, nothing more.

"You changed your name," Hannah said softly.

There was no missing the note of sadness in her voice, and perhaps betrayal. She had a right to that, he supposed. "The people who adopted me changed it. I'm Michael now. Michael Forrester."

"Michael," she repeated, as if tasting the name. "Your middle name, yes. And a new last name, too. You have a new family. But of course you do." Her eyes seemed to devour him as she reached up to smooth his cheek. "I always knew you'd grow up handsome and tall—like your father."

Michael felt his gut twist. He'd come back to do the right thing, but he wasn't letting her bring his father into this. "Lane tells me you took a nasty spill. How are you feeling?" It was an awkward pivot, but it was better than where they were heading.

Hannah managed a thin smile. A brave smile, Michael thought as she patted his hand. "You were kind to come, my boy, truly. But you don't need to stay. I'm not your mother anymore. You've got a new life now. No reason for you to relive the old horrors."

She turned her face away then, as a fresh fountain of tears racked her. He winced as Lane's nails dug into his arm, an unspoken plea to do something, say . . . something. But he was at a loss. They were strangers. Yes, she'd given birth to him, had raised him for a time. But could a few strands of DNA bridge the gap of thirty bitter years? He wasn't sure they could, or that he even wanted them to. And yet, as he stood there looking at her, so wretched and ashamed, he could feel her heart breaking, the same heart that had loved him all those years ago, that had lost a husband, and not one son, but two.

Reaching down, he brushed a strand of hair from Hannah's cheek. "We won't talk about old times," he said softly. "But I'm here now—as Michael. Let's let that be enough."

Lane flashed him a look of gratitude, dabbed at her eyes, and gave Hannah's hand a pat. "I'm just going to pop down to the nurses' station and see when you might be allowed to have something to eat."

"No," Michael blurted, knowing he must look like a deer in headlights. "I'll go. I'll do it."

"It's okay. I need to stretch my legs."

So, what? They were just supposed to *catch up* now, after thirty years?

Michael did his best to telegraph terror, but either Lane wasn't picking up on his signals, or she was flat-out ignoring them. *Stay,* she mouthed, giving him that look women saved for moments like this. *Talk to her. Please.*

And with that, she was gone.

Chapter 53

Lane

Out in the hall, Lane made a beeline for the ladies' room, slipped into a stall, and let the tears come, a damp jumble of hope, relief, and gratitude. She had braced herself for the worst when she saw Michael in the doorway. Instead, he'd surprised her with a display of compassion and tenderness she hadn't dared hope for.

And if she had shamed him into coming back, so what? She was beginning to realize that Michael coming into her life had never been about happily ever after, that she was only meant to be a catalyst in the reconciliation between mother and son. So be it. If it brought Hannah some measure of peace, she could live with that. She would have to.

Resolved, she emerged from the stall, splashed her face with cold water, and dabbed on a little lip gloss. Life went on, after all, and there were things to do. Dr. Ashton said Hannah was going to need help when she got out, the kind of aftercare Hope House wasn't likely to provide.

There were places, rehab centers, for that sort of thing, but she didn't like to think about the long-term effects of a prolonged stay in such a setting. No, there was a better option, though it wasn't one Michael was likely to approve.

At the nurses' station, she cleared her throat until a woman whose name tag identified her as Karen Walsh, R.N., lifted her head from the chart she was scanning.

"Help you?"

"I'm a friend of Hannah Rourke's, and I was wondering if you could give me any information about the kind of aftercare she'll require once she's discharged?"

Nurse Walsh smiled benignly but shook her head. "I'm afraid you'll need to speak to Mrs. Rourke's private physician about that. It'll be his decision, and they don't usually write that kind of thing down on the charts. That would be Dr. Ashton. He was in to see her early this morning and adjust her meds. He said he'd be back later today to check on her. You might catch him then."

Private physician?

Lane flashed back to last night—Dr. Ashton in his shiny shoes and well-cut black suit. She'd been too frazzled to ask how he happened to know so much about Hannah's psychiatric history. She had just assumed it was all somewhere in the hospital's records. Now she sensed there was more to it than that.

"Is Dr. Ashton not on staff here?"

"Not technically, no. Not for a long time now. But he was called in when Mrs. Rourke presented."

"And he just dropped everything and came running?"

"For Mrs. Rourke? Oh yes, ma'am."

Lane nodded distractedly as the wheels in her head began to grind. Private physicians cost money, and not a little money, either. So how was Ashton getting paid? Presumably, Medicare would pick up some of it, but a *private* physician who looked as if he'd been on his way to the opera when he was called?

"Can you tell me if Hannah has any kind of insurance? Private insurance, I mean?"

"Sorry, we don't handle the money stuff down here. We just put them back together. You'll need to go to the financial offices. They won't tell you anything, though, unless you're family."

It took several inquiries and a series of wrong turns, but finally Lane managed to locate the financial offices, which turned out to be a row of glass-fronted cubbies on the first floor.

"Are you a family member?" the middle-aged blonde asked robotically.

"I'm engaged to Mrs. Rourke's son," Lane answered without blinking. If she could lie to her mother's face, surely she could fool a hospital billing clerk. "We're, uh . . . we're thinking of having Mrs. Rourke stay with us while she rehabs, and Dr. Ashton said we'd need to make arrangements for her to have physical therapy, so I was wondering about the financial—"

The woman seemed not to be listening. Finally, she glanced up from the notes on her computer screen. "It says here all arrangements for Mrs. Rourke's care are to be made through Mr. Callahan."

"Mr. Callahan?"

The clerk eyed Lane dubiously. "Perhaps you should speak to your fiancé. Mr. Callahan is the gentleman who looks after Mrs. Rourke's affairs—her money and things."

Lane blinked at her, stunned to learn that Hannah had any money at all, let alone enough to be looked after. She did her best to recover. "Yes, of course. I guess I've never heard him mentioned by name. You don't happen to have his number handy there, do you? My fiancé is a bit overwhelmed right now, after his mother's accident, and I promised I'd get the ball rolling. You know, one less thing for him to worry about."

More than a little surprised, Lane watched the woman scribble the number onto a pink message pad, tear off the top sheet, and slide it across the desk. Snatching it up with a hastily muttered thanks, she hurried away before the woman had a chance to second-guess her decision.

Michael was just stepping out into the hall when Lane returned to Hannah's room. He looked worn out, and vaguely annoyed. "Where the hell have you been? I thought you were going to get her some food."

"I'm sorry. I got caught up in other things—when she might go home, and what she'll need when she does. I completely forgot about getting her something to eat."

"Don't worry about it now. The nurse came in to give her something for pain, and it's already making her groggy. They want her to rest, but she asked to see you before we leave."

Lane was aware of Michael behind her as she stepped back into the room. She did her best not to think about the conversation that would have to take place once they left the hospital, the one about where they all went from here.

Crossing to the bed, she laid a hand over Hannah's. "We're going for a little while so you can get some rest. But Michael said you wanted to see me first."

Hannah's eyes dragged open, heavy-lidded and already bleary from the meds. Holding out her free arm, she beckoned Lane to bend down for an awkward hug. "Thank you for this," she whispered against her cheek. "Thank you for my son."

"Rest now," Lane said softly. "We'll be back later."

She was about to pull away when Hannah's grip tightened, and she found herself staring into eyes that were surprisingly lucid. "It was no mistake, my girl. So just you hold on to him. He doesn't know it yet, but he needs you every bit as much as you need him."

It was Lane who finally broke the silence as they left the hospital. "Are you all right?"

Michael was wearing his unreadable face again. "Why wouldn't I be?"

"Because you've just seen your mother for the first time in thirty years, and she looks like she's been through a meat grinder. It's okay to feel . . . I don't know . . . shaken up."

"I'm fine."

Lane sighed. "Michael, you don't always have to put on such a brave face. It's okay to have feelings about this." She slowed as she reached her car and looked at him squarely. "You did a good thing today, by the way."

Michael pressed his fingers to his lids, as if warding off a headache. "Yeah, well, it sure as hell didn't feel good."

"Maybe not now, but it will later. Have you eaten?"

"Eaten?"

"As in food. Why don't we take my car and go grab some lunch? When we come back we'll talk to the doctor about Hannah's prognosis. In the meantime, there's something I need to ask you."

Michael eyed her warily but slid into the passenger seat when Lane opened the door. There was so much she wanted to ask. Why he'd changed his mind. What he planned to do now. What he and Hannah had talked about after she left the room. But first and foremost, she wanted to know what he knew about a man named Callahan.

At the diner, Michael ordered an omelet, Lane a club sandwich. Conversation, or what there was of it, was stilted while they waited for their food to arrive, as if they had suddenly used up all the words between them.

She could see his side. He'd been hiding from his past, from the scars and the memories, for more than thirty years. And today, quite against his will, he'd come face-to-face with all of it. Part of him—a very big part—would always blame her for that. And maybe that was fair, but nothing could make her regret the joy she had seen on Hannah's face when she had thanked her for her son. Still, it might be wise to steer clear of the emotional stuff right now.

"Michael, I told you I needed to talk to you about something."

He looked up from the thick china plate where he'd been chasing a bit of tomato around with his fork. "Yes," he said flatly, a grudging invitation for her to continue.

"I know this isn't really any of my business, but does your mother have any money?"

Michael set down his fork with a look that said he clearly didn't understand why she would ask him, of all people, such a question. "How in God's name would I know that?"

"I guess I'm asking if your father left her well-off when he died. He was the mayor, and a businessman. Presumably, he had assets."

"There was some insurance money, but that would be long gone by now. And as far as I know, most of the business holdings went to his partner. Why? What's this all about?"

Lane slid the scrap of paper with Callahan's number from her pocket and unfolded it. "Earlier, when I went down to the nurses' station, I learned that Dr. Ashton—that's your mother's doctor—isn't on staff at the hospital, that he's actually her private physician. He was called in when she presented at the emergency room."

"So?"

"So, how does someone like Hannah, who lives in a halfway house and has no income, happen to have her own private physician?"

"I have no idea."

"I didn't, either. Then, when I went down to the financial offices to ask about what kind of arrangements we'd need to make before Hannah could be discharged, the woman working there told me I'd have to check with a Mr. Callahan, since he was the one who looked after Hannah's money. She gave me his number. Have you ever heard of a Mr. Callahan?"

Michael frowned thoughtfully, then shook his head. "No."

"I think we should talk to him."

Michael pushed his plate away and carefully folded his napkin. "Are you under the impression that my feelings have changed? Because you should really know that they haven't. Visiting her in the hospital, making sure she's all right, is one thing, but I have no intention—none whatsoever—of getting tangled up in that woman's life again."

"This wouldn't be about getting tangled up in *that woman's* life, as you say. And by the way, *that woman* is still your mother, no matter what you or she might think. And she's still going to need a roof over her head when this is over—and the way things are looking, so will everyone else at Hope House. I'd like to talk to this Callahan. If he's the one who initially arranged for her to get in there, maybe he knows how to get in touch with someone who'd be willing to stand up to Landon."

"So talk to him. Just leave me out of it."

"Come on, Michael. Do you really think he's going to tell me anything? A complete stranger?" She waited a beat, until she could see that her words had registered. "He would talk to you, though— her son. You could help Hannah, and a lot of other people."

Finally, grudgingly, Michael nodded. "All right." His eyes widened when she pulled her phone from her bag. "You're going to call him now?"

Lane nodded as she tapped in the number. "Yes. So you can't change your mind."

A man answered on the third ring.

"Mr. Callahan?"

"This is he."

"Yes, well—" Lane stumbled, wishing now that she'd taken a moment to plan what she was going to say. "My name is Lane Kramer," she said finally, simple and to the point. "I'm a friend of Hannah Rourke's."

There was a long silence, the awkward void of a man caught off guard. "How can I help you?"

"I was given your number by a billing clerk at Starry Point General. Hannah was in an accident yesterday. The hospital suggested I get in touch with you, since you apparently handle her personal affairs."

"Is Mrs. Rourke all right? Is she—"

"She was hit by a car while riding her bike. She's banged up, but we expect her to make a full recovery. What I'm really calling about is Hope House."

There was another pause, then a long release of breath. "What can I do for you, Ms. Kramer?"

"You're probably not aware that there are plans to try to shut it down, very serious plans, in fact, by the mayor and town council. I was hoping you might be able to help me contact the founders, or the board, or whoever I need to talk to in order to keep that from happening. I've tried locating them myself, but it all seems very hush-hush."

"Forgive me, but may I ask why you believe I could help?"

"Well, I suppose I thought that since you must have been involved in getting her into Hope House, you might be able to point me in the right direction. I've been snooping around, writing letters, but so far I've come up empty-handed, and time is running out."

There was another long pause; then Callahan cleared his throat. "With all due respect, Ms. Kramer, I'm not really comfortable discussing Mrs. Rourke's personal affairs with someone I've neither met nor heard of."

"Would you be willing to discuss them with her son?"

"I'm sorry. Did you say . . . her son?"

Lane suppressed a smile. If that surprised him, the rest was really going to knock him for a loop. "Evan Rourke is also a friend of mine."

This time there was no thoughtful pause. Callahan's response was immediate. "Perhaps we'd better set up a meeting. Would you be able to come to Raleigh tomorrow afternoon?"

"Tomorrow?" Lane glanced at Michael, who rolled his eyes helplessly over the rim of his coffee mug. "Yes, tomorrow's fine. Say, around three?" After a quick forage in her purse, she located a pen and scribbled down Callahan's address, then ended the call.

"Three o'clock," she told Michael crisply. "At his home in Raleigh."

Michael looked stricken. "That's a five-hour drive."

"Yes, it is. And at the end of it I might finally get some answers."

Chapter 54

Michael

Michael kept his eyes on the road, asking himself for the hundredth time why he'd agreed to go on this little junket, and why, for that matter, the meeting had to be in person. He could have spoken to the man on the phone and accomplished the same thing. Instead, he was traipsing halfway across the state to discuss things that had nothing to do with him, and a woman who wasn't even part of his life.

Maybe it was guilt. Okay, not maybe. It was definitely guilt. It wasn't fair to let Lane do all the heavy lifting. The least he could do before he skipped town was make sure Hannah had a roof over her head. If this Callahan knew something that would help save Hope House, he owed it to Lane to help her find out what it was.

But that's all it was.

He wasn't a fool. He'd seen the way Hannah looked at Lane, the way she'd looked at them both, with those old fairy-tale notions of hers. He knew what she wanted—and why she wanted it. It was a way to tie him to Starry Point, to snare him back into her life, using Lane as bait. Well, that wasn't happening. She didn't get a vote, in that part of his life or any other. Blood or no blood, Hannah Rourke had been gone from his life longer than she'd been a part of it, gone so long he'd believed her dead.

But then, of course he'd believed she was dead. He'd been told so, point-blank. Had Katherine been mistaken, or had she simply lied? She'd always been squeamish about Hannah, jealous of a woman she'd never met. Was he wrong to wonder now if Hannah's so-called demise had only been a convenient invention intended to stave off curiosity? He didn't like to think so, but he'd be having that conversation soon, and it wasn't likely to be a pleasant one. His father wouldn't care one way or another that Hannah was alive and well, and back in his life. But he would have his hands full with his mother—with Katherine. Christ, he had no idea what to call anyone anymore.

"Michael, you need to turn just up ahead."

Michael's head swiveled in Lane's direction. "Sorry?"

"You need to turn at the next light. Are you not paying attention to the GPS?"

Michael turned obediently, feeling his belly grind when he saw they were now on Callahan's street. Odd, meeting the guy at his home instead of in an office somewhere, but then he didn't plan to stay long. He surveyed the enormous two-story as he pulled up the drive: soaring white columns, manicured boxwoods, meticulous stone walk. Whoever the guy was, he'd done well for himself.

He stood with his hands in his pockets while Lane rang the bell, wondering if it was too late to get back in the car and hit I-95 north, to forget that in the last seventy-two hours his life had been completely upended and was probably about to get much worse.

Lane was reaching for the bell again when the door opened, revealing a gray-haired man in tan trousers and a navy cardigan. The man slid wire-rimmed glasses down a longish nose and peered over them at Michael.

"As tall as your father," he said with a tight smile.

For an instant Michael could swear the ground had shifted. "Uncle R.B.?"

"Come in, young man."

Michael was keenly aware of Lane's gaze as they stepped into the foyer, could feel the string of questions simmering just beneath her polite veneer, but at the moment he was simply too baffled to explain, mostly because he wasn't at all sure he could.

"This is Lane Kramer," he said stiffly. "You spoke yesterday on the phone. She's a friend of Hannah's."

"Ah yes, Ms. Kramer," he acknowledged stiffly, as he took their coats and hung them on an ornate rack near the door. "If the two of you will follow me, we'll discuss this in my study."

Michael's gut churned as they trailed Callahan down a dimly lit corridor and into the study. The room felt strangely familiar. The enormous desk and leather chairs, the floor-to-ceiling cases lined with books, the decades-old pall of tobacco, all might have been from his father's study. But then that shouldn't surprise him. Ronald Callahan and Samuel Rourke had been friends since their freshman year at Duke.

"Can I offer either of you a drink?" Callahan asked, hovering near a small bar in the corner.

Michael eyed the desk and saw that R.B. was already working on one himself. "No, thank you. I'd really just like to get this over with."

Callahan frowned, then splashed a hefty draft of scotch into a glass. On his way across the room, he pressed it into Michael's hand. "Have a drink, son."

Everyone took a seat. Callahan settled behind his desk, steepling his long fingers beneath his chin. "You look like your father," he said, smiling in earnest now. "Except for the chin; that's Hannah's chin."

Michael felt Lane's gaze again and knew it was time to explain. "Uncle R.B. was my father's business partner and closest friend."

Her brows pinched together. "But yesterday you told me you didn't know him."

"Because I didn't. He was never Mr. Callahan to me. He was simply Uncle R.B., my father's best friend, and the man who drove me to Boston to meet the Forresters."

Callahan nodded, some of his smile slipping away. "It was a long time ago, Ms. Kramer."

"Yes, it was," Michael agreed curtly. "A lifetime, in fact. Now, if you don't mind, I'd like to know what this is about. What is it we couldn't discuss over the phone?"

"All business, I see," Callahan observed. "Also like your father. Very well, then."

Withdrawing a folder from the desk, he laid it on the blotter. "After your father's accident there was a lot that needed to be handled, insurance and investments, so many loose ends, and Hannah was . . . well, she was overwrought. Then later, after the fire, there was even more to be dealt with. She wasn't in any shape to handle things, legally or emotionally. And so, when approached, I agreed to . . . step in."

"Approached?" Michael repeated warily. "Approached by whom?"

Callahan removed his glasses, wiped them with a handkerchief he produced from his cardigan pocket, then perched them back on the end of his nose. "By your father."

Michael stiffened. "My . . . father?"

"Please, Evan. Let me get it out."

"Get what out? What are you saying?"

Callahan closed his eyes briefly and shook his head. "It was a hell of a storm, the kind that blow up out of nowhere on the banks. Days later, after your father . . . disappeared . . . pieces of the *Windseeker* started washing up along the jetty. The police, everyone, assumed Sam was dead."

Assumed?

The word seemed to reach him from very far away, echoing sickeningly against the walls of his skull. "Not everyone," he said stonily. "Not Hannah."

Callahan held up a hand to silence him. He was pale now, his expression pained. "Please. This isn't an easy thing to tell, though I always knew I'd have to tell it one day." From the file on the desk he withdrew a yellowed newspaper clipping and slid it forward.

Michael recognized the article that had run in the *Islander Dispatch* the day after the accident. MAYOR OF STARRY POINT PRESUMED DROWNED. He glanced at it but didn't touch it. If he didn't touch it maybe none of what he was about to hear would be true.

Lane picked up the scrap of newsprint, lingering briefly over the grainy photo, a jagged bit of stern bobbing against a stretch of rock. "It's your father's boat."

He nodded grimly. "What's left of it, yes. If you look closely you can make out the *W* on the hull."

Callahan cleared his throat and pushed on. "What you don't know—what no one knew—is that Samuel Rourke didn't die that day. He was washed overboard, but he didn't drown."

Michael barely registered Lane's hand on his arm as the blood rushed to his ears, hammered inside his skull.

It's a lie. It's a lie. It's a goddamn lie.

"It wasn't planned, Evan," Callahan continued. "Your father never set out to abandon you and your brother, or even Hannah. It just . . . happened. When he was finally picked up by a fishing boat, he was too ill to speak. By the time he recovered, everyone had already assumed the worst, and he began to see a way to escape the life he'd been so miserable in. When he called me I didn't believe it was him. His voice was different after the accident, something to do with damage to his vocal cords from being dehydrated for so long. At any rate, I thought someone was playing a joke, and not a funny one. Then he asked me to take care of your mother and look after you boys."

His voice trailed raggedly. He cleared his throat, gathering himself to tell the rest. "Please try to understand. Your mother wasn't well in those days. That made your father's life . . . difficult. So he thought, if everyone believed he was dead, why not let it stand? The search had been called off, the memorial held. In the eyes of the world, Samuel Rourke was a dead man. They believed it, and he let them—because it was a way to finally be free."

Michael set his untouched glass of scotch on the desk, his eyes frozen on Callahan's face. "Where has he been, and where is he now?"

"He died eight months ago, complications from the renal disease that plagued him after the accident. He'd been living in Canada . . . with a woman named Margaret."

Michael's head was swimming. It couldn't be true, and yet his mother's assertions about another woman kept popping to the surface. "When did they meet—my father and this woman?"

Callahan looked away, all but squirming in his leather chair. "They knew each other . . . before. She died about four years ago, from bone cancer. He was as happy as he could be under the circumstances, but he never forgave himself for what he did—for leaving you and Peter."

Michael shot to his feet, unwilling to listen to another word. "You think I give a good goddamn if the man was happy? Jesus . . . does my . . . does Hannah know?"

Callahan flinched, but managed to keep his voice even. "She has no idea. It never seemed to be the right time to tell her. Or a safe time, given everything she'd already been through. It would be a hard thing to take, I think."

"To learn her husband faked his own death? Yeah, I think that would be a little unpleasant."

Callahan sighed, clearly a man in the middle. "I don't think you've quite grasped your father's state of mind at the time. Living with your mother was killing him by inches. No one knew how to help her back then, though God knows the doctors tried everything they could think of—and some things they shouldn't have. None of it worked, ultimately. Your father was out of options. He simply didn't have the capacity to deal with Hannah's problems."

"It's a bit extreme, don't you think?" Michael fired back sarcastically. "I mean, did the man never hear of divorce?"

Callahan lifted his watered-down scotch and swirled it thoughtfully. "Your father was Catholic. Divorce wasn't an option."

"But staging his own death was?"

Lane rose from her chair and came to stand beside him. "Mr. Callahan's just trying to explain what was going on in your father's mind. None of this was his doing."

"He knew! All these years, he knew and he never told anyone."

"Yes, I did know," Callahan said quietly. "Your father was my friend, Evan. But he was also a client at that point, which entitled him to certain . . . protections. His wish was that you not know any of this until he'd been dead a full year. As his attorney I had no choice but to comply with those wishes."

Sidestepping Lane, Michael planted both hands on the edge of the desk, leaning forward until he was eye-to-eye with Callahan. "Don't shovel that attorney-client privilege crap at me. The man didn't think twice about turning his back on a wife and two sons."

"It was an act of desperation, and I can tell you with certainty that he deeply regretted hurting you and your brother."

"And my mother—did he regret hurting her, too?"

"Of course he did. He cared for your mother in his own way, just not the way a man needs to care for a woman like Hannah. And he loved you boys with his whole heart and soul. Calling him to tell him about the fire—about Peter—was the hardest thing I ever had to do. I knew he would blame himself, and he did."

Michael shook his head, thinking of his mother, of the events that had set her on the final path to self-destruction. "Not enough," he ground through clenched teeth. "He could never have blamed himself enough."

Callahan pretended not to hear. Setting aside his glass, he opened the folder on the desk, sifting through it until he found what he was looking for. "After the fire, Sam asked me to personally see to your adoption, to make certain you were placed with a good family, preferably one far from Starry Point. Then he asked me to establish a trust for Hannah. Every dime of your mother's care, the doctors, the private facilities, all of it, was paid for with your father's money. That goes for Hope House as well."

Lane's jaw dropped briefly before she found her voice. "Samuel Rourke is the man behind Hope House?"

"Was the man—yes." Callahan shifted in his chair, addressing Lane now, clearly relieved to be moving away from his friend's sins and onto his philanthropy. "By the time Hannah was ready to be ... released, the house was in pretty bad shape. Not that anyone thought her moving back there was a good idea. But she was adamant about coming back to Starry Point."

"She wanted to be near Peter," Lane said softly.

Callahan nodded. "Yes. Her doctors weren't crazy about the idea. They no longer felt Hannah required full-time supervision, but they weren't convinced she was ready to live on her own. They suggested a halfway house to help her transition. And so Hope House was born, with no one the wiser. I've been overseeing the trust ever since."

"Rourke and Callahan," Lane said, as if a light had suddenly gone on in her head. "You're R&C Limited."

"Yes. And you're the Ms. Kramer who wrote to me about Harold Landon. I'd like to thank you for that. I have some people doing a little checking, but I couldn't respond to your letter without all of this coming out. Mostly, I was trying to protect Hannah. She has no idea I've been pulling the strings, let alone that I was pulling them for Sam."

Michael turned on his heel and began to pace. "And what about me? Did I not have a right to know? He was tired of my mother. Fine. Was he tired of me, too?"

"Evan, you have to believe me when I tell you the hardest part of this for your father, harder even than losing Peter, was giving you up. He couldn't send for you, and your mother was in no condition to care for you. So he did the only thing he could. He made sure you had a family that could give you the same opportunities you would've had as his son."

Michael whirled, jabbing a finger in Callahan's direction. "Don't you dare sit there and try to defend what he did. Don't you dare do it! You're wasting your breath trying to paint him as anything but a selfish bastard. The man turned his back on his family—just washed his hands of us."

"He never lost track of you," Callahan said softly. "He knew about every graduation, every award, every significant event in your life."

"How the hell would he know anything about me?"

"From me. He asked me to let him know how you were from time to time." He slid a stack of envelopes to the edge of the desk, tapping them with the flats of his fingers. "These are for you."

Michael eyed the stack warily. "What are they?"

"Letters," he said evenly. "From your father to you. In case you ever learned the truth."

"And if I never did?"

The look he gave Michael bordered on reproach. "I don't think he really ever expected that you'd read them. I think it just made him feel better to write them, to pretend he was still a part of your life."

"He should have considered that before pulling his disappearing act."

Callahan ignored the remark. "The last of them, the one on top of the stack, arrived a week after his death."

Michael glanced at the letters but made no move to touch them. "I don't want them."

"Not now, no. But you will, Evan."

Okay, it was time to get a few things straight. "My name is Michael. Not Evan—Michael. And there's nothing in those letters I care to read."

Lane brushed his hand. "He's right, Michael. Take them."

"Fine," he snapped, swiping the top letter off the stack and stuffing it into his back pocket. It didn't mean he was going to read it, but if it got them off his back, fine. "I'll take one. You can burn the rest, for all I care."

Callahan rose and came around the desk, a weighty manila envelope in his hands. "This is a copy of your father's will. You'll also find the deed to the house, and other pertinent financial paperwork. There were no other children. Everything your father had will go to you now, except for Hannah's trust and the Hope House Foundation. I'll follow up in a few days, if that's all right, to see how you're feeling about things, and answer any questions."

Michael knew he should shake the man's hand, say thank you, say something; he just couldn't. With a vague nod, he caught Lane's eye and gestured toward the door. Lane followed him but turned back to Callahan as they reached the doorway.

"The woman—Margaret—did you know her, Mr. Callahan?"

Callahan nodded. "She was my secretary."

"Can you tell me if she happened to have red hair?"

The question clearly came as a surprise. "Yes, she did. Why do you ask?"

"A sketch of Hannah's—a mermaid with red hair. It makes sense now."

Michael knew the sketch well, had seen it a thousand times in Hannah's sketchbook, but had never connected the dots to the other woman—to Margaret. He was a boy then, ignorant of such things, and if truth be told, unwilling to believe his mother's assertions. Turned out, she'd been right all along.

"Ah yes." Callahan's expression was tinged with sadness. "Lovely things, those sketches. She had a real gift, lots of them, in fact."

Lane took a tentative step back into the room. "Mr. Callahan, I'm not sure why I'm saying this, and I'm fairly certain Michael won't agree, but I think there was something noble in what you did for Samuel Rourke—and for Hannah."

Michael stared at her, annoyed and vaguely stunned. Damn right he didn't agree. But Callahan was smiling, a tremulous blend of grief and gratitude.

"You loved her," Lane said softly. "All this time, you loved her."

Callahan removed his glasses and folded them into the pocket of his cardigan. "I couldn't help myself. She was unlike any woman I'd ever known. She never looked twice at me, though. She only had eyes for Sam. Sam knew how I felt. I suppose it's how he knew I'd look after her. We were best friends, closer than brothers, but he was never right for Hannah. The things that attracted him to her were the things that drove him away in the end. He wasn't capable of dealing with her . . . problems." He swallowed hard, his Adam's apple bobbing tellingly as picked up his glass and drained it.

"But you were?" Lane asked in a way that wasn't a question at all.

Callahan set aside his empty glass, his smile gone. "I would have liked the chance to try."

Chapter 55

Lane

I t was dark when they finally made it back to Starry Point, the air knife sharp as Lane opened the door of the SUV and stepped out onto the drive. The clouds that had shadowed them all day had finally begun to shred, revealing a spatter of crisp white stars and a bone white sliver of moon.

Michael hadn't said a word on the ride back, fuming stonily behind the wheel, his eyes locked on the road as I-40 blurred past. There had been so much she wanted to say, so many questions she longed to ask. In the end, she had kept it all to herself. He slammed the car door now, marching away from the inn, and then across the street with long, purposeful strides.

Lane followed a few paces behind, silent as they slogged through the carpet of wet leaves that blanketed the lawn. She should have seen this coming, not that she could have stopped him. Rourke House was his now, to do with as he pleased, which was precisely what worried her. She couldn't help sneaking a glance at the greenhouse, a chilling reminder of Michael's long-suppressed anger. After today, another session of venting might be exactly what he needed—and what he deserved.

But Michael didn't head to the greenhouse. Instead, he followed the weedy path up onto the front porch and sank down onto the top step, hands propped on his knees. Lane didn't wait for an invitation. Tucking her hands up into the sleeves of her coat, she eased down beside him. It was all she could do not to touch him, to smooth the deep furrow between his brows.

"What are you going to do?" she asked instead.

Michael threw her a sidelong glance. "Do?"

It was a familiar conversation. "About your father . . . the letter . . . all of it."

"I haven't the first goddamn idea."

"No, I guess not. Look, it's cold. Why don't we go back to the inn? I'll fix you something to eat."

"You can't fix this with food, Lane."

"How about alcohol?"

He managed a smile, but there was no humor in it. "No, thanks. If I start drinking now I might never stop. What I really need is to just sit here with my thoughts."

"You want me to go?"

"Yes."

"Will you promise not to go into the house? After everything, I don't think you should. At least not yet."

"I have no intention of going inside. I just need some time alone, to try to wrap my head around all this. Everything changed today. Everything I built my life around—everything I grew up believing— was a lie. I need to think about that, about what it means, and what I'm supposed to believe now—do now."

Standing, she brushed the leaves from the seat of her pants, still fighting the urge to touch his face, all shadows now in the chilly moonlight. "Don't stay too long, though. It's cold."

She was stretched out on her bed, running through the blurred events of the day, when she heard his knock. He looked miserable when she opened the door, although after the last forty-eight hours, he was certainly entitled. He said nothing as he stepped into the room, just pressed a thin white envelope into her hands. It was still sealed but badly rumpled, as if he'd been holding it for a very long time, trying to find the strength to open it.

"Read it," he said bluntly.

"You're sure?"

"No, but read it anyway before I lose my nerve and burn the damn thing."

Lane lifted her head sharply. "You can't. Not without knowing what it says."

"I know," he said flatly. "But I want to." Wandering to the window, he stared out at the darkened beach, flinching a little each time the light swept past the glass. "I used to sleep in this room," he said flatly. "Back when I was a boy. Did I ever tell you that?"

"Yes, you did. How many others were there?"

"Fifteen to twenty, give or take, all lined up like little soldiers in those skinny iron beds. The number was always changing. New kids came in; others got homes—like puppies at the pound."

Lane didn't want to think of him as a boy here, miserable and alone. She had teased him once, about yachting camp, and all the while he'd been living with memories no boy should ever have to live with. His attention was still fixed beyond the window, locked not on the horizon, but on some point in time that only he could see. Like Hannah.

"Out there," he said, tapping the glass. "Down by the jetty. That's where they found my father's boat, or what was left of it, smashed against the rocks. Everyone just assumed..." He turned from the window then, his voice cracking with thinly veiled emotion. "Everyone except Hannah, that is. People thought she was crazy. I did, too."

Lane said nothing. He needed this, she knew, but it was hard to watch, to see him torturing himself, taking even more guilt on those already scarred shoulders. She wished there was something to say, something that would help make sense of it all, but how could anyone make sense of a thing like this?

"Go on," he said, jerking his chin at the envelope. "Open it."

Lane stared at the handwriting, unsteady and heavily slanted—the hand of an old man, a sick man. A good-bye. Suddenly, she wasn't sure she wanted to be part of such a private moment.

"Are you sure you want me to read it?"

"It's a little late for discretion, don't you think?"

Lane felt her cheeks go hot, but he wasn't wrong. Dropping onto the edge of the bed, she tore open the envelope and teased out several folded pages. Clearing her throat, she began.

Evan,

I have no way of knowing if you'll ever read this letter, but like all the others, it had to be written. By now you know what I did, and why. There are times in a man's life, selfish times, I'll grant, when doing the right thing becomes insupportable, when despair gives rise to its own brand of madness.

I have never asked for your forgiveness, nor do I ask it now. I deserve no such kindness. I write only to say how sorry I am at having lost you—and Peter. R.B. told me about the fire. I died a little that day. What happened to your brother will forever be on my hands, and on my heart. Mine—not your mother's.

I have only days left on this earth, and so this will be my last letter. Know that it is written with love and regret, a final handful of words to atone for a lifetime of heartbreak. How clear the right way seems once you've chosen the wrong one. And yet, as I look back over my life, I find there is one bright spot, and that is you, my son, though I know I haven't any right to your accomplishments, or even to a place in your memory. Please know that in my heart I have never stopped being your father, and that I did the best I could for you from a distance. And for your mother, too, as you must surely know by now. She didn't deserve what I did to her. Only the weakest kind of man turns his back on a woman who needs him. I was the weakest kind of man.

The father who never stopped loving you—

P.S.—Hold nothing against R.B. He played no part in the choice I made, but has remained a faithful friend, helping me to make reparation in the only way I knew how.

Lane blinked back tears as she folded the pages back along their creases and handed them to Michael. "How will you tell Hannah?"

Michael stared at the pages briefly, then let them flutter to the floor. "I have no intention of telling her."

It was what she was afraid he'd say. "Are you sure that's the right decision? You said it yourself, all those years ago, she was the one— the only one—who refused to accept that your father was dead. After everything she's been through, don't you think she deserves to know she was right?"

Michael's face registered something approaching astonishment. "To what end? So she'll finally have proof that her husband was desperate to be free of her? That he cared more about some secretary than he did about his own family?"

Lane was careful to keep her voice even. He didn't need a lecture right now, but he did need to understand. "Don't you see? She never needed proof, because she always knew. It was everyone else who needed convincing."

"Fine, she learns she was right. Then what? She spends the rest of her life reliving it all, and blaming herself?"

"Or maybe she realizes it's time to forgive herself. She's stronger than you think, Michael. She's had to be. I'm not saying tell her today, but I think that in time the truth might help her feel vindicated."

Michael eyed her grimly. "There are more important things than being right, Lane."

"I understand that, but this isn't just about being right. It's about proving she wasn't crazy for believing what she did. And just maybe, she'll finally see that not everything that happened back then was her fault."

"Meanwhile, the Rourke name gets dragged through the mud all over again. Only this time my mother plays the tragically wronged heroine, and my father is the villain."

"The Rourke name? That's what you're worried about? Michael, no one else has to know any of this, but your mother has a right to the truth, to know that what people thought about her all those years ago was wrong. She needs that, and she deserves it."

"I was one of those people, Lane. How do I look her in the eye now and admit that?"

"You don't." She reached for his arm, surprised when he didn't pull away. "You were a child, Michael, a little boy. What were you supposed to believe?"

"I saw the wreckage with my own eyes. The pictures ran in the paper for days." He stepped away and resumed pacing, this time giving the windows a wide berth. At length, he sagged down onto the edge of the bed, elbows on his thighs, hands dangling between his knees. "All my life, I've blamed her for his death, for forcing him out of the house that day. It never once occurred to me that she might be right, that the bastard might actually be alive."

"Under the circumstances I don't think anyone would have believed differently. But, Michael, you're going to have to find a way to forgive and let go of the past."

He closed his eyes, shook his head. "That isn't going to happen."

"I know you don't believe it's possible, that you're hurting right now, but try standing in your father's shoes for a minute. You heard what he wrote. Life with your mother wasn't easy. Even she admits that. He was miserable—desperate. Right or wrong, he took the only avenue he believed open to him. He walked away from one life and began a new one. And in her way, your mother did the same thing. She gradually withdrew from the real world, where every day was a struggle, and not even the doctors could help her. Then, when the grief became too much to bear, she buried Hannah Rourke and became Dirty Mary—because it was easier to be a social outcast than a woman who'd lost a husband and two sons."

Suddenly, Michael looked very tired, tired of listening and tired of talking. "I know this all seems very clear to you, Lane. And you'd like me to say I can just put it all behind me, but it's not that easy. I lived it."

"You didn't let me finish."

Michael looked at her wearily. "There's more?"

"Yes, but you won't like it."

"I haven't liked any of this, so far."

"I think before you can forgive anyone else, you're going to have to find a way to forgive yourself. All these years, you've been blaming yourself, for not being able to make your mother well, for not being there for Peter when the fire started, for not being able to hold your family together. But none of those things were your fault. Actually, I'm not sure they were anyone's fault. Your father, your mother—all of you—did the only thing you knew to do at the time. You survived."

"So that's your answer? Just forgive myself and everything will be fine?"

He was getting surly now, like a child who didn't want to do his homework, because he didn't know how, and didn't know how to ask for help. Dropping down beside him, she gentled her voice. "I didn't say that. But there won't be room in your heart for anyone else until you try. Blame can take up a lot of space in a heart. I finally figured that out. Life is too short for grudges, the big ones or the small ones."

If Michael was listening, he made no response. It broke her heart to see him hurting so, tortured by a past that kept rearing its ugly head. Before she could stop herself she pressed a kiss to his temple. The air seemed to go out of the room as he lifted his head, his eyes full of pain and confusion—full of need. Lane felt her bones go soft, felt the warm, strong pull of him, stirring memories of another night—and the last time he'd needed her. When he reached for her she pulled away. She couldn't be there for him this time, not like that—not temporarily.

"I'm sorry, Michael, I can't. I don't want to just be a distraction, and we both know that's what I'd be, a way to keep your mind off things you'd rather not think about. I was that for you once. I can't do it again."

"Right. Got it." He stood, pushing his hands deep into his pockets. "I know you want the happy ending. And you deserve one. But I can't stay in Starry Point. Not when there are memories everywhere I look. I wasn't lying when I said I didn't want to hurt you, or when I said leaving was the best thing for both of us. It still is. That hasn't changed."

Lane nodded, trying to pretend she hadn't been hoping he'd say something else. She watched as he crossed the room and retrieved his father's letter from the floor. When he had folded and pocketed the rumpled sheets, he turned back to face her.

"I'm sorry, Lane. Sorrier than you'll ever know."

She managed another nod, then watched him go.

Michael's door swung open almost instantly in response to her light rap. Clearly, he hadn't been able to sleep, either. He stood in the doorway, a silhouette in the faint blue-white light that spilled into his room.

"Lane, it's three a.m. What are you . . . what's wrong?"

He was wearing a pair of pajama bottoms and nothing else. Without meaning to, she let her eyes run the length of him, then back again. The moment spun out awkwardly.

"Nothing's wrong," she said, finding her voice at last. "I just . . . changed my mind."

Michael found her eyes in the gloom, then looked away. "That's a bad idea."

"I know," Lane said softly. "But I'm here anyway."

"What you said before, about being a distraction—" He broke off, raked a hand through already tousled hair. "You were right. You should go back to bed."

"I can't sleep."

"They make pills for that."

"I don't want a pill."

She gazed up at him through lowered lashes. Something had changed in the dark empty hours since he'd left her room, a stirring of blood and bone that refused to be quiet, a stripping away of pride and pretense. Stepping closer, she laid a hand on his bare chest, felt the deep thrum of his heart against her palm, the warm, quick urgency of it. He wanted her, as much as she wanted him. That hadn't changed. How did she make him understand that he didn't have to be noble, that her eyes were wide open, and for now, tonight, she didn't care about tomorrow?

"Michael, you don't have to protect me. I've been lying up there in the dark, thinking about everyone telling me to fight for what I want. Well, this is what I want. Here. Now. For however many days we have left. I don't need a happy ending. I need right now."

She stared at him, waiting, then realized she had no idea what she wanted him to do or say. Part of her hoped he'd send her back to her room, that he would care enough, down in places he hadn't explored yet, not to risk hurting her again. But the other part, the flesh-and-blood part, hoped he would pull her into his arms and drag her into bed.

In the end, he did neither. With a single finger, he traced the curve of her cheek with agonizing slowness, then tucked a wayward strand of hair behind her ear. "I won't sleep with you," he said with a husky softness. "But I will stay awake with you."

"But I thought—"

"You deserve more than just right now, Lane. You shouldn't ever forget that."

Lane managed a nod, her throat suddenly too tight to speak.

He took her hand then, like a wayward child up past bedtime, and led her across the room to the large four-poster bed. The drapes were open, the stars on display out over a silver-black sea, and as she lay down she tried not to think of the lonely boy who had once looked out at that same sky as he drifted off to sleep.

His warmth was welcome when he finally dropped down beside her and snugged an arm about her waist—as if they'd been sharing a bed for years. They lay awake for a while, their bodies fitted like spoons in a drawer, until the mingled rhythm of heart and breath began to lull her toward sleep. It wasn't what she'd come for when she padded down the stairs. There was no passion in their closeness, no threat and no promise, only a quiet sense of rightness as the horizon slid toward silver and she finally drifted off.

When she opened her eyes again, the horizon was a dusky shade of pink, and Michael was gone. Pushing back the sheets, she turned to look at the empty place beside her. She had no right to expect him to be there, no right at all. He had declared nothing—promised nothing. And despite it all, she felt betrayed. Not because Michael had betrayed her, but because she had betrayed herself.

Chapter 56

Michael

Michael shrugged deeper into his jacket, turned his eyes toward the lighthouse, and picked up his pace. The sun glinted sharply off the cold gray sea, the wind biting hard as it skimmed in off the frothy Atlantic. He'd forgotten how cold the wind could be at this time of year, that there was a reason places like the Cloister shut down for the season.

He'd left Lane sleeping in his bed, the safest course, all things considered. She had looked so lovely with the morning light slanting across her face, setting all that auburn hair on fire. He wasn't sure he could trust his resolve a second time. She wouldn't understand when she woke up and found him gone, but eventually she'd thank him. Besides, he had a bit of business to take care of.

In his pocket, he found Samuel Rourke's letter, the words of a dead man and a liar. At some point, during what had been a very long night, he had come to a decision. He would destroy the letter and leave Hannah to her blissful ignorance. Would that Callahan had done the same for him. Lane wouldn't be happy, but it was his decision to make—alone. The sooner he was rid of the damn thing, the sooner he could start putting the whole hideous business behind him.

The jetty was slick as he scrambled out onto the rocks. Gradually he found his footing, determined to make it out to the end, to stand where the wreckage of the *Windseeker* had once washed up and deceived an entire town.

Overhead, Lane's gulls circled greedily, scolding him for bringing no breakfast. They floated above him as he made his way toward the jetty's end, a noisy cloud of gray and white, as he dropped down onto the driest rock he could find. He swore softly as the wet seeped through his pants, summoning Sister Mary Constantine's grim warnings about piles.

Dragging the letter from his pocket, he carefully unfolded the pages, fighting to keep the wind from snatching them. When he finally threw his father's words into the sea, he didn't want it to be an accident. He imagined how it would feel to tear the letter in half, and then in half again and again, how the bits would flutter in the wind like so much confetti, until they finally fell into the purling gray water—gone for good.

But in spite of his resolve, he held fast to the pages. It was hard to say why. He didn't need to read them. Every word was already burned into his brain. Perhaps his father hadn't asked for forgiveness outright, but he had certainly pleaded his case, trying to explain away the terrible thing he'd done, to justify the unjustifiable. The final act of a selfish bastard.

And yet he couldn't shake the bone-deep sense of loss. Not for the man his father had been, but for the man he had once believed him to be, for the memories he could no longer cherish, for the role model who died not as a hero but as a coward.

Samuel Rourke had chosen to walk away from his life, a wife who needed him, children who loved him—for another woman. It was that choice, a single moment of blind selfishness, that had led to his mother's undoing, and ultimately to Peter's death. For thirty years he'd been blaming the wrong parent.

Lane had asked him to stand in his father's shoes, to see that he'd taken the only avenue open to him, and that his mother had done the same. They had turned their backs on intolerable lives and invented new ones. Hadn't he done the same? Michael Forrester hadn't been his invention, but it hadn't taken him long to step into that new boy's skin, to leave Evan Rourke and his scars behind. Except those scars had never healed. That he was back in Starry Point was proof of that.

So, what was it all for? All the running and blaming and pretending. All the lies. For what? Despite their best efforts and years of denial, the truth had won out. What good, then, was likely to come from more deception? It hadn't worked for any of them, and for his mother least of all.

The pages in his fist had grown limp in the damp salt air. He stared at them now, wondering if Lane was right. Was Hannah strong enough to hear the truth, to read the words her long-lost husband had penned just days before his death? And if not, could he live with the very real possibility of another breakdown? He honestly didn't know. But if there was a chance, even a small one, that that truth could bring his mother some measure of peace, wasn't it worth the risk? He could leave Starry Point with a clear conscience, though when that leaving might take place he had absolutely no idea.

He had yet to delve into the paperwork Callahan had handed him yesterday, but he suspected there'd be plenty of loose ends to tie up: trusts to be overseen, assets to be transferred, the house to be disposed of. And of course, Landon would have to be dealt with, and the Hope House issue resolved. Lane would expect that of him before he left town, and it was the least he could do. The very least, in fact.

Only the weakest kind of man turns his back on a woman who needs him.

His father's words hissed hotly in his ear, grinding against his conscience like fingernails on a blackboard. The hindsight of a guilty man, or perhaps a plea to the son now beyond his reach, to be a better man than he himself had been. Whatever the intent, they were making him think, and he wasn't sure he liked the direction of his thoughts. A few days ago, putting Starry Point behind him was all he wanted. Now, quite suddenly, the idea left him hollow.

Maybe it was the thought of following in his father's footsteps, of slinking off like a coward. Or the realization that his urgency to be gone wasn't about running toward something, only about running away. His life had been empty for longer than he cared to admit, a professional and personal sham that filled his time, but little else. But it didn't have to stay that way. Now there was Lane, and a promise of happiness—if he chose to take it.

The wind picked up, sending a gust of sea spray into his face. He licked the salt off his lips, tasting his boyhood. Could he stay? In this place where everything seemed to pulse with memories, where every sight and sound reminded him of his first life—his real life? It was hard to imagine. Impossible, actually.

Lane had said it, and she was right. There would never be room in his heart for anyone until he learned to forgive. And there was just too much to forgive. For starters, there was no way to make things right with a dead man, to erase the facts contained in the letter now crumpled in his fist. The nearest he could get was to destroy it, for his sake as well as Hannah's.

But once again something stopped him, some nebulous scrap of thought that kept flitting through his head, like a moth or dust mote that refused to land. And then, finally, he had it: an image of Dirty Mary—of Hannah—perched on the dunes, waiting for the truth. Was it possible that he was, even now, holding that truth in his hands? That what his mother had really been waiting for all these years was vindication? It sounded crazy, but the longer he stared at his father's unsteady scrawl, the more convinced he became that he was right.

Chapter 57

Lane

Lane looked up from the coffeepot when the back door opened. Michael was there, his cheeks dark with morning stubble, wind-blown and slightly damp as he peeled off his jacket and draped it on a peg. Suddenly, her hands were clammy. She curled them into fists, not knowing what to say, or how to act. In the end, the oven timer saved her.

The kitchen filled with the mouthwatering aroma of cranberry-spice muffins as she extracted the pan and set it on the stove. Stalling for time, she spent a few minutes tidying: stowing oven mitts, wiping down counters, straightening towels.

"Lane—"

She cut him off with a hand as she lifted her mug. She didn't need apologies or explanations. They'd done those already. And really, there was nothing to apologize for. In fact, she should probably thank him for taking the high road, for refusing to let her make a complete fool of herself. And if he'd snuck out again, well, who could blame him after the way she had thrown herself at him?

"Look," she said, trying to sound casual as she poured him a mug of coffee and passed it to him. "Before you say anything, we don't have to talk about last night. It's done, and quite frankly, I'd rather not rehash it if you don't mind. In fact, we don't have to talk about it ever again."

He nodded, looking distinctly relieved.

"So, have you given any more thought to what to do about Hannah and the letter?"

Michael stared down at his feet, as if fascinated by the wet half-moons at the tips of his boots. "I thought about it all night, as a matter of fact. You told me I need to forgive, and maybe that's true. I can forgive my mother. Maybe because it turns out there's really not that much to forgive when you take everything into consideration. But I can't and won't forgive my father. What he did set all the rest in motion, and no letter can ever change that. So I went down to the jetty to shred the damn thing and toss it into the ocean."

Lane's mug halted en route to her mouth. "Please, please tell me you didn't."

"I wanted to—still do. But no, I didn't."

"What changed your mind?"

"Something you said once, about Hannah waiting for the truth. All of a sudden I knew the letter *was* that truth, proof that she hadn't been wrong, hadn't been crazy. Last night, you said she had a right to know, and she does. I'm going to show her the letter."

"I'm glad."

"You were right, Lane," he said quietly. "About a lot of things."

"What . . . kind of things?"

"About there being no room in my heart, for starters."

"Yeah, well, we don't need to go there again. Really. I get it."

"I don't think you do," Michael said evenly. "And I need you to. I asked you once how you know if you're where you're supposed to be. Do you remember that?"

"Yes, I remember."

Her face was stony as she braced for yet another explanation about why he couldn't stay, couldn't be the man she needed—couldn't love her. Instead, his cell phone went off in his pocket. He swore softly as he glanced at the display.

"It's Katherine returning my call. I need to take this."

Lane nodded curtly. "Go ahead. We're done here anyway."

Michael opened his mouth to say something, but the phone jangled again. Grimacing, he slipped out the back door to answer the call. Lane was actually relieved. There were only so many times a girl could be turned down before she started taking it personally. Besides, she needed to get to the hospital. Dr. Ashton had agreed to meet her at eleven to discuss Hannah's care, and a potential time frame for her release.

Twenty minutes later, she was dressed and ready to go, packing muffins into a paper bag, when Michael reappeared, still clutching his cell. His cheeks were pink and shiny from the wind, like a boy's, but his brows were bunched, his shoulders tightly hunched. Apparently the call hadn't gone well.

She tried to imagine what it would be like to have your son, the boy you'd loved and thought of as your own for thirty years, call you out of the blue and tell you his birth mother was back from the grave and suddenly back in the picture. It couldn't have been an easy conversation for either of them, but it had to have been especially hard on Michael. He was being pulled in too many directions. Two mothers, two lives, and she'd been pulling on him, too. None of it was fair.

"I'm sorry about all this, Michael. If I had stayed away from Mary—from Hannah—when you asked me to, none of this would be happening now. You wouldn't know she was alive, wouldn't know the truth about your father. And there'd be no reason to have what I'm sure was a rather uncomfortable conversation with Katherine just now."

Michael nodded. "And Hannah would still be Dirty Mary, sitting out there all alone on the dunes, waiting for the truth. Now she won't have to wait anymore. She has you to thank for that. I suppose I do, too."

"She loved you Michael—and Peter. Never forget that."

Michael said nothing as he stepped past her and began rinsing out his mug. Apparently the discussion was over.

"Well, then, I guess I'm off to the hospital. Unless . . . you want to ride along?"

He turned as he dried his hands. "Thanks, but I need to tie up a few loose ends. I'll meet you there in about an hour."

Lane blinked at him. "Really? I didn't think you'd want to see her again."

"I don't. But you were right about the letter. She has a right to know."

"Yes, but not now, Michael. I didn't mean now. She's been through too much. The accident. Seeing you. We have to wait."

"I can't wait. I need to do this now—before I leave for Raleigh."

She set down the muffins. "Raleigh?"

"I'm going back to talk to Callahan. I'll be away for a while."

"How long is a while?"

"A few days. A week. I don't know right now. There's some business I need to see to, about the house and the trusts. And I suppose we'll need to decide what to do about Hope House. Hannah's going to need somewhere to go once she's discharged."

"About that," Lane began hesitantly. "I've been thinking about something more long-term."

"Long-term?"

"What would you say to Hannah coming to live with me?"

Michael couldn't have looked more stunned if she'd proposed dancing naked out on the jetty. "To live with you . . . here?"

"It makes sense, right now. She's going to need someone to look after her for a while, and with the inn closed for the winter I'll have time to help her through rehab. After that, maybe we can find her something long-term, a place where she can move into something like a normal life if that's what she wants, and her doctors say it's okay."

Michael sighed and dragged a hand through his hair. "Lane, I can't think long term right now. I've got my hands full with the here and now."

"I know that. I wasn't pushing. I just thought—"

"What? That you could fix it? Make us one big happy family again?"

"I'm just trying to help. I didn't mean—"

"I know you didn't. I just . . . I can't promise anything right now. To anyone."

Lane lifted her chin a notch. The words stung, but they weren't new. "You've always made that pretty clear."

The clock over the sink ticked noisily as she held his gaze, a thin, mechanical heartbeat in the charged silence. He made no attempt to defend himself. But then how could he when they both knew it was true?

The moment was broken when the doorbell rang. Their eyes held a moment more before Lane turned and headed for the parlor. She wasn't prepared for the enormous Fraser fir standing on her front porch, or for the young man who popped out from behind it.

"Delivery," he said simply.

Lane blinked at the monstrous evergreen. It dwarfed the boy by at least three feet. "I'm sorry. I'm afraid you have the wrong address."

He tugged a receipt from his pocket and squinted at it. "This the Cloister House?"

"Yes, but—"

"Says right here, Cloister House. Where do you want it?"

"But I didn't order a tree. There's been a mistake."

"There are some boxes in the truck, too," he informed her. "Oh, and I'm supposed to give you this."

He pushed the receipt into Lane's hands. It took only a moment to recognize the Sewell's Hardware logo, and Dally's loopy script.

Sorry, boss, couldn't help myself. After everything that's happened I thought you deserved a Christmas tree. I charged it all to your account. If you hate it you can fire me. Don't forget to pop

Harry into the CD player. If anyone can help you forget Profes-sor McDreamy, it's Harry. D—

Sighing, she stepped aside. "Just put it anywhere."

Several trips later, the tree was surrounded by four large card-board boxes, and Lane stood shaking her head. She really did need to fire that girl. At the sound of approaching footsteps, she turned. Michael seemed vaguely astonished to find an evergreen tree had sprouted beside the fireplace.

"What's all this?"

"Dally," she said simply.

"She bought you a tree?"

"Not exactly, no. But she sent one."

"That girl's a piece of work."

Lane found a smile. "Yes, but she's a good friend."

"What's in the boxes?"

"Ornaments, I'm guessing. The inn's always closed at the holidays, so there never seemed much point in a tree. She must have assumed I'd need them. I'll return them tomorrow, or maybe donate it all to Hope House."

"You're not going to keep it?"

Lane nudged the closest box with the toe of her boot. "I'm not really in the mood for holiday cheer at the moment. Besides, I've got a ton of work to get caught up on, and a new project I'm thinking about starting."

A smile flickered at the corners of Michael's mouth, sad and a bit reminiscent. "When I was here as a boy we always begged for a Christ-mas tree, but the nuns wouldn't have it. We had a nativity scene in-stead, which, as you can imagine, fell a bit short of our boyish ideals."

"So, do you do one now?"

His expression hardened as he eyed the bare tree. "Like you said, not much point."

Chapter 58

L ane watched as Hannah took a bite of muffin and washed it
down. She was struggling to eat with her right hand, dropping
crumbs and sloshing tea, but she was looking decidedly better,
in spite of her bruises, which were beginning to turn a sickly shade
of yellow-green.

The consultation with Ashton had gone well. He was both pleased
and surprised at the pace of Hannah's recovery, and had every reason
to believe she would be released by Christmas. The sling would come
off, her bruises would heal, the scar on her forehead would fade with
time. But Lane was worried about other scars, the kind that didn't
show, and might never heal if she was wrong about Hannah's capacity to handle what she was about to learn.

She had confided in Ashton, about the letter and Michael's plans
to show it to Hannah. As expected, he had urged caution. While
vindication might ultimately prove beneficial to Hannah's recovery,
he was concerned about the timing. In his opinion, there were only
two likely outcomes: either Hannah would see the news as vindication, or she would let it push her over the brink. One way or the
other, they were about to find out.

She hadn't told Hannah why Michael was coming, only that he

was. Now, as he appeared in the doorway, she wondered if she should have at least tried to prepare her. But how? Was it even possible to pave the way for such news? If there was, she couldn't imagine what it might be. At least they'd be a call button away from help if it went badly. And according to Ashton, it might.

She caught Michael's eye as he stepped into the room, but it was impossible to label what she saw in his expression, though determination might come close. She shot him a look, an unspoken plea to tread lightly, but he was already pulling the letter from his pocket. Apparently he intended to launch right in. Stomach heaving, she stood and moved beside him. She couldn't let him do this badly.

"Hannah," she ventured, before he could begin. "There's something Michael needs to tell you, something I'm afraid it won't be easy to hear."

"Something bad?"

"Yes," Michael said flatly. "It's something very bad."

Lane narrowed her eyes at him, but to no avail.

"It's about my father."

"About . . . Sam?" Hannah's face had gone a shade paler, her bruises suddenly standing out grotesquely. "What is it? What's wrong?"

Michael unfolded the letter, carefully smoothing the pages. "Do you remember Ronald Callahan? Uncle R.B.?"

"Ronnie?"

"Yes. Ronnie. I saw him yesterday and he told me . . . he gave me this." Without further preamble, he pressed the letter into Hannah's free hand. "Father wrote it—last year."

Hannah stared at the pages a moment, examining the slanted, spidery hand. "Last . . . year?"

Michael nodded. "Yes."

Her hand trembled as she lowered her head and began to read, her swollen lips moving silently as she devoured every line, then went back to savor them again more slowly. Finally, she looked up, her eyes shimmering with unshed tears.

"Not dead," she rasped tearfully. "My Sam. Not dead."

Lane met Michael's uneasy gaze. They were both thinking the same thing.

"Hannah?" Lane said gently. "You understand that Sam isn't still alive now, don't you? That this letter was written over a year ago?"

Hannah nodded, sending a pair of hot tears sliding down her cheeks and onto the pillow. Her eyes fluttered closed as she clutched the letter to her breast. "They were wrong. All of them . . . wrong."

"Yes, Hannah, they were."

They were quiet for a time while Hannah cried herself out. After thirty years she had a right to her tears. Finally, Michael stepped to the bed, brushing the lingering traces of dampness from his mother's cheek.

"All that time," he said hoarsely. "All that time you knew he was alive, and none of us believed you. We should have listened. I should have listened."

She reached for his hand, curled bloodlessly around the bedrail now, and gave it a pat. "You couldn't have known."

"You knew."

"Of course I knew. We were man and wife. We shared a bed, a life. That counts for something." Her face softened then with a tremulous smile. "He was a good man, your father, in spite of his faults."

Michael jerked his hand back, looking mildly stunned. "How can you say that? After everything he did—the cheating, the lying—how can you lie there and say he was a good man?"

"Because it's true. And because good men sometimes do bad things. Your father loved me once, though I'm not sure he ever knew it. He must have to have stayed as long as he did."

"He left you for another woman!"

"No," Hannah countered with a shake of her pale head. "He did not. He left because he didn't know what to do with me. There's no sin in that—weakness perhaps, but no sin. The woman was just a lie he told himself—an excuse—because it was more acceptable to run into the arms of another woman than to abandon a sick wife."

"How is that more acceptable?" Michael demanded with barely controlled fury.

Hannah sighed, sagging deeper into her pillows. There were shadows beneath her eyes now. "My poor prince. You've carried so much anger, and for so long. First at me, and now at your father. But it's time to give it up."

Michael's jaw clenched mutinously. "No."

"It's no good holding on to old hurts, my boy. Your father did what he had to. It wasn't his fault."

"Then whose fault was it?"

Hannah shrugged. "Mine, maybe, or God's. It doesn't matter now. What's done is done."

Michael shook his head slowly. "Maybe that's the problem. For me, it isn't done. I've had less than forty-eight hours to digest all this and people are already telling me it's time to forgive. Well, I can't. The man did a hideous thing. I can't just let him off the hook."

Hannah pursed her lips, her expression stern and surprisingly maternal. "You can. And you must. This grudge of yours will poison you if you let it. You won't shake it on your own, though. You'll need help, someone to anchor you when the anger rears its head. You know what I mean, don't you—what I'm saying to you?"

Her gaze slid pointedly to Lane, and then back again. "It took me a long time to learn that it isn't fate that makes off with our wishes, my boy. It's us. Life gives us exactly what we need, even what we want, but we're afraid to grab it and hold on with both hands. We let go when the holding gets hard. We blame when we should forgive." She paused for the tiniest beat, locking eyes with her son. "And we run when we should stand our ground. Because we don't understand that we don't just get the life we wish for. We get the life we fight for."

The life we fight for.

The words reverberated in Lane's head, weighty, and eerily familiar. Her mother had said much the same thing. She had taken those words with a grain of salt then, but now she saw them for what they were—sound truths from two women who had lived, and loved, and lost. And who even now found a way to keep fighting.

Hannah's eyes were nearly closed now, her face shadowed with the strain of the morning's revelations, but strangely calm, too, now that it was over. It seemed, at long last, Hannah Rourke had found her truth, and perhaps a little peace.

On the other side of the bed, Michael stood with his head lowered and his hands thrust into his pockets. Had he been listening at all? Lane hoped so, because the things his mother had said, her willingness to forgive, her incredible generosity toward the man who had wronged her, had been nothing short of astonishing.

In a moment that might have sent her careening off the mental cliff, she had faced the truth with wisdom and strength, excusing her husband's cowardice and betrayal, even claiming a portion of the blame. But something told Lane Hannah's generosities hadn't been aimed at Samuel Rourke. They had been aimed at Michael. She had softened the edges of the selfish husband, painted over the faults of the flawed and careless father, in order to leave the door of forgiveness open for her son. It was an unfathomably kind gesture. And it was like her.

Michael cleared his throat. Lane glanced around in time to see him grab his coat from the chair and jerk his head toward the door.

Tiptoeing past Hannah's bed, she followed him out into the hall. "I know this was hard for you," she said, trying to get a handle on his mood. "But at least it's over now, and—"

"I'm going to take off," he said, before she could finish. He avoided her eyes as he dragged on his jacket. "It's a five-hour drive to Raleigh."

"You didn't tell me you were leaving today."

"Yeah, I guess this morning got a little messy. I'm sorry about that. It's just that a lot's happened, and I have a headful of questions that aren't going away until I get some answers. Besides, I think a little distance might be a good thing for me right now."

"Distance?"

"From Hannah. And from Starry Point."

"And me?"

Michael's eyes slid away. "Maybe. Yes."

Lane stiffened but managed a nod. "Drive safely."

"Lane—"

"No, you go," she said, holding up a hand. "You've said all you need to. We both have."

Chapter 59

It was nearly eight when Lane finally returned home. She'd put it off as long as possible, lingering until the night-duty nurse had essentially thrown her out. She tried to ignore the empty spot in the drive where Michael's SUV was usually parked. She'd better get used to it. This time it was only for a few days, but eventually he'd be gone for good.

At least with Hannah coming to stay, she wouldn't be alone. And she'd have plenty of free time before the season started to outline the novel that had been percolating in her head for the past two weeks. Michael had been right about one thing: it was time to stop hiding behind magazine articles and write something real. Who knew, maybe she'd even send him a copy when it was finished—proof that there were no hard feelings. It would be the grown-up thing to do, and it was definitely time to grow up.

Exhausted in every way it was possible to be exhausted, she dragged herself up the front steps and fumbled for her key, wishing she'd remembered to leave a light on this morning when she left. In her present mood, the last thing she needed was to come home to a house that was not only glaringly empty, but pitch-dark as well.

Inside, she made a beeline for the parlor lamp. Dally's Christmas tree towered gloomily beside the fireplace, barren and utterly depressing. Groaning, she turned away. As if her day hadn't been bad enough.

She was halfway to the kitchen before she realized the boxes Michael had stacked near the library door yesterday were gone. Backtracking, she flipped on the library light with a sinking feeling, and felt her throat tighten. Not a pencil or pad remained. Not so much as a paper clip to prove he'd ever been there.

There was no need to look upstairs—she already knew what she would find—and yet she made herself go, freezing when she reached the landing and peered down the hall toward the Tower Suite. The door stood ajar, revealing a slice of the bed where only last night they had lain awake together, staring at the stars. Her stomach lurched as she forced herself to step into the room, to take in the bureau with its hastily emptied drawers, the bathroom swept of personal possessions. He hadn't gone to Raleigh. He'd just . . . gone.

Numb, she moved from surface to surface, hoping to find a note. An apology. A good-bye. But there was nothing. How had she not seen it? Not realized he meant to run? It was why he'd been so insistent about showing Hannah the letter. He knew he wasn't coming back. Hannah had known it, too, she realized now. She had seen it, sensed it somehow, and had chosen her words accordingly. *"We run when we should stand our ground."* Only, it appeared her son hadn't been listening.

Downstairs, Lane crumpled onto the last step, hugging her knees like a sulky child. It didn't matter, really. He was always going to leave. This was just sooner. And it wasn't the leaving that upset her. It was the way he'd done it. At least that's what she was telling herself when she heard her cell phone jangle in the foyer.

Her heart bounced into her throat as she scurried for her purse, counting rings as she fumbled the thing out of its small side pocket. Her face fell when she checked the display.

"Hey, Dally, what's up?"

"Interested in a little gossip?"

Lane sighed. "Not really. Not tonight."

"I bet you change your mind when you hear what Dustin Redall just spilled."

"Dustin?"

"The cop I've been seeing? Blond hair, blue eyes?"

"They all have blond hair and blue eyes, Dally. What's the scoop?"

"Just that the police have made an arrest in all these break-ins. Three little punks from the south side—imagine that. It's hush-hush for right now, but it should hit the papers in a day or two, as soon as Breester figures out how to spin it. Which means Hope House is off the hook."

Lane gripped the phone a little tighter. "Are you sure about this? I mean *really* sure?"

"I got it straight from the horse's mouth, didn't I?"

"Why would Dustin tell you something like that?"

"He wants me to think he's a big deal, I guess. Anyway, I thought you'd want to know."

She could hear the smile in Dally's voice. She checked her watch—too late to call Callahan. It would have to wait until morning. "I always said you were better than a subscription to the *Islander Dispatch*, and you are. Dally, this is wonderful news."

"So . . . do I still have a job?"

Lane eyed the tree balefully. "Barely."

"Have you decorated it yet?"

"No."

"Come on. Don't be a grinch. It'll be fun."

Lane smothered another sigh, the shine of Dally's news already beginning to dim. "It's been . . . a bit of a day."

"Let me guess—Professor McDreamy?"

"He's gone."

"As in . . . gone?"

"I'll tell you about it tomorrow."

"I could come over if you want. So you're not alone."

"Thanks, but no. Right now I'm thinking about getting good and drunk."

"Wow, that bad?"

"Tomorrow, okay? But thanks for the update."

"Okay, boss."

Lane struggled to process the news as she ended the call. Under normal circumstances Dally's bit of gossip would have left her giddy, but now, as she thought of the other news she would have to impart to Hannah, the news that her son was gone, she found her excitement severely curtailed. In fact, the prospect of such a conversation made her want to climb into bed and pull the covers over her head. Had he thought of that, she wondered, as he was heading out of town?

In the kitchen, she excavated a bottle of Pinot from the fridge and poured herself a hefty glass. She was halfway to the parlor when she decided to go back for the bottle. Not even she could get drunk on one glass of wine.

She just prayed Dally had been listening when she said she didn't want company. It would be just like her to pop by with a box of Twinkies, an assortment of Ben & Jerry's, and a bootleg copy of *The Notebook*. The girl had a heart of gold, but at times her gestures could be a bit overwhelming, as the eight-foot Fraser fir in her parlor would attest.

She eyed the green monstrosity now with a shake of the head. So much for the romantic Christmas for two. Not that it had ever been real. She'd always known that, hadn't she? Then why did the sight of it, freshly cut and waiting to be trimmed, feel like such a taunt? For two cents she'd toss it, and all four boxes of decorations, out onto the lawn.

Instead, she sank down onto the hearth with her bottle and her glass, keenly aware of the silence that seemed suddenly to crowd the corners of the room. It had been enough once, this quiet existence. No expectations. No complications. Just a safe and solitary sameness. Then Michael had shown up, with his charming smile and his willingness to play house, and now she didn't know how to go back. She would have to, though—somehow.

If anyone can help you forget Professor McDreamy, Harry can.

Well, they'd just see about that.

Diving into the cartons of decorations with a gusto that could only be fueled by the Pinot, Lane rummaged through strands of garland and boxes of fragile glass ornaments until she found what she was looking for at the bottom of box number three—Harry Connick Jr. staring up at her with his liquid eyes and that movie-star mouth.

Wrestling the CD from its shiny plastic, she slid it into the stereo and hit PLAY, then turned up the volume, letting the jazzy rendition of "Sleigh Ride" fill the room. She eyed the tree again dubiously, the decorations she had just heaped out onto the floor. *Why the hell not?* She had wine, twinkle lights, and Harry. She could do this. She could decorate Dally's monster tree and pretend that everything was fine— that she was fine.

It had been a while but she still remembered her tree-trimming basics as she unraveled the first strand of tiny white bulbs and plugged them in. They flicked to life, warm and white, then blurred into tiny prisms as the tears finally came. With a muffled sob she sank back down onto the hearth. She couldn't do this. And she sure as hell wasn't fine.

The sound of the front door opening brought her head up with a jerk. Wiping her eyes on her sleeve, she stood, trailing Christmas lights behind her as she headed for the foyer.

"I thought I told you I didn't want—oh."

"My key was still under the mat."

Michael had the good grace to look sheepish as he stood in the doorway, holding up the key in question. He seemed about to say more when he closed his mouth and ran his eyes around the room, taking in the blaring stereo and decoration-strewn floor, the wine bottle and glass on the hearth. Finally, he pointed to the strand of lights dangling from her hand. "Are you having a party?"

Dropping the lights, she stepped past him to turn off the stereo. "As I matter of fact, I am," she answered coolly as she turned back to face him. "It's a going-away party."

"Lane—"

"Did you forget something?" she asked, not caring that she sounded petulant. "No, I doubt that. You were very thorough."

"Let me explain."

"There's nothing to explain. You lied, and then you left. I guess I should have listened. You said you'd hurt me, and you did."

"I told you I couldn't stay, and I told you why."

"You didn't say you were clearing out today, though, did you? And without so much as a good-bye."

"I didn't know. I—" He stopped abruptly, and raked a hand through his hair. "No. That's a lie. I did know. Or at least I was pretty sure I was leaving."

It was all she could do to keep her face blank as she absorbed this frank admission. Honesty was supposed to be refreshing, but this didn't feel refreshing at all. "Were you even going to see Callahan? Or was the bit about saving Hope House a lie, too?"

"No. That part was true. I was going to Raleigh. In fact, I was almost there when I turned around."

"Because you realized you'd forgotten to leave a note?"

"You're not going to make this easy, are you?"

"Well, I'm not sure what *this* is, but no, I'm not inclined to make anything easy for you at the moment."

Michael sighed. "Fair enough. The reason I turned around was that I realized I was going the wrong way. For a long time now I've known something's been missing. I just didn't know what it was. Now I do."

Lane swallowed the lump in her throat but could still find no words.

"It took me a while to get out of my own way, but I finally get that this is where I'm supposed to be. Everything that's happened—Hannah, you, the letter from my father—all of it was meant to show me the way home."

"To Starry Point?"

"To you."

He took a step toward her then, slow, cautious, as if he were afraid she might bolt. "I don't want to relive my father's mistakes, Lane. I don't want to hurt the people I care about, and I don't want to run away from what's hard. I'd rather stay and fight for the life I want."

Hannah's words. He *had* been listening.

"You left—no note, no good-bye. You just left." Her eyes filled with tears. She blinked them away. "How do I know you won't do it again?"

"Because I'm done being an idiot. I was afraid to let myself love you, afraid it would mean being tied to this place, to always living in the past. I didn't realize that's exactly what I was already doing. I've been stuck, but not anymore. Somewhere between here and Raleigh I finally figured out the only way to stop living in the past is to make a future."

"A future . . . with me?"

Michael closed the distance between them with a single step. Cupping her face in both hands, he bent to brush a kiss against her forehead, then one across her mouth, his lips whisper-soft. "Yes, with you."

A fresh set of tears welled before she could check them. "I missed you," she whispered as she blinked them away.

"I was only gone seven hours."

"I know." Standing on tiptoe, she matched his kiss, the barest of touches, then angled her head to look up at him. "Don't do it again."

He nodded, his eyes never wavering from hers.

Lane felt her heart quicken as the gaze lingered and stretched. It was a look she would happily have drowned in, smoldering and smoky gray, but it was what lay behind it that finally made her heart sing: love, need, and for the first time—a promise.

Epilogue

Mary

It's a rare, brilliant day. The sort you get sometimes at the end of March, when the air is fresh and the sky is so blue it nearly breaks your heart. Things are blooming, buds unfurling, life turning and returning—because that's the way it works. We travel the circle until at long last we come round again, to look ourselves in the eye as judge and jury.

I am not proud of the mistakes I made, or the hurt I caused, though I was not alone in that. There is blame enough to go around, I suppose, if anyone wants it. But I don't. Samuel Rourke was a good man who did a bad thing, and I forgave him long ago. And now, at long last, it seems his son has found a way to make peace with the past as well.

I feel neither sadness nor loss as I look upon this place where my home once stood, the scene of all my heartbreak and grief. I'm glad they have razed it, and buried the last of its wreckage. It should have happened long ago. But then, everything happens in its time.

I never expected so many people, but I'm glad they've come to see my boy, the prince I lost, and then found again, do this fine thing for the people of Starry Point—and for his brother. It makes my heart catch in my throat to look at him as he steps up onto the dais. He is so like his father, tall and handsome and good. And now, finally, back where he belongs.

Some small corner of my heart, the one I keep for Peter alone, breaks a little, but smiles, too, as the shovel is thrust into the earth and the new sign with its shiny brass plaque is unveiled.

PETER ROURKE MEMORIAL PARK

It's a fine thing—a right thing—and I hope, as the crowd begins to gather around the dais to shake my Evan's hand, that his brother is watching and sees this thing that is being done in his honor, that he knows he is not forgotten, not truly gone from our hearts.

Still, we must all of us go forward.

I am nearly healed from the accident now, but will not linger at the inn—an addled old woman forever underfoot. Neither will I return to Hope House, safe now from the mayor, thanks to Lane. Instead, I will have a small apartment close by, with a girl in twice a week to see to the washing and dusting—and to no doubt count my pills. I will have my drawing to fill my time, and visits with Lane and my boy. R.B. has also promised to come up from Raleigh, though I don't know why he would bother after the trouble I've been to him over the years. It shames me now to think how shabbily I treated him when we were young. He's been such a dear friend, truer and more constant than I either knew or deserved. This time I will be kinder.

There's a clamor now, cheers and applause, as my boy is finishing up his speech. I will never look at this wide green space, where a home once stood and a family once lived, and not mourn all that was lost. But I will always be glad, too, to see children at play here, and old people resting on its benches, to know that young lovers will come here to walk its paths.

I have found a kind of peace, you see—not a perfect healing, but a scarring over of the broken places, which is more than I dared hope for. Perhaps it is only the new pills, but I think not. It's a hard thing to forgive those who wound us, but harder still to forgive the wounds we inflict upon ourselves. I have done that now. I have found my bit of truth and resigned my demons to the sea.

I have sought redemption for so long, scanning empty horizons for it, only to find it has been within reach all along. I had only to let go of yesterday to claim it. Time, you see, is the enemy, a trap of our own making. The past is lost forever, a wasteland of all that could have been and never was, while the future stretches endlessly before us, always an hourglass's worth of sand beyond our reach. Today, then, is what we have left—the here and the now—to make our wishes, and to fight for the life we want.

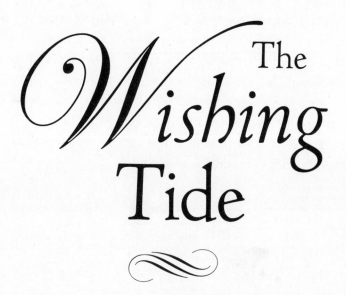

The *Wishing* Tide

BARBARA DAVIS

This Conversation Guide is intended to enrich the
individual reading experience, as well as encourage us
to explore these topics together—because books,
and life, are meant for sharing.

A CONVERSATION
WITH BARBARA DAVIS

Q. Your protagonist, Lane, owns a bed-and-breakfast called the Cloister House. Her favorite room there is her writing room, in the northeast turret. We're reminded of Virginia Woolf's "A Room of One's Own." Why is this room—both actual and metaphorical—so important to a writer? Do you have a room of your own? Do you have one space where you like to create, or can you do it in different places?

A. These days, life comes at you full blast twenty-four/seven. There are so many distractions: TV, with its twenty-four-hour news cycle, the infectious lure of social media, cell phones, e-mail, and always, always an endless list of things that need doing. Having a place that's yours alone, a kind of sanctuary where you have at least some command over what comes into that space, offers a small sense of control and helps set the tone for creativity. I'm fortunate to have an actual office, which I just redecorated, as a matter of fact, but I can usually write anywhere—the back porch, in the car, at the beach, sitting cross-legged on my bed with an old movie playing in the background. As long as there's no music. Music gets in my head and I can't hear anything else.

Q. There are three main characters in The Wishing Tide: *Lane, Michael, and Mary. Was one of them easier to write than the others? Or harder to write than the others? Did you have a favorite character?*

A. I think Mary was the easiest for me to write. Perhaps because she came to me first, and almost fully formed as a character. Her story informed the rest of the novel and set the pace for the entire story. It took several stabs to get her voice right, but I always knew who she was and what she'd been through. I also think she's my favorite character in the story. I love her strength and endurance, and also her unique brand of wisdom, which seems to allow her see and know all things.

Q. *The setting of Starry Point is fictitious, yet it's so detailed it feels real. How did you create this setting and why did you feel this book needed to be set here?*

A. For me, there's something very healing about the sea. I'm always calmest when I'm near the water, and it's where I tend to run when I feel stressed or blocked, so I suppose it felt like a place Lane would go to heal after her marriage ended. Also, I liked the symbolism of the sea ebbing and flowing, giving and taking. It plays nicely with Mary's losses, and with her ultimate healing. I put a lot of time into building my settings because, for me, when setting is done well it actually becomes a character, a living, breathing piece of the story, until you can't imagine the story taking place anywhere else.

Q. *For several of the characters in this book, there's a disjunction between their dreams and their lived reality. Do you think this is somewhat inevitable as we age and get tossed around on life's waters? Have you had to combat issues that made you sympathetic to the problems your characters faced?*

A. I think very few of us wake up at forty and find that we're living the life of our dreams. We cherish those dreams early on but rarely chart a course to get there. Life gets in the way. We need to be responsible, make a living. But I also think, as we reach our later years, there's time for second chances. The kids are grown, the pace of life slows, and it's possible to finally chart that course and go after those dreams again—but only if we want them badly enough. I empathize very much with Lane, with the disappointments of losing a baby and giving up a writing career due to criticism and lack of support. But here I am, chasing down my dream. Life can be tumultuous, even downright hard, but the human spirit is incredibly resilient.

Q. *You've now written two novels,* The Secrets She Carried *and* The Wishing Tide. *How were the experiences of writing them different? Was one more challenging to write?*

A. I started writing *The Secrets She Carried* after being laid off from a draining but very lucrative corporate job. I was terrified but determined, and so I dove in. Unfortunately, it was a complicated story with a dual timeline, and it never occurred to me to work from an outline. Needless to say, I had more than my share of false starts. It took me two and a half years to finally nail it. With *The Wishing Tide*, I was under contract, which meant I had an actual deadline. False starts weren't an option if I was going to get the manuscript in on time. So I learned how to outline. Once I had a clean, precise story arc, the actual writing went like a dream. I finished in six months.

Q. *At the end of the day, what do you hope readers take away from this story?*

A. That it's never too late to live a good life. That just because life threw you a few low blows and knocked you off your pins doesn't mean you have to stay there. You can keep fighting and eventually get to a better place.

QUESTIONS FOR DISCUSSION

1. In the beginning of the book, we learn that Lane writes magazine articles about places she's never been and things she's never done. What sense of her did you get from that bit of information? What else did you learn about Lane that seemed to strengthen those conclusions?

2. The sea has been used as a symbol for many things in literature. In your opinion, what do the sea and the tides symbolize in *The Wishing Tide*? Do they hold different meanings for different characters? If so, what?

3. Mental illness still carries a heavy stigma in our society. How does Mary use that stigma to her advantage? What do you feel this strategy says about her, and how did it affect your initial impression of her?

4. What do you feel there was about Mary that compelled Lane to overlook her quirks and appearance? Would you ever befriend a person like Mary? Why or why not?

5. Mother-daughter relationships are often complicated. Discuss the tension between Lane and Cynthia, and how their confrontation helped Lane gain insight into her past disappointments. What

role, if any, did Mary play in their ultimate reconciliation? Have there been times in your life when an outsider has offered advice that has helped you see a situation in a new light?

6. As children, our physical and emotional environments play a large role in the way we perceive the world as adults. How have events in Michael's past affected his ability to find happiness with another person? Do you agree that people who have never had positive role models in the areas of love and marriage are more likely to fail at love themselves?

7. One of the bonds Lane, Michael, and Mary share is that over the years they all suffered a life event that caused them to relinquish long-held dreams and to ultimately give up on the idea of happiness. Do you believe there are certain life traumas from which it is simply impossible to recover, or do you believe there is always a way back to happiness? Have you ever known someone struggling to heal from a traumatic event who simply couldn't let go of his or her pain? What judgment, if any, did you place on this person's failure to move on?

8. At the start of the book, all of the main characters have assumed false identities or roles as a way to insulate themselves from unpleasant past events. By the end of the book, how have Lane, Michael, and Mary come to terms with those false identities and committed to being truer to themselves? What pitfalls do you foresee as they each move forward?

9. Throughout the book, the themes of guilt and forgiveness play large roles in why each of the main characters finds it difficult to move forward with his or her life. Discuss the various ways each appears to have embraced the concept of forgiveness by the end of

the book, and the role that self-forgiveness plays in each character's emotional healing.

10. How does Michael's learning the truth about his father provide him with clarity about the kind of life he's been living and the need to do things differently? Do you believe it's possible to change your lifelong beliefs and patterns based on lessons from the past?

11. Initially, Lane, Michael, and Mary appear to have little or nothing in common. However, as the story progresses, we see that they have much more in common than we are first led to believe. Discuss the things they actually have in common and how each acts as an emotional mirror for the others.

12. A major theme of *The Wishing Tide* is that it's up to each of us to fight for the life we want, something each of the main characters stopped doing at various points in their lives. By the end of the book, did you get the sense that each has finally chosen to fight for the life he or she wants? If so, why? Do you agree with this premise?

After spending more than a decade in the jewelry business, **Barbara Davis** decided to leave the corporate world to pursue her lifelong passion for writing. *The Wishing Tide* is her second novel. She lives near Raleigh, North Carolina, with Tom Kelley, the love of her life, and their beloved cat, Simon. She is currently working on her third novel.